BLOOD AND CUSTARD

AN INSPECTOR VIGNOLES MYSTERY

British Library Cataloguing in Publication Data:
A catalogue record for this book is available from the British Library
ISBN 978-1-904109-26-6

First published 2015

The Hastings Press
hastings.press@gmail.com
www.hastingspress.co.uk

Set in Garamond
Cover design by Bill Citrine
Printed in Poland by booksfactory.co.uk

BLOOD AND CUSTARD

An Inspector Vignoles Mystery

STEPHEN DONE

For Bill

PROLOGUE

September 1952

'I'd like to go home now, please.' The boy's eyes were bright.

'What's the hurry? You're having a nice time, aren't you?'

'Yes.' He hesitated a beat. 'But it's getting awfully late...' The boy was trying not to sound worried. They were kind and now he felt guilty glancing at his precious Timex watch with the luminous dial, the hands of which were relentlessly moving forward. Half past seven already. Cripes! He felt a sinking sensation in his stomach. He wanted to leave.

'Tell you what, laddie, I'll fetch the train timetable and we can see what's the best one to put you on.' There was a confident quality to the man's voice that made it hard to do anything but agree. You just had to go along with what he said. Earlier that day he'd suggested they sneaked in behind the loco shed to get a better look at the engines. The man had said this with an amused twinkle in his eye, but it had still felt more like a command than a question. And then it had been the man's idea to go back to the house afterwards to warm up after a few damp hours spotting trains. But the boy wanted to hurry back and eat his fill in the refec' with all the other boys. It was shepherd's pie and peas tonight. His favourite.

'That would be awfully kind. They'll be worrying you see. I—I should have said where I was going.' His mouth felt dry and he quickly drank from a glass of ginger beer close to hand.

'They won't mind once you explain. When they know you were being looked after properly.' The lady gave him a cheery smile. 'And besides, you must have some of my nice cherry pie first, dearie. I bet you've not eaten all day.' She was big and rotund, with chubby bare arms blotched with tiny red veins; dimples formed on each cheek whenever she smiled or laughed — which she did frequently. A motherly sort of figure; all floral house coat and massive apron wrapped around her large, soft frame, further enveloped by the scent of baking and washing powder and warm clothes drying on a wooden airer winched high above the hot kitchen range. The boy took a furtive glance at his watch again, trying to take comfort in the dial that told him it was waterproof to a depth of fifty feet. Why couldn't she check the time and not just laugh it off when he said it was late?

He was hungry, but getting onto a train was more important right now. If they could just be walking to the station it would feel so much better. He'd had a ripping time, but there always came a point in any great day when enough was enough, and that time had come. However, his tummy rumbled, the smell of the hot pie was mouthwatering and the sweet vanilla and cornflour smell of the custard she was stirring in a milk pan was beguiling.

The man spread the timetable open on the big kitchen table and ran a finger down the columns of numbers.

'There you go: steaming hot custard, poured all over my special cherry pie.' The lady placed a bowl on the table before the boy. 'I'm sure you'll like it.'

'Thanks awfully.' He picked up the big, electro-plated spoon, noticing that it was scratched and worn through years of use and cleaning. He wanted to dive straight into the delicious pudding set before him, but his stomach was now strangely contracted and tight. He could feel a knot of tension down there, like a little balled fist pressing on his innards. It felt unsettling being in a strange house and so far away from school on this dreary, wet night. He was going to be in an awful lot of trouble when he got back. He was probably going to get caned on the palms by the headmaster for this.

'Get stuck in, then!' The man grinned at him across the table. Probably it was just the way the light from the overhead bulb reflected off his spectacles, making them like pale mirrors and masking his eyes, but something about him suddenly unnerved the boy. The sharp shadows cast on his face made him look odd, his nose longer and sharper, a bit fox-like. He looked almost sinister. No, that was just silly, and very uncharitable. The boy swallowed, but his throat was as dry as a desert. He glanced quickly down at the blue-and-white pottery bowl and stirred the hot custard, whorling a stain of bright red pie filling into the pale yellow.

Oh bother! If he was going to get a beating for being back after curfew, then he may as well get a belly full of lovely grub inside first. It would be bad manners to refuse, in any case. He tried a taste. It was like nectar. Hot and heavy with vanilla and slightly sour cherry. He dived in again, eager for more. He lifted the spoon, laden with glistening fruit that looked almost glassy beneath the yellow custardy covering, towards his mouth. But his hand was quivering, perhaps with nerves or a sudden dip in energy after a long day fuelled only by two beef dripping sandwiches and an apple. He could not stop the twitching in his arm and so, inevitably, the pie and custard slipped from the side and plopped in a long, glutinous red–and-yellow stain down his white school shirt.

There was a strange electric silence in the room, broken only by the rattle of rain against the window pane and a howl of wind down the chimney. Eyes met eyes then dropped down to the slithering gobbet of what looked like bloody custard.

'Oh, we don't like that. We don't like that at all.' Her voice was low, calm and yet somehow menacing. 'Dirty boy.' She almost whispered the words, yet they were heavy with something that frightened him.

The man closed the timetable and rested his palm upon the cover in an action that had an ominous air of finality about it. 'Looks like we won't be needing this, then.'

CHAPTER ONE

Nottingham Victoria

Tuesday 11th November. As the train traversed the impenetrable gloom of the tunnel, Fireman Edward Earnshaw glanced into the intense heat of the fire, flipping his long-handled shovel upside down and holding it just inside the narrow opening of the firebox. By so doing, he bought himself a little protection for his eyes against the white-hot heat. Satisfied with what he saw, he stood up and clanged the thick metal door shut with his steel toe-capped boot. He propped the shovel against the side of the tender and took a swift look at the water gauges, illuminated by a dim light from a tiny electric bulb. Everything looked tickety-boo. He had a good fire, helped by some decent coal in the bunker, and enough room in the boiler to add more water if the safety valves threatened to lift when they came to a stand at Nottingham Victoria.

He glanced across at Driver Hurst, who had one hand on the vacuum brake and an elbow crooked on the narrow wooden ledge of the opened cab window, watching intently for the approach of the half moon of dim light that indicated the exit portal of the tunnel at the northern end of the station. The driver was enveloped in a wreath of exhaust that had become trapped in the cab confines, rendering him like a charcoal sketch in shades of greys and blacks, with tiny white highlights for his eyes.

Eddie liked the approach to this particular station. In his book, 'Vic' was seriously impressive. It was big and grand and, on a sunny day, the light streamed through the extensive glass canopies and striped everything with bold, diagonal shadows cast by the glazing bars. This multi-platform station, with its cheerily tall clock tower, was situated in a deeply excavated hollow, the sheer faces of the rough-hewn sandstone towering over everything, amplifying the noise and holding in the smoke that steadily turned the rock black with layers of accumulating soot. He found the setting both dramatic and exciting. However, these same confines could also render the station dark and gloomy, chilled by the rush of pungent air from the yawning tunnels at each end. This was especially true on a rotten wet November day — like today.

He rested his gloved hands on the cab's side sheet and peered forward, squinting to prevent the rain from stinging his eyes. He liked the way the lamplight reflected off the slick surfaces of the platforms, which stuck out like wet tongues from the train-shed at the station's heart. The rain bounced again off the cab roof as they exited the tunnel, but Eddie was past caring. He was already soaked down one side and pretty much dry and toasty on the other — thanks to the roaring fire. A bit more rain was not going to make much odds.

He could hear the vacuum open and felt the bite of the brakes in response as Driver Hurst skilfully applied them in gentle bursts, easing back and getting a feel for the train slowing before pushing again on the stubby brass handle, polished to a gloss by regular use. The local schools were out and, as Eddie expected, there was already a gang of kids clustered under the nearest awning. Some, with the scant regard of youth for the teeming rain, sprinted forwards, ignoring the downpour, yelping and shouting and pointing, tuppenny notebooks clutched in pale hands, bare knees below shorts flashing in the deepening twilight.

'It's a namer!'

'What's it called?'

One lad was running out front and, despite his National Health prescription glasses spotting with rain drops, was the first to try to decipher the locomotive's curious name. 'It's *Un-sicky*. No, *Oomseek*. Oh, I dunno.' He twisted his mouth in puzzlement at the odd name cast in brass.

Eddie was aware of the faces looking up at him, clearly envious of his position on the footplate. They were all watching intently as he nonchalantly leaned on the cab side of his engine whilst it sailed, almost soundlessly, with the regulator now closed, into the station with just a little wisp of steam drifting around the pumping pistons and the big spinning wheels. He enjoyed the attention, although he didn't wish to make that obvious. However, he still felt the need to readjust his cap, getting the angle correct whilst peering, self-importantly and somewhat unnecessarily, along the thick tube of the rain-varnished boiler that reflected the station lights slipping smoothly along its elegant form.

'Cor, she's a belter!'

'I've not copped her!'

'Brilliant!'

'Ow d'you say that name, mister?' The lad with the rain splattered glasses was asking the question whilst he trotted at a slowing pace alongside the engine.

'*Um-See-Key*.'

'Wha?'

'*Um-See-Key.*' He gave the lads a wink as the train squealed to a stand.

'What's one of them, when it's at home?' A lanky boy with bad acne and an ill-fitting school blazer piped up.

'A Thompson B12, stupid!' A short, stocky boy with his school cap pushed back on his head gave a mocking retort.

'I know that! I mean, what's an Umseeky-thingy.'

'Dunno...' The stocky boy had no answer.

'Where is it, mister?' The boy with the glasses was now wiping them on his sleeve, but only managing to make the lenses all smeary.

'Not *where*, but *what*. It's a kind of deer; well, a type of antelope, actually.' Eddie was not exactly sure of the specifics, having never seen a picture of one, let alone a living example; but he knew that many of this class of locomotive carried the surprisingly numerous and varied names of African animals.

'I knew that,' boasted an older lad with slicked-down hair visible beneath his school cap.

'Bet you never!'

'Bet I did!'

There was an opening and slamming of doors, a brief bustle of feet, and the murmur of conversation as a good number of waiting passengers climbed aboard the up 'all stations stopper' to Marylebone. The steam-powered antelope gently sweated from somewhere below the frames, the vapour clinging as it rose, giving the impression that this elegant green machine was indeed some kind of iron beast, hot and panting after a gallop across the veldt. It was now almost pitch black beyond the end of the train-shed roof. Little signal lamps gleamed red, but one close to the platform turned at that moment to a bluey-green as the home starter dropped.

Eddie looked back along the train and saw that the guard was still helping an elderly gent aboard. Driver Hurst looked expectantly across the cab, an unlit 'rollie' jammed in the corner of his mouth. The line they were on was justifiably famous for its prompt station starts, and he was ready to get on the move the very moment the guard gave the signal.

'Excuse me, sir. Please, sir... Have you seen this boy? He's missing.' The voice was that of a woman, and Eddie was surprised by her plaintive call, not having seen her approach. Her face was upturned towards his. She was pale, and her blue eyes were watery and wide, and underlined by a smudge of tiredness like a bruise. Her cheeks were drawn and hollow and rain-spattered. She looked as though she were sickening for something.

'Sorry, luv?'

'My son. Have you seen him? He's missing. Please help me find my boy.'

Eddie was taken aback and didn't know what to say. This was so unexpected that he just looked back at her stupidly.

'I must find him. Take a look.' She thrust a large black-and-white school photograph wrapped in a sheet of shiny cellophane upwards towards Eddie, both hands gripping the thick mounting card so hard that her knuckles showed pale and bony. He noticed a wedding band and the slight flash of a stone on the engagement ring beside it on her slender finger. The innocent, toothy smile on the young boy's face combined with his mother's imploring gesture, made Eddie think he was looking at some kind of religious icon.

'Sorry. I've not seen him.'

'He went missing from here, I'm sure of it. Last Saturday. Please look out for him. He likes looking at the trains...'

'Don't we all!' One of the excited train-spotters tried to make a joke, but it fell flat. The boys had all taken a step back and were either making a point of studiously looking at the engine or shuffling awkwardly and appearing embarrassed, unsure how to react to her obvious distress.

Eddie peered once again at the image of the boy's face. The image was distorted by drops of rainwater and a fold in the transparent shiny covering. The mother stood rock-steady, arms uplifted, eyes fixed on Eddie. He felt confused and unable to meet her urgent gaze a second time. Aware that they were due to depart, he looked back along their train instead, lifting an arm in answer to a whistle and a somewhat cursory wave of a lamp glowing green as the guard stepped aboard.

'We've got the off!' Eddie was relieved to shift his thoughts away from that of the missing boy, although he was aware of the woman watching the train depart as if somehow her hopes were also being dragged away by its movement. She was holding the photograph pressed to her rain-coated breast, the boy's smiling face looking outwards. He saw all types from the cab of an engine and, fancying himself as something of an amateur sleuth, had become quite good at spotting those with money and those without. Those with good taste and those forced to wear hand-me-downs and darned and patched clothes long past their best. She was certainly not one of those rough types — who drank and smoked too much and could be vulgar — that he sometimes encountered on stations late at night. He thought she might be a bit posh. But, despite the clues suggesting the woman was neither poor nor homeless, she looked thoroughly abject and lost.

The boy with the spectacles was now keeping time beside *Umseke*, which was hissing furiously, great clouds of steam issuing in soft jets from below the front buffer beam. 'I wish I was driving her!'

'Me too.' Eddie winked at the lad. He thought he heard Driver Hurst grunt — as his contribution to the exchange — but the sound of the steam was fizzing around the cab and it was hard to hear anything. He looked back at the gaggle of boys, who had been forced to stop at the platform end and watch the train accelerate towards the gaping tunnel mouth, the wooden-bodied coaches painted in the latest cream-and-red livery that train-spotters liked to call 'blood and custard', creaking and squeaking softly as they snaked their way out of the station. In the distance a station light picked out the now-tiny figure of the mother still clasping the photograph, her rain hood and pale coat illuminated by warm lamplight, making her resemble a modern-day Madonna. Something about this little cameo punched Eddie in the heart.

Chapter Two

Talbot Lane, Leicester

The rain continued its relentless drumming. Pools of water sagged the canvas awning and strained the ropes that secured it to metal eyelets screwed into the viaduct wall and to wooden posts driven into the stony ground. It repeatedly overspilled, and in so doing released a stream of heavy droplets that fell uncomfortably close to where Sarah Ferrington was working. She tensed and closed her eyes to let the little splashes of icy water cease before quickly wiping the dirty droplets from her cheek and pushing a stray length of damp, ginger-blonde hair back behind her ear in an irritated gesture. There were buckets already full of water nearby, and the constant drip and splosh added to her discomfort, an unwelcome reminder that she needed to make the long hike to the nearest public conveniences that were anything but conveniently sited.

Miss Ferrington was chilled to the bone. Her body was aching from either sitting cross-legged and bent forward, or from lying prone for many hours on the heavy oilcloth that edged the excavation. This protected her from the worst of the damp earth, but offered no relief from the many small stones and odd-shaped lumps that pressed, unerringly, into her hips, kneecaps and elbows. But, uncomfortable though she was, she was enjoying the experience. She could only admire the way Dr Quincey, a seasoned pro and her personal tutor, worked, apparently unaffected by her own cramped position as she cleaned a short flight of steps and the corner of a stone wall they had recently revealed.

She took a lungful of musty air and shuffled herself into yet another unsatisfying position. She narrowed her eyes to regain focus in the light cast by a hissing storm lantern and the dying embers of the afternoon light filtering through a curtain of silver rain, then deployed her trowel once more, painstakingly easing the earth away from the bones it held in its clasp. Sometimes she reached forward with her left hand and used a household paintbrush to clean the curve of the cranium and the strong jaw-line she was revealing, sweeping the fine earth clear of the age-darkened, creamy-brown bones. No matter how weary, she was going to do the very best job she could. It was an honour that Professor Wildblood had given her a whole skeleton to uncover and record on her own. She could not mess up this opportunity.

She was still a student, with barely two years of experience, and yet already the professor was sufficiently impressed by her methodical approach that he'd declared: 'Whoever is lying down there is all yours, Sarah. Uncover that old soul and record everything and anything you find. Don't miss a trick! Show Denise and me what you can do.' Before she had time to mumble a few words of surprised thanks, the professor had interrupted her: 'Just another blessed Roman, of course, but since we've found the poor blighter, I feel duty-bound to record it.' He had been quite unmoved by the surprise discovery of the skeleton, huddled in its stone grave almost beneath the railway viaduct. He had been dismissive, perhaps even a little contemptuous, of what appeared to be an exciting discovery. But there were fringe benefits to his disappointment: she had been given the honour of recording the burial for the simple reason that this was not what he had hoped to find on site.

He'd staked his not-inconsiderable reputation — and, more pertinently, rather too much of the University and Leicester Museums & Libraries Committee's money — on finding the long-lost bones of King Richard III under the railway arches behind Talbot Lane. Instead of the missing monarch, the professor appeared to have found the grave of a middle-ranking Roman Briton at the corner of what might prove to be a stone-built workshop adjacent to the long-lost city walls. Each discovery was interesting in its way, but hardly shock revelations. After all, they were digging but a throw of a cricket ball away from the Jewry Wall, so one more dead Roman was not going to create much of a stir. And if it were old bones you wanted, there were plenty around the lovely old church of St Nicholas, standing amidst a small circle of gloomy trees still clinging bravely onto wet and discolouring leaves that looked like bats. Even the road cutting across the end of Talbot Road was called Holy Bones, so it was unlikely that the *Leicester Mercury* was going to make this discovery front page news, let alone give the university proctor reason to celebrate an excellent return on his investment.

Professor Wildblood had certainly chosen a place out of the public eye, despite its proximity to the city centre, hidden behind a short run of elegant, three-storey, early-Victorian houses and a clutch of untidy business premises. They were working in a scrap of scratty waste ground that hosted buddleia, discarded beer bottles, miscellaneous junk and an overriding stench of urine and tomcats beneath one of the arches of the tremendous viaduct constructed by the Great Central Railway in the dying years of the previous century.

'I wonder if they knew about this all along. The navvies and their paymasters, that is. Perhaps they just covered it over and said nothing.' The professor had shocked both Miss Ferrington and Dr Quincey with his pronouncement.

'I don't think so, because they would have been obliged to declare a burial site.' Dr Quincey was making a few notes about the section of wall she'd uncovered the day before.

'This blasted viaduct and all that went with it cut a swathe right through a rich seam of Roman remains. The loss is incalculable.' Wildblood sounded as though he held a personal grudge against the railway. 'And let's not even think about the damage to the all-important medieval period that we're interested in. I worry that there has been just too much disturbance.' As if to reinforce the point he was making, the giant, blue brick structure thundered with the sound of yet another in an apparently endless succession of heavy coal trains. The locomotive unseen above their heads was snorting and pounding with a regular, slow beat and the many four-wheeled wagons rumbled behind with a din that echoed around the close confines of the arch. 'Damn these blasted trains.' Wildblood swore with perfect pronunciation, though his curses were largely inaudible beneath the competing noise. He ran his fingers through his tousled hair. 'It cost them a small fortune of extra expense and a lot of valuable construction time declaring what they did admit to finding. As you know, the railway company had to make that viewing window at one end of the station to let people see the mosaic floor they'd uncovered. It must have driven the contractor to despair.'

'I can appreciate that, professor,' said Dr Quincey, 'but are you really suggesting that they ignored other finds in order to minimise the impact?'

'Why not, Denise? If we were building this blessed thing and paying for it out of our own money, would we act any differently?' The two women conceded the point.

'It would have slowed them down, I suppose. We've been here four days already and we're still only part way through,' Miss Ferrington ventured.

'Precisely.' He gave the two women a long stare whilst the coal train finally passed over and the low murmur of the city traffic and the relentlessly falling rain filled the void. He held up a long, bony finger. 'However, all is not lost: I think the railway contractors might just have done us a tiny favour by trying to let some things lie whenever possible. And the proof is here in this splendidly preserved burial. Perhaps Richard was also left where he lies.'

Dr Quincey smiled. 'So, some good came from the railway?'

'Possibly.' Professor Wildblood gave an exasperated puff of air from his cheeks. 'But they also trampled over everything with their great digging machines. Did they plant this monstrous pillar on top of the last Plantagenet king?' They all stared down at the bones of what was clearly not King Richard. The professor slapped the enormous construction of beautifully engineered blue brick in a futile gesture. 'I was sure he was here! Sure of it.' He fell silent after this final outburst and sloped off to his little scout tent pitched behind the back wall of a screws-and-fixings manufactory that was almost Dickensian, such was its state of dilapidation. He was going to pore once again over the financial figures in his little leather-bound notebook whilst rehearsing how to break the bad news to the dean.

'Another hour and it will be time to call it a day.' Dr Quincey was gently massaging the small of her back. She stood beside Miss Ferrington and looked down at the skull that stared blankly from her student's partially revealed excavation. The storm lantern's flame burned with a slight flicker from its poorly trimmed wick, causing the edges of the eye sockets to appear animated. It was unnerving. 'What about all this modern-day muck? Perhaps we should shift it now and then you can get a clear run at the chest and pelvis area of the skeleton tomorrow.'

Miss Ferrington slowly eased herself up from the ground and stretched her arms and flexed her shoulders in painful movements. 'Righty-o. A bit of shovel work might get some warmth back into my arms.'

'It's good to mix heavy work with delicate for that reason,' said the older woman. With the toe of her work-stained boot she was testing some of the mound of household waste and litter that still lay in uneven lumps over the greater part of her student's excavation. She was frowning. 'Why did anyone bother to carry buckets of fire-ash out here, Sarah? What's wrong with the ash can in the back alley, for goodness sake?'

'I know. I've had that friable stuff blowing in my eyes on and off these last few days. The old bottles and cans I can live with, but getting dust in my eye is the most annoying thing.' Miss Ferrington squatted back on her haunches and dug at the surface of the nearest mound with her trowel. 'It looks like someone has thrown at least two bucket-loads of ash here, then piled some earth on top. Can you see?' It was just useless detritus, but she wanted to demonstrate that she was applying her usual analytical skills to even a mundane problem. 'Why would they bother to cover fire-ash with soil? People are strange.'

'Why bother to do what?' Dr Quincey paused, shovel in hand, ready to dig it in deep as soon as her student backed away.

'To scoop up some of the compacted surface covering, which as you know is devilishly hard to cut through. Look over there, behind us.' Miss Ferrington twisted around and pointed with her trowel. 'That seems to be where the earth was taken from. I can see the shovel marks cutting into the ground.'

Dr Quincey pulled a face. 'Goodness only knows.' She could see what Miss Ferrington was referring to and also thought it a bit odd. 'Some people live like absolute pigs, I know that much. Look at all this!' She dug hard into the mound, then turned and dropped the earth and ash into a waiting wheelbarrow, her movements practised and efficient, and not unlike those of the firemen on the footplates of the locomotives passing overhead. Miss Ferrington joined her in the work and, after a few minutes, they had skimmed off the greater part of the accumulated detritus.

'Oh, cripes! I've dug too deep. There's a bone fragment.' Miss Ferrington lay down her shovel and knelt on the ground. 'Look...' She held up a short piece of bone, badly charred and fractured at one end. 'It can't be Roman, as we're not even down to the surface level of when the viaduct was built, let alone earlier.'

'And it's far too new. I'd say that's probably the remains of the filthy litterbug's dinner!' Dr Quincey was contemptuous.

Miss Ferrington inspected the bone carefully. 'It's not chicken: it's too thick. Is it lamb?' She looked puzzled. 'No, perhaps pig.' It was good practice to identify any bones, even if of no archaeological value or significance.

Dr Quincey dropped to her haunches beside her, brow deeply furrowed. 'Wait a minute, there's more — lots more. Can you see? Crushed into small fragments.' She concentrated on the parts scattered on the ground in the fine ash. 'Everything has been burnt and then ground into pieces. It was quite a meal!' Miss Ferrington noticed that Dr Quincey had lost her note of contempt and had instead adopted the serious tone she had used when they made their first important finds in a dig. Her tutor now took the bone and turned it in her fingers for a few moments, then carefully laid it to one side. Extracting her trowel from one of the large pockets on her waxed green jacket she prodded and probed, fishing out a series of little pieces, one of which was curved and distinctively shaped. 'That's neither lamb nor pig.'

They stopped and exchanged glances. Miss Ferrington had just turned up a smoke-blackened buckle in the shape of a flattened snake, along with a few strands of fabric that had somehow survived the burning where the fabric had been turned over and sewn into a seam. 'That's a snake belt buckle. My kid brother just loves his snake belt. He wouldn't part with that for anything.' She laughed nervously.

Dr Quincey bit her lower lip gently as she contemplated the curve of the bone held in her hand. 'Would you be kind enough to run along and fetch Professor Wildblood please? I'd like him to take a look.'

'What is it? Is there something wrong?'

'No—no, I don't think so.' She frowned. 'Just ask him to join us. Quickly, now.'

CHAPTER THREE

Talbot Lane, Leicester

Detective Sergeant John Trinder and WPC Jane Benson stood beneath a dripping awning, looking at the scene revealed before them with a mixture of puzzlement and mild irritation. Both were wet through. Trinder was still smarting from receiving a stream of rainwater unexpectedly released from the temporary covering. The water had trickled off the back of his hat brim and penetrated the gap between collar and neck. It was ice cold and he now felt uncomfortable and miserable. Benson was faring little better, with dirty splashes up the back of an almost-new pair of stockings and one shoe glistening with a coating of fresh, liquefied mud that looked like melted chocolate.

'I am so sorry, I should have warned you about that wobbly plank. There's been so much rain...'

'All in the line of duty.' Benson took a deep breath to try and curb her own irritation and gave the excited young archaeology student a forced smile. Her foot was soaked through and she feared the worst for her shoe. 'Who is in charge here, please?'

Miss Ferrington gave another apologetic smile, throwing in a nervous glance as Trinder slapped his hat a few times on his free hand to knock off the water. 'That would be the professor. At the back there.'

'So, you got here at last.' A tall, thin man with uncontrollable hair worn unfashionably long at the back stood up from where he had been seated on a canvas folding chair behind a trestle table close to the bricked-up rear of the viaduct arch. Professor Wildblood was wearing a tatty tweed jacket with leather elbow patches over a sagging, bottle-green cardigan in a chunky stitch with leather-covered buttons, beneath this was a cream-and-brown Viyella shirt. Shapeless corduroy trousers and leather walking boots completed the look. He walked towards them, the storm lanterns placed on the ground throwing hard shadows that brought out the form of his skull beneath weather-beaten skin. He looked gaunt and faintly alarming, and he towered over Benson. 'Took your time,' he grunted, 'we're losing precious money as each hour passes.'

'We came as quickly as we were able. The city constabulary and ourselves had to ascertain who was responsible for policing this plot of land,' Benson explained. 'And it fell to us. Apparently the land beneath and immediately adjacent to these arches is within the curtilage of British Railways.' A low rumble from above and the haunting whistle of a distant engine carrying through the incessant fall of rain seemed to reinforce her point.

'I would have expected you to be fully conversant with the situation.' Trinder was not in the mood for being polite. 'Considering that you are digging up railway property. It could have saved much valuable time if you had made the fact known to us from the start. This is a plot of land we have not had need to visit until now.'

'Of course I know! Everything we are doing here is quite above board, I can assure you of that, officer. Goodness knows the faculty had to jump through all manner of hoops before we could start work. And then there were the application forms to complete for the British Society for the Advancement of Science and then the Leicester Museums & Libraries Committee needed their own set of forms rubber stamped and signed in triplicate by some office-Johnny in the Transport Executive. I've never known anything like the British Railways Board for generating paperwork.' He gave a deep, heartfelt sigh. 'I just didn't realise it would make any difference to what type of bobby turned up, that's all.' The professor was feeling just as sour as Trinder.

'This is railway property and therefore under our jurisdiction.' Trinder left the words 'worst luck' unspoken. 'And we are not bobbies. This is WPC Benson and I am Detective Sergeant Trinder of the British Railways Detective Department. And you are?' He left a slight pause before adding 'sir?' The gap was just long enough to suggest that his respect needed to be earned.

'Professor Wildblood, head of archaeology at Leicester University.' He puffed his ample chest out and gave Trinder a steely look, then seemed to think better of this face-off and attempted something approximating a smile. Stepping closer, he offered his hand. 'This is Dr Quincey, lecturer in archaeology, and Miss Ferrington, a student.' The two women remained silent. The atmosphere was thickening by the moment. 'I think we've rather got off on the wrong foot,' Wildblood coughed. 'You see, I'm under awful pressure to get this dig finished. The clock is ticking and now — now all this!' He ran a hand through his hair and did a convincing job of looking harassed. 'I expect it will take a devil of a time to sort out.'

'That rather depends on what it is. Perhaps we can make a start.' Trinder made an effort to soften his tone, but he still wanted to get on. It was all in the line of duty, but he was still not best pleased to be standing beneath this miserable, dripping arch in a God-forsaken scrap of wasteland. By rights he should be on a train steaming down to Woodford Halse whilst looking forward to being welcomed home by his pretty wife, Violet, and their lively little boy, Robbie. His evening meal would just have to wait another hour or two in the oven and Robbie would be asleep by the time he got home. It was a scene played out all too often.

'The finds are very small and fragmentary. Not like this fellow.' Wildblood pointed to the almost-complete skeleton in the shallow grave close by. With the low angled light from the three storm lanterns throwing huge, elongated shadows upon the curving, lime-stained brickwork and etching dark lines around the cleaned bones, it was a scene of almost Gothic intensity. Benson shivered and dug her hands a little deeper into the pockets of her police-issue overcoat. 'It was Denise — Dr Quincey — who made the discovery,' Wildblood continued. 'She was working with young Sarah here, clearing modern-day detritus from above the burial.' Trinder and Benson looked towards the two women. 'Sarah is one of our brightest students. She was investigating the skeleton to gain experience. It helped make the most of a dig that was not delivering quite what we'd expected.' Wildblood had momentarily perked up as he discussed Miss Ferrington — whom, Trinder observed, flushed slightly at the attention. 'As you can see, Sarah is presently uncovering the skull. We are reasonably certain now that it belonged to a female, although we have not yet made a stab at her age, but there could be other items within the grave that—'

'Surely you did not bring us here to look at Roman remains,' WPC Benson interrupted.

'Indeed not.' Wildblood stopped in his tracks. 'Perhaps it's better if the ladies take over; they made the discovery.'

'That makes more sense.' Trinder looked across at the two female archaeologists. Dr Quincey spoke first.

'We are working about three feet below the surface we are standing on. Ordinarily, I would expect us to be around six foot down at the very least before we reach the Roman stratification, but there again, we were rather hoping to find evidence from a much later date.'

'What were you looking for, if not this?' Benson queried, glancing down at the grave.

'Our intent was to discover the remains of King Richard III. The last of the great line of Plantagenet kings, who, as you will know, fell at Bosworth, so paving the way for...' She pulled up short and started again after an apologetic upturn to one side of her mouth. 'It is important to understand that with all the late-Victorian railway construction work around here, we can presume that a lot of the upper layers have been scraped off and there is every possibility of some confusion and even destruction to the historical layering we would normally expect to find below the nineteenth and early twentieth century accumulations.'

'So, how can you be sure that what you are excavating here is Roman?' Benson asked, 'perhaps these remains are from a later date.' She had no desire to hear more than was necessary about their work, but she needed at least a basic understanding of what they were dealing with. It could be crucial in helping make the decision as to whether this was an active crime scene or something ancient. Hopefully the two diggers had just muddled up some ancient remains and she and Trinder could be on their way home in no time.

'We are skilled at reading layers of soil deposits and we also sift the soil removed for dating finds. We found some coins that give us a clear date that this is a late Roman burial.' Dr Quincey pointed at the clean grey ash they had partially removed from Miss Ferrington's excavation, which was heaped in the big, wooden-bodied wheelbarrow. 'But here we have the modern deposits in question. We are not talking about layers compacted over hundreds of years. This ash is very new. It is still light and liable to be blown away. This is a recent deposit and not something we would ordinarily even bother to pick through.'

'How recent?' asked Trinder.

'Weeks, maybe a few months at a stretch.' Dr Quincey shrugged her shoulders. 'I would be very surprised if it had been here much longer than three months.'

Trinder sucked air through his teeth and felt his heart sink. 'And it was in this ash you found the remains?'

'Yes. Miss Ferrington correctly identified all this as having no archaeological interest, but she noticed something about the deposit that drew our attention.' She looked at Ferrington, urging her to take up the story.

'I've been getting the stuff blown in my eyes these last days. It's turning my stomach to think about it now.' She made a face and Benson gave her a sympathetic look. 'But there was something that had me puzzled.' She sounded almost enthusiastic as she got into her stride. 'It's part of my training to observe and question everything about a dig site, and it struck me as curious that this ash had earth scattered on top, earth that I think was scooped from the freshly formed depression over there. Can you see?' She indicated the place in question, although as the WPC adjusted her position and felt her muddied foot squelch, she was not sure it looked any different from the undulating waste ground they were standing upon. 'It set me wondering why anyone would bother to go to that trouble.'

Trinder looked unimpressed.

'And then we discovered a bone fragment. At first I thought we had accidentally dug too deep.'

'Can we see?' Trinder asked.

'Of course. Over here.' Quincey walked across to the table, the others following. 'These are the biggest pieces we extracted, but we stopped collecting and left things as they were as soon as we identified them as human.' There was an array of small and very irregular shapes laid out upon the table. 'All badly burnt, as you can see. I would hazard that someone tried to break up the larger pieces after burning, as there are clean break lines, free of the scorching and soot from the fire.'

Trinder and Benson exchanged grim looks at this information then peered at the grey and dusty objects. They could see it was some kind of bone, but they were all so small and ill-defined that it was hard to draw any conclusions. 'You're quite sure they're human?' Trinder was clinging to the last, faint possibility of catching a train he knew would depart in fifteen minutes.

'We are, sergeant,' the professor piped up, his voice heavy with portent.

'We are skilled at identifying human bones. Although it would be advisable to have that checked in a laboratory, of course.' Quincey picked up the largest piece. 'This is one of the better-defined examples.' She held it between thumb and forefinger and lifted it so all could get a good view. 'It's the outer edge of the occipital orbit.' Trinder gave her a questioning look. 'The eye socket, sergeant; the outside of the right hand one, to be precise.'

Trinder squinted closer at the piece of bone. It was about and inch and a half in length. 'You can tell from that?'

'I can. We all can.' Dr Quincey gave a heavy sigh and replaced the bone on the table. 'But we can tell you precious little else. The fragments are so small and jumbled. There may be larger pieces yet to be discovered. Once everything is gathered and taken to a lab it may well be possible to say more, but I would not place too much hope on that.'

'Once we appreciated the gravity of the situation I got young Sarah here to telephone the authorities,' Professor Wildblood added, finishing with what might almost have been an apologetic cough.

Dr Quincey continued. 'We cannot give you the sex, time of death or cause of death. Although over the last hour or so I have tried to gauge the size of the skull from this fragment and might cautiously suggest that this was a younger person. A youth, perhaps.' The rain suddenly stopped just as she finished speaking. The effect was as though someone had just lifted the stylus off a gramophone playing a particularly loud special effects record of a torrential rainstorm. There was a tiny peep of a distant guard's whistle and the rumble of traffic along St Nicholas Street and High Cross.

'Or a child, perhaps.' Benson looked pale and her voice was quiet. There should be no difference, but discovering the remains of a young person always struck a particularly painful chord that resonated unpleasantly. Even hardened police officers with many years of experience found this tough.

'There's so little to work with.' Trinder also looked pained.

'We do have one item that might help.' Miss Ferrington held up the blackened snake belt-buckle. 'It was mixed in with the ash and has also been burnt. These belts seem to be especially popular with boys aged about six to twelve.' She gave an encouraging smile, as if eager to please the police officers, both of whom were looking downcast. 'My nephew, who is nine, wears his constantly.'

'But can we be certain it was worn by the person whose bones are here?' Jane Benson sounded sceptical, her cynical detective mind in gear.

'The condition is consistent with that of the bones.' The eager student was not going to be dissuaded so easily.

'A not unreasonable supposition, but purely circumstantial.' Trinder's voice was flat. 'Even if we could say that this buckle is associated with the remains, it hardly narrows our search.'

'How so?' asked Wildblood. 'This snake buckle points towards these being the remains of a young male. We think the skull is that of a younger person, so the two facts seem to fit. I would say that's a darned good starting point.' He appeared to want to support Sarah Ferrington's opinion. Perhaps he was hoping it might speed up the investigation process and off his dig site as soon as possible.

'Is there anything else?' WPC Benson asked Miss Ferrington. They must not be drawn into speculating about a case of such gravity.

'No. But there is a lot of modern rubbish all around and I suppose some of that could be associated,' Dr Quincey offered. 'We swept most of the detritus lying on the surface into the corner over there when we first came on site. Old Coca-Cola and pale ale bottles, rusty tin cans, yellowing newspapers, bits of twisted wire. Nothing special.'

Trinder looked at his colleague. 'This is going to need the services of the forensic team. We're going to need to check every last scrap of litter and get every piece of bone retrieved. There's little we can meaningfully do here tonight, however.' Jane Benson agreed, with more than a hint of relief in her voice. 'Post a uniformed officer here to secure and protect the site overnight, Benson. Hold the fort until he arrives.'

'Very well, sir.'

'The usual routine: nobody to enter and nothing taken off site. Everything left exactly as it is. You know the drill.' Trinder now looked at the three archaeologists, their faces pale in the flickering light. 'If you could furnish Benson with your particulars, please? She can take preliminary statements from each of you whilst we wait to secure the site. Once that is completed you may go home. We will be contacting you all in due course for fuller statements.'

'And tomorrow? I presume we cannot return.'

'No professor, the dig site is now closed and is to be considered a crime scene.'

'For how long?'

'Looking at this lot, I'd say it could be a good day or more of work. We're going to have to get someone to sift through every darned square inch of ash and soil and pick out every tiny fragment of bone.' What a nightmare, he added, sotto voce.

'Not half as much as it will be for the parents of that poor lad.' Dr Quincey bit a nail and looked white as a sheet.

CHAPTER FOUR

Leicester

'Come along.'

'Where are we going?'

The man beckoned towards the door leading to the hall. 'Through here.'

'Why?'

'Cos' I say so.' His voice was not raised but there was a steely edge to it that brooked no dissent.

The boy stood up, moving his chair clumsily and scraping its legs unpleasantly on the quarry tiles. He trembled and felt a bead of perspiration form along his brow. 'I—I'm awfully sorry. It's nothing. It will wash off. If I could just have a cloth I can wipe it off.'

'I don't think so.' The woman folded her broad arms across her expansive bosom. Double chins assembled below her mouth which was now a thin-lipped line. It was remarkable how her face, indeed her whole demeanour, could change so swiftly from warm and welcoming to hard and bitter. 'Be quiet. You need to go into the back.' Her voice was also quiet, but commanding. It was not unlike how matron spoke when she was administering some vile medicine. You had to just shut up and obey.

'I do? B—but why? I don't think I want to, thank you. I just want to go to the station now, please.'

'We don't have all night, laddie.' The man beckoned, his other hand holding the edge of the open door. 'The sooner you do as you are told, the sooner it will be over.'

'I'll put the kettle on.'

The man nodded in response. It was almost an acknowledgement of something pre-arranged. The boy felt slightly reassured by her sudden desire to make a pot of tea. He had no idea why they were suddenly acting the way they were, but surely nothing could be so very wrong if they were going to have a pot of tea. He didn't want to go out the back, whatever that implied; but he had no choice and so, reluctantly, he put one foot in front of the other as though he were sleepwalking. He felt dizzy, the smell of warm pie and custard and of clothes drying filled his nostrils. The lamp above the table seemed to be swinging to and fro as though it were a ship's lantern in a rolling swell. It was making his head swim. But no, the lamp was still. It was he that was rocking on his feet. He felt dizzy and hot and clammy by turn. The floor was trying to move upwards and then it would swirl disconcertingly around his feet like a rug lifted by the wind under the back door. The hall was cooler, with steps down into a corridor leading off somewhere deeper in the house. There was now a smell of damp and mouldy cardboard and mice in his nostrils. The man opened another door and the air became warmer. It was heavy with the smell of hot water and washing blue; of clothes steeping in soapy water. Ordinarily it was a clean and reassuring aroma, but he felt scared and was trembling.

There was something else he could smell in the air. He stumbled forwards over the worn bricks that formed the floor. Why was the man taking him in here? They had stopped in a room dominated by a huge bank of oven doors let into a broad brick chimney breast in a room with high windows blanked out by bits of cardboard and white paint. It looked like a small factory. He suddenly realised what the other odd smell was. It was similar to when his mother sent him on errands to Mr Brewin's butcher's shop. It was that horrid, dead-meat smell, but warmer, perhaps because of the ovens — which must be alight, judging by the heat being radiated from that direction. He hated that meat smell. The butcher's shop was not his favourite errand, what with all those purplish cuts of meat that felt spongy and chill to the touch through the grease-proof paper Mr Brewin wrapped them in. They must keep their meat down here. How strange: meat and washing and a hot oven. That made no sense at all. He could see big, metal hooks ranged along a metal bar fitted into the roof trusses. They looked like meat hooks, but even he knew that you didn't hang meat where it was so warm. And there was a series of big zinc pans steaming quietly. It was all very curious.

'We had a nice day didn't we, sonny?'

The boy gave a slow shake to his head to try and clear his thoughts. He felt confused. The man was speaking to him and he must answer. 'Y—yes. Thanks awfully. Why are we here?'

'What was your favourite?' The man was standing beside a big, metal-topped table and sharpening a rather long knife on one of those odd sharpening sticks that you held in the other hand. The boy stared in mute fascination. He'd never understood how these sharpeners worked. He tried once and nothing happened, no matter how hard he clattered the two together. Why was the man doing this? The boy was going to ask, but thought better of it. Instead he answered with as much enthusiasm as he could muster. 'I saw *Ocean Swell* first thing! That was brilliant.' He paused. This was before they had met, and sounded perhaps ungrateful. 'But I'd never seen *Derby County* or *The Happy Knight*,' he added hastily. 'They were my top cops! Thanks awfully. I'd never have seen them if you hadn't taken me to the loco shed.' It felt safer talking trains. He patted his jacket pocket and felt the bulge of his Ian Allan Combined Volume. It was reassuringly heavy and, knowing that the pages were carefully marked with so many neat underlinings was nice. This made him feel a bit more secure. One of the boys at his school carried his prayer book at all times, and that made sense in a way, if perhaps rather too serious for his own taste. But having to hand the names and numbers of engines he knew, or longed to know, gave him a sense of things being in their place. It brought order to a world now lurching into something strange and most definitely *dis*ordered. He realised he was missing the strict, almost suffocating, rules of his boarding school.

The man was still flashing the shiny steel blade up and down the sharpening thing. He was fast and clearly knew what he was doing. The blade made a metallic slicing sound that set the boy's teeth on edge. 'Me too.' He gave a brief smile; just a flash, like a torch clicked on then off. 'And don't forget *Butler Henderson* — whoever *he* is!' He laughed. The boy tried to do the same, but what came out was little more than a pathetic croak. The man sighed, as if regretful. 'What a pity such a nice day ended on a sour note.'

The boy looked away. The knife was unsettling him and he couldn't understand why the man needed to sharpen it right now. 'I'd better clean my shirt, if I may.' He tried to sound confident. 'There's a lot of hot water down here, isn't there? Is that why we're here?' He caught sight of a bright red pack of Frisky Soap Powder. He'd not heard of this brand before. On the box was a pretty lady holding a basket of clean laundry under her arm. He liked her playful smile and mauve-blue eyes.

'You don't need to worry about that. Not now.' The man ran a fingertip along the blade and pulled a face as though it had cut him. 'Ouch! That's as keen as mustard.'

CHAPTER FIVE

Off the Glenfield Road

Jane Benson was seated on the top deck of the number sixteen Leicester City bus as it slowly waddled along King Richard's Road, the soft suspension accentuating every pothole along this busy thoroughfare. The window was steamed over and raindrops spattered on the outside of the glass sparkled like diamonds in the oncoming car headlamps. It was no distance to her stop and usually she was more than happy to walk home, but after her extended and tiring day she just wanted to get home as quickly as possible and rest her wet and aching feet.

She eyed her mud-encrusted shoe gloomily and kicked a cigarette butt aside. It was going to require a lot of cleaning and then take ages to dry, resting against that almost useless coin-operated radiator Mrs Mason saw fit to provide. Her heart sank at the thought of the succession of shillings required to feed the hungry heater and, in a desire to drag her thoughts away from this dispiriting image, she wiped some of the condensation clear on the window and looked out at the many shuttered shops lining the road. She watched a young man in a cloth cap and white scarf race along the pavement, feet splashing in the puddles. Evidently he thought something — or someone — was more important than wet feet. A pretty girl waiting in a bus shelter, perhaps? A couple huddled under a large, black umbrella were walking arm in arm. They appeared untroubled by the teeming rain, perhaps welcoming the excuse to be close, despite the downpour. Theirs was the slow and deliberately extended walk of lovers, making the most of each other's company and the weather be hanged.

She felt a pang of something akin to jealousy and suddenly wished she'd taken up smoking. Her work colleagues seemed to find solace in the act, although she reckoned she inhaled more than enough smoke from the steam trains each day, and this on top of the sickly house-coal fumes that always hung low over the Leicester rooftops. The air inside the bus also seemed to be composed largely of combusting Woodbines. It made her cough, but maybe she was missing something. She'd noticed as it approached that her brown-and-cream bus was carrying a bold advert for Capstan cigarettes — perhaps she should take the hint.

She leaned her forehead against the cool glass. God, it was stuffy in here and the combination of heat, condensation and ever-present smoke was oppressive. She was feeling glum. The long days at work and her poky bedsitting room were dispiriting, but neither was the root cause. The reason was all too clear. Although she usually tried to keep the painful truth repressed, tonight the stark reality was staring back at her like the slightly haunting reflection of her face in the window. It was that lack of a certain someone in her life. A man. A lover. Perhaps this imagined beau was even now waiting outside the De Montfort Hall to take her to a show, or maybe he had suggested the cinema. Perhaps he might even run carelessly through puddles in order not to be late in meeting her off the bus.

She remembered that *Don't Bother to Knock*, starring Richard Widmark and Marilyn Monroe, was playing at the Savoy in Belgrave Gate. She would like to be taken to see it by an eager man with rainwater splashed on his trouser legs. The film's title and the poster were scandalously provocative and they struck a chord that was perhaps a little too close to home. She allowed herself to imagine her fictional lover not bothering to knock, but coming straight upstairs to visit the lonely girl — not in room 809, as the poster declared, but in the back bedroom at number 17 Mostyn Street. Come to think of it, he'd better not make a sound on the way up those creaky stairs, let alone knock, as Mrs Mason would send him packing with a flea in his ear. She managed a wry little smile at the image.

Snapping out of her reverie, she stepped off the rear platform of the bus on Glenfield Street and walked to her digs. Opening the front door it smelled of that unpleasant polish Mrs Mason always used on the linoleum in the hall. She hurried upstairs, unwilling to encounter her landlady. Whilst fiddling with the key in the lock she was aware that the tiny room at the end of the short landing, which had stood empty for the last few months, now had a thin line of light glowing beneath the door. She paused momentarily to wonder who the new lodger might be and, as she did so, the door swung open. She found herself looking straight at a man with glossily slicked hair, a neatly trimmed moustache and a strong jaw-line. He was snappily dressed in a grey suit and a black bootlace tie, and his shoes were an outrageous black-and-white design.

'Oh!' She immediately regretted her overreaction and made to step into her bedsit.

'Sorry, I didn't mean to startle you, doll.' He had a deep voice that sounded as though it had been matured by a hefty intake of cigarettes and alcohol.

'Not at all.' She silently recoiled at his impertinence. She was no *doll*, thank you very much. 'It's just that the room has been empty a while, so I was not expecting anyone to be inside.' She broke eye contact and found herself smoothing her black woollen police overcoat and looking again at her filthy shoes. They had probably trailed mud up the stairs. She was going to get an awful ticking off.

'I can see why takers were not forming an orderly queue. It lacks most of the creature comforts and then just about everything else on top. Ha! Saying that, I can see that there are some fringe benefits to staying here.' His eyes twinkled cheekily as he eyed her up and down.

She felt herself getting hot. She needed to take her hat, coat and gloves off promptly. It was a chill night outside, but that bus had been like an oven and she was overheated. 'If there are any, then it's not our landlady's cooking.'

'That bad, eh?' He winked. 'Pardon my manners.' He extended a hand and stepped closer. 'Max Hawkes.'

'Miss Benson.' She gave his hand a very light squeeze for just a moment. 'Are you staying long?' She made a point of keeping her voice neutral.

'For a few weeks. Maybe longer. It depends.'

'Depends on your work, I suppose?'

'Got it in one. My line is insecure. Easy-come, Easy-go, as the song says. I've got to snap up the offers when they come, take my chances when I can and see what comes out the other side. I spend most of my time with half an eye on securing the next job.' He opened his hands as if to say 'what can you do?'

'I see.' She decided he was in insurance. Probably one of those creepy door-to-door salesmen. His suave good looks suddenly appeared false and unappealing, and his shoes were in dreadfully bad taste. She gave him a fleeting smile that was polite whilst communicating that she had no wish to deepen their acquaintance. 'I hope everything works out for you, Mr Hawkes. If you will excuse me, it's been long day.' Without waiting for a reply she stepped into her room.

An hour later she was seated beside her sash window. A bowl that had been filled with Heinz tomato soup was on a table little larger than one used for card playing. A steaming mug of tea was close to hand. Her stockings were rinsed out and draped over the frame at the end of her bed; her shoes, stuffed with yesterday's *Leicester Mercury*, were left to dry slowly and turn white with salt stains. She did not have the heart to do anything more with them tonight. She felt tired and empty.

The discovery of bones that could be those of a child was something she felt keenly. It cut into her with a ferocity that ached. The emotion welling inside was one of anger more than sorrow; anger that someone could take a young life and then burn, smash and discard the remains with such contempt. What emotion could explain such a despicable act? Was it hatred? This was shaping up to be a crime of such cruelty it was hard to stomach. An accidentally lethal blow landed in a stupid moment on a boozy night outside the Eclipse in Eastgate was terrible, but she found it easy enough to understand how it could happen. Likewise the hit-and-run death on a smoggy night described in yesterday's newspaper was tragic, but quite explicable. But this?

She sipped her sweet tea and enjoyed the warmth as it slipped down. Closing her eyes she tried to shut out the image of the skull fragment in Dr Quincey's fingers. She was only partially successful, as this was replaced in her mind by the face of that young uniformed constable that Trinder had found from somewhere and ordered to stand guard. The lad appeared barely old enough to be out of short trousers and his face was as pale as a newly peeled potato. She'd left the poor lad standing forlorn and alone under the dripping awning down a grubby narrow back alley behind Albert's Screws & Fixings Supplies and a spare parts place for cars, his eyes nervously flicking down to the skeleton in the open grave.

She opened her eyes with a start. She'd almost nodded off. There was a haunting, lilting melody filled with minor notes crawling around the room. She looked around, puzzled at the source, then pulled back the scrap of colourless curtain and pressed her nose to the cold glass. The tune was coming from outside. The downpour of earlier had eased to a light precipitation that produced a misty aura around the few spots of light along the house-backs. The trumpet was beautiful. A melody full of yearning, romantic and yet also sad. It was exactly the sort of tune she wanted to hear at this moment, and after just these few minutes she could feel it wash like a salve over her soul.

But where was it coming from, and who was playing? She wondered if it could be a gramophone record; but no, it had stopped mid-phrase, only to start again from the top. It was someone practising. She lifted the lower sash, to see and hear more clearly, caring nothing for the loss of precious heat. The long rows of cramped back yards with their high brick walls and tiny privies, and the back alleyways in between, stretched out in a monochrome dullness. A few kitchen lights glimmered and the occasional upper bedroom curtain glowed, but otherwise all was still. The sound was drifting up from below. She leaned forward on her arms and, after a moment of adjusting her eyes, could make out the toes of two shiny shoes and the swaying rim of the trumpet bell in the open doorway of their outside loo. My goodness, it was the impertinent Mr Hawkes. He was weaving a magical musical spell over this drear November night.

She smiled and shook her head slowly. What a surprise. A travelling salesman who could play trumpet, and with feeling, too. Despite her hair dampening and her spectacles slowly clouding with the airborne mizzle, she remained as she was, quite entranced. He played three tunes, until the impromptu concert was rudely brought to a halt by Mrs Mason throwing open the back door.

'Mr Hawkes! Your time is up.' Her strident voice was like a nail rubbed down a sheet of tin. 'Ten minutes and not a second more. I think I made myself quite clear on the point and you are straying dangerously over the limit.'

'Time already?' His voice sounded sad. 'Of course. I shall come in right away.'

WPC Benson pulled away from the window and eased the sash down as quietly as she could, letting the curtain fall into place whilst keeping one fold back with her fingers. As a rule, she was no curtain twitcher, but there was a first time for everything.

CHAPTER SIX

Leicester Central

The British Railways Detective Department, despite its impressive name painted in cream Gill Sans lettering on the outside of a blue-painted door, consisted of little more than two offices, a cramped interview room that had been converted from a store cupboard, and a small entrance vestibule.

The larger of the two offices was filled by rows of ageing metal filing cabinets, an over-subscribed hat and coat stand and two gigantic desks dating back to the opening of the railway; these were shared by DS John Trinder, DC Blencowe and the two women constables, Jane Benson and Lucy Lansdowne. Mrs Mavis Green was notionally the DI's secretary, but in practice acted as both gate- and house-keeper. She effectively presided over everything from behind her own desk that was dominated by a massive black typewriter at which she clattered relentlessly and with a surprising degree of aggression. Adding a welcome splash of glamour to this rather dour working environment was a colour portrait of the two princesses, Elizabeth and Margaret, pinned to the wall above her head. This would no doubt be joined next year by one of the new young queen in her coronation robes at Westminster Abbey. When not pounding the keys of her typewriter, Mrs Green was inducing the kettle to boil on a lethal-looking gas ring, taking telephone messages or sternly fending off visitors she felt were not sufficiently important to warrant entry.

The most junior member of the team was PC467 Simon Howerth. His place in the pecking order was to be perched on the end of the desk shared by the two WPCs, a berth he had occupied since joining as the new recruit in 1950. However, as he spent the majority of his time running about from one place to another at the beck and call of the others, this was not proving an undue hindrance.

Just a thin partition wall away, Detective Inspector Charles Vignoles was seated behind his desk within his small, private office, sited on the platform side of the main station block. The exposed hot water pipes running beneath the bay window that overlooked the station concourse were humming and offering welcome heat accompanied by the distinctive smell of dusty hot metal. He had his chair tipped back on the malfunctioning tilting mechanism that often threatened to send him toppling over backwards if he did not remain perfectly balanced. Comfortably reclined, with a near-empty cup of coffee to hand, he was inspecting a colour centrefold in a recent edition of *Railway Magazine* that lay open across his knee. With a smoking pipe jutting from the corner of his mouth and glasses perched on his nose, his was the contented and enjoyable appreciation of something that interested him deeply.

DS Trinder observed all this through the partially opened door, and cleared his throat in anticipatory warning before knocking once and stepping smartly inside, without waiting to be asked. If the door were ajar, then Vignoles was available to be disturbed.

'You will want to know about last night, guv?'

'Ah, good morning John.' Vignoles gave a quick glance towards his sergeant. 'Take a seat.' He took another look at the magazine, sadly aware that these stolen moments before the proper work of the day commenced were over. 'Not sure what I think about all this.' He furrowed his brow. 'I perhaps need to have a look for myself, before I make any rash pronouncements.'

'I'm pretty stumped too. But how do you know, guv? Did Jane speak with you this morning?' Trinder sounded puzzled.

'Jane? I doubt she has an opinion on the subject. Never had her down as much of a locomotive buff.'

'Not sure if I'm quite following you.'

'The new standard classes of locomotives the British Railways workshops are currently rolling out.' He tapped the glossy print. 'This Robert Riddles fellow, who designed them, is making some pretty bold claims about what benefits they deliver. Reckons they're far easier to maintain and more efficient to run. Added to which there are many standardised components right across the classes, which will offer up further savings. Clever.' He nodded appreciatively. 'All in all, quite an impressive package, and yet, I just don't know what to make of them. Some look rather too "Trans-Atlantic" for my taste.' He gave his pipe a thoughtful puff. 'I suppose one will get used to them, given time.' Trinder could now see that Vignoles was talking about the print of a painting in the magazine. The artist had adopted an elevated position that displayed a grand array of dark-green-and-black steam locomotives of varying sizes carefully positioned as if outside a locomotive shed on an open day.

'So...' Vignoles closed the magazine and laid it to one side, then swung around to face Trinder, planting his feet firmly on the old brown linoleum floor. 'Those bones under the viaduct. Was it a wild goose chase?' He held a note of hope in his voice.

'No. It looks rather grim, actually.'

'Ah.' His idle consideration of the new locomotive designs was definitely over.

'It's going to be tricky. We've got almost nothing to work with.'

'But they are human remains?'

'I'm afraid so, guv. The archaeologists who found them seem to know their stuff and are convinced they're human. Recently deposited in what looks like fresh domestic fire-ash.' Vignoles raised a quizzical eyebrow at this revelation. 'Been there no more than a few months at the outside, but they reckon they could be a lot newer. I'd be inclined to agree.'

'We'll need a second opinion. Get on the blower and see if the Leicester Constabulary lab boys can take a look.'

'I've been on to them already and they should be on site any time now. And I've detailed two uniformed constables to collect all the rubbish and junk in the area. We're going to need every scrap we can find, on the off-chance there's a clue in there somewhere.'

'Good man. So what have we got?'

'Little more than a pile of ash that looks fairly recently deposited. I'd estimate about two or three bucket-loads. According to the archaeologists, the ash then had soil thrown on top in what could be interpreted as an attempt to cover up the deposit, although this was largely removed by the time we were on site, so I couldn't confirm that. Mixed into this ash are a great many human bone fragments. These are burnt and perhaps further crushed, and all very small. Pretty useless, to be honest, but there was enough for one of the lady diggers to suggest we're looking at the remains of a young person.'

'How young?' Vignoles was watching Trinder intently.

'They could not indicate the sex, but when pushed suggested perhaps a nine- to twelve-year-old. Give or take a year or so. I know, it's awfully vague. But, there is also this...' Trinder handed Vignoles a small brown envelope, which he duly opened whilst Trinder continued speaking. 'A snake belt-buckle with a few red and blue threads. It has also been fire damaged.'

'It could be associated with the bones?'

'Possibly. One of the diggers, a girl student called Sarah Ferrington, speculated that this might be worn by a boy. She offered that as a clue to help us.' He raised an eyebrow.

'Fancies herself as an amateur detective, eh?' Vignoles turned the little piece of cheap, soot-stained metal around in his hands. 'It's a start I suppose. Nothing else?'

'Not as yet. Perhaps we'll get something in the litter scattered about the area. But the site has been badly trampled and the surface deposits have been largely cleared and shovelled into mounds and then two deep excavations made. All in all the area has been contaminated and messed around as thoroughly as one could imagine.'

'Perfect. What about those who made the discovery?'

Trinder flipped his little black police notebook open and consulted the scribbled notes he'd made the night before. 'Professor Alfred Terence Wildblood of Leicester University is heading a small team. This consists of Dr Denise Quincey and the eager Sarah Ferrington. They used two council labourers to make the preparatory cuts in the ground. These men also laid down duck boards, put up a temporary canvas awning and erected what looks like a scout tent for the professor to use as his office. The men are no longer on site and won't be again until the professor closes the dig. I don't sense anything suspicious about the archaeologists at this stage.'

'If ever there was a group of people likely to discover bone fragments in the ground, it is surely them. If one of them wished to conceal the remains of a murder victim, they'd be darned stupid to choose their own dig site. Still, you'd better check them over for form's sake and see if anything catches your eye. Get the names of those workmen and give them the once-over whilst you're at it. Probably a wasted effort, but we'd better be methodical and follow every angle we can.' Vignoles put the snake belt-buckle on a clear patch of desk and toyed with his now-dead pipe whilst speaking. 'We don't have a time of death, nor even the day or week. We've no idea when this person went missing. Worse still, we know next to nothing about the victim except he just might be young and just might have worn a snake belt. All of which means we can't start to establish if any of these people have alibis. Darn it, why did this have to land on my desk?'

'A few yards further away and it would have been over to the constabulary.' Trinder and Vignoles exchanged a rueful glance. 'I've sent Jane to do some door-to-door, but she's hamstrung for the same reasons. She can do little more than ask around and hope for the best.' Trinder shrugged his shoulders apologetically. 'I'm not expecting results.'

Vignoles nodded in agreement. 'The question is, who is missing a child? Assuming that is what we are looking at here. An adult with no friends and living alone might conceivably vanish and nobody notice for a considerable length of time, but surely that's not likely with a young boy. Or girl.'

'I agree. It makes my blood run cold just thinking about it. But I've not seen any missing persons' bulletins about a missing child doing the rounds. Thankfully, they're rarer than hen's teeth.'

DI Vignoles considered the valid point Trinder just made and inspected his untidy desk with a mounting sense of unease. Had his notoriously messy filing system resulted in missing an important call for help? 'Can't say I've seen anything either, but I'd better sift through this lot just in case I've overlooked something.' He quickly rifled through a precarious mound of paper, but was instantly becoming impatient, angry with himself for being so casual. Looking up, he saw the young constable passing the open office door.

'Howerth! I've got a job for you!'

'Yes, sir.' Simon looked startled. He was not often called into the guv'nor's office and, now he was in there, he noticed that neither the DI nor the sergeant looked in a particularly good mood.

'The sergeant and I have a crime scene to visit. Whilst we're out, go through this lot and see if there have been any communiqués regarding missing persons, especially children. Then look on all the notice boards. Check with your fellow officers. We need to know if there's an active hunt for a missing young person.'

'Yessir!' Howerth could hardly believe his luck. Tasked with going through the undoubtedly important papers on the detective inspector's desk was a sign that he was winning his trust. 'Is there anyone in particular I should be looking out for, sir?'

'Just anyone missing, from anywhere, irrespective of age.'

'Including Nottingham?'

'What an odd question, constable. Did the DI not make himself perfectly clear you were to look for missing persons from absolutely anywhere, Nottingham therefore included?' Trinder looked annoyed.

Simon's face glowed red. 'Of course, sarge. It's just that, um...' He stopped, losing courage, correctly surmising that he was in danger of making himself look foolish.

'Spit it out.' Vignoles had stood up and was reaching for his heavy winter coat. 'Has the cat got your tongue?'

'It's just funny. Funny-odd. Well, not funny at all, I suppose.'

'We don't have all day.' Trinder glowered.

'Sorry. It's just that I was having a pint with my mate Eddie last night...'

'Ah. The terrible twosome reunited.' Vignoles adjusted his hat in preparation to leave, but allowed a flicker of a smile, despite the gloomy feeling starting to take hold about the grim discovery so discomfortingly close to their own station.

Simon and his friend Edward Earnshaw had what they in the service liked to call 'form'. The two had an extraordinary history of getting into all manner of scrapes and hair-raising situations, some of which had proven to be extremely dangerous. However, despite appearing like annoying stones in the detective's shoes, the two lads had unquestionably helped solve a number of important cases and so, one thing leading to another, Vignoles had decided it might be better to channel Howerth's enthusiasm along more appropriate, and legal, channels. Whilst it was a massive gamble that did not meet with universal approval, PC467 had duly started his apprenticeship in their office.

'We meet once or twice a week. Work rosters allowing.'

'The point being?' Trinder was impatient.

'The point is, sarge, Eddie said he was accosted by a lady at the Vic yesterday afternoon as he was coming in on the all stations stopper to...Well, never mind to where. He said this lady came up to him showing him a photograph of a schoolboy and asking if he'd seen him. She was really upset.'

The three fell silent as this information sank in just as an unfitted freight train clattered through the station, the little six-wheeled tender engine puffing furiously at the front.

'A missing boy.' Vignoles exchanged a look with Trinder, who appeared equally taken aback.

'That's what Eddie said. The photograph she had was of him in school uniform.'

'And this was at Nottingham Vic?'

'Yes.'

Vignoles looked furious. 'Sergeant, do you know anything about this?'

'First I've heard about it, guv.'

'I wonder what else I don't know about!' Vignoles lifted his eyes to the skylight above their heads, drawn by the noise as it was hit by a sudden heavy downpour of rain that sounded like small pebbles being dropped onto the filthy glass. 'Howerth, find your chum Eddie and tell him to call in and see us. Today. Do that now, you can get on looking through all these papers afterwards. We need to know more about that boy, and trace the mother.'

'Righty-o. I have Eddie's work diagram for the week so we can work out when to meet up for a pint. I should be able to work out where he is now.'

'Good. Tell him to report to us as soon as he is able.' Vignoles shooed the constable out of his office.

'In fairness, that may have been her first, maybe her only, appearance at the Vic,' Trinder ventured.

Vignoles ran a hand over his chin, his initial annoyance subsiding. 'We must drill into everyone that this is exactly the sort of thing I need to be told about. Badger would haul me over hot coals if he got wind of it.'

Trinder nodded sympathetically. They both knew that Chief Superintendent Badger was a notoriously uncompromising boss who seemed to delight in catching them out. 'What now?'

'I want to see the crime scene. Send Lansdowne to Nottingham and she can ask around for this distressed mother. There must be others who encountered her that day, and surely she left a telephone number or address so people could pass on any information.' He stopped, one hand on the door handle, and looked pensive. 'The problem is, John, what do we tell the poor woman when we find her? Do we break her heart based on the most inconclusive evidence imaginable, or do we play our cards close to our chest and deny we've found the remains of what just might be her boy? That feels wrong.' They looked at each other and neither felt willing to decide. 'Sometimes I hate this job.'

CHAPTER SEVEN

Off Talbot Lane

'Is there anything you can tell us?' After a peremptory exchange of greetings, Vignoles cast his eye around the excavation site whilst simultaneously addressing the senior Leicester City Police Forensics Officer, Simon Beaumont. Trinder was still giving the recalcitrant canvas awning a suspicious look and ensuring he didn't receive a dousing similar to that of the evening before.

Despite the muddy access route and the quantities of exposed earth, Beaumont was clad in an almost spotlessly clean boiler suit worn buttoned up to a white shirt collar and regimental tie beneath. He was evidently the meticulous sort. Before answering the DI's question, he sucked air between his teeth by way of forewarning Vignoles there was going be no quick breakthrough. 'We've recovered a considerable number of tiny bone fragments that will offer up nothing. We do have a small number of larger fragments that, at a stretch, might tell us something about the victim. But not until we give them time and attention.'

'DS Trinder warned me it was going to be a tricky one.'

'I'm afraid so, inspector.' Beaumont gave Trinder a quick glance that suggested he approved of the sergeant's caution. 'It will prove impossible to give a sex to the remains. If we find a good run of teeth then we have a better chance of course, but it is going to be very tricky.'

'Are these not the remains of a young lad?' Vignoles appeared to be surprised, and glanced from Beaumont to Trinder in quick succession.

Beaumont pursed his lips in an expression of mild disapproval. 'I've heard the pronouncement of your lady archaeologist, but I would advise caution. Her pronouncement is perhaps premature.'

'So we could just as easily have an adult female?'

The forensics officer shrugged his shoulders. 'It may indeed prove to be that of a youth, but there again it could be a young female. You will need to call upon other detective powers to resolve this one based on what we have so far.'

'But if I pushed you?' Vignoles needed something, anything, to work with.

'I don't like being pushed, Mr Vignoles, but I might hazard that the person is younger rather than older, and certainly small in stature.' Vignoles pulled a pained expression whilst Trinder slapped a hand against his damp coat in frustration. They needed more than this. Beaumont held up a gloved finger. 'Thankfully, bone evidence is not all we have. Come and get your detective brains engaged.' He led them to the table previously used to lay out Roman remains and at which the other two members of the forensics team were inspecting and bagging the usual kind of rubbish found gathering in any abandoned corner of a city. 'There's all sorts of stuff here that your officers swept up.' The uniformed officers in question were keeping guard over the entrance to the crime scene whilst trying to stay dry from the steadily pattering rain; both were watching impassively. 'They trawled up quite a haul, which we are currently assessing.' He proffered a piece of leather threaded through a scorched buckle. 'This is worth further consideration.'

'Is that part of a bag?' Vignoles asked.

'I'd say it's a buckle and strap from a leather satchel. A typical school satchel,' Beaumont replied.

'Looks like it was good quality, heavy leather. It might have been expensive.' Trinder was happier now they had something to inspect.

'I agree with your analysis, sergeant.' Beaumont gave another little nod of approval. He liked the DS. 'We have another, larger piece of the satchel here.' He opened a brown paper bag. 'One of the front pockets. The thickness of the leather has prevented it from properly combusting.' He lifted up a substantial piece of scorched dark chestnut leather, and although badly damaged it was instantly obvious what it had once been. 'Even better, from inside, we recovered some crumbs and a sweet wrapper. It was a Glacier Mint.'

'Which could suggest a young lad,' said Trinder.

'Or lass. Or an adult. I admit to quite liking them myself, so what does that prove?' Vignoles was unimpressed.

'I love them — when the sweet ration allows.' Beaumont cracked a smile.

'No help at all, then,' Vignoles countered. 'Fox's might manufacture their mints in Leicester, but they sell them all over the country. No use at all.' Vignoles was now looking at the neat rows of broken bottles, crushed tin cans, odd bits of rusty wire and a number of cigarette cartons arrayed on the archaeologists' table. He saw nothing to inspire him.

'Ah, but we also have *this* little beauty!' The forensics officer opened a small envelope and proffered a rectangle of card. He was obviously enjoying revealing each item in turn, spinning out the evidence with relish. It was an Edmondson railway ticket.

'From inside the pocket of the satchel?' Trinder asked.

'Indeed.'

Vignoles was immediately interested and, taking it carefully from Beaumont, gave it closer examination. 'Platform ticket for Grantham, issued on 24th September this year.' He turned the slightly scorched ticket gently between his fingers, listening to the crows cawing in the treetops and the distant sound of buffers of an unseen train clattering in the station. 'We've got a starting point. Good work.'

'You buy a platform ticket if you're meeting or seeing someone off from the station in question. So the person who bought this one must have lived in Grantham.' Trinder looked animated.

'A reasonable supposition,' Vignoles agreed. 'Or in the country or a village with Grantham as the nearest station. Its usefulness over, it was dropped into the pocket and forgotten. It gives us a location and a time when this person was alive. Presumably, any ticket used for travel from Grantham to Leicester at a more recent time perished along with the body.' He stopped and took a deep breath. 'Of course, we are still having to make a giant leap of faith that this burnt offering and ticket were owned by the same person whose ashes are here.'

'But if these are his, then the killer was careless. He tried to destroy the evidence, but was not thorough. Perhaps he was in a hurry. He might have made other mistakes, too.' Trinder was trying to find a way forward.

Vignoles didn't answer. He took a final look at the litter on the table. He was wondering if their energies might be better spent in Grantham. 'Thank you.' He nodded to the forensics officer, then addressed Trinder. 'Let's find Benson.'

It did not take long to locate the WPC. She was standing beneath a large black umbrella beside the pale-blue-painted wooden gates opening into one of the small business premises crammed into the lee of the viaduct. The gates were being shaken at that moment by a heavily laden coal train passing high on the viaduct. The big mineral engine was lifting exhaust high into the air and a shower of fine cinders dropped onto the umbrella's fabric like tiny hailstones. Jane had stepped to one side to allow a navy blue-and-cream Foden DG delivery van to reverse into the yard of Talbot Motor Factors Ltd. The driver had only just that moment cut the engine and it was ticking quietly as it started to cool; the smell of exhaust still lingered. Benson indicated that she would like to speak with him and the driver looked mildly surprised, not only at being accosted by a pretty lady in uniform, but by the sudden appearance of two stern-looking men in long, dark overcoats and brimmed hats who were rapidly approaching.

'What's up?' He was perhaps wondering if this was the preamble to a mugging.

'I wonder if you could spare a few moments.' Benson gave him a winning smile to put him at his ease.

'If you make it quick, love: I've got a delivery to collect.' The man had a crumb stuck to his lower lip, which he wiped away with the back of a hand that held what looked like a tightly balled paper bag. Perhaps it had contained whatever he had just been eating.

'We won't keep you long, Mr—?'

'Tibbott. Mike Tibbott.'

'Just a routine enquiry. There has been an incident behind these premises.'

'What sort of incident is that, then?' He gave Benson a quizzical look.

'A very serious one.' Vignoles was standing on the other side of the driver, giving a slight nod of acknowledgement to Benson before speaking. 'We prefer not to say more at this stage about the exact nature of the incident, but would be grateful for any assistance you might be able to offer.' He flashed his warrant card.

'Oh, right. Well, I'm not sure I can be much help, but fire away!' He spread his hands wide and gave a shrug of his shoulders.

'Are you a regular visitor here, Mr Tibbott?' Benson asked.

'I call in once or twice a week. Sometimes more, sometimes less. Depends.'

'At regular times and days?' Benson asked.

'Not really. I get a shout and come and collect stuff, then deliver it out and about as needed.' He nodded towards the building. 'They make parts for motor cars. Supplying the motor trade around the county. My company, Draper's...' he pointed to the bold name on the side of his van, 'we pick up from all kinds of places, taking stuff around as needed.'

'*Kar Kare is Our Koncern.*' Trinder was reading the advertising line beneath the owner's name. His incredulous expression made it clear what he thought of it.

'I know. It's bloody awful — pardon my French, miss — but the boss is mad on all this advertising stuff and swears by it.'

'I'd swear at it.' Trinder was unimpressed.

'Do you stay on site long?' Benson asked.

'Not really.' Tibbott hesitated before adding. 'Well, you know. If time allows, I do take the odd cuppa and have a little sneaky ciggie with some of the lads.' He gave a conspiratorial wink to Benson. 'Just a fag break.'

'You know the employees here?' Vignoles asked.

'Yep. Not that there's many. It's only a small place.'

'So you might notice if something unusual happened around and about?'

'What sort of "unusual"?' He was puzzled by the inspector's question.

'We are interested in any unusual activity around the back of the premises. Under or beside the viaduct arches.' They all gave the monstrous structure a glance, as if somehow it needed acknowledging. The blue engineering brick was slicked to an almost oily black by the falling rain. 'Prior to the arrival of the archaeological diggers, that is.'

'Is that who they are? I did wonder.' Tibbott shook his head as if unable to understand why people would even consider such work. 'You mean back there, under the arches? I wouldn't know anything about there. I stick to the yard, loading my wagon. It's just wasteland and junk.' He seemed to be looking for somewhere to throw the paper bag, and decided to toss it inside the cab of his vehicle.

'So you are familiar with the area in question?' Benson probed.

The driver hesitated and looked at the ground, pulling at an ear lobe.

'It would be wise to speak up.' Trinder had been observing the exchange and felt the driver was holding something back.

'Look, it's nothing that will help your investigation.' He looked sheepishly towards Benson then faced Trinder.

'We can decide that,' Trinder responded.

'Of course.' He laughed. 'The, er, facilities are a bit primitive in the works. A bit, er, pungent, if you catch my drift. So, if any of the lads get caught short we just nip around the back. When there's no one looking, of course. You know...against a wall.'

Vignoles was not interested in his toilet habits, but they might make Tibbott a useful witness as a result of his surreptitious visits under the arches. 'Have you had the need to step around the back during the last month?'

'I can't say I was keeping a record!' He laughed. 'I dunno. A few times. Two, I suppose. But, like I said, there was never anyone about. But now, with that lot working there, we've had to take our chances with the facilities provided.' He wrinkled his nose to illustrate the hardship involved.

'You didn't perhaps pass someone leaving the area?' Trinder asked.

'No. Sorry.'

'Might you have seen anyone carry a bucket or two filled with fire-ash around there?' Trinder added.

'No.' Tibbott gave Trinder a strange look.

'Or a school satchel perhaps?' Trinder knew this was a long shot. It had most probably been burned off site.

Tibbott was shaking his head. 'Can't help. Sorry.'

It looked as though there was little else the delivery man could give them and so Vignoles thanked him and Benson noted his name and address in her little book and they let him get on with collecting his delivery. At that moment the heavens opened once again.

'Let's get out of this blasted rain. You can carry out the door-to-door when it eases off.' Vignoles urged Trinder and a grateful Benson out of Talbot Lane and hurried them back towards Central station. As they walked he told Benson about the fragment of satchel and the Grantham platform ticket.

'It's a good start, sir. If we can find that lady in Nottingham and she confirms her son had such a bag, then I suppose we will at least know who it is.' She tailed off. The miserable weather was already darkening the streets and turning the roads to a glossy sheen that reflected the interior lights of a passing bus. The rain was dampening their spirits enough without thinking about the desperate misery for that unfortunate mother if they had to tell her the worst.

'Have you found anything of interest?' Vignoles fired the question at Benson whilst cleaning his glasses on his handkerchief for the umpteenth time that day.

'Nothing, sir. The men in the auto spares factory told a tale similar to Mr Tibbott's. It does rather explain the unpleasant odour under the arches.' Benson wrinkled her nose in an expression of distaste. 'But nobody saw anything and their stories all match. There were few people at home along the lane, but those who were saw and heard nothing that jumps out. But we don't even have a time and date, sir. It makes it awfully hard.'

'Well-nigh impossible.' Vignoles stopped. They were now inside the covered street level booking hall of Central station. 'Did anyone mention especially noxious bonfires? No, that would not do. But a garden incinerator, perhaps?' It was not really a question, more a case of Vignoles thinking aloud.

'Incinerator?' Benson raised a carefully plucked eyebrow. 'Why would they?'

'We found ashes. Everything had been burnt by a great heat.'

'Of course. I'll go back after six when more people are home from work. I can ask about that.'

'Perhaps a neighbour has been burning rubbish recently.'

'And ask if anyone smelt charred pork,' Trinder suggested.

Vignoles and Benson looked quizzically at him.

'It is what burning human flesh supposedly smells like. Pork. So I'm told...'

Benson looked green about the gills.

'Sorry, Jane.'

Vignoles changed tack, aware that whilst they were speaking quietly, this was no subject for a public arena. 'WPC Benson, I want you to map out Talbot Lane on a blackboard. Place each house and business on the map and list all names associated with each. Start to block out the immediate area, then expand outwards beyond the far side of the viaduct into places like Bath Lane and the neighbouring streets. Blencowe can help. Start with the site of the bones and work outwards. I need to know who lives and works where, what times they come and go. Try and give me some structure. Try and give me anything!'

'Righty-o, sir.' Benson cheered a little. This kind of meticulous and detailed work was something she and Blencowe enjoyed, but more importantly it took her a step away from the image of burning flesh.

'Plot any salient facts, any names or events about those occupying each of the premises and see what that throws up. Sergeant Trinder, open up a case file. I'd better break the bad news to the Badger. I just wish I had an idea of what I'm going to tell him.'

CHAPTER EIGHT

Leicester

He felt sleepy. A deep weariness had crawled into his body, removing the ability to flex any muscle. It was impossible to lift his limbs. It was so much easier to just lie there...

His head had lolled to one side to rest against the grainy, rough edge of the zinc hip bath he was immersed in. He found he could not move it. Why bother to even try?

Why was he in a bath? There was no need to take a bath... But he could hardly find the energy to hold even this thought, let alone give it proper consideration. It was so warm and deep. Completely enveloping. He could not quite tell the difference between his body and the water, so equal were the temperatures. It was as though he were completely at one with the bathwater, as though he were seeping into it, slipping into the water and mixing...

Oh, but he was so weary. It must be time to go home... home... His eyelids drooped and closed.

A few moments passed that could have been an hour, or perhaps it was no more than a second or two. There was no way to tell. He forced his eyes wide open and, in a jolt of last-ditch energy, tried to focus on the chair with his jacket draped across the back. His ABC...where was his little book? Was it safe...was it...? He could not keep his mind on anything. With a struggle he managed to open his oh-so-heavy eyelids once again. The pretty girl on the Frisky soap packet. Smiling at him. Calm and reassuring. He liked her. If she thought everything was OK, then...

His body turned slightly, the bath now fuller than before as he slumped deeper into it. His final flickering glimpse was of his shirt ballooning out in the water, free of the waistband of his shorts. Why was it red? All red... Was he bathing in cherry red pop?

His jaw hung slack. After about five minutes a hand reached down and closed his eyes.

CHAPTER NINE

Leicester Central

'You wished to see me, inspector?' Mrs Green had showed Eddie Earnshaw to the office door, but he hesitated on the threshold, waiting to be invited inside.

'Ah, Fireman Earnshaw.' Vignoles looked up from the short list of notes he was assembling in preparation to typing out a briefing document for Badger. 'Take a seat, young man.'

DS Trinder had seen Earnshaw arrive. He also entered the office, dragging a battered wooden chair to one side of the desk and sitting down. He gave Eddie a brief nod by way of greeting.

'You got here promptly.'

'No trouble, sir.' Eddie took off his grease-top cap and started turning it around in his hands. He had brought a strong whiff of burnt carbon into the room. His blue overalls already stained black-and-grey as testament to a very early start in Leicester shed. 'Simon got a message through to Mr White — he's our foreman — that you wanted to see me. I was preparing to fire a trip out to Coalville and back, but because the request came from yourself and sounded urgent, Mr White arranged for another lad to take on my roster and he let me ride footplate on the next engine off shed.'

'That was most accommodating of him.' Vignoles knew all the shed foremen along the line and made of point of developing a good relationship with each. They were strong characters who held considerable sway over a great body of men and their willing co-operation in some of the more curious requests he had been known to make over the years had proven vital. The Leicester shed foreman had always been helpful in the past. 'I shall pass on my thanks for his assistance. He has saved you and me a lot of time.'

Eddie looked slightly nervous. He stole a few furtive glances around the room. This was perhaps only the second time he had been inside the inspector's private office, and it was still the same cluttered Aladdin's cave that he remembered. It came with the most bizarre assortment of curios crowding the shelves and other flat surfaces. Apparently, most were unclaimed lost property items. He was drawn to an oddly shaped lump of steel that was acting as a paperweight on the centre of the desk between himself and the detective inspector.

'I understand that at Nottingham Victoria you were approached by a lady asking after her son.'

'Yes. Has she found him?'

'We don't know. We are trying to identify her. Unfortunately, she did not report the incident to the railway police. Did she mention her or the boy's name?'

'No. We were about to depart, there was no time.'

'Can you describe her?'

Eddie pulled his eyes away from an inverted v-shaped slice of what looked like a piece of rail, and pulled a face. In so doing some white lines appeared on his soot-blackened visage as he chewed over the problem, the colouration to his skin the result of his dusty, fire-raising duties earlier. 'I only saw her for a few moments and was concentrating on getting ready to depart. And it was quite gloomy, even with the station lamps. She was not especially tall and she was quite thin. Thin and pale.'

'What was she wearing?' Trinder prompted.

'A light coloured raincoat. With a belt. I think it was a pretty good one.'

'How do you know that?' Trinder queried.

'Sometimes you can tell when you see better-made clothes, can't you?' Eddie looked flustered. He prided himself on being observant, but in this formal situation, with two detectives staring expectantly at him, he was no longer so sure of himself. 'Her shoes were shiny and well cared-for. They were dark blue. Or maybe black. It's hard to be sure in that light. Her eyes were blue. Yes, pale blue. I do remember that, as she stared at me and it was unsettling.' He glanced down at his heavily work-stained boots that were leaving grey ash on the floor.

'Anything else?'

'She had one of those pixie-hood things on her head. Not a hat. A plastic rain hood.'

Trinder made a note. 'What about her son?'

'It was just a picture of a boy in a blazer. With a gap in his front teeth.'

'It was a school photograph?' Vignoles asked.

'Yeah, I think so. Very formal. Just head and shoulders. But quite big.' Eddie used his grubby hands to indicate a rectangle approximately ten inches by eight. 'It was covered in see-through cellophane to stop it getting wet.'

'What did she say about him?' asked Vignoles.

'That he was missing, and she needed help to find him. She went there because he likes watching trains.'

'At Nottingham Victoria?' Trinder interjected.

'I suppose that's what she meant. That's where we were.'

Trinder nodded, but looked puzzled. A platform ticket in Grantham, human remains in Leicester and a boy last seen in Nottingham.

'So, she asked you to keep a look-out. Did she say how to contact her, or give any indication or clue about where she lives?'

'Oh dear, no. I suppose she might if we'd had time, but we were just about to leave and there was another distraction, too: a big group of train-spotters were crowding around the loco whilst I was trying to see if the guard was on board and giving us the right away.'

'Train-spotters, eh?' pondered Vignoles, 'Do you think any of them might have been connected with the lady or her son?'

'I don't think so. She was just caught up among them. The lads had run along beside the engine as we rolled in, you see, sir.' Eddie stopped as he caught Trinder raising an eyebrow and was unsure if this meant that the sergeant expected Eddie to have made efforts to stop the over-excited schoolchildren from running and perhaps putting themselves in danger. 'They were asking me about the name of my engine, and then suddenly there she was.'

'Might you be able to recognise any of them again?' Vignoles tried one last shot.

'Hm... One had National Health specs on. There were a few older ones who stood more at the back. But if I know anything about these spotters, they'll be back in the same place every day.'

'Fair enough,' said Vignoles. In the few moments of silence that ensued Eddie leaned a little closer toward the desk and cautiously put a hand on the lump of metal. 'Is that a piece of Vignoles rail, sir?'

'It is, indeed.' Vignoles smiled. 'Designed by my namesake. It was presented to me some years back and I confess to being rather proud of it. A little survivor from that wondrously odd broad gauge railway Mr Brunel dreamed up.'

'I've never seen a piece of that before.' Eddie suddenly put on his cap, sensing that the interview was over.

'Thank you for your help, Fireman Earnshaw. Keep your eyes peeled, and if you see either mother or son, make sure you tell us immediately.'

CHAPTER TEN

Mostyn Street

At number 17, landlady Mrs Mason was clattering pans in the back kitchen with the radiogram turned up louder than usual. This cacophony was all the louder because she had left the kitchen door ajar. Clear warning signs that she was in a foul temper. Benson could hear the distinctive sound of Mr Churchill's voice making a broadcast. The Prime Minister's familiar, half-swallowed vowels and chewed-up words that sounded as though he were inebriated were being delivered in typical, bitten-off sentences and punctuated by oddly-timed pauses and words stressed seemingly at random.

'...I'm talking about. The way people-are-beginning to think, now. The different classes have all rubbed shoulders in this war. Because of the bombs, and evacuation, much more than they did in-the-last-one.'

Jane Benson began to ascend the stairs, taking in the ugly, patterned carpet whilst wondering why the PM was still talking about 'this war'. It had ended years ago. He was so out of touch. They were entering a new 'Elizabethan' age with a young and pretty queen and exciting new clothes and furniture and wallpaper patterns in the shop windows — even if few could afford them. She didn't need to be endlessly reminded of the war, although looking at the distinctly pre-war decoration of Mostyn Street, perhaps he was pitching his words at people like Mrs Mason.

'...we'll all. Come out of this a-bit-different. To how we went in...'

She reflected on the inescapable fact that Mr Churchill, once the nation's saviour and darling, was getting old. Those less charitably minded claimed he was losing his marbles. Or perhaps he was just clinging on with more than a hint of desperation to those lost years of national triumph. Whatever the truth, some of his pronouncements these days were far from universally popular.

Opening her bedroom door she turned on the ceiling light. A weak glow came from the single bulb suspended from the ceiling. Placing two brand new packets of tea on the little table, and still aware of the booming voice downstairs, she quietly applauded the fact that at least the PM had finally ended the tea ration. A small mercy and one that improved her life demonstrably more than almost all the other stuff those politicians huffed and puffed about in Westminster. She fiddled with the radiator and, once it fired up, stood with her coat on and waited for the welcome fingers of warmth to start pushing aside the great dull weight of cold air inhabiting the room. With a bit of luck Mrs Mason would either turn the radio down or the news would end and they could share in Mrs Dale's Diary of endless domestic dullness.

'A penny for them!'

Jane Benson jumped like a scalded cat and spun about. She, too, had left her door ajar and now, leaning casually and impertinently against the doorframe, was the new lodger. 'Oh my goodness, Mr Hawkes, you gave me quite a start!'

'Apologies, Miss B.' With two fingers he tipped his hat further back on his head in an action that was almost a mockery of an army salute. He cracked a broad smile. 'You look deep in thought. Something troubling you?'

'Of course not.' Her response was instantaneous. 'I was just...' She had to consider her reply. 'I was just waiting a moment for the radiator to warm up, that's all.' She stepped a little closer to the door, enough to subtly block the way in.

He might be impudent, but he was observant. She was indeed preoccupied, and not about Churchill and the price of tea; nor did she much care why Mrs Mason was in a grump that evening. She was preoccupied by the revelations of the last twenty-four hours. The thought of those charred remains was hanging heavy over her in a way that other investigations had rarely done before. It was still early days, and yet already she sensed there was something callous and cruel in the air. On the way home she had found that memorable phrase from Macbeth circling about in her head. *By the itching of my thumbs, something evil this way comes.* She believed that she could smell the evil. Of course, the profound cold beneath the viaduct arch and the accompanying stench of damp, dug-over earth, rotting rubbish and sour urine could explain that. She faced him squarely and folded her arms in a gesture which implied that the subject of her thoughts was closed to further interrogation by the cocky man slouching in her doorway.

'Ah, so you also have one of those blasted radiator things too?' He gave a low whistle, then dropped his voice to little more than a murmur. 'She doesn't like to spend much on creature comforts. That thing eats shillings like a hungry dog.'

She couldn't help but smile. 'That's true.' They heard a sudden clatter of plates. 'Dear Mrs Mason seems to be in a right stew over something. I'd steer clear of her if I were you.'

Hawkes stood upright and fished a packet of Player's from his fashionably baggy trousers. 'Smoke?' She declined, but for the second time in as many days wondered if she were somehow missing out. He lit up in a well-practised move that looked as if it were learned from watching the Rat Pack. 'I appreciate the warning, Miss B, but it comes too late.' He flashed a cheeky grin. 'I confess I might well be the reason for her making that racket,' he confided, keeping his voice low. He threw an exaggerated glance towards the top of the stairs, then took a long drag on his cigarette. 'I got tired of the ten-minute limit and took advantage of her going to the shops to put in some extra practice.' He exhaled smoke noisily like a steam engine at the buffer stops.

'Practice?' Benson took a moment to process the information. 'Oh, the trumpet.'

'Sure thing! And not in the darned wind and rain sitting on that draughty toilet seat.' The lazy way he was speaking was obviously affected and inspired by listening to how jazz musicians spoke in films. 'I discovered she's got a few half-decent discs gathering dust in the front parlour. You know, I'm thinking she's a whole different kind of bird when she stops boiling cabbage and gets those hideous curlers out.' He winked and she could not help smirking at the image of Mrs Mason letting her hair down. 'So I slipped on a long-player by Miller, whacked up the volume and jammed along.'

'Jammed? I'm not sure I understand.'

'Ad-libbed. Made up some phrases. OK, so it was not strictly a jam session. That's when the boys invent something live and then we mix it up, taking turns to see where it goes and not caring too much if it takes us down a blind alley. No, I just threw the hook line around some. I hung my own melody variations around the rhythm section and around Miller's trumpet line.' He took another noisy drag on his Player. 'Of course, it was just a cut I was playing along to, so they couldn't respond. It's best when each soloist alters the melody a little to keep everyone on their toes, each taking a turn to pull the tune some place new. But it was a bit of fun.'

Despite her best intentions and dark mood, she was intrigued. She did not quite understand the words he was using and suspected he was talking jazz, which was something she had never understood, being the preserve of earnest university graduates in black roll-neck sweaters and college scarves, but it was interesting listening to Hawkes. And surprising. It was something new and fresh, perhaps challenging, and she was in the mood for a new experience. 'You were playing in the front parlour, not in the outside privy?' She sounded almost in shock, her eyes wide with surprise.

It was true the room in question was supposed to be available for 'recreational purposes' by the lodgers, but it was so unwelcoming and drear, with the fire never lit, that she never felt inclined to enter and so the door remained permanently closed. She was not convinced that Mrs Mason even used it except perhaps on high days and holidays. Most probably she only did so if someone died, when it would become a temporary funeral parlour. It had about as much warmth and appeal as a chapel of rest.

'You played along with a record?'

'Yep! Full volume.'

'Oh, golly gosh. Then she walked in on you?'

'You got it. I lost track of the time and flipped the disc over and was working my way across most of that side, too. Got as far as *Little Brown Jug* and then the plug was pulled. And it really was pulled, Missy B!'

She laughed, choosing to ignore the outrageous nickname he had dreamed up that made her sound like a boat. In fact, she laughed so hard she almost bent double and felt tears welling. It was such a welcome relief from the tension building inside. She held a hand in front of her mouth and tried to compose herself. At this rate she was going to join Hawkes in her landlady's bad books if her laughter drifted downstairs. 'How funny! I wish I'd seen her face.' She finally managed to stop laughing, but was still smiling. 'Are you in a band?'

'In a manner of speaking. I was lead trumpet for a while in a nice little outfit down London way. But then it fell on hard times and things got, er...complicated...' He paused, as if reconsidering what he was about to say. 'I lost my place and felt the need to move on. A change of scene. It happens. I mainly do session work these days and take short-term placements with any house band that will take me. I spend a lot of time on the road following the next payout.'

'And I had you down as a travelling salesman.'

Hawkes guffawed. 'A salesman? Jesus wept, I'd rather starve than sink that low.' He looked at his wristwatch. 'Heck, I've gotta scoot. Won't do to be late in my first week.'

'You're working this evening?'

'I'm in residence all month at the Green Cockatoo. If I get a lucky break, I might get to stay until the new year. You should come down. It's a pretty mean house band. We can lay down some good sounds.'

'Oh. Er, no. No, thank you, Mr Hawkes.'

'Another night, then?' He reached for a battered black leatherette-covered case with bright metal corner protectors and fasteners, which he had placed on the floor not far from his bedroom door.

'I'll think about it.' She suddenly lost the smile that had been lighting up her face for the past few minutes. It would be wiser to look cool and disinterested. She hoped she came across as perhaps a little stern and forbidding, dressed as she was in her policewoman's uniform and overcoat. She had no desire to give this over-confident man any encouragement. An itinerant musician working in a sleazy jazz club was hardly the sort of person she wanted hanging around her bedroom door of an evening.

'Suit yourself. Auf Wiederseh'n, sweetheart!'

With trumpet case swinging at his side, Hawkes trotted down the stairs, adjusting his hat with his free hand. WPC Benson, face burning and inwardly reeling from his cheeky parting shot, slowly closed her bedroom door on the smells of boiling veg and the sounds from the still-chattering radio rising from below. She filled her little kettle with icy water and wondered at the odd emotion making her heart beat so fast.

CHAPTER ELEVEN

Nottingham Victoria

WPC Lansdowne's patience in patrolling the two big mainline stations in Nottingham had paid off: the desperate mother clutching a photograph of her missing son had been found. Her name was Deidre Dutton; her missing son was Gordon. They'd got some facts to work with, at last. But names also made everything that bit more personal and potent. With a heavy heart, Vignoles told Trinder they were off to Nottingham Victoria.

The stationmaster stood on the platform awaiting their arrival. He was a conspicuous character, familiar to the regulars and noted for his impeccable dress code and an obsession with punctuality. As expected, the man wore a spotless, black, long-tailed jacket, a glossy top hat and grey-and-black pinstriped trousers, set off by shoes that reflected like mirrors. A gold watch-chain was looped between two small pockets on his waistcoat. He looked like the father of the bride waiting anxiously outside a church — or an undertaker, perhaps. His sallow face and grave expression lent weight to the latter image.

'DI Vignoles; DS Trinder.' The stationmaster spoke stiffly and lifted his hat in greeting, but thankfully fell short of clicking his heels. 'You will find your young lady constable in my office, doing her level best to lift the spirits of a certain Mrs Dutton.' He cleared his throat. 'The unfortunate lady is taking it rather badly. Miss Lansdowne has done a sterling job in preventing her from losing self-control.'

'Under the circumstances, one can understand her feeling overwrought,' Vignoles observed dryly. He had never warmed to the stationmaster, feeling he lacked humanity.

'Has she frequented your station often?' Trinder asked.

'Only four times that I am aware of. However, she has taken her turn around others in the district.' He gave a short cough, lifting a balled fist to his mouth. 'She had taken to loitering around the place late in the evenings.' He gave the detectives a look that was heavy with disapproval. 'An ill-advised stratagem, and one that we simply could not allow to continue. It presented quite the wrong image, both for herself and the station. Frankly, I'm relieved that you two gentlemen are taking the matter in hand.'

There seemed nothing to add to this observation as they walked along the platform, their attention caught briefly by a noisy gaggle of children running towards a shiny, green locomotive that had just pulled to a stop on an adjacent platform. Vignoles was reminded that a boy, much like one of those now scribbling down numbers, might be dead and his mortal remains all but destroyed. He took a few deep breaths and steeled himself for what was likely to be an uncomfortable encounter.

The two detectives were ushered into a functional but immaculately clean office with a fire roaring in an elegant, cast-iron grate. The stationmaster kept his gloved hand on the brass doorknob. 'If you will excuse me, there is a group of truanting schoolboys in danger of running amok. I must speak with them forthwith. I shall be close at hand should you require my services further.' He raised his hat briefly and closed the door without further ado. Herding schoolkids was clearly preferable to consoling a tearful mother.

WPC Lansdowne stood up as they entered. 'This is Mrs Dutton, sir.' She indicated a sad-looking figure huddled in an armchair in front of the merrily blazing fire. She was nursing a cup of tea in her hands. 'Her son, Gordon, was last seen on the morning of 24th September, leaving his school in Grantham.' As Lansdowne spoke Mrs Dutton stood up, spilling her tea, but barely gave this a glance. 'Have you found him? Can I see him?' she blurted excitedly, her tear-filled eyes looking frantically towards the closed office door, clearly expecting it to fly open and her son to appear.

'I am DI Charles Vignoles, and this is Detective Sergeant John Trinder.'

'Yes, I know who you are, the WPC told me.' She seemed distracted and barely made eye contact; focussing instead past Vignoles and towards the door as she nervously pushed a strand of hair from her forehead. 'Have you not brought him?'

'I'm very sorry, Mrs Dutton, I am afraid we have not yet found him. I apologise if you were given false hopes.' Vignoles stopped. Looking into her moist, blue eyes, he began to plan how much to reveal to her. He had no proof that the remains they found were his, and so he should not assume, or imply, that the boy was dead. And yet he needed to ask Mrs Dutton some questions that would undoubtedly cause her to become upset. He felt himself standing on unsure ground. 'You say Gordon went missing in Grantham on 24th September?'

'Yes.' Mrs Dutton looked at him eagerly, as if this date meant that her son was safe. She was unaware that the date and the location matched the platform ticket found in the satchel pocket. Vignoles had to look away and collect his thoughts. The match was not proof of the identity of the remains, but was a strong piece of evidence. There was a large, framed picture, a sectional drawing of a Robinson Class 2 locomotive, gracing the wall above the fire immediately behind Mrs Dutton and so was directly in Vignoles's sight-line. He was struck by the way the drawing appeared strangely reminiscent of a medical diagram of the human circulatory system, with each of the many pipes, tubes and steam passageways of the sliced-open loco hand-coloured in blues and pinks like veins and arteries. Time seemed to stand still, although it was probably only a second that passed, before Vignoles continued. 'I would like to ask you a few questions about your son, if I may.'

Her glistening eyes rapidly flitted between those of Vignoles and Trinder, searching theirs for some glimmer of hope, but, finding no comfort, were then cast downwards. 'Of course.' Her hands were shaking, threatening to spill more tea on the stationmaster's previously spotless floor.

'Perhaps you might like to sit down,' Vignoles suggested. Mrs Dutton nodded rapidly then did so, moving stiffly, as if her body hurt. Noticing the school photograph with its waterproof cover resting beside the leg of the chair, Vignoles asked her if he could see it. She put her tea aside and lifted up the picture.

'Gordon is a bright, intelligent boy. We have high hopes for him, inspector. He excels at mathematics and physics. He's already quite a high flyer at school and could follow my husband into civil engineering. The housemaster says he's turning into a good cricketer, too, and might even make county level...' She broke off and gave a nervous cough. 'He's not a naughty boy, inspector. He's not the type to run off and make us worry.' She welled up and dabbed at her eyes with a pretty, lace-edged handkerchief.

'I'm sure he isn't.' Vignoles gave a kindly smile. 'Can you perhaps offer any explanation as to why he may have acted so out of character?' He tried to ameliorate the unavoidable sting of his question. 'There may be a perfectly innocent explanation for his absence.' Vignoles tried without success to think of a suitably 'innocent explanation' to offer her as an example, but his mind strayed back to the scene beneath the viaduct arch. He could feel a vein throbbing in his temple as he looked from Mrs Dutton's red-rimmed eyes down to the smiling face of the boy, with his pudding-basin hair cut and the gap in his teeth that Eddie Earnshaw had correctly recalled. 'I need to ask you some more questions, and I apologise if they upset you.'

'Anything to get him back.' She blew her nose miserably.

'When did you last see Gordon?'

'The afternoon of Saturday 17th, right here, on this station. That was the last time...' She stopped, appeared to be about to sob again but instead took a series of rapid shallow breaths and continued. 'I heard from him a few days later. He's a boarder. Full term, but with occasional weekend release days. We met here and took a stroll around the town, and then went to the Palace Coffee House for a cream tea. His favourite.'

'Where is that?' Trinder asked, taking notes.

'Clinton Street West. It's run by a Greek couple. Lovely people. They don't spare the cream, either.' They all smiled in a forced manner. 'I don't like to indulge him too much, but it's not as if it is every day we go there, and so we had quite a spread.' She managed another half-smile at the happy memory. 'I wanted to be sure that he was settling in at school. Term had only just recommenced, but one worries. You might think me silly, but one just likes to check.'

'And was he settling in?' Vignoles asked. 'Might something have happened that has made him run away, perhaps?'

'No, he seemed very happy. He was looking forward to the coming term, although maybe not to cramming Latin.' She tried to laugh but it came out as a cough and had to compose herself before continuing. 'Then I walked him back here and we watched a few trains come and go, as he likes to do. I don't mind, as I quite like them, too. There were some rather nice engines; he told me their names and recorded them in his train book. Then I saw him off on his train back to school. He had a day pass-out by pre-arrangement with the headmaster.'

'Where does he board?'

'Bishop Osmond,' she said, with a tinge of pride. Clearly, they were expected to be impressed by the name.

'And where is that?' Trinder had his pencil poised.

'In Grantham.' Vignoles noticed Trinder's jaw tense as he made a note of the town. 'It is a somewhat small establishment, but held in very high regard,' she added, as if to explain away their ignorance of the school's existence. 'It is rather expensive, but my husband sets great store on a proper education. As do I, of course.' Vignoles noticed the slight pause before she added her own endorsement. 'My husband commands an important position, so we can afford to give our son the best.' She ran her fingertips over the photograph as she spoke, the cellophane crackling under her touch. Vignoles could see it was a cut above the average school portrait, being professionally lit and composed. It doubtless cost a pretty penny. Another expense of private education. The boy was wearing a smart blazer with a complex heraldic crest sewn onto its breast pocket. 'Why haven't you found him, inspector? Why ask me the same questions over and over?' She sounded suddenly angry. 'I suppose you've been brought in because the other lot are getting nowhere.' Her sore-looking eyes flashed at Vignoles.

Vignoles was puzzled. Who were the 'other lot'? 'I'm sorry, Mrs Dutton, but this is the first we have heard about your son's disappearance.'

Lansdowne filled him in: 'Um, excuse me, sir, perhaps I should have said earlier, but the constabulary in Grantham is already handling the investigation.'

'Good. I was rather hoping that matters were already in hand.' Vignoles sounded genuinely relieved.

'Don't you work for Mr Geary, with the Grantham police?' Mrs Dutton seemed to be surprised.

'No; we are railway police. The officer in question must serve with the Grantham Constabulary — the ordinary police, if you like.'

'Well, a fat lot of good they are,' opined Mrs Dutton. 'As far as I can see, he and his rather high-handed superior have got absolutely nowhere. They seem to think my husband is involved. The very idea is preposterous. And insulting.'

'Is that why you have been making your own enquiries?' Vignoles asked.

'I have to do something. I'm going out of my mind sitting at home on my own all day and hearing no news.' She paused and took a deep breath, as if controlling her emotions.

'Has your husband also been out searching? I should like to speak with him, too.'

'No. Jeremy has just begun working on a million-pound project in Scotland. His presence there is critical, absolutely critical. He has no choice but to stay for at least another week. The timing could hardly be worse.' She clenched a fist tightly.

Vignoles was startled by this revelation but did not let it show. 'Is there any chance at all that Gordon may be in Scotland with his father, or making his way there?'

'He isn't there, and Jeremy would tell me immediately if he turned up. Oh, inspector, do you think he could be on his way to Glasgow?' Her face suddenly lit up with optimism.

'Where does Mr Dutton work when not in Scotland?'

'I can't see how that has any bearing on things.'

'We like to get all the details. It helps us understand how things stand with all those involved.'

She hesitated and looked momentarily discomfited, but then drew herself up and answered. 'Hull-Stuart & Partners. The head office is in Nottingham, on Stanford Street. He's a senior civil engineer and has a very important contract in Glasgow that will run for the next nine months or so. He has to live on site for weeks at a stretch.'

'On 17th, did Gordon definitely return to his school?' Trinder was taking notes and creating a timeline.

'Oh, yes. He is very competent with trains and timetables. The deputy housemaster telephoned to confirm his safe return. It was a week later that he went missing.'

'When you heard from him after your day out in Nottingham,' Trinder continued patiently, 'what exactly did he say?'

'He sent a postcard thanking me for the scrummy cream tea. He writes a few lines most weeks. It was nothing much. Boys are not really letter writers, are they?' She gave a wan smile. 'The card was a view of Grantham station. I think he bought a bulk supply of the same picture last year and has been slowly using them up.'

'He said nothing that made you suspect anything was wrong?' Trinder followed up.

'Nothing.'

'Can you think of any reason why Gordon would go to Grantham station on 24th?'

'How do you know he was at Grantham station that day? You said you were unaware that my son was missing until now.'

Trinder realised his faux pas and looked desperately at Vignoles for guidance. Mrs Dutton was upset, but still observant.

'You mentioned that he liked trains and so that seemed like a reasonable thing for a lad to do on his own on a Saturday morning in a town with a famously busy railway station.' Vignoles was extemporising. There was no need to upset Mrs Dutton with information about the platform ticket, the satchel and the human remains. Well, not yet.

'You are good judge of character, inspector.' Mrs Dutton gave him a searching look. 'Mr — that is, Detective — Geary discovered that Gordon had asked permission to go to the station that morning. Quite a usual request, as it transpires. He was probably looking at trains, as you rightly surmise, as this is his passion. The school approved, and even encouraged it. He was in the school's Railway Society.' Her voice tailed off and she blew her nose.

'When did the school advise you that Gordon was missing?' Vignoles asked.

'The headmaster telephoned me on the Sunday, 25th.'

'He wasn't alarmed at Gordon's failure to return on the Saturday? If he was on a day release that makes no sense.' Vignoles frowned as he tried to understand.

Mrs Dutton looked uncomfortable at having to admit that a school of such high repute and high fees had made a blunder. 'You are correct. But there was a — er — well, a misunderstanding.' She pursed her lips into a thin, pale line. 'The evening duty master did not worry about my son's absence that night because, I am given to understand, there was a mistake in recording which boys had day passes and which had weekend ones. The mistake was noticed on the Sunday, and that is when they realised that Gordon should have been back on the Saturday. It is scandalous.'

Vignoles looked grim. 'Does Gordon have a leather satchel?'

'Oh yes, a very good one. A fine piece of craftsmanship. I like to hack across country most weekends on my horse, and the saddler I use for my tack also makes bags and satchels, so we had one made specially. Have you found it?' Her hopes were raised once again.

'We have found a satchel, but we don't know if it is Gordon's. It is very badly burnt and only a small section survived the fire.'

'Burnt? Fire?' Mrs Dutton went as pale as alabaster. 'Where? Oh, Lord above.' She was trying to control her breathing, whilst staring at Vignoles with a look that turned his insides to ice. 'The school said that he had taken his satchel and his little railway book with him. The boys in his dorm were certain about that.' She suddenly brought her hands up to her face, each one clasping a washed-out cheek. 'Oh, dear God, what has happened?'

'Please calm yourself, Mrs Dutton. We don't know if the satchel we found is your son's. Did he own a red-and-blue banded snake belt?'

Her eyes widened and she gave a short nod and then pushed her handkerchief against her mouth, almost cramming it inside, both hands now balled into bony fists, knuckles showing cream through her skin. Her distress was painful to observe, but the facts were matching up.

'We found the buckle of such a belt near the small piece of satchel. There is evidence of a fire, but the exact details are as yet unknown to us.' Vignoles paused, giving the poor woman time to take this in before he delivered the coup de grâce. 'I must advise you that we have also found some human remains. There is nothing to identify them, it's just ash and a few bone fragments. We have reason to suspect it could possibly be the remains of a youth, but there is nothing to prove that it is your son.'

A deathly silence fell. It seemed to press in on their heads like an invisible weight. Nobody moved or said a word. Mrs Dutton slowly pulled the handkerchief from her mouth and took a couple of deep draughts of air, holding it inside then slowly expelling, trying to regain a measure of control. She never once took her pale blue eyes off Vignoles. It was unnerving. Finally she spoke, her voice barely above a whisper. 'Where did you find him?'

'In Leicester, close to the Central station. But I must reiterate that we cannot say for certain that what we have found is connected with your son. Only that the circumstantial evidence suggests this is a possibility. We must investigate further. Don't give up hope yet.' Mrs Dutton nodded, her eyes closed as though in silent prayer. After half a minute's silence, she opened her eyes and spoke.

'Did a building catch fire?'

'No; we found all the items underneath a railway arch, on a piece of waste ground.' Vignoles paused as he weighed up how much information to reveal. 'We suspect the body was burnt at a different location, as yet unknown to us.' Vignoles winced. He was being pedantically accurate, with all the cold detachment the police needed to adopt, but it made the hideous truth seem all the more repellent.

'How utterly sordid. Under a railway arch. My boy.' Mrs Dutton broke her unwavering gaze at last, crumpling physically in the chair. 'How could... how did he end up... like that?' She wavered between believing her son to be dead and believing that he could not be. 'No, it cannot be him. Why would he be in Leicester? It's not him! It's not!' This thought helped her to regain her composure.

'You cannot think of any reason for him to go to Leicester?'

She shook her head.

'Did he perhaps ever mention wanting to visit Leicester?'

Another shake of her head.

'Mrs Dutton, we found a platform ticket issued at Grantham station in the piece of satchel. It was dated that Saturday, 24th.' Trinder paused, thinking how to phrase his next question tactfully. 'Assuming the satchel is his, then he may have bought the platform ticket. And then he went to Leicester, which might suggest he travelled there without a ticket.'

'Impossible. He is a good boy. We taught him right from wrong. He would certainly never cheat the railways. He loves the railways. Besides, he receives a generous pocket money allowance, so he would not even need to dodge a fare.'

'Perhaps he has a school friend who lives in Leicester, who invited him to visit for the day?'

'No. He knows nobody there.' Trinder wondered how she could be so sure. She could not possibly know the home towns of all the boys in her son's school, or even his dorm.

Mrs Dutton's shoulders convulsed and she now wept openly. WPC Lansdowne, her heart filled with pity, poured her a fresh cup of strong tea from the aluminium teapot of a utilitarian design favoured by the nationalised railways, spooned in a healthy dose of sugar to combat shock, and stirred it thoroughly.

CHAPTER TWELVE

Grantham station

It was easy to understand why someone might wish to buy a platform ticket and spend time on Grantham station. At least, that was Vignoles's view of things, despite the squally wind laced with rain now blowing fiercely across this low and exposed part of the East Midlands.

'Yes, John,' he remarked to Trinder, 'a young lad or lass armed with a duffel bag — or a leather school satchel, for that matter — containing a bottle of dandelion and burdock, dripping sandwiches and an apple, could happily while away many hours watching the succession of splendid trains passing through here.' He surveyed the myriad rails, points, crossings and signals that seemed to fill the whole landscape laid out before them. 'The fastest expresses through here are hauled by the finest express engines in the land.' This last statement was perfectly illustrated by the stormy passing at that moment of *Ocean Swell* hauling a non-stopping express in a whirl of connecting rods accompanied by the whirring, churning beat of rapidly pounding pistons leaving a pungent trail of smoke now being shredded on the canopy dagger boards and around the footbridge.

Trinder was not convinced; he observed that he thought the station was 'bloomin' cold', whilst ducking his head into the wind and holding his hat on that bit tighter as yet another vicious squall of rain rattled into them. It stung his face.

Certainly, it was an almost-straight corridor of a station that invited the elements to blow with savage intensity along its lengthy platforms, despite a run of awnings and low buildings on either side. The lack of adequate shelter was exacerbated by the extensive expanses of railway marshalling yards on both sides that offered no protection. Vignoles, however, seemed oblivious to the wind. His attention was drawn towards a pair of tank locomotives bustling about as they shunted a considerable number of wooden open wagons into order on their respective tracks.

Grantham was unusual in that it had two engine sheds in close proximity — one far older than the other, but both still in daily use. It was an arrangement that ensured there was always a considerable number of locomotives coming and going and standing outside awaiting their next call of duty. It made for a pungent mix of smoke, steam and ash, which blew across the platforms and into their faces. However, for those in love with the steam locomotive it was something approaching nirvana. Vignoles offered this opinion, whilst gazing upon the curvaceous form of an engine known simply as '60700' that was poking its distinctively shaped nose out of the older shed doors. It resembled an A4 Pacific, a type unmistakeable for its stylish, Bugatti-inspired streamlining, and which included the now-famous world speed record holder *Mallard*. However, this particular engine was slightly larger, and was truly a 'rare bird'. Vignoles temporarily pushed aside the dark reason for their visit and took a few moments to consider its intriguing form. The air-smoothed smoke-box front was opened out like the gaping mouth of a giant, beached, metal fish gasping for air, but despite this ungainly attitude the engine retained a unique beauty.

Trinder held steam engines in lower esteem, although he could appreciate that some of the more glamorous examples held a certain appeal. He just turned up his coat collar higher and dutifully took in the scene. Yes, this engine was a bit different from those trundling through Leicester and Woodford Halse, but he still hoped they would soon be conducting their enquiries out of the rain. And a cup of hot tea wouldn't go amiss.

They had some minutes on their hands whilst awaiting the arrival of DS Geary, who would no doubt give them the full gen on the Dutton case. Vignoles had wanted to get a feel for the lay of the land of Gordon Dutton's local station and, for that reason, when he telephoned Geary from Nottingham Victoria he suggested they meet on site rather than in the police station. Trinder felt he had now sufficiently got to grips with both the location and its adverse climatic conditions and was privately chewing over the content of some of the motor-car adverts in the *Leicester Mercury*, which he'd been reading on their journey across to Grantham. Each promoted the latest exciting products of Humber, Sunbeam and Morris. One day, he and Violet will have saved enough for a deposit on a nice little Morris Minor. With considerable relief, Trinder spotted Edward Sissons, the stationmaster, motioning to them with a raised hand from the opposite platform. It was time to seek refuge from the elements.

'Gentlemen, this is DS Geary,' said Sissons, 'and this is my chief ticket clerk, Richard Mayes. Together with the clerks working under him, Richard probably sees more people face to face than any of us. Although, as DS Geary is aware, I regret that we have not been able to shed much light on his investigation.'

After the usual exchange of introductions, greetings and handshakes, the group stood in the empty general waiting room commandeered for their meeting. A cheery fire was dancing in the grate and they gravitated towards it, drawing on its welcome warmth. Soon, steam began to rise from their damp clothing. Two bold posters rendered in garishly bright colours and peopled by healthy women in bathing suits depicted Great Yarmouth and Mablethorpe as gloriously sunny summer holiday destinations but these now looked rather out of time and place. It was not yet 2pm, but the gas mantles were already lit, rendering the dreary grey day outside the rain-speckled windows even darker and more unappealing.

'Please avail yourselves of this room. Mayes and I shall retire to my office next door and leave you gentlemen to talk police business in private. If you feel we can offer any assistance, do please ask.' The stationmaster and the clerk closed the door on the damp wind outside, and those remaining felt the temperature immediately rise.

'I understand, gentleman, that you may have some information pertinent to a missing person's enquiry we're handling.' Geary was short, young and very pale; as he spoke two apple-red circles appeared on the dough-white skin of his cheeks. 'I could do with something more to work with. Mr Sissons and Mr Mayes have offered what help they can, as have a few others but, frankly, we've hit a bit of a wall.'

'We may have something for you,' Vignoles replied. 'We have found human remains adjacent to Leicester Central, beneath a viaduct arch. Just ash and bone fragments. They were poorly hidden, but in an infrequently used space. By sheer luck, some archaeological excavations were recently commenced, and perhaps, without their expert eyes and diligent inspection of the ground surface, the remains might have stayed undiscovered for many years, possibly forever. We believe the remains to be fairly recent, although dating will prove very tricky. Virtually nothing can be safely concluded about age or sex. We are, therefore, obliged to rely on circumstantial evidence, such as objects found in the same place.'

Geary nodded thoughtfully before responding, mentally processing all this startling new information. 'That is interesting. I suppose it could change everything, but if there is so little to go on. What brought you here?' he asked Vignoles. 'What links these remains to Gordon Dutton?'

'There are some small items that survived what we presume to be the same fire as cremated the body, and due to slightly fortuitous circumstances we have already spoken with Mrs Dutton.' Geary looked surprised. 'From that meeting we feel that these items can be associated with her missing son. There is also a connection to this station, hence my suggestion that we meet here.'

'What have you got?'

'The items were found on the same site, but due to the remains being mainly ash and shovelled into a wheelbarrow and away from the place of burning, they can be connected only by proximity. It means we are straying onto tenuous ground, but we have no other option open to us.' Geary remained silent but licked his dry lips as he listened. 'We have a belt-buckle and part of a leather school satchel. The satchel is at the forensic lab. We also found this. It is burned, but as it was within an outside pocket of the satchel it was protected by the heavy leather.' Vignoles opened an envelope and produced the singed platform ticket.

Geary placed his briefcase on a nearby table and gave the ticket a quick once-over before handing it back. 'The date is significant. Anything else?'

'The piece of belt-buckle.' Once again Vignoles dug into his overcoat pocket and extracted an envelope. He passed this across and Geary looked inside. 'Quite distinctive and with a number of red and blue threads still attached.'

Geary gave a slow but knowing nod as he gave it close inspection. 'One moment, gentlemen.' He closed the envelope and handed it back, then extracted his black, police-issue notebook from his suit jacket pocket and checked something on a page of densely written notes and gave an abrupt nod as he confirmed a detail. He looked grim. 'Perhaps we should sit down.'

After taking their places around a table close to the fire, Geary started to speak. 'As you know, we have a missing lad on our casebook. You have spoken with the mother, Mrs Dutton?'

'Yes. She had taken to patrolling Nottingham Victoria, asking if anyone had seen her son,' Trinder replied.

'Is that so?' Geary assimilated this fact, which was clearly new information. 'I don't know what she told you, but let me give you the facts as we understand them.'

'That would be helpful,' Vignoles encouraged the young detective.

'Gordon Dutton. Age twelve-and-a-half. Full time boarder at Bishop Osmond Prep. Reported missing to ourselves early on the morning of Monday 26th September, but believed to have vanished sometime on 24th. I am sure you will not need me to point out that such a delay can have serious consequences. It's a crying shame, but there we have it.' Geary shrugged his shoulders. 'My chief superintendent has his own thoughts about the reasons for the delay, but I'll come back to that. The Duttons live in Borrowash. That's in Derbyshire,' he added, helpfully.

'I know of it,' Vignoles offered.

'The father, Jeremy, is a civil engineer, and probably banks a good salary. No doubt he has aspirations for his boy and is shelling out a hefty wedge each term as Bishop Osmond commands fees that would make your eyes water. Since the start of September, however, Mr Dutton has been away from home, lodging in Glasgow.'

'Do you think there is any significance in the timing?' Vignoles asked. 'We were struck by the fact the father has yet to leave Scotland to comfort his wife at this distressing time.'

'That puzzles us, too, and got my guv gunning for the father, although I for one can't see how he's directly involved. Mr Dutton has not been in Borrowash, nor indeed outside of Glasgow, since his son started at the school. This certainly makes him a bit of a cold fish, but it would put him far out of the frame for a crime that took place down here, perhaps in Leicester. But, in the light of what you've discovered, we might want to lean on him a bit harder to be sure of his side of things.'

Trinder made a note. 'It must be difficult for him. Being unable to get down here.'

'One imagines so, but he gives little away; at least, not over the telephone. We've not met face to face. He's ex-army: Royal Engineers, and a tough old boot by the sound of it.'

'You are convinced he has a strong alibi for the Saturday to Sunday that Gordon went missing?' Trinder asked.

'If, as you are saying, the lad has been killed and disposed of in Leicester on 24th or after, then I would say he is in the clear. One idea we have been considering is that Gordon is alive and well and up there with his father, but in hiding. This might be a bitter family feud being played out, with the son as a willing pawn.'

'That would be cruel on Mrs Dutton. And perhaps criminal: wasting police time on a manhunt that is pointless,' Vignoles responded.

Trinder paused in his note-taking. 'All is not well in the family?'

'Things are not as they seem on the surface,' Geary replied.

'Ah...' Trinder nodded. 'Families, they are usually at the heart of crimes of violence.'

'We don't yet know if it *is* a crime of violence. He is reported as missing, that's all.'

'Fair point. Could you describe the circumstances of Gordon's disappearance?' Vignoles wanted to take things methodically.

'He left the school around 10am that Saturday, with his leather satchel, wearing grey shorts held up by a blue-and-red banded snake belt. So the articles you described are most interesting, and can be considered as strong evidence. He was also wearing a white shirt, a grey pullover and a duffel coat.' Geary checked his notes as he spoke. 'Oh, and his school cap. Strict regulations demand the cap be worn at all times in public, even on a day off.' Trinder scribbled in his notebook. 'He told the duty master he was going to Grantham station to watch trains and one of Mr Mayes's clerks remembers a boy of about twelve wearing a Bishop Osmond uniform and cap. However, after that, the trail goes cold. We suspect he boarded a train, possibly without a ticket, as neither Mayes or his colleagues remember selling him one. Of course, it could have been purchased in advance or at another station. We have no witness to him boarding a train, however, which is frustrating.'

'And with so many trains calling here it will be impossible to hazard a guess where he went,' observed Trinder.

'Precisely. However, there are two scenarios we are considering.' Geary paused. 'I think one of these can now be scotched. My boss, DCI Sharpe, was of the opinion the Dutton boy did a runner to join his father in Glasgow. The pre-purchased train ticket idea would work, as would the lack of clothes or belongings taken by Gordon. The father could purchase clothes up there. Alternatively, the lad did a bunk to strike a blow at both parents and is hiding out somewhere nearer to home.'

Trinder looked puzzled. 'Why would he do either of those things?'

'Like I said, we think all is not well at home,' Geary responded. 'The Duttons are just play-acting at happy families. My guv'nor reckons the lad favours the dad, but I'm not so sure. But your discovery seems to offer another scenario for what happened when he boarded a train here on that Saturday.'

'What do think that might be?' Trinder asked.

'That he met someone, as yet unknown to us, and boarded a train away from here in company with that person. Again a pre-purchased ticket, or one bought at another station and brought along by this unknown friend could explain how the boy travelled without buying a ticket here. It's just as likely, in fact more likely, that he just bunked his fare and took his chances like so many boys do.'

'Yes, we thought of that, but the mother is adamant that her son would never defraud the railways.'

'Any mother would say that,' Geary countered.

'Perhaps he was going to a prearranged rendezvous somewhere else,' Vignoles added.

'We have considered the idea that he went looking at trains elsewhere with an older boy, although again we have no likely candidate. Maybe he went looking for a bit of excitement and adventure further afield. Maybe he went to Leicester.' Geary stopped. 'But what happened then?'

'You have no indication as to where he may have gone and with whom?' Vignoles asked.

'Frankly, none at all. Of course, he could have been lured down to London to join all those other lost boys loitering around Piccadilly Circus of a night.'

'He's too young for that, surely?' Vignoles looked horrified.

'They get younger by the day. Trust me. I travelled down to see for myself. It's a vile, sordid life of exploitation and violence. And some of them are awfully young. The Met don't know how to deal with it.' Geary took a moment to consider this before continuing. 'Wherever he went, we favour the idea that he was encouraged by someone he trusted. Someone older is my guess. Perhaps he befriended an older train enthusiast. As to what happened after he left Grantham, we are stumped. No sightings, no trail. Nothing.'

Gloomy looks were exchanged. 'We don't know what happened to him that day and evening, only perhaps the outcome,' Vignoles said. 'And even then we must be cautious. The implication is that we have found his remains, but we cannot be sure. The type of satchel he owned is a classic design; countless schoolchildren own them, and those belts also seem to be very popular.'

'But how many snake-belted school children with satchels buying platform tickets for Grantham station end up dead?' asked Geary.

'Exactly. Something worries me. If Gordon had a pass out only until early that same evening, how was it the hue and cry didn't go up that night? Mrs Dutton said there was a mix up. Have you shed any more light on this?' Trinder looked up from studying his recent notebook entries.

'Did she, now?' asked Geary, intrigued. 'The headmaster actually phoned Mrs Dutton on Saturday evening. Twice. At 8.30, and again just before eleven — 10.56, to be precise, as the headmaster noted the times on his jotting pad. He told us he was unhappy placing a call so late but felt the circumstances demanded it.'

'So the school was aware that the boy was missing on Saturday?' Vignoles interjected.

'They knew he was not on the premises that evening, but made a vital error. They believed that he was staying over at his parents' house or with a friend. She is correct in saying that the school had muddled up their records of who was out for the day and who was out for an overnight stay. But they eventually called her to clarify the matter the same evening, but with perhaps not the sense of urgency that was required.'

'But she was not at home?' Vignoles asked.

'No. Or leastways, she was not answering the phone.' Geary paused. 'And so the headmaster tried again at 7.30am on the Sunday. No answer once again. They finally spoke to her at nine that morning and the decision was made to call the police first thing the next day, the Monday, once Mrs Dutton had spoken to her husband and after the school had made more enquiries in the Grantham area and amongst his fellow boarders. The school even talked with Mr Sissons here, knowing that Gordon was intending to visit the station. Whilst concerned, their first thought was still that he had stayed overnight at someone's house and failed to inform them and it would all soon be resolved. I think that was not an unreasonable supposition, if perhaps a flawed one. The father, incidentally, had not left his hotel details with the school, so they could not telephone him themselves.'

'Interesting. What about the mother during this time? What explanation did she give for not being at home?' Vignoles asked. He had picked up an anomaly in Deidre Dutton's account of her movements on the Saturday night.

'When we questioned Mrs Dutton she claimed to have gone to see her neighbours for a glass or two of port and lemon and a few hands of bridge, staying there until just before eleven. She then slept heavily and was not awakened by the headmaster's first call at 0730.'

'But you don't believe her?' Trinder asked.

'There are inconsistencies in her story. My boss thinks she may have a secret lover.'

'With hubby away and son at boarding school, she certainly has the time and the privacy,' Trinder observed dryly.

'Indeed. He suspects the Duttons are estranged but keeping up appearances. They have a good standard of living and she is perhaps wise enough not to throw that away.'

'Do you think the father, in concert with the son, might be pulling some sort of nasty trick? Getting his own back on her?' Trinder suggested.

'My guv'nor thinks so,' Geary replied. 'But I think your discovery blows away that theory.'

'Presumably the neighbours have backed up her story?' Vignoles asked, toying with his unlit pipe.

'Partially...' Geary checked his notes again. 'That's the thing about alibis, sir: they only ever seem to go part of the way. We spoke with Mr and Mrs Wellbeck, and she was definitely at their place playing cards until about 1030, although neither can recall the exact time she left. She had just a short walk home and would have been in the house well before 11pm. If that was so, then why not pick up the call from the headmaster at 1056? We challenged her and she claims to have got her timings muddled as she was not wearing a watch and says that she went straight to bed and dropped off to sleep immediately. Her friends cannot confirm where she went after leaving their place, of course, only that she left on foot, and she lives about six to eight minutes walk away. Maybe she went somewhere else, or went home but ignored the ringing phone.'

'That puts an interesting spin on things,' Trinder observed.

'Her private life, complicated or not, does not appear to explain what happened to her son. Unless you think she is implicated,' Vignoles shot an enquiring glance at Geary.

'We have no suspicions about her wishing Gordon harm. If anything, her reaction since he disappeared suggests she is feeling guilty for not taking the call from the school that Saturday night. It is sitting badly with her conscience.'

'It might explain her patrolling Nottingham Vic station if she's feeling guilt-ridden, although I am not sure why she's fixated on Nottingham. Here would surely make more sense.' Trinder observed. Vignoles and Geary acknowledged the point. 'I'd like to know more about both parents. Get under their skin and find out what's really going on.'

Geary gave a little nod of agreement then changed tack. 'There is one item you could look for at the crime scene. Gordon was a loco spotter and had a little train book. It was hard-backed, with a hundred or so pages. It is called an 'ABC' and was written by someone called Alan.'

'I know of these books. Ian Allan — with two 'L's — publishes them. Do you know which edition it was?' Vignoles asked.

Geary checked his notes again. 'This year. 1952,' he added pedantically. 'It's called a "Combined Volume", apparently. Does that mean anything, sir?'

'It does.' Vignoles owned a copy of the same book.

'Find his book and you probably find the lad,' Geary added. Trinder exchanged a look with Vignoles. They were both thinking of the piles of rubbish and wastepaper under the arches. Could this book, or at least its burnt remains, still be there?

'Do you know if he liked Fox's Glacier Mints?' Trinder asked.

'What schoolboy doesn't?' Geary replied.

'We found a wrapper along with the ticket...' Trinder tailed off. The pathetic banality of a used sweet wrapper somehow made the possible death of the schoolboy feel more real and shocking. Nobody spoke for a few moments. The wind howled in the chimney and the coals ticked in the grate as a heavy goods train approached, the long rake of box-vans rumbling and chattering behind, making an ill-fitting window rattle in the sash.

'I would like to bring the stationmaster and his ticket clerk in to join us.' In response, Trinder left the room to fetch them. Moments later the two railway officials were seated on chairs pulled up around the fire. Vignoles addressed Sissons first.

'You were aware that Gordon Dutton frequented this station?'

'Yes, sir. He did. Together with hordes of others — and thereby hangs the problem.'

'Which is?'

'That we get too many of them. This train watching is an innocent enough hobby, but when a small army of noisy and excitable kids descends on one's station it causes operational headaches.' Sissons shook his head as if remembering all manner of difficulties.

'And it annoys the hell out of our passengers,' Mayes added, bitterly.

'The point being?' Vignoles looked puzzled.

'The point being, that Mr Sissons had to put his foot down.' Mayes gave his boss a deferential look. 'Sorry, I am not explaining this very well. When this number-taking craze was limited to just a handful we could let them come and go and did not bother to sell them platform tickets as this freed us to look after the proper, fare-paying passengers. But it became unmanageable. Making them buy a platform ticket trimmed back the numbers — at first. But after a few weeks they soon bounced back, dutifully handing over their cash and we were back to square one. I wonder how they have so much money to squander. Parents spoil their kids rotten these days.'

Vignoles grunted a reluctant acceptance of the point being made. It was widely reported that some stations were becoming overly full of young people running up and down platforms, across bridges and crossings and creating what was seen by some users as a damned nuisance. 'The spotters are likely to be local children?'

'Yes. There are some who come in by train, of course, but they are usually young men and older gents.'

Vignoles and Geary exchanged glances. Perhaps one of them was the older man they had theorised about.

'Can you remember selling Gordon Dutton a platform ticket on that Saturday, 24th September?' Vignoles asked.

Mayes looked regretful. 'I cannot. Some boys lodge in the mind's eye, of course. You know, the ones with particularly sticky-out ears or suchlike; and then you get a few girls, and, because there are so few, they are more memorable. But most just look like a sea of blazers, school caps, shorts and pudding-basin haircuts. However, one of my clerks was sure Gordon was there that day, in his school uniform, and thinks he may have sold him a platform ticket; but he had other, far more important matters to deal with and cannot elucidate further.'

'I recall the lad being here on numerous occasions, but on which specific days it is hard to say,' Sissons added. 'I truthfully cannot say for certain if he was here on that particular Saturday.'

This confirmed what Geary had said and Vignoles knew there was nothing more they could offer, no matter how willing they were. 'If you should remember anything, no matter how small and seemingly inconsequential, please do let us know. You can telephone me at Leicester Central. Thank you for your time, gents.' He checked his watch: there was a train due soon. He stood up, the others followed his cue, and they all walked towards the door.

Geary was looking pensive, chewing over what he'd heard. 'I reckon it is him, the boy, under the arches.' He spoke quietly, so only Vignoles picked up what he said. 'But if so, then how the devil did he end up in Leicester?'

'I must agree: things are pointing that way,' Vignoles concurred, as he placed his damp hat back on his head. 'I propose that both of our forces, railway and civvy, adopt that line of enquiry, but I suggest you keep the missing person's search open for now — just in case. There is still a good chance the boy will just suddenly turn up.'

Geary nodded. 'I will speak to my guv. With his permission, I shall prepare a copy of our case-notes and have them sent over to you.'

'Thank you. In the meantime I will report our initial thoughts to my super, and will speak with your DCI in due course.'

They stepped out of the waiting room and into a sharp squall. After shaking hands and saying goodbyes, DS Geary hurried away, briefcase tucked under one arm. Vignoles and Trinder stood deep under the platform awning and watched the approach of a powerful-looking tank engine which was hauling their train. The wind whipped the exhaust from the chimney as quickly as it appeared. Mayes was walking away from them when he suddenly stopped and turned about. 'Inspector!' He called across the wet and windy space between them, his voice fighting to be audible above the hiss of the advancing engine. 'I am sure it has no relevance, but the one person I do clearly remember on that Saturday was a lady carrying a bag of freshly baked Chelsea buns. In fact, she gave me one. It was quite delicious.'

The two detectives looked at Mayes, unsure what to say in response. The train came to a halt with a squeal of brakes and a hiss and the noise levels dropped appreciably. 'Can you describe her?' Vignoles asked after a short pause.

'Fiftyish. Quite a plump, jolly sort.'

'Do you know her name?' Trinder asked.

'Afraid not, sergeant. I just remember she had a massive handbag and from inside this she produced a brown paper bag full of buns.' He laughed. 'She came to the ticket window. I think she was making a train enquiry. Or she did buy a ticket? Sorry, I wish I could be more specific, but I was offered a bun and I have to say that was what stuck in my mind.' Mayes looked sheepish, aware that the stationmaster was giving him an odd look. 'I just wondered if she might remember Gordon. Maybe she gave him a bun.'

'Well, we'd need her address in order to ask her,' said Trinder, his hand already on the carriage door handle.

'Oh, sorry, yes, of course you do.' The ticket clerk looked deflated. 'Well, if I see her again I will definitely put you in touch with her. Or vice versa.'

Vignoles and Trinder stepped up into the carmine-and-cream-painted coach, not feeling much the wiser after this well-meaning interruption.

CHAPTER THIRTEEN

Borrowash

Vignoles rang the doorbell then took a step back, the better to take in the large, semi-detached house the Duttons called home. Actually, they called it *Bellevue*, according to the tasteless, curly wrought iron and timber name-plate fixed to the wall. Trinder was also sizing up the place, inspecting the front garden, which looked newly laid out in a very contemporary style with a large rockery filled with tiny plants nestling between the heavy stones. The owner was an engineer and he thought it showed. Although trying to look like a natural outcrop somewhere in the Alps, it was actually a skilfully constructed concoction of expensive and carefully chosen rocks, artfully assembled with more precision than perhaps was necessary. The lawn, even on this drear November, was immaculate and only marred by a small gathering of fallen leaves. The gates to the drive and path were in white decorative wrought iron; they appeared to be new and matched the kitsch name-plate.

Trinder looked at Vignoles. 'I reckon they have a gardener. Maybe he's looking after more than just the herbaceous borders.' He raised an eyebrow, but before Vignoles could pass comment, the front door opened.

'Good day, Mrs Dutton.' He raised his hat.

'Oh, my goodness.' She looked startled to see them and steadied herself against the door.

'May we come in? We just need to ask you a few more questions. We won't keep you long.' Vignoles moved a foot closer to the doorstep in a well-practised move that made it quite clear that she had little choice but to acquiesce to his request.

'Is there any news?' She stepped back as she was speaking and both men entered, taking care to wipe their feet on the doormat. The highly polished parquet floor would show the rain and mud.

'I am afraid not. Is there somewhere we can talk?'

'Yes, in here, please come through.' She ushered them into a large dining room where five elegant chairs covered in a tasteful striped fabric woven in greys and mustard yellow stood around a large, round wooden table polished like glass. A silver candelabra holding three tall red candles stood in the centre beneath an ostentatious crystal chandelier dangling from the ceiling. Two alcoves painted in mustard yellow held a busy assortment of ugly porcelain figurines.

It was an expensively decorated and furnished room. The Duttons were certainly not short of money.

'Do take a seat.' Mrs Dutton crossed to the sideboard, opened a decorative box and fished out a cigarette. A heavy lighter with a base of polished black stone stood close by and she lifted this to set the cigarette alight. Her hand shook slightly. 'Sorry. That was impolite. Would you like one?'

The detectives refused. She seemed to be tempted to lift the stopper from a crystal decanter of sherry, but appeared to think twice about this and now sat down, rather heavily. Vignoles noticed that one of the four matching glasses standing nearby on the sideboard was out of place and a stain of tawny brown liquid at the bottom betrayed its recent use.

'We need to ask you about the evening Gordon went missing.'

'What on earth for?' She puffed out smoke impatiently. 'Always questions, questions, questions. What about some answers? How about telling me where my son is?' She was tense and ratty.

'I'm sorry. It is the nature of our job. I understand you went out on the evening he went missing. Is that correct?'

'Yes. To see friends. I am allowed *some* recreation.' She threw a defiant look across the table. 'It was our bridge night. We always meet up. Nothing unusual about that, is there?' She was brusque and spoke perhaps too quickly.

'And your friends Mr and Mrs Wellbeck can confirm this?' DS Geary had supplied the names, and he wanted Mrs Dutton to be aware that they were well-informed.

'What is this? You're surely not suggesting that I or they have anything to do with Gordon's disappearance?'

'We are trying to resolve a few anomalies,' Vignoles replied.

'Anomalies?' She narrowed her eyes and took a drag on the cigarette. Her confidence was ebbing away.

'What time did you leave the Wellbecks?' Vignoles paused. 'Precisely.'

'About ten. Or ten-thirty. Maybe later.' She wafted a hand around, as if this would smooth over the vagueness of her reply. 'I was not paying attention to the time, why would I? And I was not wearing a watch.' All three looked at the tiny gold watch glinting somewhat ostentatiously on her wrist. 'I'd forgotten to put it on that evening.'

Vignoles gave an indulgent smile. 'You did not glance at a clock at your friends' house?'

'I may have. I—I can't remember. What's happened since has confused me. What time I left the Wellbecks is hardly my main concern.' She rubbed a temple and did a convincing job of looking harassed.

'Don't worry, we can ask your friends more about this.' Vignoles sounded reassuring. 'I'm quite sure they will be able between them to recall the exact sequence of events.' Again Vignoles paused and watched as Mrs Dutton drew heavily on her cigarette. He deliberately took his time. 'Actually, they are quite adamant that you left at ten-thirty-four. Terribly particular, is Mr Wellbeck. As I am sure you know.'

'Well, there you go, then.' Mrs Dutton shrugged her narrow shoulders, staring at the glassily polished table top.

Trinder looked up from his notebook. 'The Wellbecks live at 39 Acacia Close. Earlier, we walked from there to here. Without hurrying, it took eight minutes. Allowing for the fact that your footwear that night might have been less rugged than ours and allowing that perhaps you took your time, in order to get a little fresh night air, it may have taken you ten minutes.'

Mrs Dutton looked at the fingernails on her right hand, but remained silent.

'So if you left their house at ten thirty-four, you must have been home by ten forty-five. Ten-fifty at the latest. Would you agree?' Trinder had his pencil poised, ready to make a note.

'If you say so.' She gave Trinder a defiant look.

'You came straight home?' Vignoles asked.

'Of course.'

'But the headmaster telephoned you just before eleven. Why did you not pick up the receiver? He let it ring for some time.'

'I was asleep. I didn't hear it.'

'Fifteen minutes after returning home? So deeply asleep you did not hear it ring?' Trinder looked incredulous.

'Perhaps I took longer to get home.'

'Why might that have been?' Vignoles asked.

'I don't remember. Why do you keep on so?'

'Because it seems that deep sleep was not the reason you failed to take the call,' Vignoles answered.

'Did you meet someone on the way, perhaps?' Trinder took his turn. The pressure was building.

Mrs Dutton flushed, her cheeks turning a colour in stark contrast to her usual deathly pallor. 'What are you implying?'

'We just need to get everything straight. You cannot explain why you failed to answer your telephone at either 11pm or 7.30am.' Vignoles had lost all warmth from his voice.

'I—I probably went out for a paper in the morning.'

'To your usual newsagent?' She nodded, but it was half-hearted. 'We shall ask him to confirm this.'

'Er, now I come to think of it, no, I didn't get a paper. I must have been bringing in the milk. Yes, that's it. Or maybe I was putting out the empties.' Her hand holding the cigarette quivered slightly.

Vignoles frowned. 'But it takes only a few seconds to bring in or put out a milk bottle, and your telephone is right by the front door. I notice you have a wire basket with the name of your dairy on it at the side of the step, just as we do.'

An uneasy silence fell.

'It's time to tell us the truth, Mrs Dutton. Was someone else here, late that evening, and in the morning? Someone who inhibited you from answering the telephone on both occasions? Someone you did not wish to be distracted from?'

She flushed red again. 'What an insulting insinuation, inspector!'

'Is it? Are you denying that you had company?' She looked about to respond angrily again, but Vignoles held up a hand. 'Mrs Dutton, we are not here to moralise but to investigate your son's disappearance.' She darted her free hand around her throat and swallowed, clearly shocked by the stark reality of his statement. She extinguished her cigarette, stabbing the little stub repeatedly into the ashtray. This took some time. When she spoke it was flat and quiet.

'How did you find out? Did Francis blurt it out? The fool.'

'Francis who?' Trinder asked.

'Look, I'd rather the neighbours didn't know. And the Wellbecks. Needless to say it would not look good at Bishop Osmond.' She stopped and chewed her lower lip as she contemplated the awful fact that her son might never return.

'All that concerns us is the truth. What your neighbours or the school think is no matter to us,' Vignoles reassured her. 'Is Mr Dutton aware of what's going on?'

'Not the gory details.' She stood up and fumbled in the box for another cigarette. 'We agreed to keep things civil. No names, no dates, no details, just...' She turned to face Vignoles and blew out a stream of smoke as she spoke, her voice stronger. Resigned to confessing to something she knew could no longer be suppressed. 'My husband and I have not had relations of a romantic nature for some years.' She looked at the ceiling. 'Doubtless you will make your own judgement against me. A respectable married woman carrying on like a cheap tart.' Her voice quavered. 'But, for what it's worth, it was he who left me. In heart and soul, certainly, if not quite in body. Three years ago. I still loved him. I did all I could to stop him sliding away from me, but to no avail. He became a stranger to me. Once I knew with certainty that he found his pleasures elsewhere, my affections cooled. Our marriage is nothing now. Annulled in all but name.' She paused and looked at Vignoles as if demanding a response.

'The state of your marriage only concerns us as far as it impacts on your son.'

'Gordon knows nothing of this. He is an innocent. Away at school, enjoying his studies and happy as Larry watching steam trains.' Her voice broke, but she managed to control herself. 'My husband is away for long periods, which helps, and we feign normality during the school holidays, for Gordon's sake. The house is large and we can have separate bedrooms. So, there you have it.' She looked at the wine coloured carpet and fell silent.

'I see.'

'Do you?' She gave Vignoles a stare. 'Frankly, after years of being ignored and abandoned and helpless to do anything about it, I find myself in this humiliating situation. I am not pleased with myself. And no, inspector, I do not like being furtive and secretive. It is horrible, sordid. But I also have the right to be comforted and it is hard to not respond when someone shows me a little kindness.'

'I can appreciate that.' Vignoles was genuinely sympathetic.

'We agreed it was best for Gordon's wellbeing that we maintain an outward respectability.' Her eyes were wet. She suddenly stood up and turned her back on them. She fumbled for a handkerchief, blew her nose and then walked across to the sideboard and this time did not hesitate in pouring out a stiff measure of sherry. She gulped half of it down. 'It suits *him*, of course.' Her voice was hard. She turned about and leaned against the sideboard. 'I am his perfect decoy. Oh yes, the good little housewife looking after the smart executive home whilst he works days and nights away to give us a good life.' She gave a bitter smile whilst waving the glass to encompass the expensively furnished room. 'No doubt you will be grilling him as hard as you have me? That should put the cat amongst his pigeons.' She gave a short, harsh laugh then downed the last of the sherry. 'Yes, I was home when the headmaster called that night. I had hurried home, to meet my lover. When the telephone rang early in the morning, I thought it was my pathetic husband calling from Glasgow. Oh God, how I've regretted not taking those calls!' Tears coursed down her cheeks unchecked. 'Can you imagine how it feels to know that whilst I ignored the phone calls in order to be with my lover, the school was trying to tell me that Gordon was missing?' She banged her fist in frustration, turning her back to them. 'I was sick for days with the worry and the guilt, thinking that my selfish actions might have delayed the search for him.' She leaned on the sideboard, head hanging down, and took some deep breaths. 'Am I responsible? Did my selfish behaviour drive him away? Please tell me it's not so. It's killing me...'

CHAPTER FOURTEEN

Woodford Halse

John Trinder and his wife Violet were sitting in the back kitchen of their home near the bottom of Station Road in the railway village of Woodford Halse. It was a rented shop with living quarters set in a terrace of two-storey, red-brick shops that dipped steeply towards the massive twin overbridges of the former Great Central Railway's London Extension railway line. The gates and access road leading to the station itself lay almost opposite Violet's dressmaking shop, and this close proximity to the busy trunk railway ensured they could effectively tell the time by the passing of the trains. Even now, deep into the evening, heavy iron ore-filled wagons were sending little shivers through the fabric of the building with their passing.

The kettle was singing on the hob, and Trinder was busy shining his work shoes at the kitchen table. Yesterday's newspaper was spread open to protect the surface, and with his shirt sleeves rolled up and collar unbuttoned, he was patiently dipping the end of a cloth into a little water in the upturned lid of the tin of black boot polish. Picking up a little polish on the dampened cloth, he continued rubbing and burnishing the leather into a super-high gloss. It was a long process, but he relished the time and care required. He prided himself on having perfectly presented shoes with a shine matching the Brylcreem in his equally carefully parted hair. With a half-smoked cigarette in the corner of his mouth, he was a picture of concentration. But he was not thinking about shoe blacking.

His guv'nor used the act of cleaning, filling and smoking his pipe as an aid to chewing over thorny matters, and Trinder did much the same when he polished his shoes. Sometimes they just needed a quick once-over with a brush and cloth and then he could relax by playing some of his precious 78 rpm records (quietly, so as not to awaken their little boy). When the discs were spinning he could switch off from his detective duties, perhaps also studying a record review in one of the musical periodicals he took. But this relaxation was for when there was nothing pressing at work that demanded extra consideration away from the hustle and bustle of the office. And so, whilst Violet dried and put away the dishes from their evening meal and prepared a pot of tea, he put in some serious thinking as he cleaned the effects of rain and mud from his shoes.

He certainly had plenty to think about. There was the interview with DS Geary in Grantham and the subsequent trip out to Borrowash and the none-too-gentle session challenging Mrs Dutton. It had proved illuminating, although he wondered if they had not given a frantically worried mother a rather torrid time. Then again, she had lied, and any detective worth his salt knew they must push aside the usual niceties. It was their duty to probe into any chink in the armour of lies and deceit and spring it open to see what lay underneath. Geary had been right in his hunch, but, for whatever reason, he'd just not scratched hard enough. Well, they'd got a result of sorts and both he and Vignoles felt reassured that the mother was not responsible for her son's death. One name could be ticked off the possible suspect list. Not that they actually had a list, as such.

But that was not all he had to think about. Shortly before finally leaving the office for home, Vignoles had taken a call from the forensics lab, and the long and the short of it was that they had concluded to the best of their abilities that the bone fragments were those of someone in their early teens, possibly. Give or take a few years either way. It was impossible to say which sex. That was it. Horribly vague, but it was pretty much what the lady archaeologist had first suggested.

There was one ray of light. The lab scientists had also found a fragment of jawbone with five teeth intact and advised that if the dental records of a likely victim could be located, there might be a chance to make a more accurate identification. It was still a long shot, but it was the best they were likely to be bowled.

As Trinder burnished the toecap of his shoe, he reflected that the Duttons looked the sort who would have their son registered with a National Health Service dentist. There was big push to get all children's teeth checked these days and schools were being quite assertive about this. Trinder had even seen the Northamptonshire mobile dental surgery van travelling the roads on its way to the more remote schools in their area, so there was every chance that something similar had happened over in Grantham. He would get on the case tomorrow. A private boarding school would surely have a matron or nurse who could lay her hands on the lad's dental records, or at least know where they might be found.

Not that Trinder had any doubt it was Gordon Dutton. Everything was leading the same way, even if they had as yet to find conclusive evidence. He grimaced and gave the shoe some extra-hard rubbing as if trying to purge some of the anger welling up inside as he wondered at the mentality of a child killer. How could anyone do such a thing? He was just a harmless young lad off to look at trains. Who could kill and burn a child, and for what possible reason? It made his head pound. The perpetrator of this heinous crime must be deranged. Mad. Insane. There was no other explanation.

Trinder felt a steely determination to hunt down the killer, whatever his mental state. He wanted to clap irons on the wrists of this monster. That was why he was a copper. He might not always be able to put things right, but he could see that criminals got what they deserved. In this case, a rope around the neck and a trapdoor beneath the feet. He gave a stubborn water stain a burst of intense burnishing.

'Difficult day, love?' Violet was pouring hot water from the kettle into the teapot.

'I've had worse. Possibly.' He attacked the leather for a moment before continuing. 'We've got a new case, and it's giving me a lot to think about. Some of it very unpleasant.' There followed a little shake of his head. 'Not a good subject for after-dinner conversation.' He inspected one of the shoes more closely to see if it met his demanding standards.

'You can tell me, John. I'm made of pretty stern stuff. I didn't marry a detective thinking your job was just sitting in an office filing bits of paper.' She put a crocheted tea cosy over the pot and brought it to the table. 'My guess is there's a body.' She gave him an arch look and he made a point of not responding. 'You always try to avoid telling me about those.' Trinder still didn't reply, but his silence served only to reinforce her belief she was right. 'Ha! I'm right, then. But there's no need to bottle it all up.' She rested a hand on his shoulder for a moment then sat at the table. 'A trouble shared...'

Trinder still did not reply, giving some final rubs to the now-glistening leather. Finally satisfied, he placed the shoes neatly side by side on the newsprint. They looked like two huge black beetles made of glass. After wiping his hands on a cloth, he sat back in the wooden kitchen chair, which gave a little creak. He glanced up at Violet as she filled two cups with strong tea. She knew he was building up to something and it was no use hurrying him along. He flipped open a carton of cigarettes and shook two free. 'Want to join me?'

Violet shook her head. 'No thank you.' She only smoked occasionally, usually when in a group of friends. With cigarette alight, Trinder took a lungful and talked as he exhaled, tipping his head back and jetting the smoke in a stream towards the ceiling. 'It might be a young lad. Not absolutely sure, but everything's pointing that way. We have his name, but cannot be confident it's him. Forensics have done their best with what little we found.' He stared at the burning end of the cigarette, eyes narrowing as he watched the tobacco glow and turn to ash. There was silence for a few moments. 'We've got tiny bits of bone, a few teeth, a fragment of satchel, a piece of a belt, and a platform ticket. Not much. All found beneath a railway arch in Leicester.' He tapped the cigarette on the edge of the ashtray. 'Ashes to ashes.'

'I can see why you were deep in thought.' Violet took a moment to consider his words. 'This sounds rather an unusual case.'

'Assuming it is who we think it is, then the boy was only twelve. Last seen on Grantham station.' He dragged on his cigarette.

'Poor lad.' Violet contemplated for a few moments. 'I assume it couldn't have been some kind of accident.' Anticipating what was likely to be a gloomy answer, she reached for the cigarette carton and selected one.

'Well, there were no signs of a conflagration in the area so we have to assume the ashes were carried there. He was burnt at one location and moved to another. That suggests it was premeditated.'

'How frightful.' Violet frowned as she leaned forward to light her cigarette from her husband's. 'What about the parents? Are they suspects?'

'The mother looks to be in the clear. We gave her a bit of a grilling today and she cracked. She's got a fancy-man on the side. The son was packed away to boarding school and husband works away from home for months at a time. We'll have to talk to lover-boy, of course, but I'm not expecting any criminal intent. The impression I get is that they had more pressing carnal matters on their minds. She's been all but abandoned by the husband for another woman, but they keep up appearances as a happy couple. It can't be easy.'

'What about the father? Is he in the frame, as you police put it?'

Trinder rolled his cigarette between his fingers as he considered his reply. 'Might be. DS Geary of the civvy police in Grantham started the investigation. He seems a decent chap. A good enough copper, I suppose. But I want to question a few things he told us. I don't want to speak ill of a fellow officer, but they seem to have got themselves in a bit of a tangle. His guv'nor is suspicious of the father, even suggesting that the lad is being hidden in Glasgow with the dad as a cruel prank on his wife. I'm pretty sure we've blown that theory apart, but if the father is their focus, then why have they not done a proper interview with the man? They should have been on the parents like hawks. It only took us a few minutes of pressure and the mother cracked and told us about her fancy-man.'

Violet nodded thoughtfully. 'You and Charles are always saying that you need to look at family and friends first when it comes to...' she dropped her voice to almost a whisper, '...this kind of thing.'

'Exactly.' Trinder gave her an understanding look. He stood up, and walked across the kitchen and switched on the radio beside the big cream-and-green enamel bread bin. After a few moments the valves warmed up and the gentle tones of a dance track filled the room with an upbeat tempo. He adjusted the volume so it was not too loud whilst still offering a softening barrier between their words and their innocent son sleeping next door. They would still be able to hear Jimmy if he awakened. Feeling more at ease with the music playing, he sat down again. 'To be fair, the Grantham constabulary did not know the Dutton boy was dead. The father is in Glasgow.'

'Surely a perfect alibi?'

'On the face of it. But they've spoken to him once on the telephone and I am still struggling with the idea that the father's work is so pressing he cannot come south to be here whilst his son is missing.'

'Gosh. That's barely credible,' said Violet, shocked.

'I'm struggling to accept it. However, we are told he is leading a multi-million pound project and this is the critical start-up period, so perhaps he genuinely cannot leave. But something does not quite add up in my mind and I want to speak to him face to face. See what reaction we get when he discovers that his son was lying beneath a railway arch whilst he was too busy with his work.'

'Perhaps he is involved and the job is a smokescreen.'

'A distinct possibility.' He sighed. 'I sense there's more to this than meets the eye.' Trinder recalled the gloomy scene under the dripping canopy and cold railway arch with flickering lantern light and the Roman skeleton. It was an unsettling image. The kitchen window was suddenly assaulted by a gust of wind bearing heavy raindrops, and they could hear the rain starting to hiss on the paved back yard. He swigged some tea. 'The guv'nor and I are just feeling our way forward at the moment and we must be wary of getting carried away and making two and two add up to six. It can be dangerous to assume too much, read too much into a situation until more facts are established.' He stopped and drained his mug. 'Ach, enough of work and all this gloomy talk.' He closed his eyes for a moment hoping to sweep away the worries nagging at him. 'I quite like this song.' They listened to the voice crooning across the airwaves.

'Is it *Here in My Heart*?'

'That's right. It's by Al Martino.'

'They've played it a lot in the last few weeks. I've been making that dress for Miss Johnson over in Banbury all week, and this has been in the background quite often. It seems appropriate somehow, what with it being her wedding gown, because it's now imbued with a wish for her intended to be here in her heart.' They both smiled, relieved to be talking about something more uplifting.

'Please don't forget to call into Exley's tomorrow for the *New Musical Express*, will you? It's an important edition, as they're going to publish the first top twelve selling singles in a chart. I really want to know what tops the poll!' Trinder's eyes were bright. He loved music and buying records, although his purchasing power had somewhat diminished since the arrival of a very expensive-to-run little boy. Despite these cutbacks, he had still amassed an impressive collection of records, each one carefully stored in a paper sleeve in strict alphabetical order.

'Don't worry. Mrs Exley has been on full alert this past month, ever since you first mentioned it. She's never seen you miss a copy yet.' Violet refilled their teacups. 'You'll be able to judge better than me, but based on how often Al Martino is getting played, he surely has to be in with a good chance.'

CHAPTER FIFTEEN

Leicester

He surveyed the scene. Everything looked 'shipshape and Bristol fashion', as the saying goes. The tin bath was returned to its place, suspended from a great iron hook set into the wall, with a few last drips of water landing softly on the floor below. The quarry tiles were damp, having been scrubbed clean with sugar soap and scalding water, and the pinky-red terracotta colour was deep and rich. He pulled a face and looked pensive. The grouting between the tiles was stained dark, despite his best efforts. Maybe the ironmonger would sell him some more caustic soda, as it would be good to get this bright. It would be wise to eradicate those tell-tale lines. Mummy was always going on at him about it. Well she should try doing it, then! He did all the dirty work, and what thanks did he get? Still, the oven was hot and the heat welling out from its stove-blackened front would soon dry the floor and he could then better assess how the grouting looked. It should be less obvious when completely dry.

Otherwise, all was in order. The meat cleaver was polished to almost a mirror finish. The knives were back in their drawer, each blade well sharpened. It made it so much easier when they were razor-sharp. He'd learned that the hard way! He shook his head as he remembered the first time. What a hash that had been! Blood everywhere, and such hard work with dull-edged blades. He'd got a flea in his ear for all the mess. He'd probably deserved it, of course. But he was better than that now. He was a pro. He allowed an unpleasant, self-satisfied smile to form on his lips. That second-hand book on butchery had proved a lifesaver. He laughed at the irony. Portioning up a pig was not so different really from a boy. It was all just bone, muscle and lean meat. And then there was the offal. He made a face. He hated that. Made him want to puke.

He made a mental checklist by counting off on his fingers each task completed. She demanded he left nothing to chance and would be down soon to see for herself. Woe betide him if he'd missed something. He wrung his hands nervously and bit the inside of his cheek, which was starting to get sore. He didn't want that wet cloth stinging his face again. It hurt more than you could imagine. Or maybe she'd inflict one of those horrid Chinese burns on his arm.

But if he did as he was told then all would be fine. He sniggered like a child. They were too clever for the police; they could outwit them any day. They were the best. That was why he was leaving a few sneaky little clues, just for fun. He looked towards the door, feeling guilty at even allowing himself to think such naughty thoughts. She'd go mad if she knew.

He'd better get a move on. Just a few last scraps to burn. It wouldn't take long, but it was best to do it in stages. Trying to do too much too quickly left some bits poorly combusted. He couldn't be too slow about it either, mind. What if someone called around unexpectedly? He licked his lips. A voice in his head was nagging away, asking if he might have miscalculated with those buckets of ash. It was one thing to have a bit of fun with the coppers, but perhaps he'd not covered his tracks quite well enough. He sat down heavily and rocked on the hard wooden chair as worry started to run its icy fingers down his spine. Perhaps he ought to go back. No, he couldn't now, not again. Not with people working there. How on earth had he managed to choose a place that was about to be dug over? A forgotten corner of the city that now looked about as busy as Piccadilly Circus. And now the police were on the scene. That was not in his plan. Not so soon, anyway. After a few months, when the trail had gone cold, it would be different. He could leave a clue or two and watch how they ran around trying to interpret it. He bit his fingernails to the quick, working methodically from one to the other across both hands.

The newspapers were still quiet. But what was happening? Had they found anything? He felt queasy and rocked faster, eyes squeezed closed. If Mummy heard the police were on to it and realised he'd been lackadaisical, she'd be very angry. He could almost feel the punishment coming. The anticipation was almost worse. The police must have found something. 'A very serious incident', that older detective had said. But what had they found? He cursed softy and put his hands on his head and held it tight, trying to quell the throbbing.

After about a minute he opened his eyes and blinked. He regained his equilibrium, the panic over. He looked down at the items on the table and started to cut the school tie into small squares with a long pair of dressmaker's shears.

Snip, snip, snip. Nice little pieces that would catch and burn in a moment.

Now for the cap. He felt his thumb getting sore where the loop of the metal handle of the shears was starting to rub. They were losing their edge, even after running them over the grinding stone.

It was all this lining and gold braiding. He should really unpick the cloth badge from the front before cutting into it, but instead felt a sudden urge to hack at it. The shears baulked at the thickness of the cloth. Again and again he attacked it, hate and confusion burning in his brain until the embroidered design of a clerical man in robes with a pointy bishop's mitre on his head was sliced in two. That felt satisfying. He needed to destroy each piece with his hands and then let the roaring fire do the rest. Sweeping all the pieces of cloth onto a folded newspaper he walked over to the oven and tossed the brightly coloured pieces inside. They caught almost immediately. Blue and green flames licked enthusiastically around the rapidly combusting fibres.

He felt a tingle of excitement. It was thrilling. Not that he could tell anyone. He so wanted to share the almost physical excitement of what he'd done. He wished he could boast about how clever he was, to see people admire his skill and dedication and to recognise the effort he put into the project. His attention was drawn to an angry, almost manic, buzzing sound, coming in short, aggressive bursts from somewhere above. He looked towards the sound, and in a thick net of cobwebs high above the enamelled lampshade, he could see a big, black spider wrapping a madly protesting bluebottle in its sticky web. Serves the fly right for flying about so late in the year. He smiled in admiration. The spider was neat and controlled in its actions and there could only be one outcome. The fly's buzzing was getting quieter and less frequent.

That's what he was doing. Putting out little sticky threads just like that cobweb, and drawing them in. Showing them just how smart he was. He could play a lovely little game with that older man. Like the spider and the fly. He stood for some time, the intense heat of the oven overwhelming him, almost hurting against his body. Narrowing his eyes, he suddenly pulled the chair across to below the lamp, and with a rag in one hand climbed up and neatly swiped spider and fly and cobweb up into the rag. He crushed it tight, then stepped down and tossed it into the fire.

Chapter Sixteen

Locarno Milk Bar, Leicester

Jane Benson and Lucy Lansdowne were walking along Guildhall Lane. The gas lamps were creating halos of light in the fine drizzle and, as they approached the Guildhall itself, with its timber framed walls leaning at all angles, they could see how the antique window glass formed gentle swirls and distortions to the pretty lights within. It looked as though it were being prepared for an evening function. They snatched glimpses of waitresses in black dresses and white aprons and caps busy beneath the chandeliers. Leicester Cathedral next door had one of its great wooden doors standing wide to welcome worshippers to evensong. Cars swooshed towards them, headlamps cutting beams of light through the steadily thickening damp night air.

Work was over for the day and Jane had suggested they went for a drink. She wanted a break from the daily routine of the bus home and another night in her rented room with just the wireless or that library book she was not enjoying for company. Her colleague and friend, Lucy, could be vivacious company and always seemed full of energy and life, happy to break into a pretty peal of laughter at the slightest excuse. She also seemed to be largely untouched by the almost oppressive gloominess of this endless November with its incessant rain or chest-constricting smog. Jane, however, was feeling her spirits literally dampened by the dreariness and suffocating pollution that seemed to gather like poison gas down each street and alleyway. She needed some distraction and, although they had spent the day working together, Lucy was still just the company she needed this evening. What's more, she could be relied upon to know exactly the right place to go on a Thursday.

'There's a new place opened on Loseby Lane. I've not been yet so it will be good to give it a whirl. It's a milk bar.'

'Is that like those American diners we've seen in films?'

'I suppose it might be — though this is Leicester, remember!' They both laughed. 'You can get most things there apparently — tea, coffee, Coca-Cola or a milk shake. No wine or spirits or anything like that, though.' Lucy paused, waiting to cross St Martin's East, and took the opportunity to look at Jane. 'Or would you rather we took a glass of wine somewhere else?'

'No, let's try the milk bar. I need a change.'

'Attagirl! I hope our uniforms won't look too out of place.' Lucy made a rueful face.

'That's true of anywhere we go. In films, American diners always have motorcycle cops lounging around, so I think we might look the part.' They both laughed.

Loseby Lane was a long and slightly wiggly street which appeared narrower than it really was by the tall buildings of many shapes and styles that lined each side. The architecture varied from humble shop fronts to grandiose edifices in carved stone, interspersed with the totally decrepit and woebegone; some buildings were still in need of repair after the attentions of the Luftwaffe in the early 1940s. The shops were now either closed and shuttered, or the shopkeepers were busy taking in the last of their goods placed outside on wooden crates. A tuneless whistle on the lips of a flat-capped lad as he carried a freestanding advertising board inside and a cheery 'good evening, girls' from another as he wound back the canvas awning into its slot above his greengrocery shop window accompanied their splashy walk down the narrow pavement.

The Locarno Milk Bar threw a generous spread of bright, fluorescent light onto the glossy, wet street from its picture window. As they drew closer, there was a drift of music from inside. The bright and clean frontage, in cream with red letters, had a brash appeal. It was a flash of startling modernity; a tiny sliver of American-style living dropped like a landmine from a silver Boeing Superfortress into the heart of this stolid, red-brick, Midlands town of terraces, poky shops, many-windowed corset factories and smoking chimneys.

'It looks delightful.'

'Here comes the rain again.' Lucy urged her friend forward with a hand on her elbow.

'And they're playing *Singin' In the Rain* on the jukebox.' The door clattered shut behind them as they entered the bright Formica, chrome and red leatherette interior. It was filled with music, smoke, condensation, chattering voices and the hissing of a huge, stainless steel coffee machine that took up the greater length of the bar area. A minute later they were seated on bench seats with two clear Pyrex cups of 'frothy coffee' on the table between them. Lucy was measuring out a teaspoon of sugar from the glass and chrome dispenser. 'Sugar. And lots of it.'

'How on earth do they get enough to be so profligate?' Jane gratefully took her turn and measured out a generously heaped spoonful. 'Yummy. This was a good choice. I like it already.'

'It's open till ten.'

'That late? Apart from dingy clubs and the pubs, there's nowhere open after five. Leicester locks down and looks about as dead as the proverbial dodo of an evening. Especially on a mucky night like this.'

'Ooh, I like these...' Lucy turned the trendily transparent cup gently on its saucer. 'Anyway, Jane, enough prevaricating. What's up? I can tell there's something.'

She shrugged. 'Nothing. I'm all right.' She made a point of inspecting the wildly patterned table as if they were discussing interior design trends. 'I just felt like a change. It's good to break the old routine every so often.'

'Are you sure it's just that? You've not looked yourself these past few weeks.' Lucy stirred sugar into the beige liquid, enjoying the way the froth swirled and left a tidemark.

'Is it that obvious?' Jane took a sip of coffee as a distraction, but was inwardly pleased that her observant friend had already cut to the chase. 'I am a bit out of sorts. This rotten weather doesn't help.'

'A symptom, but not the cause?'

'I suppose so.'

'And the cause is — what? Work? This viaduct affair is shaping up a bit grim.'

'No; I'm used to unpleasantness of that sort. We've seen enough over the years.'

'You've done a great job telling me what's *not* the matter.'

'Do you ever feel like life is passing you by?' Jane asked, with a weary sigh. 'I just go to work, come home, eat dinner, rinse out a few things, listen to my landlady's radio broadcasting *Mrs Dale's Diary* on the BBC, then go to bed, week in; week out. There has to be more to life than this.'

'Like romance?' Lucy smiled.

'That's something you only see in films or read of in books. Every day I see trains going to exciting places. They stop, the doors open and shut, everyone climbs aboard, off on a journey somewhere. Except me. I just watch them steam away.'

'I'm not so sure Sheffield and Hull are such terribly exciting destinations.'

'You know what I mean.'

'I do. The analogy is good. Or is it a metaphor?' She furrowed her brow for a moment. 'Frankie's always boarding trains and then transport planes over to the Rhineland. I sometimes wish I could join him.'

Lucy had been walking out with an architecture student for a year, although his studies were now on enforced hold whilst he worked out his National Service in West Germany. Their time together was infrequent and short, not aided by his living with his parents in Mansfield. However, the arrangement didn't seem to cause Lucy too much hardship. She thought a long courtship had its advantages, and besides, her beau had to get back to his studies the moment he was released from the army: he needed to get qualified before they could even dream of buying a place together. 'I don't envy him, though; it sounds pretty grim out there. Draughty guard-houses and lots of flat and dreary countryside.'

'Like Lincolnshire, but full of Germans. Haha. Just to see the Rhine might be quite nice though. Just the once. It would make a change from the smelly old Soar.'

'Most of the bridges across the Rhine are still wrecked, with great bits of decking sticking out of the water where they fell. Frankie likes to sketch drawings for new bridges, just to keep his hand in.'

'How very practical. Maybe they'll give him a job over there, rebuilding them.'

'They'd better not! If he was there permanently it might scupper everything.'

'How's he finding it?'

'He doesn't say a lot: they discourage including too much information in letters home, but I think he feels a bit sorry for them. The Germans, that is. Strange how things change, isn't it. There we were, a few years ago, fighting them to the death and now he's feeling guilty at how they're forced to live. They took a fearful pounding from our bomber boys. The towns and cities are ruined beyond anything we can imagine. He says Cologne was flattened, except large chunks of the cathedral.'

'Probably what they deserved. Eye for an eye, and all that.'

'You can't spend your life feeling angry and aggrieved about what's over and done with. Frankie reckons they're hard workers who knuckle down and do what's called for without complaint. He says it won't be too many years before West Germany gets back on her feet and will do better than any of us. They're an inventive lot.'

Jane was not in the mood for discussing German economic recovery and passed this over. 'When's he home?'

'Christmas.'

'I bet you can't wait,' said Jane, with a heartfelt sigh. 'Must be lovely to have that to look forward to.'

'Absence makes the heart grow fonder.' Lucy gave a wistful smile. 'So, what about you? No beau on the horizon?'

'Nothing to report, WPC Lansdowne. I'm just an old maid. Left on the shelf.'

'Don't be silly! You're a catch.'

'Try telling the world that. I look in the mirror and, well, I don't even come close to the mannequins in the magazines. And these things don't help. Remember the old saying? Men seldom make passes at girls who wear glasses.'

'Pah! You've just the figure for an evening gown. Perfect hourglass. Not like me: all bones and angles.'

'Hourglass? Yeah, I've got a bust the same measurement as the depot code for Leicester engine shed. I get reminded every time I see 38c on the front of an engine.' They both giggled.

'You were made for the silhouette in vogue now. If only I was so lucky.'

'I've seen you dolled up for the evening and you turn heads wherever you go, Lucy. Anyway, even if my bust-line meets a fashion editor's approval, it's hidden beneath our truly delightful uniform that smells of old Labrador when it's damp and makes me look like a sack of potatoes. The next time I fish out my one good frock from the back of the wardrobe it will be full of moth holes and a century out of date.'

Lucy laughed, then looked serious. 'You just need to get out and about more, socialise a bit. This milk bar is so cheery and lively. Who knows who you might meet here?'

Jane's eyes strayed across to a group of young men talking noisily at a table over the way, breaking into laughter that was far too loud and staged. They were cocky and annoyingly brash. She wrinkled her nose.

'Hm. Perhaps they're not the best examples,' said Lucy,

Jane fiddled with her cup in a thoughtful manner. 'Have you ever heard of the Green Cockatoo? I think it's a jazz club.'

'Dive, more like. And quite notorious. Why do you ask?'

Jane felt crestfallen. 'Oh, someone mentioned in passing that the resident band is very good. And I quite like jazz. I think.'

'So, who is he?' Lucy's green eyes shone bright with interest.

'Who said it was a man?'

'You did.'

'I never!'

'I've not been on the force all these years for nothing.'

Jane knew she'd been rumbled. 'Don't jump to conclusions, but a new lodger moved in to my digs and he plays trumpet there.'

'So — there *is* a man!' Lucy clattered her cup swiftly onto its saucer and leaned closer across the shiny Formica. ' Spill the beans.'

'Hold your horses. He just happened to mention that he plays at the Green Cockatoo and suggested I pop along some time.'

'Ooh! A date? He asked you out?'

'No, not a date. He's an itinerant jazz musician. Utterly unsuitable for me as a romantic prospect, I assure you. But I heard him practising and he plays well.'

'Ah-ha. Purely a musical interest then? In jazz. Which you have never mentioned before.' Lucy looked at Jane sceptically. 'I'm surprised your landlady lets him practise on his trumpet. I thought you said she was an old grump.'

'She makes him play in the outside lavvy!' Jane explained, pulling a face. They both burst into giggles, releasing the pent-up tension of their job and, for Jane, a welcome relief from the growing sense of loneliness she felt was in danger of engulfing her. Life suddenly seemed full of light and colour and possibilities.

When the pair recomposed themselves, Lucy looked across at Jane with a twinkle in her eye. 'So, is he handsome?'

'How about you judge for yourself?'

Chapter Seventeen

Leicester Central

Vignoles had spent an unsatisfactory morning meeting with Chief Superintendent John Badger. He'd been given what could only be called a 'grilling' by his boss, who had been singularly unimpressed by his initial report on the Dutton case.

Badger had spent more time arguing about why they had to take on the case than discussing any material progress Vignoles and his team had made. It was clear that he regarded investigating the last mortal remains of (what was, in all probability) Gordon Dutton as an unpleasant chore that was likely to drag on interminably whilst draining them of valuable manpower and resources. It was already looking as though it would prove a tricky case to solve and it would probably only serve to bring unwanted publicity and bitter complaints from a grieving family, who would, as such families invariably did, end up finding fault with the police as a outlet for their grief. Badger had overseen a few such traumatic murder cases and they always seemed to create resentment, no matter how conscientiously his men did their duty. Child murder cases were to be avoided, usually by passing them to one of the civvy forces. To that end they had wasted time wrangling pointlessly over the boundary divisions of their department and that of the Leicester Constabulary.

However, the city council and the railway authorities had drawn the lines of demarcation long before the remains had been dumped under the viaduct. Badger had no choice but to agree that Vignoles was to handle the investigation, with Trinder in support. Having crossed that Rubicon, Vignoles was forced to admit that things had not moved on terribly quickly, although he had argued valiantly that making a reasonable stab at an identification under such trying circumstances was a feat worthy of commendation. He stressed their hope that the teeth might lead to a positive ID. Badger had countered this by asserting that, since the boy was already known to be missing, and this was being actively investigated by the boys in Grantham, all they had done was join up the dots. It was a valid point.

'You'd better knuckle down and get on with it, man. I need results.' Badger's Yorkshire roots sometimes betrayed themselves when he was angry and his polished Received Pronunciation was momentarily discarded. 'And give me summat to throw to the press, or they'll be hounding us like nobody's business. Talking of whom, how exactly are you proposing to play this "body under the bridge" business with our friends from the Fourth Estate?' He gave Vignoles a withering stare. 'Get the tone wrong and we'll have busybody nosey parkers queuing around the blummin' block to take a look whilst the hacks have a field day with King-bloody-Richard and references to princes walled up in the tower!' Badger had paused in his rant and, lifting one eyebrow, squinted at Vignoles. 'No joke intended. And did you say they've got a blasted Roman lying down there as well?'

'A whole skeleton.'

Badger groaned and slapped the table with his soft, kid-leather gloves, which he was holding. 'No, we can't have this turning into a ruddy sideshow.' He let out a long sigh and collected his thoughts. When he next spoke, he was quieter and more controlled; all trace of Yorkshire disappeared as he considered the reality of what they were dealing with. 'We're going to have to be circumspect, Vignoles. Box clever. Give the press the bare minimum for now. And you get busy and find something better to work with. And be sharp about it.'

By the end of the meeting, Vignoles was feeling a small glow of inner satisfaction. He had convinced Badger that only a *chief* inspector possessed sufficient gravitas to perform such a tricky press conference. Moreover, Badger could handle it in a manner that would brook no awkward questioning, whose bare statements would be taken at face value. As Vignoles expected, his boss's ego had been flattered and his mood visibly improved as he took the bait. It was agreed therefore that, at the press call that afternoon, Vignoles would sit tight-lipped and silent in the background.

Meanwhile, his team was pressing ahead: Trinder was chasing dental records; Benson and Blencowe were creating a map of the crime scene and surrounding area, placing the names of the known occupants of every residential and business property on each building plot. Painstaking work, but Vignoles felt sure that only by mapping and plotting in this way could they have any chance of tracing a witness or, better, the perpetrator. Someone must have seen something. The crime scene was right in the heart of a busy city and, even in the dead of night, there was usually somebody walking a dog or passing by in a car or on a bicycle. And yet they were still waiting for their first credible witness.

Freed from the meeting at last, Vignoles stood outside the detective department front door and drew on his pipe, glad of the fresh air. There seemed to be a hiatus in the rain, although dark clouds lay in the direction of Abbey Park, suggesting that more was on the way. He rocked on his heels and watched a nicely polished V2 class engine get its heavy passenger train on the move towards Marylebone. It snorted, huffed twice and, with just the briefest hint of wheel slip on the greasy rails — expertly caught by the driver — accelerated from the station, dark exhaust pulled to one side by a rising wind that enfolded one of the pair of giant water tanks at the far platform end. The wooden coaches creaked and, as the brake carriage at the rear of the train passed him, he caught a glimpse of a smudge of a face beneath a peaked cap and heard the metal click of the guard's window being lifted and slammed shut. The train wended its way across the lengthy viaducts and interesting variety of bridges that carried the railway on its super-elevated route above the city roads and rooftops, slicing between the red-brick hosiery and shoe factories with their chimneys pointing upwards like slender fingers. The clean, carmine-and-cream coaches offered a brief dash of vivid colour, but they were now engulfed by the trail of dirty smoke. The city needed strong sun to animate it, and so today it was colourless.

Vignoles daydreamed about the coming summer, when he and Anna might be able to escape to the seaside. It seemed hard to believe that sun and warmth could ever return to the land. Despite the shocking events they had stumbled upon, he still held fond memories of their week last August on the sunny coast of Wirral. He remembered the light bouncing from the waters of Liverpool Bay and the pale, golden shimmer of the sands. A far cry from the dark, syrupy flow of poisoned waters crawling along its narrow, man-made channel close by, heated by the great bulk of the power station with its buzzing wires. Thoughts of muddy liquid gave him the idea to walk across to the mobile refreshment trolley, where he bought a cup of insipid coffee. It was hot and wet and that was about it.

He needed to plan his next actions and a change of scene for a few minutes might clear his head and aid his thinking. There were a lot of tasks ahead, the most pressing of which was to meet with the elusive Mr Jeremy Dutton. He had proved hard to pin down. His secretary had so far fobbed off all requests with stories that he was in a meeting, or unreachable somewhere on site. Vignoles was tempted to put the man at the top of his currently empty list of suspects, based on nothing more than his irritating Scarlet Pimpernel tendencies.

Striding purposefully along the platform, Vignoles fought off the desire to put his head around the door of the goods despatch office and distract his wife from her work. They had met on this very platform back in 1943. She was a young lady whose eagerness to 'do her bit' to help the war effort had launched her into a world of paperwork: she found herself logging vast quantities of goods traffic. It was important to maintain a proper level of professionalism within the station environs and, whilst Vignoles had autonomy in his working day, his wife however was closely supervised by a stern, humourless fellow who forbade anyone to distract his clerks from their work.

Vignoles plunged his hands into his overcoat pockets and, dipping his head slightly against the light rain borne on the wind, resigned himself to stealing but a fleeting glance at the back of Anna's head through the grubby window as he walked down to one of the platform ends, where a handful of dedicated and somewhat older train-spotters was clustered, dressed in dark jackets and coats that made them look like a gulp of cormorants on a wet rock. They offered quiet companionship. Unlike the constant noisy chattering of schoolboy enthusiasts, they made only the occasional observation on a train movement or a timing variation, but were otherwise happy with pencil, notebook and private communion with the workings of the railway. As he drew closer he recognised one of them, but for a moment could not remember his name, nor where he knew him from. The man turned in response to hearing Vignoles's approaching footsteps.

'Oh, hullo inspector!' He seemed surprised. 'What brings you down here?'

Got him! Vignoles mentally made the connection: it was the van driver that WPC Benson had quizzed outside the automotive parts factory. The secret urinator on the supporting pillars of the viaduct. The man who'd seen nothing. 'Good morning. One could ask you the same thing.' Vignoles nodded knowingly at the little, hard-backed book open in the man's hands. The rows of numbers, some of which were underlined in blue or red ink, were easy to see. 'I didn't have you down as a spotter.'

He closed the book as if embarrassed. 'My guilty secret, Inspector — er...'

'DI Vignoles.' He held out his hand.

'Mike Tibbott. I don't go telling everyone. Some people are a bit sniffy, for some reason.'

'I know what you mean. Got any good cops?'

'Nope, I've only been here a short while, so just the usual sort. I've seen them all except that V2 just now which has sneaked down from somewhere in the north-east.'

'In good condition, too.'

'Tip top.'

They stood companionably, watching a heavy coal train clank towards them, hauled by a work-stained ex-War Department engine. After the guard's van passed, its chimney smoking heavily, Tibbott asked, 'Have you got any further with that business you were looking into?'

'We've made some progress.' That was circumspect, he thought, remembering the Badger's command.

'I've been thinking about it. You got me wondering, you see. It sounded serious. I mean, three of you on it, and then the bobbies standing guard after, and by the time I was called back next day it was full of people.' He raised his eyebrows. 'And then I heard it was a young boy you found.'

'From whom did you hear this?'

'One of the lads at the factory. I was collecting a delivery and we were talking about all the commotion. I think he got it from the bobby guarding the site. The "crime scene", as we would call it.' The man nodded, as if he were himself part of the investigating team and mulling over the finer points, whilst Vignoles silently groaned. The man fancied himself as an amateur sleuth. 'Is it true? You know, about the boy.'

Vignoles felt irritated. Why couldn't the uniformed lads keep their big traps shut? Never mind, it was going to be front page news after the press conference, so perhaps it made no odds. 'There is a missing boy, and we found human remains, which may have been those of a youth.'

'You know for certain?'

'No.'

Tibbott looked taken aback. He turned things over in his mind for a few moments. 'The body must have been in a right old state, then,' he whispered, wincing a little.

'We must get our facts straight before saying too much,' Vignoles replied evasively. 'Have you remembered anything more?'

'Sorry, no.' He saw his chance. 'Perhaps if you told me more it might jog the old memory cells. When do you think this happened? What sort of person you are looking for.'

Vignoles recognised Tibbott's game. He pondered for a moment. Maybe he was genuinely trying to be helpful; and there was a remote chance that he, or one of his chums in the factory, might remember a detail that could prove useful. 'We think the victim could have been a train-spotter. Perhaps he even came here, stood right here.'

'You don't say! Bloody hell!' Tibbott looked aghast. 'Makes you wonder.'

'What?'

'P'raps I've stood next to him. Or you might've. Not knowing, like.'

'How well do you know the boys who frequent this station? Would you recognise any of them?'

Tibbott shook his head slowly. 'Nah, I don't give a monkey's uncle about other spotters, as a rule. I keep myself to myself. Some of the young ones are a nuisance.' He looked thoughtful. 'Hey, do you think he might have been a member of the Ian Allan Spotters' Club?'

'He certainly had one of those...' Vignoles pointed with the stem of his pipe towards the combined volume in Tibbott's hand. 'He also had a brown leather school satchel and a red and blue belt holding up his shorts, and was last seen in a navy blue duffel coat and a school cap in bottle green. Does that sound familiar?'

Tibbott's eyes widened slightly as he took in the details, but he shook his head. 'That could be almost any schoolboy.' They fell silent for a moment. 'Tell you what, inspector, I'll ask around. I get out and about and I stop off at stations when I get a spare moment. Maybe someone'll remember him.' He resembled an eager terrier.

'Please leave the questioning to us. This matter needs to be handled carefully.'

'But we need — you need — to catch this villain.' Tibbott's voice was raised, but he checked himself in response to a couple of heads turning and dropped to a whisper. 'I'm just saying, I could enquire. Help you out.'

'I appreciate the offer, but we can't have the public weighing in like vigilantes.'

'Just a quiet word. Ask if they saw the lad with someone. Because I bet there was someone else involved.' Vignoles did not respond, but his silence spoke volumes. He considered the proposal. He could not prevent Tibbott from asking questions, and they did need a breakthrough, wherever it came from. 'All right, but keep it very low key and report anything interesting to me immediately. Under no circumstances confront anyone or act on any information you might hear. I shall decide if something is relevant and whether we need to follow it up.'

Tibbott nodded seriously.

'We'll be releasing all we know in the evening editions of the *Leicester Mercury,* including the missing lad's photograph.' Mrs Dutton would have to be forewarned, but it made a lot of sense to publish it. And if Gordon was alive, seeing his face might prompt someone to come forward.

'So... you have a name and a face,' Tibbott remarked. 'You knew more than you let on, inspector.' He fiddled with the book, riffling through the many pages over and over, the columns of numbers interspersed by the odd grainy, black-and-white photo were jumping and wriggling as the pages ran through his fingers; flashes of red or blue running up and down the columns, depending on which numbers were underlined and in what colour. Tibbott suddenly stopped, closed the book and thrust it into his coat pocket. 'Look at the time! I'd best be getting on.' Without further ado he hurried down the platform and — Vignoles assumed — to his van parked outside.

Chapter Eighteen

Leicester Central

Vignoles returned to the office. He stood gazing at the large blackboard upon which DC Blencowe and WPC Benson had drawn an impressively accurate street map of the area radiating from a spot, marked with an X, where the remains had been found. Each house or business was drawn out and coloured chalks had been used to add dots of colour or notations in neat handwriting. It was a masterpiece of draughtsmanship.

'You've put in a lot of work here. Well done.'

'Thank you, guv, but to little effect, I fear.' Blencowe stepped away from the board, a stub of blue chalk in his hand. 'The blue dots mean we've interviewed the occupants and got nothing. A cold blue felt appropriate.'

'There's rather a lot of blue,' Vignoles remarked, with a pained frown.

'Indeed, guv. Green means "pending"; that is, we've not managed to find anyone home yet. There's a fair few of those. Red means a possible hot lead, but don't get too excited: Jane and I are struggling to find you anything convincing. We've been scraping the barrel to get those three red dots on there.'

'So, what have you got?'

Without prompting, Benson stood up from the desk nearby, where she had been cross-checking some notes with what looked like a street directory. 'This one is a dog walker who saw an old man carrying two heavy shopping bags. Very poor visibility in the rain and it was dark and the man was wearing a hat pulled down low. He would struggle to recognise him again.'

Vignoles grimaced.

'I did warn you it was bad, guv,' said Blencowe. 'We've a similar sighting of a man unloading a motorcycle and sidecar combination late one evening. He was in oilskins, helmet and goggles and it was again raining — of course. The old lady who saw him through her lace curtains usually wears spectacles, but she'd left them in the kitchen.' Blencowe indicated the street in question, which was a short walk from Talbot Lane.

'If he is our perpetrator, he's given himself quite a walk. Why not park closer and reduce the risk of being observed? He could have got his machine down the side of the car parts factory.'

'I agree. It makes little sense.'

'We have yet to speak with a Mr Davies, who lives here...' Benson indicated a property on West Bridge, on the far side of the crime scene. 'Neighbours said he'd been burning what smelt like rubber for a couple of nights about the time Gordon Dutton went missing. Mr Davies has been hard to pin down since we learned this.'

'That definitely needs following up.' Vignoles gave a sigh. It was not an inspiring haul, despite the obvious diligence of his officers.

'Guv, does this case remind you of the Barrow Hill Mystery?' asked Blencowe.

'The what?'

'About two years back. It caused quite a stir at the time, but perhaps it didn't make the papers here.' Blencowe stroked his beard thoughtfully. 'I've got family across that way, see, so I get to read the local papers and hear all the gossip. On top of that, I've got a chum on the Derbyshire Constabulary who was in on it. Strictly speaking it was not exactly in Barrow Hill Roundhouse as such, more out the back and over the wall, so the local bobbies dealt with it. But everyone calls it the Barrow Hill Mystery, as that was the nearest place.'

'I'm all ears.' Vignoles had no idea where this was leading, but Blencowe was a solid, dependable type not generally given to time-wasting.

'Thing is, they found charred remains. Tiny bits of bone and the odd tooth among the ash. Heavy rainfall and wind had damaged the scene. They ended up with absolutely nothing to go on.'

'Human remains?'

'That's right, guv. But far less than we've got. They never found a single clue. Nothing. It's still unsolved; they were never even able to say with certainty whose the body was. It struck me there's a similar feel about the two cases.'

Vignoles considered this for a moment. 'I can see your point. But if it is unsolved, it can't help us.'

'Not on the face of it, but...' Blencowe shot a look at Benson as if for encouragement. '...I took the liberty of asking my chum there to look out the paperwork and have it sent here.' He pointed to a stack of cardboard files tied together with ribbon.

Vignoles raised an eyebrow. 'How did they generate so much paper if they got nowhere?' He looked unimpressed.

'They interviewed everyone. All the staff at Barrow Hill, all the loco crews and all residents in the area. They made requests for details of missing persons. It was a real fine-toothed comb job.'

'To no avail.'

'Correct. If you agree there is a similarity between the *modus operandi*...' he spoke the Latin with overly careful precision, followed by a nervous clearing of the throat, '...then it might be worth cross-referencing. Having two crimes that appear similar might throw up something in common that makes no sense when taken alone.'

'It would take days. Just look at it all!'

'It is a risk, sir, but we're pretty much done on the mapping, and between us we might be able to whizz through it pretty smartish.'

'All right. The others can muck in when they're free. I'm not sure I can approve more than a day; two at most.'

'We'll start right away.' Blencowe looked pleased, despite Vignoles's obvious lack of optimism. It was something fresh to work with.

'Have you interviewed the council workers who prepared the dig site?'

'Not yet, guv, but we have them on the list,' Benson replied.

'OK.' Vignoles then noticed that Mrs Green was waving a scrap of paper above her head, clearly signalling for his attention.

'Your telephone calls have paid off.' She called across to him. 'One of his staff called to give us his train times.'

'Whose train times?' Vignoles asked.

'The Dutton man. His secretary has advised us that he would like to meet the investigating officer as a matter of extreme urgency; in fact, the moment he steps off his train.' She handed him the sheet, which had been torn from a pad she kept beside her telephone, reserved specifically for taking down notes from calls.

Vignoles thanked her and read the few lines. 'So the mysterious father finally makes an appearance. And, to the best of our knowledge, this is the first time he's come south since his son went missing.'

Mrs Green made a disparaging grunt. 'His priorities are clearly not the same as mine. Seems everyone is interested in this poor mite except the father.' She returned to her typing and the force exerted on the keys as she pounded out a sentence made it clear just how far Mr Dutton fell short in her estimation.

'Better late than never. A reception committee will be waiting, he can be sure of that.' Looking at the train's arrival time, he would have to miss Badger's press conference if he was to have any chance of meeting a key witness. That thought brought a big smile to his face.

CHAPTER NINETEEN

Leicester 38c

The Leicester & Nottingham Union Canal ran like a broad stripe of dirty sump oil through the heart of Leicester. It flowed sluggishly between banks of almost colourless grasses, the surface steaming with the scalding water pouring from the cooling ducts of the massive power station that loomed over the site, its tall chimneys filling the sky with artificial cumulus clouds. Eerily pale wraiths of steam curled above the foul water that slipped past the backs of red-brick terrace houses, the multi-windowed clothing factories and the high walls and grand warehouses of the Great Central Railway goods yard. The cityscape was further punctuated by numerous belching chimney stacks belonging to iron foundries and grubby industrial premises of indeterminate use, whilst standing tall and proud above all else was the surprising shape of a smoke-blackened Statue of Liberty, gamely lifting her beacon to the smoggy skies above the Liberty shoe factory.

A grey heron stood motionless on the far side of the canal, almost perfectly camouflaged in its leaden plumage, one leg lifted and bayonet beak pointing towards the unappealing water. Two mallards paddled quietly, perhaps enjoying the unexpected warmth of the water on their bellies. Filthy, yellow-grey smog curled from countless chimney pots, only to linger low and oppressive in the misty drizzle the day had adopted. It was a depressingly gloomy late November afternoon, and one that stank strongly of sour water, coal smoke and engine exhaust.

But it was going to take more than this to dampen the enthusiasm of Billy Arnold, his younger brother Richie, and their best chum Jimmy Jebb. Their school blazers and caps were glistening with a silver sheen from the tiny droplets of moisture, and their legs were mottled like corned beef in the chill air. So what if it was cold and damp? There were lovely steam engines to cop, and the thrilling rumour around the schoolyard had been that the 'top of the cops', none other than *Flying Scotsman,* the most famous and beautiful engine in the whole wide world, was on shed. It was going to take a lot more than British drizzle and the threat of a burly railwayman yelling at them to hold these three back from bunking into Leicester shed. If they copped her it was going to make going to school tomorrow all the more pleasurable. They could proudly show the magic underlinings in their little spotters' books, and maybe even crow about having 'cabbed' her. They could tell a white lie on that last point. Nobody would be able to say they hadn't. There was just the small matter of how to get into the shed without being seen.

The canal towpath took them close to the rear edge of the engine yard, but a tall brick wall, topped by curls of vicious, rusty barbed wire, festooned with bits of ragged newspaper and knotted bindweed, prevented ingress. Without a stepladder, this barrier also made looking over the top impossible. However, they could see the upper walls and roof of the four-lane engine shed and the top of the coaling stage. Even more tantalising were the many plumes of smoke now rising in the still air like the breath of giant beasts of burden.

The tang of coal was on their tongues and slipping down their throats and the delicious smell of hot locomotive and burning carbon drifted over the brick barricade, mingling with the stench of the canal and an almost vestigial hint of sweetness from the Fox's sweet factory. The bulk of the Midland Railway bridge loomed over them to their left, at that moment grumbling at the sound of an imperfectly seen Black Five making the crossing. The engine number proved impossible to discern because its cab sides were so filthy. That was annoying. But the loss of this run-of-the-mill workhorse was no matter when they considered the enticing possibilities of what lay beyond the narrow wooden picket gate that offered the only way in. All manner of delights lay across the expanse of dangerously open ground leading to the shed and stabling lines crowded with engines.

The gate was locked. 'We can climb over, easy!' There were nods of agreement. 'We'd best be careful, because if we're chased it'll be awkward getting back over quickly.' They were standing hard against the wall, desperately resisting the urge to peer over the gate. 'Hold back, lads. We can't risk anyone seeing us until the last moment. If we stand here for too long they'll spot us coming over.' Billy Arnold was the eldest and they treated him as their leader on this top secret raid into 'enemy territory' after school and before a tea of Heinz baked beans on toast. His word and experience counted.

'But we've got to get inside! I can't miss the *Scotsman*!' Jimmy sounded almost desperate.

'Don't worry, Jebbers,' said Billy, giving him a playful punch on the upper arm. 'We've just got to be a bit clever. Now remember, we're commandos on a secret mission. Over that gate is occupied territory. It's dangerous, so keep low and out of sight.'

'We've got to work really fast.' Jimmy's toothy smile flashed.

'But be accurate with the numbers.' Billy waggled a finger.

'I bet they've got sentries patrolling.'

'Lots of them! Don't move until my signal. I'll lead; you follow. Got it?' Billy was enjoying his sense of importance.

'But it's not really dangerous, is it? If we get caught, nothing will happen, will it?' His younger brother was sounding less confident now the moment was upon them.

'Well...' Billy considered his answer. 'Let's just say it's better we don't get nabbed.'

'Oh.'

'Just run like the clappers if I say so.'

Richie Arnold was not reassured, and Jimmy's eyes were wide as saucers as the older boy elaborated. 'It all depends. Some of the men can be a bit rough, but others are quite friendly. Just don't give them your real name and address. That way they can't send a copper round to tell you off.'

Jimmy blanched. 'My dad'll kill me if that happened.'

'Who Dares Wins. We don't cop *Scotsman* without a bit of risk.'

'I heard it were easier to get in around the front way,' said Jimmy, hopeful for a safer option.

'Quicker to get in, but quicker to be sent packing. You'd get a few minutes at best as you're in full view, and besides, there's another danger that way. A really bad one.' He gave the others a sly look, ensuring he had their full attention then glanced warily towards a solitary man dressed in black walking slowly towards them along the tow path. He looked uninterested, but he might be railway police. They needed to stay alert. 'If you want scary, then trust me lads, that's the way to find it.' He rolled his eyes melodramatically. 'You go along a cinder track for a while. It's used by loads of railwaymen to get on and off shed. You're off railway property and you're right near the main line, which is wizard. But it's dark and it's lonely and there's this house all on its own, with a really horrid old man inside.'

'I've heard about him.' Richie was nodding his head in a knowing sort of way.

'He's evil. Scary as hell.' A pause for effect. 'He lurks in his shed right next to the path, ready to jump out and grab you. And he's always burning smelly stuff in his garden. Stinks rotten. He frightens the living daylights out of you — deliberately.'

'Don't like the sound of him,' said Jimmy.

'He hates us spotters the worst. There's a lad in my class who got hit with his walking stick.'

'Get away!'

'It's true. And he grabbed him so hard it left his prints on his skin.' Billy enjoyed scaring them. 'Horrible, huge, red fingermarks,' he added, with relish.

'Shall we try this gate?' Richie was won over. He looked around and saw just that man watching from some distance away, hands in pockets. But he was not coming any closer.

'Attaboy. Right, we must now synchronise our watches. It's exactly 4.20pm.' There was no need for this, but it added to the sense of adventure. 'Pencils ready! Notebooks open! Here we go!' Billy leading, they took turns to climb the narrow wooden gate and drop down on the other side.

'Run to the back of that B17 engine standing near the turntable!' He didn't wait for a reply, but launched himself across the ash and clinker and pot-holed tarmac, doubled over as he ran, school blazer flapping below his tummy, due to the ungainly gait adopted in the belief that bending low would miraculously render him invisible. He could hear the slap-crunch-slap of his fellow shed-bunkers' shoes following just as he reached the locomotive tender. This appeared massive once up close and it smelled of brake dust and exuded an extra few degrees of coldness. The grease-smeared disc of the nearest buffer looked unfeasibly large beside his face. He hunkered down next to the axle box of one of the wheels leaving space for the others to slip in beside.

'We did it!' Jimmy's higgledy-piggledy teeth showed white. His school cap was wedged between a pair of sticky-out ears, lending him a comical aspect. He was crouched the lowest of the three, looking back towards the little gate they had just climbed. 'I'll watch our backs for guards!'

'Good lad. Keep your eyes peeled. Listen for boots on gravel.'

'Wilco,' Jimmy hissed.

'I've been scouting this way in for days.' Billy looked pleased with himself. 'Let's cop this beauty, then get in deeper.'

'I want to cab her,' his brother announced.

'Not yet. We could be chucked out before we've even got started.' The older Arnold brother sounded serious. 'We do footplates last. Get the numbers first and have fun after.'

The younger Arnold pulled a face but still nodded in agreement. His eyes surveyed the gloomy scene around them. He was close to the track, the rails leading off towards the turntable ran between rusting lumps of abandoned machinery, piles of old brake blocks and standing pools of unpleasant-looking liquid reflecting the first pale glimmer of a yard lamp. The drizzle seemed to intensify, bringing down a further veil of gloom on the scene.

'We're wasting time.' His brother stood up, but remained close to the black shape of the locomotive, stepping only far enough away to get a clear view of the cream numbers on the cab side. He dictated these aloud as Jimmy dutifully made a note in a tiny notebook with a stub of pencil.

With Billy leading, the three schoolboys darted along the flank of the loco, carefully avoiding the dribble of steaming water from the copper injector pipe. They reached the turntable well, keeping the long wall of the shed building running to their right. Behind this lay unknown delights: outlines of unidentifiable engines, dimly visible through almost opaque glass in the metal-framed windows. It was going to be a challenge to get inside. They crouched beside a stack of oil drums and looked across at the massive bulk of the coaling stage, each trying to make out the numbers of three filthy, heavy mineral engines standing below its coal holes. Two men were moving about inside, but neither looked their way. Numbers duly noted, it was time to tackle the main event.

'Four down. Here goes...'

They pressed close to the shed side wall and peered around the corner. Close by, a small J52 tank locomotive was poking its nose out of the brick structure, but this drew little more than a contemptuous glance as it was a regular sight on their local patch. Jimmy noted its number anyway, forming the characters neatly and perfectly in line with those already on the page. 'Six-eight-eight-three and nine.' He spoke aloud as he wrote the number down.

'You've seen her loads of times!' Billy was peering cautiously into the pungent cathedral of steam that lay tantalisingly close, one arm extended behind him, signalling to the others that they should stay where they were. They were in a dilemma. Ranged in front of the shed were at least six locos, but deep inside were far more. Which to tackle first. And where was *Flying Scotsman*?

Billy opted for going inside. The neat lines of engines were smoking in a sultry manner, and the acrid fumes drifted into the long, wooden smoke-troughs slung from the roof; but, despite this primitive air-cleansing, the air was smoggy and the electric roof lamps, encased in dark green enamel shades, were casting bright lines through the thickened air to create correspondingly deep pools of shadow. The scene was monochromatic, the powerful chiaroscuro rendered in the greys, muddy browns and blackish mauves of a great art master. Everything stank of metal shavings, oil and Swarfega. Billy sniffed the air. 'Mm...I love that smell.' With that, they darted inside, a frisson of excitement like electricity flowing through their young bodies.

'Watch out!' Richie pushed them behind a stack of wooden crates holding oddly shaped bits of metal stacked close to the inside wall. Two men in overalls and flat caps, with almost-identical stubs of cigarettes burning in the corners of their mouths, crossed one of the walkways between the nearest row of locos. They were soon out of sight.

'We have to work fast. I'll take the engines on the right; Richie, you take the left and Jimmie, you keep lookout.' Billy strode down the nearest line, scribbling down the details of a woebegone Tango freight engine that was clearly in need of attention. A 'Not to be Moved' sign in red-and-white enamel jutted from a lamp bracket on its front buffer beam, but this was superfluous, as the connecting rods were lying neatly alongside its small driving wheels.

They edged their way forwards, the shed full of alarming sounds: the bang of a hammer and the tuneless whistle of the man who might be using it; the distant murmur of a radio. An unseen locomotive grumbled and hissed somewhere. Someone yelled 'Dave!' twice, making the boys freeze in their tracks, veins pumping in their temples, adrenaline coursing freely. Dave didn't answer, and so they moved on.

Richie muttered aloud, 'Is there a namer? I want a namer.'

'I want *Scotsman*!' replied Jimmy, peering underneath a humble, six-wheeled tender engine, hoping he could spot the wheels of something considerably bigger and more glamorous beyond.

Billy stopped. He held his hand aloft, clutching his tatty little notebook open, revealing pages of numbers scrawled at untidy angles. 'Everyone get down!' He ducked low and crouched behind the rear wheel of a powerful Pacific tank loco. 'That might be her.' He hissed the words.

'Where?' Jimmy's voice was too loud.

Billy frantically waved a hand. 'Shush! Enemy guards surrounding her.'

'That's torn it.' Richie peered around his brother's shoulder.

'I want a look.' Jimmy piped up. All he could see was the rear cab steps of the locomotive they were sheltering behind.

Billy was trying to decide what was best. 'Right, lads. We can't get closer, but scoot across this opening and into the cab of the engine ahead. Keep really low inside, and we might just be able to get a good view from up there.'

Once again adopting his stooped running gait, the elder Arnold brother dashed across the space between the two locos, not daring to glance over at the three men standing close to the front of the magnificent engine that had lured him into this perilous place. He was soon at the steps of an engine called *Hartebeeste* and reaching high to grab the base of its handrails. Engines were huge when you got up close and he was stretching to get a grip. The other two were close behind. He heaved himself upwards. His face appeared on a level with the wooden cab floor, which was scattered with coal dust and some tiny splinters of wood. The floor also came with a massive pair of boots at the bottom of two legs encased in blue overalls. Billy slowly raised his head. A huge bear of a man was looking down at him. The giant's eyes widened a fraction and there was a brief moment when Billy thought he might even crack a smile. But that moment passed. A nasty sneer formed on his face. 'Who the hell are you?'

'I—I was just trying to see *Flying Scotsman.*'

'Yer wha'? Get out of it, you little bugger!' A steel toe-capped boot was planted dangerously near Billy's face. The boy recoiled and dropped down the steps without warning and in so doing, crashed into his brother, knocking him to the floor.

'Mind out!' The younger boy was about to hurl abuse at his clumsy brother until he too saw the reason for the undignified dismount. 'Oh cripes!'

'They've rumbled us!' Billy was not hanging about, already showing a clean pair of heels. 'Come on!'

Jimmy stood still, looking bewildered. 'But we've not seen...'

'Oi! What are you lot up to?' A strong baritone voice boomed across the shed. A man in a clean set of dark blue overalls, a buttoned-up railwayman's jacket and a peaked cap was standing at the end of their line. He looked important — and angry. 'Come back here!' He advanced towards them.

The three lads needed no further warning. They ran out of the shed and back towards the picket gate, feet pounding hard on the crunchy ash. There were a few shouts from inside the shed. The way ahead looked clear and their young legs were swift, but their hopes were soon dashed. A short, muscular railwayman with a dark moustache and thick, black eyebrows was walking briskly across from the coaling stage. He was carrying a huge fire-shovel in a menacing manner and his scowling features told the boys he was not coming over to pass the time of day.

'Gotcha!' He placed himself in their way, legs splayed slightly and the shovel grasped in both broad hands horizontally, like a Viking war axe.

'Sorry, mister. We were just trying to see *Scotsman*,' Richie said politely and with contrition.

'We didn't touch anything. Honest.'

The man spat on the ground and twisted his mouth into an ugly shape. 'You're trespassing. And up to no good, I bet.' He shifted his position, hefting the shovel in a quick, smooth motion onto a shoulder, its obvious weight clearly nothing to this powerful man. He stepped closer. His breath stank of cigarettes. 'Sod off. Scram!' With his free hand he pushed Jimmy in the chest, making him recoil. He then formed a fist and made as if to punch Billy under the chin. 'Bugger off, right now, or I'll beat the living daylights out of yer!'

Quivering with a mixture of fear and shock, their legs like jelly as they tried to climb the picket gate, anxiously looking back with frightened eyes at the man who stood like a gunslinger in the now dark yard, rain falling in millions of fine droplets, the boys stumbled onto the towpath and then ran like the wind, forcing a big woman wrapped in a winter coat and clutching a handbag to step aside and press herself into a stand of dead cow parsley to let them pass. They hardly noticed her. They were now laughing wildly with the sudden release of pent-up tension and adrenaline-fuelled delight of what had been a thrilling shed-bunk. They'd got away with it, and it felt good.

CHAPTER TWENTY

Leicester Midland

Vignoles and Trinder formed a small reception committee for Jeremy Dutton. They had no description of him, but they knew on which train he was due to arrive at Leicester Midland station. They waited expectantly on the platform. There was a visible stir amongst the many waiting passengers, some picking up luggage, others shuffling nearer towards the platform edge in readiness, as the hissing locomotive glided towards them through the teeming rain. Vignoles quickly noted that it was *Hawkins* of the Jubilee class, but then turned his attention to identifying Dutton amidst the melée of disembarking passengers. For a minute or so there was a confusion of coats, hats, scarves, bags and umbrellas with steam swirling in between.

As the crowd thinned, a trim man in an expensively tailored cashmere overcoat, wearing a Homburg hat and clutching a small, leather weekend case, attracted their attention. He was standing still, with people passing each side of him as a river flowed around a rock. His eyes were as small and dark as currants and his neatly trimmed salt-and-pepper moustache didn't quite conceal the sneer that seemed to play around the corners of his mouth A self-contained and confident man, his upright bearing suggested he maintained something of his recent military past.

'Mr Jeremy Dutton?'

'That is I. You will be the detectives I wish to speak with.' His voice was strong but strangely emotionless. Vignoles made the introductions and perfunctory handshakes were exchanged. He was intrigued by Dutton's reply. It was assertive, almost a command.

'I shall require a full case review of your progress in finding my son, if you please.' His voice had a steely edge. 'I trust you have something definite to report. I did not travel this considerable distance for empty promises.'

'Since you spoke on the telephone with DS Geary some days ago, there have been some developments,' Vignoles replied. 'If you would like to accompany us to somewhere more private, we can—'

'You can tell me right now, right here, inspector!' Dutton interrupted.

'What I have to say is of a most serious nature, sir; it would be better to—'

Dutton interrupted again. He did not seem alarmed by Vignoles's solemn tone. 'Come on, out with it, man.'

'Very well. We have found human remains and have reason to believe that they are those of your son.' Vignoles spoke quietly. 'I am very sorry, Mr Dutton. It would not have been my choice to break this news on a railway station.'

Hawkins gave a sharp whistle and barked into motion, throwing a cloud of vapour around the three men. The timing was perhaps fortuitous, allowing Dutton a few moments to fully absorb the gravity of Vignoles's words whilst this distraction was so close by. His jaw muscles contracted a number of times and one eye twitched. He flicked a tiny piece of hot char from his cheek, cleared his throat and composed himself. 'I now appreciate the urgency of your many messages left at my Glasgow office.' He made it sound as though they were talking about a business conference.

'There is a pub across the way, sir. I imagine you could use a restorative drink.'

'Yes, it was a long journey and a double whiskey would be most welcome.' Dutton's voice was flat, and they all remained silent as they exited the elegant station, stepping from beneath the grand porte-cochère packed with taxis and private cars and onto Conduit Street, then crossing the London Road and into the Hind.

Seated in a quiet corner beside a glowing coal fire, three pints of Everard's on the table and a double whiskey in Dutton's hand, they resumed. 'Where did you find the remains?' Dutton tossed half the amber liquid down his throat. 'You would do me a service if you tell it as it is and don't pull your punches.'

Vignoles explained everything about the discovery of the ash and bones and other remains.

'They won't find that murdering crook down there!' Dutton sounded contemptuous.

'Sorry?'

'The hunchbacked king. They're looking in the wrong place. Fools.' He shook his head slightly in disbelief. 'I very much hope you will show more guile and skill in hunting the killer of my son.' He downed the last of the whiskey and gave Vignoles an unfriendly stare. 'I notice you said the remains are *believed* to be those of my son. Don't you know for certain?' There was an unpleasant curl to the side of his mouth.

'We have only a few scraps and clues to act as pointers.'

'But are these scraps good enough for you to make that assertion?' His eyes were sharp and alert.

'We believe so. It is a slow process, as I am sure you can appreciate, Mr Dutton. There is still a possibility that it is not Gordon, but we feel sufficiently convinced to declare our hand and treat it as murder. We are ruling out natural causes or an accident because the remains and items found that we associate with your son had been moved from another location after the deceased had died.'

'I see.' He chewed this over for a moment. 'Has my wife been informed?'

'She has. But surely you have spoken with her? She has known for some time...' Vignoles was taken aback.

'I have been rather busy.' He gave his pint a taste.

'Your work seems very time-consuming,' Trinder observed dryly.

'Yes, it is.' Dutton then launched, with some relish, into a description of the impressively expensive road construction project that he was overseeing. It was a multi-faceted affair involving the clearance of slum tenement buildings and the creation of a flyover bridge and many road junctions, amongst other elements. Vignoles stopped him mid-flight.

'We don't need to understand the complexities of the project you are managing. Our focus is on Gordon.'

'As I should hope it is.'

'I would have thought that considerations of slum clearance and concrete mixing might have taken a back seat. Under the circumstances.' Trinder weighed in again, with a slightly sarcastic tone that seemed to light Dutton's blue touchpaper.

'Do you imagine that a single moment has gone by without my thinking about my son?' Dutton replied. 'Worrying and hoping for his safe return. Well, do you, constable?' His voice was calm and controlled, but the attack was stinging. 'My God. What are you? Unfeeling robots?'

Vignoles shot Trinder a look of slight reprimand. Trinder continued, but in a more conciliatory tone.

'We do not think that, sir. But what does puzzle us is that once you received news — belatedly, because you neglected to leave contact details at Gordon's school—'

'An unfortunate oversight,' Dutton interrupted, 'I had a great many things on my mind. An important and time-constrained contract for Her Majesty's government, in point of fact.'

Vignoles pressed the point: 'Once you heard he was missing, there appears to have been little or no response from yourself. I find that somewhat hard to countenance.' He had planned to be gentle with the man but, like Trinder, felt his hackles rise in response to the man's pomposity and his apparently lukewarm concern for his missing son.

Dutton sipped his beer before answering. 'I had spoken with the headmaster, with my wife, and with the commendably eager DS Geary. I was advised that every effort was being made to find my son. I placed my trust in the proper agencies doing their jobs correctly and thoroughly and keeping me abreast of developments. There was nothing I could achieve by coming home.' He gave Vignoles and Trinder a stare that challenged them to answer back. They held their tongues. 'I was assured that door-to-door enquiries were taking place and that every avenue of investigation was being followed. What good would it serve to drop a vital piece of publicly-funded civil engineering at a critical moment just to stand around like a spare part?' His look did not soften.

'Point taken,' Vignoles replied. He changed tack. 'When you heard that Gordon had gone missing, what were your initial thoughts? Were you surprised?'

'Of course I was. He is not the sort of boy to go gallivanting off somewhere.' Dutton paused. 'He'd know better than to try a stunt like that. I'd cut his allowance instantly.'

Vignoles believed it. 'So you immediately ruled out the idea of Gordon running away?'

'I can think of no credible reason for Gordon to abscond from school. He was happy there.'

'He told you he was?' Trinder asked.

'One can sense these things. What you have told me rather suggests he met some other fate, does it not?' If Dutton was feeling any emotion he disguised it with another sup of beer. 'He has not run away, but has been murdered. You said it yourselves.' There was a slight tremor in Dutton's hand.

'His remains suggest he may have met with a violent end, but not how he came to find himself in a position of danger that led to this shocking conclusion,' Vignoles explained. 'The situation may have started quite innocently. We understand he was train-spotting at Grantham the morning of the day he vanished.' Dutton snorted contemptuously but made no other comment. 'Can you think of anyone at his school, an older boy perhaps, that he might have accompanied on a trip to Leicester? Perhaps they went chasing trains then got into some difficulty here.'

'You think a fellow schoolboy took his life?'

'We must consider every option. We have no information pointing towards this scenario, but perhaps you might?'

'I don't. I hear Gordon's school chums' names mentioned when he is at home, but I have never met them. I don't know if any live in Leicester.'

'I realise this next question will sound odd about a twelve-year-old, but can you think of anyone who might wish to do him harm?'

'Obviously not.'

'How is your relationship with Mrs Dutton?' Trinder asked innocently. 'Sometimes boys get it into their heads to run off — and thereby accidentally into danger — because they are reacting to an atmosphere in the family home.'

'Everything is perfectly fine.' Dutton's voice was dry and clipped. He drew himself up and sat back in the chair, deeply affronted.

'Mr Dutton, the nature of this enquiry demands absolute honesty from all concerned. Untruths can prove most awkward when exposed, as they invariably are.' Vignoles spoke gently but he was scrutinising Dutton carefully.

'I don't like the tenor of your questioning.'

'We cannot afford to be polite,' Trinder responded.

'Would you characterise your relationship with your wife as close. As man and wife?' Vignoles insinuation was deliberate.

Dutton extracted a silver cigarette case from an inside pocket of his finely tailored suit jacket, the movement exposing a flash of startling crimson lining. He took his time lighting up, and then finally answered. 'All right. I admit that things have become somewhat frosty between us in recent months.'

'Mrs Dutton suggested longer.'

'Did she? Time rolls on so quickly. People change... drift apart. My job commands the greater part of my time. I live for my work and...perhaps my wife...' He tailed off with a shrug of his shoulders. 'She has a comfortable home, a generous housekeeping budget and a son whom she adores.' He stopped, gazed at the floor and cleared his throat. 'I have provided for my family. They want for nothing.'

'Is there another woman?' Vignoles asked.

'No, there is not.'

'Your wife suggested otherwise.'

He raised an eyebrow, but maintained his air of aloofness. 'I see. Then she is wrong. I would like to think that she did at least confirm that our home life, when we are together, is free of strife or argument.'

'She suggested that things were civil.'

'Which shows that my son had no reason to take flight.'

'You have been in Glasgow since when?' Trinder asked.

'8th September. I took Gordon — that is, my wife and I took Gordon,' he corrected himself, pointedly. 'To his boarding school and then I travelled north later that day.'

'And you have not left Glasgow since that date, until today?'

'Correct.'

'I trust your fellow workers, your secretary and other staff can vouch for that?' Trinder asked.

'You are starting to sound as though you consider me a suspect,' Dutton remarked, raising an eyebrow. He flicked some ash into a nearby ashtray as though offended.

Vignoles suddenly had an idea and threw in an unexpected question to gauge Dutton's reaction. 'Have you ever been to Barrow Hill?'

'Never heard of it.'

'It is a railway shed not so many miles from Chesterfield.'

'No: I can state categorically that I have never been there. But, since you mention the subject of railways, can you explain why the railway police are leading this investigation?'

Chapter Twenty-one

Leicester

'But you planned it weeks ago.'

'Months, to be pedantic.'

'There you go, then.' Anna put her hands on her hips. 'If you really think it necessary, telephone the office now and see if anything has developed. Reassure yourself that everyone is doing what you need them to, then you can have a couple of hours' leisure. Do you good!'

'I suppose I could...' Vignoles wanted to be convinced.

'And, for goodness' sake, go for a pint or two afterwards because, knowing your luck, something will happen tomorrow morning and you'll be back in the office all day, on a Sunday. So take the chance while you can. You are *allowed* to have a few hours respite, darling.' Anna was adamant.

'But this is a murder investigation.'

'And you are doing all you can.' Anna leaned back against the kitchen table and folded her arms in a gesture which implied that he had better take notice. 'You said yourself you are only at the fact-finding stage. What would you do today if you didn't go? Just sit at your desk waiting, in case someone turns something up. If they do, it can wait a couple of hours. And if it were something really urgent, they could get a message read out over the tannoy at Filbert Street.'

Leicester City was playing Huddersfield Town that afternoon, and back in the summer, when the fixtures had been published, Vignoles had put a red line under the games he especially fancied watching. So far he'd managed to get to just one, and it would be nice to fit another in. He'd invited Tim Saunders, the shedmaster at Woodford Halse, to accompany him. 'November 15th is my Saturday off, Charles,' he'd said, in a jolly fashion, 'I know that, because I've just decided! I'll put a cross on the calendar and, if anyone wants me in here that Saturday, they can jolly well take a long walk off a short pier!' Saunders rarely got away on a Saturday afternoon and usually had to content himself with a radio broadcast over the loudspeakers in the noisy shed or, more usually, with just reading the pink sporting edition of the local paper.

Anna was right. He could not let Tim down by cancelling so late. And besides, the Foxes were playing well. If they could somehow poach a win from the current league leaders, they could reach the dizzying heights of third in the table. True, it was going to be a tough battle to do so, but one to savour. Heck, that swung it — he was going!

* * * *

'Right, lads. Yesterday was good, but none of us copped *Scotsman*.'

'I did!' Jimmy Jebb blurted out. 'Just a glance.'

'A likely story,' Billy replied, sceptically.

'I did!' Jimmy's cheeks burned.

'Well, we didn't, so we're going in again.'

'But Billy, won't they be onto us now?' Young Richie was looking anxious again.

'They will, so today's bunk is going to be straight in, get *Scotsman*, and straight out. Bang! No hanging around.' His eyes were full of excitement.

'Is that why we're going the front way?' Jimmy asked.

'Yep. I got word she's standing right outside the shed this morning, so we don't even have to go very far in. We might even see her without having to get past the gate, which would be perfect. I just hope she's still there.'

'Cor!' Richie was sold on the idea. 'Dead easy!'

'Didn't you say this way was dangerous? What about that weird old man?' asked Jimmy, chewing his lower lip.

'But we know he's there, so we'll be prepared!' He tried to sound convincing. 'You know, like anti-aircraft defences. The enemy ack-ack fire is waiting to meet us, but we still press on to the target, ready to take avoiding action.' There were knowing nods of assent as the two younger boys understood his wartime analogy. They could imagine flying Lancaster bombers over Germany. 'Let's get a move on.'

Billy led them around the street corner and onto a cinder path lined with vicious brambles that stretched out long fingers of thorns above dank stands of dying nettles and sooty grass. They trudged in single file down the path, which soon swung close to the main running lines of the railway, with just a wonky wooden fence and more thorny vegetation between them and the track.

They were also close to Filbert Street and, aside from the sound of a passing goods train hauled by the familiar old engine they saw most days, there was a low murmur from behind the identical rows of brick-built terraced houses. It was the sound of many thousands of people walking and talking as they approached

~ 126 ~

the stadium. The constant drumming of feet was punctuated by the occasional car horn and the rasping sound of wooden ex-ARP gas rattles being twirled but, despite the audible presence of so many football supporters, there was nobody on the cinder path. It was a surprisingly lonely spot, even though it was close to so many dwellings and the bustling railway. The boys negotiated a dog-leg in the path, avoided the wet fronds of a lifeless-looking buddleia, and then stopped.

There it was.

It was just as Billy had described it: a dreary, ugly old house set in its own untidy yard. A solitary survivor from what once had been a row of dwellings before the Luftwaffe demolished the rest. It looked unloved. Almost as if shunned by the massed terraces that lay some way back, hiding behind their own yard walls and stands of scrappy saplings and bushes. The scene was softened and smudged by the drizzle and the sickly smoke of thousands of coal fires. The old house was a hunched, mean-looking construction. The windows were boarded over or veiled by ancient lace curtains of such a filthy tea colour that they looked rusty. The slate roof was slick and shiny and sagging badly in the centre and there were weeds sprouting from the leaking gutters.

But what drew their attention was a tarred, timber shed close to the front corner of the low wall edging the property. The shed's windows were so caked in grime and covered by encroaching ivy that it was impossible to see if there were curtains behind masking a light inside. A skein of smoke curled from behind the shed from an unseen source. It reeked of burning refuse and was the colour of pus.

'Is that it?' Jimmy's eyes were like saucers.

'It gives me the shivers.'

'Cor, what a pong! What's he burning? Stinks horrid.'

'Keep it down, Richie. We don't want him to know we're here.' They squatted behind a clump of briars and peered at the house. 'Just a few yards and we're past, and then it's straight on to the shed. Can anyone see the old codger?'

'He must be out the back, making that smoke,' Richie suggested.

'Or in the shed. Ready to pounce.'

'Only if he sees us,' Billy replied. 'We can sprint to the front wall and hide tight and low. He can't see us if we stay below the parapet. Here goes!'

They were soon crouched in sodden grass, pressed hard against the wall, scuffed black shoes in a pool of oily grey water. It was most unpleasant and they could not stay there long. They were aware of the ominous presence of the house and the looming bulk of the shed so close on the other side of the wall. Billy sneaked a quick glance through the bars of the front gate. 'All clear!'

They wasted no time, but Jimmy, once he had passed the gate, stopped and twisted about. He knew he shouldn't risk it, but he peered around the gatepost with one eye. He had a better view into the space behind the shed. There were piles of rubbish, an old tin bath, scraggy weeds and yet more overgrown shrubs. He could also see part of an iron stove serving as an incinerator; it had a slender chimney with a funny metal cap on the top, shaped like a witch's hat, and it was this that was emitting the foul stench. It was an oddly compelling view and yet there was something frightening about it. Jimmy did not want to be caught by the ogre who lived there, and yet he also wanted a glimpse of him. However, despite the signs that someone had been there recently, nothing moved. The blank windows of the house stared back at him. He felt as though he were being watched, the hairs on his neck rose. He ran to join the others.

* * * *

The crowd was thickening; a sea of grey- brown- and green-clad humanity moving relentlessly towards the stadium in a powerful clatter of boots, shoes and even clogs, on slippery cobbles. Some slight relief was offered by the occasional blue-and-white banded scarf, or a rosette-shaped favour pinned to a lapel. Drizzle settled on the acres of woollen clothing like millions of microscopic jewels. A slight steam hung above them as their massed body-heat fought against the winter chill, enhanced by the smoke of countless cigarettes and pipes. The temperature was falling and the low streets were already blurring with the encroaching evening smog. But Vignoles and Saunders could hardly be happier.

They were discussing the impending game, each rehearsing the possible options and tactics that might see their team secure a precious win. Then, with that delicious perversity of football, the other took his turn to offer a counter argument of all that could — and surely would — go wrong; the pitfalls and failings of the Foxes and why they must not raise their hopes too high and should expect disappointment, only for the other to strike back with a spirited defence in that endless cycle of anticipatory debate, which was also being played out by numberless others now crowding the streets and filing through the clattering turnstiles.

Vignoles and Saunders were unlikely companions in many ways. Differing in views on just about everything; they could debate anything from football to politics to the price of bread, and rarely agree. To an observer it might appear a fractious relationship in danger of spilling over into argument, but that was far from the truth. Each held the other in high regard and their sparring was just that. Landing hurtful punches was never the intent. It was friendly but challenging debate. They also shared an appreciation of railways, Saunders adopting a solidly pragmatic standpoint, coloured by a life of trying to keep the locomotives in his charge in good repair; Vignoles holding a more romantic view, despite meeting with troubling and distressing scenes as part of his job as a railway detective. And they both followed Leicester City, although they characteristically disagreed on how the team should play, how it was managed and who it should or should not buy. Even the result of a match could spark a healthy discussion over a pint about whether it was deserved or not. In other words, both men were thoroughly enjoying forgetting the day-job for the duration of the afternoon.

Vignoles stopped outside the narrow entrance slit in the side of the stand and bought a fourpenny programme from a vendor with a canvas bag filled with the slim publications slung across his shoulder. He noted the reassuringly familiar cover in cream and dark blue that sported a charmingly amateurish drawing of three City players cheerfully running onto the pitch, ball safely clasped under the captain's arm. They looked like strapping, well-groomed fellows. He held the programme aloft. 'They look nothing like our lot!'

Saunders laughed in agreement as he took his place in the queue for the turnstile and Vignoles fell in behind, taking in the smell of Woodbines and a whiff of meat pies and hot Bovril. He could almost taste the post-match pint. Ah, Saturday at quarter-to-three. Perfect.

Vignoles halted suddenly in their shuffling progress, forcing him to apologise to a man who had shunted into him from behind. Was that Tibbott over there? Yes. There was the same blue-and-cream delivery van with the stupid advertising slogan, and the man himself leaning against its front wing, with a newspaper cone of chips steaming in his hand. So, he was a train enthusiast *and* a fellow

Foxes follower. Quite a coincidence. Tibbott was perhaps thinking much the same thing about Vignoles, as he appeared to be looking his way, his face a model of concentration. But something struck Vignoles as odd. He turned to watch Saunders squeeze through the turnstile, then gesticulated and mouthed silently that he would join him in a few moments. Much to his friend's puzzlement, Vignoles left the queue. Was Tibbott watching him? Vignoles dodged through the crowd, moving against the tide, reaching Tibbott as he was about to climb into the van.

'We meet again, Mr Tibbott.'

'Indeed, inspector. Going to the match?'

'Clearly. And yourself?'

'Unfortunately not. I was delivering in the area and got caught up in the crowd. So I got myself some chips.' He gave a sheepish grin. 'Well, better get moving!'

'Won't be easy with the roads so clogged. You can't move an inch. In fact, it would be dangerous to even attempt it. Best wait a few more minutes and it will be clear after kick off.'

'I suppose you're right.'

'You should be careful. The traffic police won't like you parking your van here on a match day.' Vignoles suddenly wondered why he was risking missing kick off to engage Tibbott in a foolish exchange leading nowhere and he regretted having started it.

'Righty-o. Noted.' Tibbott laughed as if relieved. 'Actually, er, now you're here, there's something I wanted to mention.'

'Make it quick.'

'That lad, the one who's in the paper today; could he have gone down to Leicester shed on the day he was done for?'

'We don't know, but why do you ask?'

Tibbott gave a knowing nod of the head. 'I thought as much. Yep, that adds up.' He puffed out his chest, as if pleased with himself, then leaned close and spoke quietly. 'Have you talked to that old man Twist, who lives down that way?'

'No. Who is he and why should I?'

'Lance Corporal Leslie Twist. War wounded and an ugly sight. Scary.' Tibbott's voice could not be heavier with implied meaning. 'Fought in the Great War. It did nothing for his personality, that's for sure, as he's a right nasty old bugger. Twist by name and twisted by nature.' He nodded knowingly. 'Or so I've heard.' Tibbott paused and observed Vignoles closely, as if waiting for his gratitude. This was not forthcoming and so Tibbott continued. 'He lives down by the engine shed, all on his own, in a tumbledown place with nobody around.' Tibbott leaned in even closer, his breath reeking of vinegar and chip fat. 'It's lonely down there, especially with these dark evenings.' He raised an eyebrow that implied more than was said. 'Now, I'm not casting aspersions, inspector; I'm just saying, you never know.' He tapped the side of his nose.

'I see,' sighed Vignoles. 'What sort of things have you heard?' He felt his heart sink. This is what came of letting members of the public get involved. It might be well intended, but this tale-telling tittle-tattle was not what they needed.

'It could just be idle chatter, but he's got a reputation for hating train-spotters. I heard a whisper he's slapped some of them about.' Tibbott stood upright and his voice was back to its usual level. 'Makes you wonder, doesn't it?'

'Thank you, Mr Tibbott, that may prove helpful,' lied Vignoles, knowing that such a mixture of malicious gossip and hearsay rarely was. Now the local paper had run the story he was probably going to hear more unsubstantiated nonsense over the next few days. Rumours, misunderstandings, even personal vendettas, all delivered as tip-offs that were invariably far off the mark.

'If you would now excuse me, I have a match to watch. Good day to you.'

'Twist.' Tibbott pointed a finger at Vignoles. 'Don't forget the name. Twist. As in Oliver.'

'I shan't.'

Vignoles headed back, making better speed now he was joining the rapidly diminishing numbers passing through the turnstiles. There was a thrilling roar and a hum of anticipation coming from within the ground. The teams must already be out on the pitch. Standing in the short queue, he began pondering at the chances of Tibbott being there on exactly the same day — one of only two days that he visited the stadium at Filbert Street. What were the odds against that? But, before he could dwell on this any longer, he was being asked to hand over money in exchange for a ticket.

'Is everything all right?' Saunders had been waiting for him.

'Yes, sorry, call of duty, I'm afraid.' Vignoles fell in beside Saunders. 'Right, come on lads! Pull your socks up and give them a game...'

* * * *

The boys made good speed to the perimeter fence of the engine shed without further problems. All three were enjoying the exhilaration of having evaded the unwelcome attention of the ogre, their muddy knees and hands and damp socks going unnoticed.

'Well done, lads. And just look at that beauty!' They followed Billy's pointing finger. Unmistakeable and indeed, beautiful, in her coat of blue express engine livery was *Flying Scotsman*. Sitting pretty some distance from the front of the shed, with wisps of steam that indicated she was being made ready for use.

'Yes! Got her! Got her!' Jimmy was literally jumping up and down with excitement.

'I reckon she's just come off the coal stage.'

'Can we get any closer?' Richie was leaning over the fence as far as he was able. 'She's the best.'

'Better not. Look, there's a gang of men over to the side there. We'd get a flea in our ears, for sure.'

With a grudging acceptance that this was probably wise, they settled down to some serious contemplation, taking in how the steam showed almost luminescent against her rich blue paint in the rapidly fading light. The locomotive had been polished and burnished with oily rags until her bodywork boasted a glorious, rich sheen. A deep roar came from behind them. A strange, thrilling, animal sound that tumbled over the rooftops like a wave.

'Sounds like the kick-off. Wish I was there.'

'Gladder I'm here!' Jimmy added.

'We can bunk in for the second half!' Richie suggested.

'We could try. What d'you reckon, Jebbers?'

'Not me. I've got to get home.' Jimmy looked momentarily crestfallen, but a sharp toot from *Flying Scotsman*'s whistle drew his attention away from missing the football and back to the wondrous iron horse just as her driving wheels started to turn. This was why he was wet and grubby and risking a box around the ears for coming home in such a state.

'She's moving off!'

The engine took gentle huffing breaths as she rolled towards them, the driver leaning from the cab, apparently keeping a close watch on something on the valve motion. As the engine drew closer he looked up and, catching sight of the three lads, sportingly lifted a hand in salutation. They waved back. What an honour to have the engine driver acknowledge them! Then she was gone. Pale puffs of steam mingling with the mist and the rising steam from the power station gathering over the Soar.

They spent a while trying to discern the numbers of the other locomotives in view and then Jimmy reluctantly turned away. 'I really need to be getting home.'

'It's getting dark, so it should be a piece of cake getting past the ogre's house.'

They trotted back down the path, trying to urge some warmth back into limbs now stiff and reluctant to move. The house was in darkness, with just a sputtering gas lamp on a cast-iron post beside the cinder track casting a slight glow to the far side. The stench of burning seemed to be even more intense and the smoke was rolling more quickly from behind the black cube of the shed. From this, a chink of yellow light showed where the door was ajar.

'He's inside!'

'Cripes!' Richie was breathing hard.

'What we gonna do?' Jimmy was looking to see if there was someone else going in the same direction to offer them protection, but the little path was deserted and the fence and dense vegetation was preventing them from walking along the edge of the railway lines. There was no other option. They went for it, feet pounding on the cinder path; breath rasping. They were close to the front gate and it was looking good. Five more seconds, perhaps six, and they would be safe.

But he came at them.

He seemed to take shape from the dark shadows collecting around his foul dwelling. The clothes he wore were black, as though formed from the very walls of the tarred shed out of which he seemed to step, face and hands appearing to be sculpted from the swirls of stinking smog. And what a strange, misshapen face it was. Two staring eyes above a mouth that was little more than a knife slit through inflamed and unnaturally smooth skin, stretched taut like a drum. It was a nightmarish vision that struck horror into the three boys.

'I'll have you!' One of his hands locked onto Richie's arm and gripped it hard, like the pincers of a giant lobster.

'Owww...'

'I saw you! Sneakin' about!' He lashed out at Jimmy with his walking stick and struck the boy a sharp blow on the shoulder. Twist was a thin man and clearly disabled, with a leg in a heavy metal cage, but he was far from feeble. He lifted the stick again as though to send it crashing down on Jimmy's skull, but Richie fought back

~ 133 ~

using both hands to prise the surprisingly vicious grip from his arm and, in so doing, managed to spoil the old soldier's aim.

'Let me go! You're hurting me!' Richie yelled as he wrenched at the narrow, bony fingers.

'Take that!' He now slashed at Billy's heels, causing the boy to stumble and lose his balance, feet skidding on the mud and gravel until he tumbled heavily into a clump of dirty nettles. 'Vermin!'

Richie had now freed himself. He pushed Jimmy forward but Twist raged after them, his voice hoarse and cracked. He was a strange figure in a flapping black overcoat, flailing his stick about his head, and with a filthy army cap set at a ludicrous angle across his brow. The three boys ran, stumbling and scrambling until they finally got into their stride, then hurtled down the lane with Twist's foul curses following. The ogre could do little more now than hurl ugly words into the rain and the darkness.

Ten minutes later Jimmy said goodbye to the Arnold brothers and reluctantly watched them turn the corner and head towards Filbert Street, where they intended to take their chances at sneaking in for the last stages of the match. The pair knew all the weak points in the security, and which gatemen sometimes turned a blind eye when ticketless young lads slipped in at the tail end. Whilst a part of Jimmy wanted to join his mates, the truth was he'd had enough excitement for one day. The thrill of seeing *Scotsman* and the terrifying encounter with that crazy old man had combined to leave him exhausted and hungry. It was growing cold and dark, and the rain was back. He couldn't wait to get home; he wanted a hug from his mum, and he longed for bread and dripping in front of the roaring coal fire.

He checked his pockets. Yes, he still had the money for his ticket wrapped in a grubby handkerchief. And there was his pencil and his penny notebook. Oh! But where was his Combined Volume? It was bulky and had some weight, so it took only a few moments of frantically patting his pockets to realise that it was missing. He repeated the exercise, to no avail. He could feel tears pricking behind his eyes. How could he have been so careless? All his numbers — lost! Months of work — lost! He slapped the pillar box he happened to be standing beside in sheer frustration. Why had he even taken it along? He'd wanted to savour all the way home the anticipation of underlining the two words *Flying Scotsman* using his best pen as neatly as possible. This was an act not to be hurried. There would be no rushing, no smudging of the ink. But now it was lost. He must have dropped it when that madman attacked them. That had to be it. They had run and laughed in nervous excitement and relief and nursed bruised arms and shoulders and examined nettle stings and searched for dock leaves, and he'd just not thought about it. There was no alternative: he'd have to go back and look for it.

He stared nervously at the empty street corner. If only Billy and Richie were here. The smog was thickening by the minute. This would surely protect him. The entry onto the little path looked very unwelcoming. But he could do it. He *had* to do it. The book was more important than... than *anything*. His mum would understand why he was late for tea. He swallowed nervously and felt his hands tremble, but took a deep breath and, with great reluctance, forced his feet to take him back down the cinder track...

CHAPTER TWENTY-TWO

Leicester Central

'Hello, lovely. You missed your train?'

The boy nodded. He'd been studying the timetable pasted outside the station entrance on Great Central Street.

'Ah well, never mind, eh? There'll be another along soon, I expect.' She gave him a reassuring smile.

'In an hour-and-a-half.' He looked thoroughly miserable. Normally, such a wait on a station platform would be his idea of heaven, but he was hopelessly late getting home and was tired, cold and hungry. The idea had lost its appeal.

'I expect your folks will be wondering what's happened to you.' She could see tears making his eyes glisten. He nodded hurriedly but could not answer for fear of sobbing.

'That won't make the train come any faster, will it now?' He shook his head, feeling overwhelmed by his situation. He started to shiver. 'It won't be nice, you sitting there all on your own for all that time. Cold, too. And I bet you're famished. Tell you what, I've got some lovely, fresh-baked pie back at my house. I live ever so close. Just a step along from here and there'll be a nice, hot fire to warm yourself. What d'you say?'

'Thanks, but I'd better not. I was told never to...' He stopped himself and looked embarrassed.

'Your mum taught you not to talk to strangers? Quite right, too!' Her smile created dimples in her cheeks. 'But you can trust me, because I'm not a stranger; everyone knows me! I only live just across the way. And my son will see you right for your train. He knows all about them; he even has all the timetables.'

'Really?' Jimmy felt cheered by this news; the lady was kindly and motherly, and she had a son just like him; a fellow spotter, too. He sniffed back the tears and wiped his nose on his sleeve.

'Your mum will be pleased as punch to know you were safe and warm and dry, and not hanging around a lonely, dark station all on your own and then getting home looking like a half-starved cat!' She laughed. It was a nice sound.

'Come along, then. My boy'll be waiting.' She put an arm around him. 'Don't you worry about a thing.'

Chapter Twenty-three

The Green Cockatoo

My fur got stole,
But, Lord ain't it cold,
But I'm not gonna hollah,
Cause I still got a dollar,
And when I get low,
Oh-woah-woah, I get high...

The singers had powerful voices and the single spotlight was making the emerald green fabric of their perfectly tailored sheath dresses shimmer. With shoulders bare and slender arms gloved to the elbow, they were a glorious sight. One was a bottle blonde; another had raven black tresses; the third had hair of flame red, with lipstick to match. Large, paste earrings dangled as they swung their hips to the powerful back-beat. Their harmonies were tight, riding high over the rich tones of the brass section.

Jane Benson and Lucy Lansdowne were enthralled. It was hot as Dante's Inferno in the Green Cockatoo and the air was thick with smoke and the smell of scent, aftershave and sweat. The band was on a low stage, the drums and double bass sending pulses through the timber joists like a freight train over rail joints. Every table was full and the small dance floor could not comfortably hold any more couples, though they were dancing in enforced close proximity. Behind the music was a wall of chatter and laughter.

My man walked out,
Now you know that ain't right,
But he'd better watch out,
If I meet him tonight,
I said when I get low,
Oh-woah-woah, I get high...

Jane leaned forward and shouted in order to be heard. 'I say, they're very good!'

'I love Ella's recording, but these girls are even better!' Lucy agreed, hardly taking her eyes off the three captivating young women just feet away from their table as they lifted their left arms high into the air, right hands on hips, in a stance that drew a roar from the back of the room. Hawkes was standing on the opposite side of the stage, but in between the artfully waving limbs and swaying hips, they had a good view of him as he bent his knees slightly and lifted the trumpet, to better fill the room with sound, in perfect synchronicity with the trombonist beside him.

Lucy gave her friend an approving look, but Jane was pretending to only have eyes for the redhead standing immediately in front of her.

All the bad luck in this town has found me,
Nobody knows how trouble goes
around and around me...

The band punctuated the 'woahs' and 'ohs' from the three singers with short passages from the trombonist, the rhythm guitarist and finally Hawkes, on trumpet. He stepped forward and played a short solo, executing it expertly and with feeling and was rewarded with a burst of applause as the blondie sang a solo.

I'm all alone
with no one to pet me,
But the old rocking chair's
never gonna get me...

Jane realised she was grinning like a Cheshire cat. She picked up her gin and tonic and took a sip.

'He's good!' Lucy yelled. 'Really looks the part!'

'Looks can be deceiving.'

'You wouldn't say that if he serenaded you below your window!'

Jane rolled her eyes. Their heads were almost touching in order to hear each other's words. 'He'd get a pan of cold water on his head if he tried!' she said, but she was laughing.

She was enjoying the evening far more than she'd expected. Hawkes or no Hawkes. The glamorous singers, the jazz music, the (doubtless sophisticated) chatter of the audience, punctuated by sudden peals of laughter, and the smokey, slightly sleazy atmosphere were quite thrilling to her, and she felt unusually animated, almost as though she were more alive than usual. She watched the dancing couples moving together in a hot huddle, some of them necking quite outrageously whilst almost standing on each other's toes, and felt a tingling realisation of the possibilities open to those brave enough to take the plunge. Real life was right here, right now, in the Green Cockatoo. It was not quietly reading a book whilst nursing a cup of cocoa before turning in for yet another early night.

The song came to an end and the appreciative audience began applauding furiously and wolf whistling in ear-piercing shrieks. The vocalists bowed gracefully and beamed huge smiles at each other in acknowledgement of a job well done. The first part of their set was over and they filed off, exiting the stage through a rather shabby green velvet curtain. A gramophone record started to play over the loudspeakers.

'Oh no, he's coming over. What shall we do?'

'You can introduce me, for a start.'

'Evening, girls!' Hawkes looked pleased to see Jane and her mystery companion. 'Mind if I join you?' Without waiting for a reply, he pulled out a chair and sat down, his hat tipped well back on his Brylcreemed hair. 'Looks to me like those G & Ts need a bit of stiffening up.' With perfect timing he caught the eye of a passing waiter and silently mouthed the order. 'So doll, who's your lovely friend?'

Jane flushed, but Lucy raised a perfectly pencilled eyebrow a fraction in surprise at his compliment. Jane thought him a little impudent, but introduced Lucy, adding, 'She is also a policewoman. We work together.' She hoped that might make him think twice about referring to them as dolls.

'You don't say?' Hawkes was caught off guard only momentarily. 'I'd better be on my best behaviour, then, haha!'

'Yes, Mr Hawkes, I think you had.' They all laughed and Jane emptied her glass. Another was on the way and she thought it would look unseemly to sit with two glasses in front of her. As the alcohol warmed her blood and the noise and heat and heady atmosphere of the club enveloped her, Jane realised she was actually enjoying herself. She glanced at her friend, whose eyes flashed back at her with a subtle expression of delicious delight. It was an exchange not seen by Hawkes, who was just at that moment busy handing money to the waiter.

CHAPTER TWENTY-FOUR

Belgrave & Birstall

Charles and Anna Vignoles found seats in a saloon brake coach for their short morning ride from Belgrave & Birstall station, in the leafy northern edge of the city, into Leicester Central. The Monday morning commuter train was hauled by the same Gresley A5 type tank engine usually seen on this duty and attracted only a cursory glance from Vignoles as it steamed beside the island platform. Daylight was struggling to gain ascendency over the endless, low clouds that pressed down above them. The rain gave the deep maroon coaches an eggshell finish that caught the pale gaslight.

The coach was not overcrowded and so they managed to sit some way from the other commuters with their morning newspapers flapping and re-folding above crossed legs. There was a gentle murmur of sleepy conversation above the soft clickity-clack of the wheels as the engine almost coasted down the gentle gradient towards the city. Anna removed her hat and made some adjustments to her glossy black hair. 'You look pensive, Charles. Was it that telephone call?'

'Yes.' He was brushing the heavy wool of his overcoat in a distracted manner. He'd fielded a call to their home only minutes before they were due to leave. 'Another boy has gone missing.' He paused a beat. 'From Leicester.'

'Oh Madonna. When?'

'Saturday evening. Last seen outside Central.' He looked as though he had been winded.

'Our own station.' Anna looked pale. 'But that means two boys have...' She left the sentence unfinished.

'He's not come home yet, that's all.' Vignoles spoke too quickly and his voice was abrasive. The strain was already starting to tell. 'Sorry.' Anna shook her head. She understood. He fell silent, collecting his thoughts. Staring out of the rain-smeared window at the countless rows of chimney stacks, he noted that some were already bearing shiny new television aerials. Since the date had been announced when Princess Elizabeth would be crowned the following year, their number had increased month on month. Vignoles's breath was fogging the glass, traversed by rivulets of condensation. A bedraggled black crow flapped slowly between two trails of smoke that hardly moved in the windless dawn. At last he spoke. 'I hope these two cases are unrelated.'

Chapter Twenty-five

Leicester Central

'What do you make of it, Vignoles?' Chief Superintendent Badger looked sombre. He had just concluded a run down of the situation and was perched on the edge of his chair, kid gloves clenched in one hand so tightly that his knuckles whitened. His smart cap and swagger-stick rested amidst the confusion of the desk.

'I'd like to hear more from Jimmy Jebb's two school chums, though I don't imagine they will have much to add.' Vignoles was fishing in the dark.

'By the sound of it, they left Jebb alone and that was the last they saw of the poor blighter.'

'And thereby hangs the mystery. What happened to him once he was left alone?'

'Quite.' Badger threw his gloves down onto the desk. 'The Leicester Constabulary will try to obtain a fuller statement from the two brothers once the initial shock has passed. They were all attacked by this Twist fellow earlier that day. Look into it.'

Vignoles stroked his chin. How very odd this was. Tibbott had mentioned the same man not an hour or so before Jimmy Jebb and his chums had their altercation with him. It was uncanny. Worse still, he'd been tipped the wink about the man but had gone to a football match and done nothing. Vignoles realised that Badger was still talking.

'Do you know this man, Twist?'

Trinder shook his head and looked at Vignoles, awaiting his response. 'Not personally,' Vignoles answered. 'He's not come up on our radar screens, so to speak. But curiously, his name was mentioned to me by a member of the public on the same day Jimmy went missing. It sounded like silly gossip, and the informant was at pains to not make any specific claim, so I brushed it off.'

'Most unfortunate.' Badger was not pleased.

'It was merely vague, unsubstantiated rumour, sir. It would have been well-nigh impossible to justify needling the man based on that alone.'

'Accepted.' Badger conceded the point.

'However, in light of the boy's hostile contact with Twist and his subsequent disappearance, I will follow it up.'

'What were you told?' Badger was not enjoying hearing that they might have collared this man before he'd had time to strike.

Vignoles shifted uncomfortably in his chair. 'The old man is supposedly bad-tempered and is said to have an aggressive streak towards train-spotting boys. He may have assaulted one in the past, although the informant was unwilling to give names, dates or any other specifics.' Vignoles cringed. An uncomfortable silence filled the room. Trinder was now giving his boss a look of wide-eyed shock. He spoke first. 'You mean we've got a prime suspect, sir?'

'We must be circumspect, sergeant.'

'Hang circumspection! Get down there and haul him in. Grill the old sod and don't be too nice about it, either.' Badger snapped. 'This information might be pertinent to both Dutton and Jebb, and you sit here asking us to be circumspect? A little lad has been abducted, probably fiddled with, and murdered. Bloody hell!'

'To be fair, sir, we do have to look before we leap. It was about as vague as it can get. It could be malicious false witness. We could be laughed out of court if we act based on just that alone.'

'Prove it, either way.' Badger was unmoved.

'Who gave you Twist's name, guv?' Trinder asked.

'The very willing Mr Tibbott. You may remember WPC Benson questioning him on Talbot Lane. The van driver. He seems eager to help. Over eager.'

'Good for him.' Trinder nodded approvingly.

'I just hope the press don't find out you'd been tipped off and failed to act, Vignoles. I hardly need remind you that we give press conferences in order to broadcast the fact that we need all the help we can get from witnesses.' Badger sounded weary as he spoke. 'The idea being that we then act when they come forward with information. Never mind, we know now.' Whilst still irritated, the storm was blowing over.

'If deemed good enough information, we act. In my judgement, it wasn't.'

'Yes, yes, I accept that.' Badger had vented the tension inside and now spoke more calmly. 'However, in the cold light of today, we now know that Jebb's friends were attacked by Twist. They're bruised and cut to prove it. So make him squeal. Wring it out of the man. We can justify being heavy-handed. There could be grounds to bring an assault charge against him, too.' Badger dropped his voice and looked at Vignoles. 'Act swiftly. You might save the poor lad's life.'

CHAPTER TWENTY-SIX

Leicester

'You two start upstairs. PC456?'

'Sir?'

'You take the downstairs. 788, have a look in that shed.' Trinder barked the orders to the four uniformed constables. He was feeling edgy. They had a possible double child killer in custody and needed evidence to prove it.

'What exactly are we looking for, sarge?' PC456 enquired. He liked a clear set of instructions and needed to understand exactly what was expected of him.

'Anything to suggest a child has been here. I don't rightly know, so if you see anything that you think a miserable ex-soldier shouldn't have in his house, give me a shout and we'll take a gander.'

The constable nodded in acknowledgment. Not long afterwards there was the sound of a shed door being given a series of hefty kicks to break the lock and PC788 called across the yard. 'Sarge! Come and look at this. It's a rubbish tip. And it stinks.' He wafted his gloved hand before his nose.

Trinder peered into the dingy interior and took in the ancient floorboards, barely visible between bales of old newspapers and magazines bound by twine. There were stacks of filthy clothing, planks of timber propped against the walls and torn cardboard boxes filled by what looked like empty bottles and rusting tin cans. An ancient motorbike lay beneath some sacking. It was claustrophobic with clutter and the stench of something rotting. 'Best get started then. Those clothes bundles over there, take them apart and look for anything resembling school uniform or anything that might belong to a schoolboy. Even if it's just a scrap.' Trinder shared the constable's feelings about the grim task and turned gratefully to follow Vignoles to the front of the house, where the door was open wide. The smell emanating from inside was, if anything, worse than in the shed.

'It's going to be like looking for a needle in a bloomin' haystack,' remarked Trinder, despondently.

Vignoles grunted and paced down the hall. 'Find me something to suggest two young lads having been here recently. Ignore anything else.' He was speaking to the constables who were tentatively picking their way between yet more mounds of rubbish and clearly in need of guidance. 'Twist lives alone and probably has few or no visitors. See what plates and cups have been used. Look for a blanket or a makeshift bed.' He wrinkled his nose with distaste and stifled the temptation to retch. The house was an utter hovel. It was probably infested with all manner of unpleasant crawling things and goodness knows what infectious diseases. He could feel his scalp start to itch beneath his hat, but kept it wedged firmly on his head. 'We'll tackle the kitchen, John.'

Trinder followed reluctantly into the lean-to construction at the back of the house. The two men stood underneath the dim light offered by a single low wattage bulb that Vignoles flicked on, using a handkerchief. He had no wish to touch the greasy switch, even with his leather gloves. A square of cotton could be boiled and sanitised later. The light did little to lift the gloom. If anything, it accentuated the worst aspects of the miserable galley. An ancient, wall-mounted gas water-heater that looked positively lethal dripped into the sink, where a green stain formed from what was a long-term leak. There was an unwashed plate, a fork and a knife, a black teapot and a mug of indeterminate colour, a few small pots with sugar, salt and pepper, but little else. Trinder lifted the lid on an enamelled tin and grimaced as he revealed the stub of a mouldy loaf inside. An empty tin of sardines gave off a fishy smell, but this was almost preferable to the aroma of sour milk and rotting cabbage.

'The living conditions of a poor old man.' Vignoles sighed. He almost sounded disappointed that there was nothing to suggest an abducted boy or two had been there.

Trinder tried the back door, which was unlocked but quite effectively secured because it had dropped on its hinges and the damp had swollen the wood, so it was wedged tight. He gave it a thump with his shoulder, flicking the resultant dirt off his jacket with his handkerchief, and they stepped back outside, relieved to inhale what in contrast felt more pleasant: a soupy mix of house coal and bonfire. The smog was collecting once again over Leicester, sucking the light and colour from what was still only late morning. They could see PC788 poking around with a long stick in some half-dead bushes on the other side of the yard. He had decided that this was more productive than battling through the mounds of detritus inside the shed. 'This place has a bad atmosphere,' Trinder observed glumly, whilst hunting around for a similar stick. Prodding and turning over the foul contents of Twist's house was definitely something to be done at arm's length.

Vignoles agreed. If ever a house reeked menace then this was it. He was not normally given to such emotions and silently reminded himself that, as detectives, they dealt strictly with facts. It was all very well feeling spooked, but the clock was ticking and they needed evidence. Turning around to assess the rear of the tumbledown house, he felt sure they were going to find something that would tear a hole in Twist's defence, even if the kitchen had so far drawn a blank.

The problem was the old soldier was proving to be an uncooperative, foul-mouthed bugger. So far his only crime seems to have been failing to take a hot bath for at least six months, by the state of him. By his own admittance, Twist was no fan of children and was happy to tell the police that he actively frightened off any foolish enough to stray too close. But this was a very long way from murder and the calculated disposal of a body by secret cremation.

In truth, there was something about the damaged old man that worried Vignoles. The circumstantial evidence made Twist look like a suspect, but his overconfident and cocky manner suggested that he had nothing to hide. He just growled and laughed and sneered by turns at every effort they made to catch him out. He was almost enthusiastic in his ranting at the stupidity and ignorance of modern youth. Despite his pent-up rage at the injustices of war and the way society shunned him for his dreadful deformities, he was curiously open and frank. Dammit. They needed something incriminating before they tackled him again. At least by the time they next met, Twist would have been forced to take a hot bath and to submit to the delousing spray whilst in custody. He'll also have been given some clean clothes. All this would make it possible for Trinder and him to stay in the same room as Twist for more than a few minutes.

They heard a shout from PC788, by then squatting down by a remarkably ugly incinerator. He was using a torch to peer inside the mouth. Vignoles felt his pulse quicken. An incinerator was exactly what he'd asked Benson to look for a few days previously. This one was big, almost industrial in scale, and could probably kick out a fair heat when fired up. He and Trinder exchanged a knowing look. Neither needed to say it aloud: both were thinking that it was just the right size to consume body parts with ease. They set off across the yard, carefully stepping over or around broken flower pots and bits of rusting corrugated iron.

'I reckon there was a fire in here yesterday, sir,' the constable explained. 'But there's something inside I need to get a better look at.' The constable narrowed his eyes in the hope of shutting out the pale grey dust that was starting to lift as he moved his hand around inside, grimacing as he touched a hot ember. 'Aye-aye, what have we here, then?' He pulled out the spine of a small, hard-backed book with a few stumps of scorched pages remaining where they were stitched tightly into the binding. 'The rest turned to ash as I touched it, sorry.' He held out the remains in his cupped, gloved palms for the detectives to inspect.

'I know what that is.' Vignoles dug into his overcoat pocket and pulled out a book instantly recognisable as being the same size and shape, and where the damaged one was not heavily blackened, the colour and print matched exactly. 'Both Dutton and Jebb had exactly the same edition as mine.'

'Is that one of the train-spotting books you mentioned?' Trinder's voice was excited.

'Correct. DS Geary was quite specific that Dutton owned this edition, and Jimmy's school chums reported he also had one and had brought it along on Saturday.' Vignoles put his copy away and carefully picked up the burnt fragment. 'If the owner is anything like the rest of us, then we might be lucky...' He carefully eased the delicate section of pasteboard cover away from the page beneath and smiled.

Trinder leaned in closer. 'It's handwriting, guv. It says Jimmy, then a capital jay followed by an e; the rest is burnt and unreadable. Surely that has to be Jebb.'

'It's pointing that way, John. We shall be able to identify his handwriting by matching it with his other school books.'

'Then we've got him! The twister's bang to rights.' Trinder was clearly excited. 'Jolly good work constable!' he remarked, but suddenly fell serious. 'But does that mean young Jimmy has met the same fate as Gordon Dutton?' He and Vignoles gazed at the black and rust stained incinerator and Trinder felt his stomach heave.

A locomotive drawing close to Leicester Central suddenly let out a loud whistle and redoubled its efforts after slowing for a distant approach signal. This acted as a break to their contemplation of the sinister furnace, the opening of which now looked even more like a gaping, toothless mouth.

'Right, bag this up, sergeant and get the men to redouble their efforts.' Vignoles spoke first. 'Looks like we're on the home stretch, but I'll need more than this. There may be something of Gordon Dutton's here too.' He addressed the constable. '788, close the fire door and cordon off this area. This is now a crime scene. Nobody goes near until we get the forensic boys in for a proper look.'

'Yes, sir.' The constable's eyes widened as he began to understand the enormity of what he had stumbled upon. 'And keep looking around this place before the day gets any darker.' Vignoles turned to Trinder. 'Mr Twist has some very serious questions to answer.'

Trinder nodded grimly. 'Damn right he does.' He was itching to have another crack at the vicious, murdering monster now they had something that definitely linked him to one of the missing boys.

CHAPTER TWENTY-SEVEN

Leicester

'Let me go, let me go! I don't want to be here.' Jimmy Jebb's eyes were bloodshot; his voice mumbled and weak. He was quivering with fear and exhaustion and his throat was so parched it could hardly open. Despite this, he was trying his best not to show it. They became so angry if he showed fear, even more so if he cried. And he had cried a lot. His arms and back were bruised, his jaw swollen on one side, and his wrists were rubbed raw by the rope tied around them. He could taste the metal tang of blood and his tongue knew a tooth was loose. How could he explain all this to his parents? They'd be so cross with him. 'I won't say nothing. I promise. Just let me go!'

'Good lad.' He got a wink for his pleading and promises, but nothing else. 'When we're ready. You've to wait until we decide when it's time.' The man's voice was emotionless. It was this lack of feeling that so confused and frightened Jimmy. Why didn't the man understand that he had to go home? He just delayed, made excuses and left him for hours and hours locked in this place that smelt so strongly of soap and drying clothes that, when taken together with the heat, made him feel faint. It was suffocating. That oven was roasting. And why did they have to hit him when he cried?

'W—when will it be time? Please tell me.' He closed his swollen lips and tried to force back the stinging tears.

'Now, now, what's with all these questions, then?'

Oh God, she was back. Jimmy felt his spirit crushed. Left alone with the man, there were moments when he felt a bond. They talked engines and stations and steam sheds. At least, the man did the talking and he listened and grunted and tried to nod encouragingly and make positive sounds whilst trying to quell the searing pain from the beatings. When they talked trains he could almost imagine everything was normal. If he could just convince the man to take him over to the station, any station, it would be all right. He would be able to shout, to tell someone, to get free.

The woman pushed her face too close to his and ordered him to be silent, or she would tie that cloth soaked in soapy water around his mouth. It made him retch and struggle for breath when she did that. The cloth was tight and constricting, too. It was terrifying trying to gulp air as panic overwhelmed him.

She frightened him. He reckoned her son was scared of her, too. Her domineering bulk and endless sickly smiles and sweetly spoken rubbish about her baking sounded lovely at first. The mothering and cosseting had been nice for an hour, on that first evening when he was so cold and hungry and feeling miserable. It had been perfect. Just what he needed. But she never stopped. And her smiles came wrapped with a horrid sting. She was strong and could be so cruel. There was that strange light in her eyes and a set to the jaw that was stubborn and hard as she twisted his arms up his back, pulled his fingers so far backwards he thought they would snap.

'No need for all this fuss, or you know what you'll get.' She looked at her son, who dutifully picked up a cloth from out of the steaming copper on the range. He let it plop back into the water. The point was made.

'I just want to go home, please.'

'You don't need to be worrying about that. Leave everything to us.' She gave a dimpled smile as false as that painted on a clown. And she knew just where a dimpled fist could strike the kidneys to make him spew his guts and lie on the quarry tiles almost unconscious. 'Are you thirsty?'

He shook his head. He was desperately thirsty, but felt the urge to defy her, to refuse anything from her. He'd rather die of thirst than give her the satisfaction. 'I just want my mum.' The words were a faint croak.

She turned to her son. 'Have you decided where?'

He nodded. 'I have. And this time it's a real corker! Sheer genius, even though I say it myself. You'll be very pleased with me.'

'It had better be good. Get back to the top of your game, because you sailed a bit close to the wind last time.'

'I did?' He looked worried, lower lip compressed between his teeth.

'What do you take me for, some kind of fool? I can read the papers and listen to the radio news like the rest of them.' She waggled a finger at him. 'A right mess you've made, by the look of it, and now it's plastered all over the front pages.'

Jimmy was turning his head from one to the other as if watching a tennis rally. At least they were leaving him alone whilst this went on. But what was in the newspaper? What were they arguing about?

'Not too clever, my boy. Are you quite sure they're not getting too close to us?' Her eyes were cold and the smile had vanished.

'I was going to explain, honest. They don't have a clue. I know it might look bad, but we're still calling the shots.' He smiled. 'You can trust me, mam. I'm going to lead them a merry old dance. It'll be such fun!' He looked at her with an imploring expression. 'That's why we need to do it again so soon afterwards. I've got it figured in my head. It'll really confuse them. Put them into a proper nose-spin.' He made himself look bigger, like a street pigeon strutting after a mate on a city pavement.

She eyed him curiously. 'You'd better be right. Are you sure you did exactly as I told you?'

'I didn't mess it up last time, despite what you've read. In fact, it was very clever. I was a little worried when they first started digging, but things have gone our way nicely. I hold the ace cards and can outwit them. Just you see!'

'Well, that's all right, then.' She sounded mollified.

'This one will be inspired. It will go down in history.' He gave a self-satisfied nod of the head. 'It's time we pushed ourselves to another level. Show them how clever we are. They'll write books about this — about us — one day.'

'Got it all worked out nicely, have you, son?' The smile came back.

'Every last detail. Just say when.' He rubbed his hands together with glee and gave Jimmy a strange look.

'Mind how you go and don't you make any silly mistakes.'

'Yes, mam.' He rolled his eyes.

The mood between the pair thawed as the little storm passed over almost as quickly as it had started. She looked down at Jimmy. 'You wanted to know when you would leave, dearie.' He nodded. 'Well, we've got some good news. How about tonight?' The dimples formed, but her expression turned Jimmy's blood to ice.

CHAPTER TWENTY-EIGHT

Leicester

'Do you understand why you are here?' Vignoles opened his second interview with the old soldier.

Twist shrugged his shoulders and scowled. It was a disturbing sight. He was a thin, tortured creature, a physical match to his surname. The skin on his face was stretched unnaturally smooth and blotched bright pink and red, even though so many years had passed since his remedial surgery. His lips were almost non-existent; his mouth little more than a slit that opened and closed like that of a huge fish. One lazy eye appeared to be permanently pulled wide as if in acute surprise at something happening slightly to one side of whoever he was looking at. His lank hair hung in long, damp fronds down the back of his skull. One leg, gripped by a vicious-looking metal cramp, was stretched out to one side of the table. A whiff of carbolic soap and the chemical tang of insecticide dust hung in the air; both were preferable to the unwashed stink that hung in the air during the first interview. Vignoles was aware that Twist would be easy to dislike and it would be equally easy to pin blame on such a figure. He must tread carefully and not assume they had the perpetrator before them.

'How about you tell me again? Haha! To be honest, boss, I've had myself a nice hot bath and a tasty bowl of soup, so ta very much and I hope you won't be charging me for the pleasure.' He chortled with a sound like water gurgling deep in a pothole. 'Being hauled away in a police car aside, I've been treated tolerably close to civil, when all's said and done, though I'm wondering where these clothes came from.' He clawed at his clean but baggy, threadbare shirt.

'They're a sight better than those you arrived in,' Trinder remarked, irritated by the ingratitude.

'But they're not mine. And they don't fit.'

Vignoles declined to discuss the suspect's sartorial needs. 'You are here to answer questions about the disappearance of James Jebb, known as Jimmy. We have reason to believe that you met him on the evening of Saturday 15th. Is that so?'

'That'll be the little bugger I nabbed outside my house. Why are you interested in him, then?' Twist's horribly distorted face made an expression that suggested genuine curiosity.

'The boy has not been seen since.'

'What's that to do with me?' Twist grimaced. On a dark night a face like that would terrify any child.

'Because you had confronted him the day he went missing,' Vignoles explained.

'I gave the little bugger a flea in his ear and sent him packing. That's it. Got a fag? I'm gasping.' He scratched under an armpit. 'This itchy powder reminds me of my army days: we used to be deloused there, an' all. And a cup of tea would go down well.' He winked at Trinder, who bridled at this attempt at matey familiarity, then glanced at a uniformed PC standing against the back wall, who shuffled his feet in response. He didn't like Twist's tone, either.

'Tell us exactly what you did to Jimmy, and...' Trinder placed an unopened carton of State Express 555 cigarettes on the table between them, '...you can have one of these.'

Twist wriggled in his chair, moving the leg that was encased in the heavy frame. 'Expensive ciggies. They're paying you too much.' He leaned forward and his fishy mouth spat out the next words in a sarcastic tone. 'This your idea of clever interview technique, is it? Done all the training courses, have you, detective?' He cackled. 'As it happens, I think a fag's the least I'm owed for being prodded and poked and shaved and made to wear someone else's kit!' He flung himself back in his chair and called loudly to the PC. 'And where's that cuppa? Two sugars, mind!'

'You've got a cheek,' muttered Trinder. Twist was far too full of himself, and he suspected the old man was secretly enjoying the attention. 'You can have a smoke and a cuppa, and as much sugar as you want, soon as you've told us the truth about Jimmy.'

Twist settled into his chair as if making himself comfy for a long stretch of time. 'So, I only get them if I'm a good boy.' His voice was syrupy and mocking, like that of a taunting schoolboy. This was rather ironic, considering his reputation for despising them. It was perfectly pitched to annoy the three officers, like a scratchy nail down a blackboard. He waited for a reaction.

Vignoles leaned forward. 'No. I think that's how *you* work it. What is it? A bag of glacier mints to lure them in? Or maybe a bubblegum? How do you get boys into your house, Mr Twist?'

'Eh?' For the first time Twist looked serious. 'What you on about? Bubblegum? Phah! Leave that stuff to the Yanks. Mints? Rot yer teeth!' He pulled his mouth wide and peeled back the vestigial lips to reveal a startlingly good set of teeth. 'Ask them into my house? I hate the little buggers. Ask anyone.' He glared at Vignoles.

'That lad walked right up to my place, bold as brass, and started sniffing about like a dog. Just like a dog, on all fours, snuffling about in the dark.' He turned and spat a vile-looking gobbet onto the floor, making Vignoles and Trinder wince with disgust.

'Kept standing up then ducking down, thinking how he was clever and that I couldn't see him.'

'Sounds like he was looking for something that, presumably, he had dropped during your earlier altercation. Why did that anger you so much?' Vignoles asked.

'I don't like them lads. Always up to no good.'

'Was that why you attacked Jimmy and his two friends earlier that same day?' Trinder asked. He felt his temper rising and his voice was hard.

'Skulking about, they were. Giggling and staring and peering into my place. I just shooed them away.'

'Two of them have cuts and bruises that prove you did more than that. Without provocation, you assaulted them and struck out at them with your walking stick,' Vignoles said firmly.

'Probably fell over when they ran off.'

'You admit that Jimmy Jebb returned later, alone, and that he made you angry. Did you attack him a second time, Mr Twist?'

Twist dropped his voice so it sounded almost conspiratorial. 'I spotted him, though it was pitch dark. My army days gave me more than a burnt off face and a rotten leg.' He nodded sagely, as if sharing a state secret. 'Months of sentry duty taught me well. When you're on look-out over no man's land you get really good at seeing in the dark. Your life depends on it.'

'So, what did you do?' Vignoles dropped the level of his voice to match Twist's.

'Jumped out!' Twist suddenly slapped the table hard, making Vignoles involuntarily recoil. His gnarled fingers were almost touching the cigarette packet. Vignoles was annoyed. He had been taken by surprise, and in the arena of an interview, where dominating the space and keeping tight control of the suspect and the questioning was key. It was vital not to betray any weakness or doubt, and the old soldier had just gained a small advantage. Twist winked. He knew exactly what he was doing and was enjoying it. The PC unfolded his arms and adjusted his feet, readying himself to advance and pin the man in his chair if necessary.

'I can't chase them, but I know how to wait for the right moment to strike,' Twist chortled, with an unpleasant, phlegmy sound. As if to illustrate his point, he suddenly swiped the cigarette packet and held it close to his pointed chin triumphantly; a wicked grimace cracked across his distorted face as he sniffed it, breathing in the aroma of tobacco.

'Give that back!' Trinder stood up, his chair toppling over with an inelegant crash, leaving him standing and leaning over the table, but he was unable to effectively do anything unless he entered into an undignified tussle that was likely to end in a stalemate and some badly squashed cigarettes. The constable rushed forwards, but Vignoles waved him away.

'I just want a fag, that's all.' Twist fiddled with the packet, his misshapen, bony fingers struggling to extract one. Trinder balled his fists, but a look from Vignoles told him to recover some dignity and right his chair. 'I'm answering all your questions, and you promised me a smoke for it. They were tormenting me! Torture, I call it. Have you ever heard of the Geneva Convention?' He stuck a cigarette in his mouth but had no means to light it. Vignoles saw the opportunity to change tack. He'd give Twist the reward first, and hope he'd return the favour by telling them what happened.

'Light the gentleman's cigarette, sergeant.' Trinder followed the order grudgingly, believing that Twist should get nothing till he cooperated.

Vignoles let Twist take a deep drag on the cigarette and saw him visibly relax. He recommenced the interview. 'When Jimmy was searching for something, and it annoyed you, what did you do? Explain exactly what happened.' Vignoles was studiously calm.

'Cuffed him round the ear, of course.'

'You hit him?'

'Nah; I could've felled him if I'd wanted to: landed a punch and laid him clean out. But I just cuffed the little sod. It stings, that's all. Frightened the living daylights out of him, though, I thought he'd piss his shorts! Hahaha!'

'You assaulted Jimmy Jebb for the second time that day?' Vignoles kept his voice level.

'A clip round the ear isn't assault. Happens every day: schoolmasters, bus conductors, stationmasters, even you bobbies do it. Gotta keep the little buggers in order.'

Vignoles declined to comment, preferring to keep the questioning on track. 'What did you do after that?'

'Nothing. He scarpered. Ran like a hare.'

Vignoles opened a box file which, until that moment, had been ignored by everyone. 'I don't think that is quite correct, Mr Twist.' As he opened the file, a faint whiff of bonfire was released.

Inside, as if lying in state, was the surviving fragment of Jimmy Jebb's train-spotting book. A few crispy, blackened pieces had flaked off the charred spine. 'Mr Twist, how did this come to be inside your incinerator? It is the remains of a book that belonged to Jimmy.'

'Oh, well done! Your boys are so good at their detective work, inspector. They've done you proud. I found it Sunday morning, outside my gate, in a puddle. It was soggy, ruined, useless.' He paused and shrugged his shoulders. 'So, I chucked it on the fire. He can always get another one.' He lifted both arms in the air for a moment in a pantomime of surrender. 'OK, I give in. I admit it: I should have told you from the start. I knew his name and address: it was written inside the book. But I do like a bit of entertainment.' His one good eye winked.

Vignoles could feel his face burning. Twist was entertaining himself, playing games, with not a shred of concern that the boy was missing, possibly abducted, maybe even dead.

'Why do you hate boys?' he asked.

Twist jabbed a bony finger on the table, his voice suddenly losing the mocking and mirth. 'Same reason as you've dragged me in here like a bloody criminal.' He glared at Vignoles, his hand shaking slightly. 'Look at me: I'm a freak, that's what you all think.' Twist's words were accurate, and they caused an uncomfortable silence to fall. 'The boys hate me. Call me horrible names, throw stones at my windows — which I can't afford to repair — and they knock on my door and run away. Sometimes they set fire to stuff.' He fell silent.

The atmosphere had suddenly become still and intense. Trinder seemed to have stopped breathing. Vignoles offered Twist another cigarette, opened a box of matches and struck one. As it flared the sound, though small, seemed to fill the room. Twist leaned forward and took a moment or two to get his cigarette alight.

'I'll tell you a story.' He took a few urgent puffs. 'I had a cat. A sad old stray. Nobody loved that mangy old bugger. But I did, and he loved me back. I called him Felixstowe. He had a torn-off ear and a closed-over eye. We recognised something about each other, I suppose. A lovely, kind, loyal old fella he was. Wanted nothing but a bite of food and to curl up in front of the fire with me. No questions, no insults. No judgemental looks. He just fixed his one green eye on me and purred.' Twist dragged heavily on the cigarette, hand now quivering more strongly. 'Do you know what they did to him, inspector? Those lovely, darling schoolboys you're so worried about?' He looked at Vignoles and Trinder in turn. 'Shot him with an air rifle and strung him up by the neck with a bit of rusty wire. Hung him off my doorpost. Couldn't have been dead: the pellets only hit him in one back leg. So he hung there till he died. The murdering bastards.'

'I can imagine that was very distressing.' Vignoles spoke sympathetically. Twist shrugged and looked at the floor. 'And you think Jimmy Jebb or his mates did that?'

'Nah, maybe not them, but their type did. So I took to frightening them off. Get in first, and scare the little sods away.'

'You served in the Great War?'

'I don't talk about that.'

'How were you wounded?'

Silence.

'Were you on the Western Front? It must have been hell.'

Twist considered this for a moment, then quietly, almost reluctantly, he answered. 'Passchendaele. It was a mortar shell. I was lucky — so they keep telling me.' He smoked for a moment or two. 'Sometimes I wish I'd bought it at the time, along with my mates. Three of them gone. Lost in a flash. I'm supposed to be grateful to be alive.' His voice sounded weary and sad.

Vignoles, aware that sympathy and understanding were proving more productive than interrogation, laid it on even thicker, hoping to create the conditions for a full confession. 'You are a war hero, and these youngsters taunting and showing no respect would make anyone in your situation feel bitter, even angry.'

Silence.

'I can well imagine how very easy it is for a thoughtless, ignorant lad to say or do something that just tips you over the edge; that makes you finally snap and lose control for a moment.'

Silence.

Trinder spoke next. 'Did Jebb say something stupid? Call you a name? Taunt you?' He was calmer and focussed now; he saw how Vignoles was playing the man and followed suit. 'You lashed out without thinking. Perfectly natural. Perhaps you hit him harder than you meant to? We'd quite understand that, you know. Easy done.'

Twist lifted his head slowly to face them, his strange, molten face with its crinkled skin in folds around his chin making him resemble a tortoise. 'Listen chum, I could kill a man with my bare hands. But only if I intended to; never by accident. I was shelled in my rabbit hole in the ground for months on end. I was sniped at, mortar-bombed again and again. We got gassed. And you think some daft kid is going to make me snap?' He stubbed out the cigarette on the table and stared straight at Vignoles. 'Right. I've had enough of this. I want to leave.'

'What about Gordon Dutton?' Vignoles suddenly threw in the new name, hoping this time to use surprise to trip up the old soldier. 'Did he say something stupid or insulting that deserved a cuff round the ear?'

'Never heard of him.'

Vignoles extracted a copy of the school photograph that had been lying face down underneath the box file. He turned it over and slid it across to Twist. 'You might not know his name, but you will remember his face.'

Twist shook his head and looked puzzled. 'Never seen him before in my life.'

* * * *

'The trouble is Anna, I'm inclined to believe him, even though he quite pulled the rug out from under our feet.' Vignoles took a sip of beer then placed the glass on the Ercol side-table beside his armchair. 'He was perfectly frank about scaring Jebb and the other two boys. He even admits to frightening him off later when he came back on his own, apparently looking for his Combined Volume. We questioned him about his movements on the day Gordon Dutton vanished and he swears blind he never left the house except to buy tobacco and a pint of milk — oh, and a tin of his favourite pilchards. We tracked down the shopkeeper, who confirmed all this. Blencowe and Lansdowne enquired around Central station and the surrounding area, but nobody remembers Twist being there. And trust me, he's very memorable.'

'Did you say he has a gammy leg?'

'Yes. Wrecked by a mortar shell. He's quite badly crippled and his face is disfigured. You would not forget him in a hurry.' Vignoles took some more beer. 'That's another thing working in his favour. He can hardly walk. He stumps about his back yard and hobbles slowly to and from the corner shop and that's about it. When he startled the gang of lads, he only caught one of them because he was hiding in the dark and stepped out suddenly, deliberately to surprise them. But he couldn't give chase. So I can't see how he could dispose of a body. Also, I've got nothing to link him to Dutton.'

'But you found Jimmy Jebb's train book in the fire? That's highly suspicious, surely?'

'On the face of it, but Twist explained it away very neatly. Said he'd found it and disposed of it.' Vignoles let out a long breath of air, before inspecting his pipe. 'He was quite happy to admit that he clipped Jimmy around the ear, and made no attempt to deny assaulting the three boys earlier that afternoon. The man appeared to feel no guilt about it. Either he is the most arrogant killer I have ever met or he is not our man.'

Anna was sharing the bottle of beer. She took a sip from her glass. 'Perhaps that's his strategy. Be as bold as brass and face you out. He freely admits to some aspects of the scenario, but denies the really bad part.' Anna looked thoughtful. 'Judging by your confusion, it sounds like his plan is working. He's playing you, Charles.'

'Hmm... John and I wondered about that. Is he a wily fox or just a crotchety old man?' Vignoles shook his head. 'Anna, I'm starting to doubt myself. He looked a dead cert for the killer, but we can't build a case that would get to court. We had to release him as there were no grounds to hold him any longer. We could charge him with the assault, but the boys haven't reported it to us.'

'Did Twist seem bright?'

'Oh yes. His brain is working perfectly. He gave us a bit of a runaround, and toyed with me like a cat with a mouse.'

'He won a point or two in the opening rallies, but now it's time to regroup and change your strategy. Challenging him head on didn't work: he was ready and waiting with answers prepared.' Anna became animated as she spoke, sitting elegantly in the chair opposite her husband, holding a glass of amber beer that caught the firelight. 'If he is the killer, then he will have planned his responses to your questions. So, find his weak spot and play on that.' She gave Vignoles an encouraging, almost playful look over the top of her glass.

'You're quite right. I was taken off guard far too easily. I wonder if his personal situation, all his injuries and afflictions, made me feel awkward and a bit too sympathetic.'

'He knows human nature. We naturally feel sorry for those in a worse situation than ourselves, especially those who were injured or maimed serving their King and country in wartime. But even a war hero can be a child killer.'

'Indeed, and it was strange that he twice pointed out to us that he could kill a man if he chose to.'

Anna nodded sagely. 'Another clever ploy. It's a double-bluff. He thinks that, if he tells you he could kill if he wanted to, you will think that if he was a killer, he would never reveal that.'

Vignoles pulled on his pipe and leaned back in the armchair. 'You are quite right. But there are still some practical problems to tussle with. His lack of mobility, for one. I cannot see how he could carry or easily manhandle a body, even a child's body, in order to dispose of it.' His pipe filled the air with a sweet-smelling smoke, which Anna always enjoyed. 'But perhaps I'm going about this all the wrong way. I need to think how a man in his situation would solve that problem. Ash is relatively light so, once cremated, transporting human remains is not an issue. Whilst not the quickest walker, he can nonetheless walk, and a bucket of ash is not impossible for him to carry. But it seems like a long haul to Talbot Lane. Why not choose the wasteland around his own home?'

Anna could think of no immediate answer to this. 'How did you get on to him?'

'Via two routes. When Jebb went missing, his parents contacted his friends, the Arnold brothers. They described the alarming encounter they'd had earlier in the day. Twist had lashed out with his stick at them, and grabbed one roughly by the arm. We assume this is when Jebb lost his train book. If Twist is telling the truth, it seems that the boy went back alone later to try and find it.'

'Why was he on his own?'

'The group broke up because Jebb had to get home for tea, but the brothers wanted to sneak into the stadium and see the end of the match.' Vignoles managed a wry smile. 'Just in time to see the Foxes celebrating a 2-1 win. Ah...' He allowed himself a few seconds' indulgence to re-live the moment that the whistle was blown. 'We assume that, after they parted, Jebb realised he'd lost his book and went back for it.'

'Poor lad. And the other source?'

'Earlier that day, hours before Jebb disappeared, a member of the public — a van driver called Tibbott — gave me what he considered to be a tip-off regarding Gordon Dutton. He said that Twist had a reputation for hating schoolboys and for being violent. He had no details, no names, dates, places, witnesses, so it just sounded like the usual baseless rumour-mongering that we hear all the time. We first encountered Tibbott whilst questioning people door-to-door about the Dutton case, close to the crime scene. Then I ran into him on the platform end at Central, where he was spotting trains. He said nothing about Twist on these occasions. It was only when I bumped into him by accident at the football stadium that he told me about Twist.'

Anna shook her head. 'Don't tell me he's a Foxes fan as well as a train enthusiast! You have much in common with this Tibbott fellow!' She laughed, and was glad for an opportunity to do so, no matter how slight the reason, to lighten the atmosphere. She always enjoyed discussing her husband's work after dinner in the evening, but his cases were often rather grim, which created a solemn feeling in both of them. To draw a line under the discussion and to break Charles's pensive mood, she gave the fire a vigorous prod with the poker. As the coals re-settled and the flames again danced cheerily, she turned to him with a big grin. 'Shall I open another bottle?'

Chapter Twenty-nine

Mostyn Street

WPC Jane Benson poured boiling water into the brown-and-cream teapot, then fitted over the top a knitted cosy that had been a gift from her mother last Christmas. It was garishly striped in pink and blue — a combination that had Benson worrying that her mother was dropping a subtle hint that it was high time she thought about marriage and the possibility of a boy or a girl. It certainly had a babyish quality that looked faintly incongruous in her room.

'Sugar?'

'Two, if I may.' Hawkes was sitting rather stiffly in the only armchair and looking far less relaxed than previously. Perhaps the English tea ritual made him uncomfortable. He was more at home ordering gins and tonics or rums and colas, as he had done with alarming alacrity and frequency at the Green Cockatoo. He watched with exaggerated intensity as Benson poured milk from a jug and then handed him a porcelain cup and saucer decorated with red roses, which she had picked up in a second-hand shop. It looked too delicate for Hawkes. He held the saucer rather high, with the cup too close to his face, as he took an exploratory sip to test the temperature.

'I don't suppose tea is quite your thing,' Jane giggled, 'but I don't have anything stronger — unless you find a glass of the sweet sherry Auntie Glenys gave me more to your taste.'

'Tea is perfect. Honestly.' He took a sip, then carefully balanced the cup and saucer on an arm of his chair. 'Did you girls enjoy the evening down the club?'

'What I can remember of it.' Jane made a rueful face. 'I think Lucy and I got a bit squiffy. Please tell me I didn't make an absolute goose of myself.' She bit her lower lip.

'Not a bit.' He winked. 'You upheld the good name of the British Railways police perfectly.'

'Thank goodness. I had a pounding head the next morning.' She sipped her tea.

'In my book, a clear head the next day means the atmosphere at the club was dead and the company worse.'

'I'm not sure I can agree about that. I shall be keeping a closer tally on your trips to the bar next time.'

Hawkes smiled. 'So, there will be a next time?'

'Maybe. Would you like some fruitcake?' She changed the subject abruptly. 'It's homemade and awfully good.'

'A man never says no to homemade fruitcake.'

She opened the tin on a little table beside the window, lifted out a rectangle of dark cake, partially wrapped in greaseproof paper, and cut two fat slices.

'Did you make it?'

'My mother made it. I'm not really the baking type; besides, living here makes it hard.'

'Our landlady would not take kindly to the competition.'

She handed him a slice of cake on a plate. 'She rather frightens me, if truth be told.'

'Her cooking frightens me. That lamb she murdered today was beyond belief.' They laughed. It had been an especially inedible meal and the aroma still lingered. They had both recoiled at the stewed prunes and condensed milk to follow, and retired instead to Jane's room for tea and fruitcake. This gave Jane an opportunity to talk with Max Hawkes privately without appearing too forward. She had left the door open, a clear signal to their landlady that no monkey business was intended. Hawkes would have preferred the door closed, but he was doing a good job of appearing content. Jane thought he looked so funny, seated in her saggy old armchair. He was slumped low, with knees lifted high because the tired springs in the seat were giving in, and an effete porcelain cup in his hand. He reminded her of a cheeky schoolboy in the headmaster's study, on his best behaviour.

'So, what did you make of my band?' Hawkes took a mouthful of cake as he waited for her answer.

'I was pleasantly surprised. It was better than I expected. Oh, sorry, that sounded awful!' Hawkes was watching her with an amused expression. 'The three girl singers were knockout.' Jane paused to take a bite of cake.

'They're a swell outfit, that's for sure,' replied Hawkes, adopting the American slang he so loved.

'And you played very well.'

'Ach, I'm just a journeyman trumpeter. Nothing more, nothing less. How about this Friday? Can I expect to see you two lovely girls back at the Cockatoo?'

'Depends on my shift that day. We cover the whole twenty-four hours, Friday nights included, of course.'

He gave a little shake of his head, as if amused by something.

'What is it?' Jane asked.

'Ah, nothing, nothing.' In fact, he was feeling far more self-conscious than he'd expected, now he'd actually managed to get an invitation into an attractive lady's bedroom. Heck, that was quite a step forward. Since the first moment he set eyes on her in that severe police uniform, he had felt desire for her. She looked even more attractive now, wearing clothes that hugged her hourglass figure and a feminine perfume. It was bewitching. If only she wasn't a policewoman. What was he thinking? 'It's just that...' He tailed off.

'It's not like you to be bashful. Speak up. Is something wrong?' She suddenly checked how her skirt was lying and that her cardigan was still demurely buttoned up.

'You look absolutely perfect. Quite lovely.' He stopped and neither reacted, but a slightly awkward silence started to grow.

'I've never taken tea with a policewoman before.' He grinned sheepishly.

Jane laughed. 'We're no different from anyone else. We drink tea — we even eat cake!' She took a bite of hers and a sip of tea, as if to illustrate her point.

'But you aren't the same as other girls.' He paused for effect. 'You could arrest me.'

'Now, what naughty things have you done that I could arrest you for?' she teased, peering over her spectacles.

'Nothing! Honest.' Jane felt a certain lack of conviction in his voice, but he suddenly followed up with a joke of his own: 'I have to hold my hands up, officer, and admit to rather liking this cake. And I also like sitting here, sharing tea with you.' He gave her a cheeky wink and his self-confident tone returned.

'Thank you, kind sir.' She was still smiling but something inside told her to hold back. Was it all jesting? Or did she see him hesitate with his response? It was a little confusing. 'More tea?'

'Love some.'

After she poured more dark liquid from the teapot, their eyes met momentarily and each looked about to speak, but something held them back. Jane sat more upright on her hard chair and replaced the teapot on the table.

'I have to go away tomorrow. Only for one night. I have an evening audition in Sheffield, so I'll stay the night with a friend.'

'An audition for another band? Sounds exciting.'

'Not in the least; after the first few you start to dread them. Even if I pass, it's only for a week's work. I'll probably just doss at my friend's for the duration. It's far less romantic and glamorous than people may imagine. I'm catching a train from Central. That's where you work, isn't it? I'll be there around ten in the morning.'

'I shall be busy, of course.' She spoke too quickly. 'We have two rather awful cases on our hands. There's a lot to do and time is pressing.' She stopped. Talking shop was not what she intended.

'Those missing boys? I read about them in the paper, but I'm sure you can give me all the gen.'

'Yes, it is them; but I cannot discuss the investigation.'

'Could you just tell me one thing, though, because I am puzzled about it: why are these two missing boys a railway matter?'

She hesitated. Her job suddenly felt like it was crashing over her head like an unwelcome wave of cold water. 'Let's just say there is a railway connection to both cases and so we found ourselves picking them up, but we do sometimes work in concert with other forces.'

'I see. They're disturbing cases, that's for sure. Two young lads in short succession.' He gave a low whistle. 'One presumed dead and the other... What are his chances, do you think?' Hawkes stopped himself. 'Oh, sorry; of course, you said you can't talk about it. But it's hard not to be interested.'

Jane felt pleased that this louche jazz player found the cases so moving. She found herself liking him more for having the sensitivity to care about the missing boys. 'I really don't know.' She gave a long, heartfelt sigh. 'We just have to work hard and remain hopeful.' She fell silent, mulling over the conversation she had had with her colleagues. They had all come to the same simple, stark conclusion: time was of the essence and as each hour passed without finding Jimmy, the chances of him turning up alive diminished. The problem was, what to do next? They were still clutching at straws and, until a strong witness came forward, or a decent clue was found, it was just more foot-slogging by all the uniformed officers the city could muster and endless processing of tiny scraps of information and analysing reports of sightings, the majority of which always proved useless. It was painfully slow and very frustrating but, without any idea of where the boy might be, they were impotent.

'I rather like railways,' said Hawkes brightly, in an attempt to start a conversation about something they had in common but which she was not barred from speaking about. 'Musicians travel a lot. I spend half my life either on trains or loitering on wet and draughty platforms. Just my suitcase and my trumpet, a hat, a coat and a smoke. Alone and yet not alone.' Hawkes sounded thoughtful, although Jane was unsure where this reflection was leading.

'There's always someone close by on the railway,' she replied, 'even if you cannot always see them. The signalman in his box, the whistling porter, the engine crew, the guard along the corridor, the other passengers...'

'I like the odd sounds and the smell of engine smoke. I sometimes play a few tunes if there's no one around. The acoustics can be good.' Jane looked dreamy. This was what she wanted to hear. Hearing a solo on a jazz trumpet on a late night shift would improve her mood. 'You certainly see a lot of things whilst waiting on a station at all times of day or night, Jane. You really see life being played out.' He paused. 'And some of it's not so pretty. Mind if I smoke?'

'Go ahead.' She took a moment to decline as he offered her one. Now was not the time to start smoking. She would look gauche and end up red-faced and spluttering.

He lit a cigarette. 'There are some mighty odd people, too. You see the lonely and the lost, the dangerous and the sinister. The drunks on Friday nights being rowdy on the way home. The shady dealers in dark corners of the big city stations, the spivs, the hookers. Sleazy businessmen with girlfriends half their age. Heck, you name it, they're out there.'

'We often follow in their wake,' Jane remarked, 'picking up the pieces.'

They sat in silent contemplation for a few moments. 'So, do you have anyone in the frame yet? In the missing boys case?'

Over the course of the conversation, Jane warmed to Max Hawkes and felt he was a kindred spirit. It would not hurt to say a few words to him about the case, but she would keep things vague, not give away any details. 'We thought we had a suspect in connection with one boy, but it looks less certain now. So it's back to the drawing board, by the look of it. And we need to get our skates on to have any chance to help the other.'

'Gosh, it must rile you terribly when you see how the papers get everything so wrong.'

'Wrong? What do you mean?'

'The *Mercury* got the facts wrong, didn't they? Oh, of course, you haven't read it yet.' He reached over and picked up the late edition that Benson had put aside to read after dinner. It was still folded. He flicked it open to reveal the front page headline news about the missing boys. Alongside two school portraits of the lads there was a formal image of a businessman in a suit and regimental tie. Hawkes tapped the picture. 'This man — Jeremy Dutton. They reckon he's only just come down from Glasgow, having been there since 8th September. But that's not right, as you know.'

Jane looked puzzled and leaned in closer to read the account. Their shoulders were almost touching. His aftershave smelled lovely.

'No, no, the paper is correct: he did not come back home until October.'

'I do hate to contradict you, doll, but I know it ain't right. I travelled down from Preston on Saturday 24th September with this very man. We shared a compartment, just the two of us. It was a long journey, so we chatted to pass the time and got quite chummy.'

'Are you quite sure it was him?' Jane asked, feeling a strange fizz of excitement.

'On my mother's life.'

'And you are quite sure about the date?'

'Yes.'

'But that's the day his son went missing. Are you certain, because this is really important?' She fixed her eyes on Hawkes, searching for any hint of doubt in his expression.

'A hundred percent. I've only travelled from Preston to here once this year, so I am not confusing it with any other occasion. Oh, and I can show you where it's written in my diary: the time of the train and everything. I recognise him from the photo. He told me he was a civil engineer working in Glasgow. Building roads, or something dull like that. I was not terribly interested, but then we got onto music and it turns out he likes jazz. He would have been in Nottingham early that evening. I know it doesn't matter all that much; I mean, he's the boy's father, so he can't be a suspect.'

'Listen, I need you to come to our office tomorrow and make a formal statement. And make sure you bring that diary! It could be crucial evidence.'

Hawkes gave a wan smile and smoked for a moment. There was a slight upturn to one corner of his mouth. He was starting to regret being so eager to correct the newspaper. Making a witness statement meant having to give the police his name and address, maybe other details. How much would they want to know?

'You can't believe he killed his own son.'

'That is highly unlikely, but anything that does not match up needs investigation. I really cannot say anything more about the case.

I've already said too much. Come tomorrow, please, to the detective department office, just off the main platform. You are going there anyway, to catch your train. Just come half-an-hour earlier. Pretty please? For me?' Her smile could have melted an iceberg.

Hawkes agreed. He genuinely wanted to help the case get solved, because he despised people who interfered with kids. And if he helped Jane to solve the case, she was likely to be very grateful.

'I'll be there at nine-thirty, I promise.'

Jane felt overcome with exhaustion. 'I'm sorry, the day has rather taken it out of me.' She gave him a kindly smile and stifled a yawn. 'Please don't think me impolite, but I start work at six.'

'Of course not. I'll leave you in peace now and see you in the morning.' The thought of that made him smile.

They stood up and Hawkes thanked her for the tea and cake. He wasn't sure if it was all right to lean in and plant a chaste kiss on her cheek, so decided to err on the side of caution. Jane felt relieved that he hadn't tried to be familiar with her. She stood in the doorway and watched as he walked the few strides to his room, then turned away and closed her door. Her head was throbbing and she felt almost weak with weariness. She was glad to be alone. She had enjoyed the attention, but what on earth was she doing with Max Hawkes? He probably had a girl in every town. His type always did. Didn't he admit he was going to sleep at a friend's house? Yes, he used the word 'friend'. He deliberately didn't reveal if this person was a man or a woman.

Twenty minutes later she was tucked up in her single bed, pondering the bombshell news about Dutton. Then she started to fret about Hawkes coming into the office. He might mention that they were alone in her bedroom that evening. Worse, he may reveal that she was discussing police business with him. Oh, botheration! Still, nothing could be done about it now. Perhaps she should listen to something soothing, like *Bedtime with Braden* on the Light Programme.

A chink where her curtains did not quite meet allowed in just enough light from the street lamp for her to see the silhouette of her teapot and cups, and the used side-plates with crumbs upon them. She felt a pang of something inside. A thrill of pleasure, mingled with regret. There was a faint trace of aftershave lingering in the air. She was glad that she hadn't cleared the tea things away. They brought a welcome sense of companionship into her room.

CHAPTER THIRTY

Leicester Central

'Thank you for coming in at such short notice, Mr Dutton.'

'I presume you have news about my son, inspector.' His voice betrayed no emotion.

'Yes, Mr Dutton. The dental records came back positive. Two fillings helped them make an exact match for Gordon. We can now be certain that the remains found were your son's. I am very sorry.'

Dutton closed his eyes for a few seconds, letting the news sink in. He spoke quietly. 'And have you found who was responsible for his death?'

'There has been an important development. A surprising one, that we need your help with.' Vignoles examined some notes on his desk, spectacles perched low on his nose, as if checking a detail before speaking further. Trinder sat impassively to one side.

'Then I am all ears.'

Dutton was immaculately attired, down to his regimental tie and what looked like gold cufflinks. He exuded respectability and a fat salary. Crossing one leg over the other, he carefully adjusted the lie of his trouser fabric to ensure that the cloth covering the knee was not stretched out of shape. Vignoles noticed a whiff of cologne.

'When we spoke yesterday, you told us that you had not left Scotland since 8th September. Is that correct?'

'Yes.' Dutton casually extracted a silver cigarette case and flipped it open. He offered Vignoles and Trinder a cigarette of an expensive brand. They declined. He lit one, took a deep drag and exhaled slowly. 'May I ask where this is leading?'

Vignoles paused and held Dutton's gaze through the blue skeins of smoke. 'Did you, in fact, travel from Glasgow to Nottingham on Saturday 24th?'

Dutton tapped his cigarette into the ashtray before him. His movements were calm and precise. He said nothing, but brushed an imaginary speck of dust from the sleeve of his jacket.

'We have a witness.' Vignoles made a show of checking his notes, although he was fully conversant with what they said. 'He shared your compartment, and you chatted. You told him your name and about your contract in Glasgow. He has a very clear recollection of all the details and could pick you out in a parade. He states that you alighted at Nottingham Victoria.'

Dutton held his silence.

'Your wife has confirmed that you did not return home that night.' Vignoles met the engineer's cold little button eyes. 'Where did you spend the night, Mr Dutton?'

Dutton looked straight at Vignoles but still declined to say anything.

'You have a very loyal team about you in Glasgow, I must say. They hold you in high esteem.'

He finally spoke. 'Yes, they are a fine outfit: top hole, to a man.'

'And woman. Your secretary, Miss Reeves, was well chosen; she did a sterling job of defending both your privacy and your good name.' Vignoles paused a beat. 'But she is at heart an honest woman, and once she realised that DS Trinder was investigating your son's murder, she quite correctly spilled the beans. Loyalty only goes so far, one finds. Perjuring herself in a murder case was not part of her job.'

Dutton's jaw clenched a few times and he scratched his left earlobe. He smoked in silence for a while. Neither detective pressed him to speak. He was hemmed in, so they decided to be patient and wait for him to confess. After a long silence, all he said was, 'I see.' He stubbed out the cigarette and frowned as he stared at the floor. He was thinking hard.

'We know you came to this area on the same day that your son went missing. You then lied about being here, and now that we have caught you out, you are refusing to explain yourself. Your continued silence will leave us no alternative but to assume that you had something to do with his death.' Vignoles pushed his glasses back into place, carefully laid his pen beside his notes, and sat back, staring into Dutton's eyes accusingly.

'It is quite monstrous to suggest that I had anything to do with my son's death.' He spoke quietly, but with a conviction that rang true. 'Whoever committed this terrible crime must be criminally insane.' He paused, his expression changing quickly from anger to anguish. 'My wife is taking it hard. Drinking a touch too heavily. And when she's not drinking, she's walking the streets showing all and sundry Gordon's school photograph. I fear her nerves are in tatters.'

Vignoles nodded sympathetically. It was time to make the man feel as though he were amongst sympathetic people to whom he could speak freely, open up and share his burden — whatever that turned out to be.

Dutton cleared his throat. 'It's — well, it's all rather awkward. Things are not as they should be in my marriage. We are more like brother and sister these days, inspector; we lead our own separate lives, if you understand what I mean.'

'Yes, we are aware of your marital situation. We also know that your wife spent the night of 24th September at her home with another man. He has confirmed that he left her at nine forty-five on the Sunday morning.'

Dutton flinched, but quickly composed himself. 'I suppose I cannot blame her.' He stared at the cream-painted wall for a moment. 'You must not judge her too harshly. It is I who am the guilty party: I placed her under intolerable strain. She was doubtless feeling lonely and unloved. You see, inspector, we did not wish to apply for a judicial separation: we could not bear the public disgrace. Nor did we want Gordon to suffer the shame of coming from a broken home. We both agreed to keep our marital problem a secret; to maintain a proper level of outward decorum. I deliberately sought work that required me to live away for weeks at a time. We sent Gordon away to school so he would not feel the lack of a father on a day-to-day basis. I took my leave to coincide with his being home during the school holidays, to give him a semblance of normal family life. We wished to ensure that our names remained respectable in the eyes of our peers. However, if she is now inviting men to our home in such a brazen manner, I wonder if that was a wasted effort.' He looked mildly irritated.

'So, Mr Dutton, can you please now confirm that you took a train south to Nottingham on 24th September?' Vignoles continued to press him on this point.

'Yes, all right, I confirm it. But I shall say no more.'

'The fact is, Mr Dutton, you need an alibi. You have to reveal your exact movements on that day. And I mean specifics: times and locations, the names and addresses of anyone you met.' Vignoles paused a beat. 'Let's begin with your reasons for going to Nottingham.'

Dutton gave a heavy sigh. He felt cornered. 'I had a... a certain private matter to resolve. I needed to keep it hush-hush.' He lit another cigarette, but his movements lacked the calm fluidity of a few minutes earlier. 'Exposure would ruin me, and the subsequent loss of income and social position would inflict untold damage upon my wife and son.'

'Please elucidate further,' said Vignoles. 'Was this matter of an illegal nature?'

'Yes — well, one aspect is illegal and utterly deplorable, the other, well, I do not consider it should be a reason for persecution.'

Vignoles was intrigued to know what illegal activities someone like Dutton, with his high education, his handsome salary and his pride in being seen to be an upright citizen could possibly be involved with. 'Do continue.'

'I am conversant with the laws of the land as they stand, though I disagree with them. My actions that weekend were an attempt to keep something completely discreet and hopefully remove a problem with as little fuss as I could. I slipped down to Nottingham for just one night. A trip that Miss Reeves and one other trusted colleague in Glasgow did their utmost to conceal, although neither knew the reason for my absence.' Dutton took another long drag and exhaled slowly, touching his silver cigarette case lightly with his free hand. 'I had a rendezvous that evening, at a pre-arranged location. It was a... er, well, a business transaction, shall we say. As it is completely unconnected with my son's disappearance, I do not see why I should reveal any more than that. I am entitled to some privacy.'

'I'm sorry, Mr Dutton, but that won't do,' Trinder replied. 'We need to know who you met. That person is your alibi for that evening.'

'Yes, I rather feared that was the case.' Dutton weighed up his response. 'All right. I stayed in the Park Hotel. You will find me in the register, under the name of Smith.'

'Original,' Trinder responded.

'I checked out at seven-thirty on the Sunday, hurried to the station and was on my way north.'

'You still have not told us the nature of the meeting,' Vignoles reminded him.

Dutton sighed heavily. 'Over the years I, well, I have... I have come to realise that my, er, interests...' he coughed nervously, 'my desires, that is, were no longer focussed on my wife.'

'So you were having an affair?' Trinder asked.

Dutton paused a moment. 'Not exactly. More a series of short liaisons with a number of different persons. Over several months. There you have it. I dare say it all sounds rather shabby and sordid to you. But I'm not seeking your approval. That is what I want... what I need.'

'And you met with one of these, er, "friends" that night?' Trinder asked.

'Look, sergeant, if I'd run off with a sergeant major's wife, I'd have come clean about it, got a divorce, made a decent settlement on my wife, and that would be it. Nobody would think anything. But these encounters...' He paused to consider his words. 'Well, they need to be kept strictly secret or you chaps might come knocking in the night and haul me up in front of a justice of the peace.'

'But it is not illegal to have a series of affairs, Mr Dutton. Nor even to consort with prostitutes,' observed Trinder, surprised that Dutton was so ignorant of the law.

'But it is an offence to consort with men,' Vignoles observed. 'Am I correct?'

'You are.' Dutton stared at the floor.

Trinder was stunned. He had not foreseen this twist in the tale.

'And I was being blackmailed by an avaricious little crook with no scruples or human feeling. He was most certainly not defending public morals, as he risibly claimed.' Dutton gave a bitter laugh. 'He wanted a hefty sum to keep my private life private. So that, gentlemen, was why I was in Nottingham. To hand over a sizeable slice of my savings to a dirty little blackmailer.'

CHAPTER THIRTY-ONE

Leicester Central

'Do we believe him, guv?' Trinder was seated in Vignoles's office, a welcome pot of tea close to hand.

'With regard to his possibly meeting his son, the times and places do not match, John. Gordon bought a platform ticket in the morning at Grantham, then appears to have bunked his fare to travel to Leicester, where he met his fate. Dutton alighted at Nottingham at 5pm, though we have no proof of where he went after that. If he was going to meet Gordon in Leicester, why get off at Nottingham?'

'The fact that Dutton has revealed that he engages in illegal acts of gross indecency with other men leads me to believe that he has nothing to do with Gordon's death. I don't think that any man would admit to doing something so repugnant and immoral if it were not true, guv. Most especially not to police officers, bearing in mind Section 11 of the Criminal Law Amendment Act.'

Vignoles nodded.

'It's impossible to corroborate the story about the blackmailer,' Trinder continued. 'Obviously, Dutton cannot prosecute the man without revealing his sordid secrets to the press, the public, and his employer, which would completely ruin him; but he refuses even to give us his name.'

Vignoles shook his head slowly and puffed on his pipe. 'It never ceases to amaze me what messy lives some people lead. The lies, the deception, the damned charade.' He swivelled in his chair and stared sadly out of the window onto the busy station platform. A local train formed of two maroon, narrow-doored suburban coaches was disgorging a clutch of passengers. Two glamorous young women with fine hats and gloves and long woollen coats, holding narrow umbrellas and wide handbags, were chatting close to the office window. Vignoles noticed their red lips, meticulous make up and expensive coiffures. That was a charade, too, in its own way. A kind of stage make-up enabling them to act out their own imagined versions of themselves. He stopped himself: he was being ugly and cynical. This case was getting under his skin if he could start to see harmless innocence with such jaundiced eyes. They were just two pretty girls heading to London for a spot of shopping. He spun back round to face Trinder. 'Right. Back to business! How do you see our suspect list?'

'Well, guv, it's getting shorter. The Duttons are in the clear. If Mr D was paying off his blackmailer in Nottingham, he can't have been in Leicester at the same time his son was taken. Mrs D's fancy man is a non-starter. She says he's never met the boy, and doesn't even know where he goes to school, let alone that he'd be in Grantham or Leicester that Saturday. So that leaves Twist.' Trinder paused and weighed up his next words. 'He may be curmudgeonly, but there's something about his story about Jebb that almost convinces me. And I can't see how he is connected to Gordon Dutton.'

'But Twist is wily and could be spinning us along. We need to have another look at the man, but not head-on. He countered all our questions and deflected them skilfully, which could suggest he's planned his responses, expecting us to call,' replied Vignoles, remembering Anna's words.

'You could be right, guv. It's a clever tactic to admit to much of what we threw at him, but not the really serious stuff.' Trinder sounded more upbeat.

'I'm not sure we can get permission to take his house apart more thoroughly without first strengthening our case against him, but maybe there's something we've missed in all that mess. I wonder if he might have had help? If he had an accomplice, that would get over the difficulty of how he could have carried a body.' They looked at each other without much enthusiasm. They had no one in their sights as a possible accomplice: Twist appeared to have no friends. 'Let's go through all the evidence once more. I know we've been over it a dozen times, but there must be something there.'

'We have a firm date and close time-band for Jebb, and a date for Dutton going missing, but not for his death. We know he started out on Grantham station and ended up in Leicester. At what point did his fun day out turn into something nasty?'

'Any ideas?' Vignoles was happy to let Trinder try and make sense of it.

'Looking at the timetables and speaking with Bishop Osmond School, he had to be back at 5pm sharp to avoid a ticking off. That's assuming the school had made a proper record.'

'Accepted.'

'Can we assume that he travelled to Leicester voluntarily, guv? Was he alone, or did he meet someone at Grantham who took him to Leicester? The booking clerks at Grantham sold a few tickets to Leicester that day, but nobody sinister sticks in their mind. Someone looking like Twist certainly would.'

'If Gordon went to Leicester voluntarily, he should have left there by three-thirty at the latest, to get back to Grantham for five.'

'And we have no sightings of him in Leicester,' said Trinder, looking deflated. 'It is curiously like that cold case Blencowe mentioned.'

'I'd forgotten that. Has he found anything to connect it to the Dutton case?'

'I think he drew a blank.'

'No surprise there.' Vignoles checked his watch. 'The Central's just opened for lunch. Maybe a pint will inspire us?'

'I hope so, guv!'

CHAPTER THIRTY-TWO

Leicester

The house smelled of warm sausage-meat and greasy, hot pastry.

'Where will you go this time?'

'I thought I'd try something really daring.' He gave her an arch look with a naughty twinkle in his eyes. 'But also somewhere appropriate, seeing as the lad liked trains.' He tapped the side of his nose significantly. 'There's a theme developing. I have a master plan.'

'Ooh, but you're a clever one. We were a bit...' she turned down the corners of her mouth, '...casual at first. Just here and there. Whatever fancy took us. But I like it better now.'

'But we were learning back then. Just starting out. Now we've hit form. You know, I can see this serialised on the radio: each week they slowly unfold the story...' He drifted off into a reverie whilst he wiped around the deep, enamelled sink one last time.

'Get away with you. That's just being fanciful.'

'Not a bit of it.' He looked into the distance as if into the future. 'The listeners would be so shocked. Repulsed, but unable to turn off! Each episode they'd hear a bit more and gasp at the sheer audacity of what we've done!' He grinned and returned to working away diligently with his cloth around the base of the taps, ensuring there were no stains that could prove a giveaway. 'If only we could see their faces. All sitting around the radio thinking that they're snug and safe — then discovering that we're out there, waiting!'

'Ooh, you're giving me the shivers.' She smiled indulgently and rubbed her arms. 'You always said you wanted to do something that would get everyone sitting up and taking notice.'

'You bet. Carving our names into history.' He suddenly looked sad, as if a switch had been thrown. 'Front page news. All over the country. We might even be on the BBC. Maybe it would even be news in America! Imagine that — world-wide notoriety! I don't suppose they'll ever know, though,' he said, wistfully, 'because we're just too smart. Which seems such a shame. We can hardly make history if they never discover who did it.' He gave her a furtive look before turning back to the taps. His eyes were secretive and shifty.

'Oh, Michael, you are a tease! Of course they'll never latch on. But we know, and that's enough. That's how it is. Our little secret.' She folded her arms and smiled. 'So, where are you going?'

'Never you mind!' He started to wring out the cloth, his powerful hands forcing every last drop from the material. 'All will be revealed when I'm back. It's safer that way.' He sucked air between his teeth. 'Aye, but I'll need my wits about me, and a bit of good-natured banter to deflect attention. I have to keep those working there off the scent.'

'It sounds dangerous.'

'Dangerous, and wickedly naughty.' They both laughed.

'Just don't go thinking you're smarter than you are!' She did the waggling finger routine, the outstretched digit an inch from his nose. It was like a red rag to a bull. He hated it when she did that. 'Now, you mentioned having to win over the others. What others might they be?'

'Those working at the place I'm off to now.' He sounded sulky as he checked his watch. Never mind what Mummy thought, he was just about to make everything a little more thrilling. He wanted to read more in the papers. He wanted to hear people talking about it; guessing and wondering, whilst he lapped up every word. The lads in the factories and garages were all talking about it and asking his opinion. What a thrill. 'There's bound to be a few lads around the place. I have a delivery to make. One of the senior men there has a car that's playing up and so I'm taking a spare part down for him. That's how I got the idea, you see. I'm expected there and they know my face. Nobody will think anything of me unloading a box from my van.'

She nodded approvingly. 'Good boy. Tell you what, take a bag of those little sausage rolls I made. Hand a few around. Stay for a cuppa. Then everyone will remember you chatting and being friendly.'

'That could work a treat. The smell of those rolls is making me hungry after working so hard. Even with blades as good as those, it takes some doing. And stoking that fire is blummin' hard work.'

'I know, dearie. Tell you what, you can have one now. But leave the rest alone! You need them for that job.'

Chapter Thirty-three

Leicester Central

'Sir?' DC Blencowe struck his knuckles on the open door.

'Yes?' Vignoles looked up from the crime file open on his desk. He was making notes of various points to follow up. Outstanding details they still needed to check. This was the sum total of his and Trinder's brainstorming efforts after a pint of best bitter had oiled the cogs of their brains the day before. It was a dispiritingly short list, and the only conclusion he reached was that they were failing to make any significant headway with either the case of the murdered schoolboy or the case of the missing schoolboy. Or were they the same case? That was perhaps the most unsettling aspect of all. Were they dealing with someone systematically picking off boys? Was Jebb dead as well? He threw down his pencil and looked relieved by the distraction. 'Come in, constable.'

Blencowe was holding some sheets of paper in one hand. 'I've found something I'd like your opinion on, sir.'

'Uh-huh. Pertaining to what?'

'It could pertain to both boys, although it's actually from the Barrow Hill case.' Vignoles let his spectacles drop to the end of his nose and gave Blencowe a querying look but remained silent. 'I know you told me to put all that stuff aside, sir, but things are a bit slow, as you know, and it's been nagging away at me like toothache and what with the files sitting on my desk all the time, I could not help flicking through them again.'

'Let me see.' Vignoles didn't need to hear an extended apology.

Blencowe selected and then handed across one of the papers he was holding. It was a witness statement taken by the Derbyshire Constabulary. Vignoles quickly scanned the statement, which was very short and written in a crabbed and rather ugly hand. He was about to ask why he was supposed to be interested in this unremarkable document when his eye caught the name of the witness. He looked up to find Blencowe staring at him.

'Interesting, don't you think?' The younger man's big frame towered over the desk.

Vignoles reread the statement. 'But he saw nothing, heard nothing.'

'But that's just the point.' Blencowe actually rose and fell on his heels as he replied. 'It's not what is said, but who is saying it. The fellow has cropped up in the Barrow Hill murder, was on the site of the Dutton murder on a number of occasions, and then he puts us on to Twist. He was also close to where Jebb went missing and about the same time.'

'Michael Tibbott.' Vignoles lay the paper down on top of the crime file, which happened to be open on his own typed report on Tibbott's tip-off about Twist. He chewed the name over for a moment. 'What do you think this signifies, Blencowe?'

'Either these are completely random events and unrelated, or there is some significance that we must investigate. Four unrelated events is a lot of unrelated events.' Vignoles winced at the sentence construction, but accepted the truth behind it. 'So, sir, I conclude there is a reason. A very deliberate sort of reason why Tibbott keeps turning up like this. Happenstance can't account for it, surely.' Blencowe stroked his beard.

'It certainly looks suspicious, on the face of it.' Vignoles drummed his fingers on the desk a moment as he processed this information. 'But let's work it through. He's a van driver. He goes out and about, and frequently. Therefore, there is a higher probability of his being just about anywhere.'

'He collects and delivers from the Talbot Lane premises and has done for some years, I agree. But it's funny how he knows what's around the back.'

Vignoles puffed some air out. 'Not really. Their lavatories are foul. Nipping out the back onto a bit of wasteland seems quite reasonable. And others do the same.'

'That is also true.'

'Why was Tibbott at Barrow Hill?'

'He was making a delivery of car parts to a garage close to the crime site. It all checks out.'

'So he has a perfectly good reason to be there?'

'Correct.' Blencowe held up a finger. 'And that is why nobody spotted anything amiss at the time. The perfect alibi.'

Vignoles was struggling to see where this was leading. 'He also had a perfectly legitimate reason to be at Talbot Lane.'

'And once again we saw no reason to investigate him further.'

'What am I missing?'

'Each event looks innocent and is made legitimate by a provable reason for him being there,' Blencowe explained. 'But then we ask ourselves, why was he on Filbert Street when you saw him there before the match?'

'He said he had been making a delivery.'

Blencowe raised an eyebrow and looked slightly smug. 'Well, I made some discreet enquiries at his workplace. His boss is an accommodating sort, happy to help us with routine enquiries, no fuss and no questions.' Vignoles made an approving gesture and asked Blencowe to continue. 'And guess what? Tibbott had no deliveries within a half-mile of the stadium that day. I can show you on our chalk map all his deliveries that day. He had no need to travel down Filbert Street. Tibbott surely knows the streets as good as any cabbie after so many years in the business. It just does not wash.' He looked triumphant.

'Good work, Blencowe. Nobody would deliberately place their vehicle in the midst of a football crowd without good reason.' Vignoles suddenly felt a little prickle of electricity run through his body. Could Tibbott have gone there specifically to pretend to bump into him by accident, so he could tip him off about Twist? But how on earth could Tibbott have known that he would be there? He dismissed the idea. 'Go back to Tibbott's boss. I want to know all his movements for the whole of that Saturday, before the football match and after, when Jebb vanished. I want to know where he was right until he got home and into bed, but that could be harder to discover. I also want to know his movements on the day Gordon Dutton went missing. But be discreet: don't tell his boss why you are asking, and tell him that your inspector doesn't want Tibbott to know we're asking about him. It is essential that he suspects nothing.'

'Yes, sir; I quite understand the protocol.' Blencowe looked excited.

'Just remember, there is nothing here to suggest he is a killer. Don't lose sight of that. If we play this wrong he might go to the press complaining that good, honest citizens who try to assist the police run the risk of being wrongly accused themselves. That could damage our reputation and the Badger would have my guts for garters.'

'Yes, sir.'

'Is the sergeant out there?'

'He's conducting an experiment with Mavis.'

'He's doing what?'

'I can explain!' Trinder had appeared at the office door. 'Our session down the Central Hotel got me thinking things over and I had a bright idea.'

'Then you'd better come in and tell me what it was.'

'Has Blencowe explained about his breakthrough?' Trinder gave the officer in question an approving glance.

'I'd not call it a breakthrough yet, but it is a legitimate line of enquiry.' Vignoles could sense that Trinder was also excited about Tibbott. He felt the need to dampen the over-enthusiasm of both officers.

'Tibbott seems too eager to help, if you ask me. I think he's keeping a close eye on the investigation. Monitoring our progress — or lack of it. And feeding us a red herring with Mr Twist. That was a stroke of genius. A nasty old codger who is known to hate kids. And I fell for it hook, line and sinker.' Trinder paused and sighed, annoyed with himself. 'Perhaps he laid in wait for a lad to go past Twist's house, then abducted him, killed him, and laid the blame on Twist.'

'It is close to where you saw him in Filbert Street, sir.' Blencowe added, voice heavy with meaning.

'Because of Tibbott,' Trinder continued, 'we've wasted time and effort sifting through a ton of junk in that vile house. And I've been thinking about Jimmy Jebb's train-spotting book, guv: maybe Tibbott deliberately put it outside the house; laid it as bait, hoping the old man would pick it up and take it inside. Then he tips us off and we find the book. Twist gets framed for murder.'

Vignoles was silent. He was staring at his own report on the encounter with Tibbott. The man had parked his van just yards from where Jebb was last seen by his friends. Maybe he had been lurking; watching; waiting. Not waiting for Vignoles but for the streets to empty so he could strike, safe in the knowledge that, for about two hours, the area would be deserted and he could snatch any small boy who happened to be on his own. It had been sheer accident that Tibbott had met him outside the ground. No wonder the man had been eyeing him from across the road, eyes bulging as if on stalks. He'd probably almost choked on his chips when he realised who was standing right in front of him. Vignoles nodded to himself as he worked through the sequence of events. Tibbott, if he did indeed abduct Jebb, must have done so shortly afterwards. The thought made Vignoles shudder.

'Do we have nothing on file about Tibbott, John?' Vignoles asked quietly.

'We've not found anything on him, guv,' Trinder replied. 'Do you agree he's a suspect?'

'I want to know more about him first, so don't even think about pinning two abductions and a murder on him. What were you up to with Mrs Green?'

'It was an experiment. We've spent days going through all the witness statements received and all the house-to-house enquiries and other scraps and, as you know, nobody appears to have seen anything suspicious, despite these abductions taking place in a crowded city. So we asked ourselves: why might this be? Two reasons jumped out. Firstly, the abductor was somehow forgettable. Almost invisible, you might say, like a corporation workman, for instance. If you see two men digging a hole on your street, odds are, you take no particular notice. A week later, you wouldn't remember their faces, let alone when they started digging. Who could identify them in a lineup of men dressed in flat caps and donkey jackets? Same goes for a delivery man.' Vignoles was filling his pipe and paused momentarily in the act as he heard this, then waved a hand for Trinder to continue.

'A delivery man comes and goes irregularly, different days, and different times of day. Anyone would be hard pushed to remember whether he was there on any given day, let alone the time. What's more, he is a familiar, trusted face; he does not look anything like what people imagine a child killer looks like.'

Vignoles struck a match and concentrated on watching the flame catch the dry tobacco. 'I'm not sure I know what one of those looks like, but I see what you are driving at.' Vignoles tried an experimental puff on his pipe, then tossed the smoking match into the ashtray.

Trinder looked at Blencowe, who waggled the sheaves of paper in his hand. 'It bothers me that nobody saw either boy being abducted. My theory is, someone did see it, but didn't recognise it for what it was.'

Vignoles had his pipe fully alight and puffing merrily, a sure sign he was listening intently. 'Go on.'

'I ran a little experiment, guv. I asked a family friend and her twelve-year-old son to come to the station at a set time, he in school uniform and she dressed plainly in a manner that drew no attention. At the appointed time I asked Mavis to come out onto the platform with me; I fed her a story about wanting to watch someone and needing her as a cover so we just looked like an ordinary man and wife. We passed the time of day for ten minutes, chatting about Al Martino being at the top of the hit parade and other things. My friend acted her part: she approached the boy and spoke with him for a few minutes, then they left the station together. When Mavis and I stepped back inside, I asked her to describe who she had seen on the station and what they were doing. It was most illuminating. She had a hazy recollection of the boy, got the colour of his uniform cap wrong, and said he was aged anything between eight and fourteen. She remembered seeing him alone, then with a woman she assumed was his mother, but she can give me no description of the woman. In short, she offered nothing that would stand up to cross-examination. That they walked off together after a short rendezvous escaped her attention altogether. Why? Because it all looked so innocent and unremarkable. There was no reason for her to remember it. I'd asked four lads from the engine shed to play other parts, and Mavis remembered them in great detail, though she didn't know any of them. One had played the role of a shady-looking character in a long trenchcoat with his hat pulled low over his brow to hide his eyes, and who was continually checking his watch. She gave me a superbly accurate description of him. Likewise, she remembered many details about my other accomplices: three loutish youths smoking and making a lot of noise on the opposite platform.'

Vignoles listened but said nothing, letting Trinder complete his story.

'I know it was very basic, guv, but I think it demonstrates that people do not remember the normal and unremarkable. They remember the weird, the shabbily or garishly-dressed, the sinister, the rowdy.' Trinder looked excited about his revelations. 'Now, I think Blencowe and Benson have made a startling discovery. Amongst these apparently useless reports from the public, there is, in fact, a wealth of observation. We may have been guilty of assuming that these boys were dragged away kicking and screaming, or that they were lured away by a creepy or sinister-looking man. We've been hoping for a witness to say that he or she saw an older boy or man arguing with a younger boy, possibly dragging him along, or perhaps accompanied by a scared, worried, or reluctant-looking schoolboy. But none has. In fact, we don't have one witness sighting of a man or youth walking or travelling with a boy.'

Vignoles thought he could guess where Trinder was going but he kept quiet and simply nodded from time to time.

'Now, Blencowe has something to show you, guv.'

Blencowe had carefully laid out seven small typed notes in a row. Each one was a witness sighting, composed of just a few short lines; each was dated and signed. Blue pencil had been used to mark each short commentary as having been read and then dismissed. However, a large red question mark had been added, presumably at a later time. 'Initially these were dismissed and filed away as of no interest,' said Blencowe. 'But, after talking with the sarge, we went through everything once again and grouped all the sightings according to their location, time and date. We dismissed nothing this time; instead we looked for common threads, regardless of whether they seemed likely or not. We just wanted to put the events into groups. The thing is, sir, something rather strange came up.'

Vignoles was simply observing Blencowe and Trinder. He wanted to hear their theory before performing his own examination of the evidence. One day — he hoped — one or both of them would become detective inspectors and part of the training was to let them try to work things out on their own sometimes, without him puppy-walking them at every turn. 'Go on,' he said, encouraging his protégés.

'Well, sir, we are starting to think there might be a female involved. An older lady, in her fifties or thereabouts. Described as having a larger frame. "Generously proportioned", as one witness put it. Always with a huge handbag, and possibly carrying food. One observer says she was seen handing out cake to a schoolboy. The important point is that a lady matching this description was seen with boys who might have been Dutton and Jebb, although their descriptions of the boys are vague, hence why initially the reports failed to command our attention. The dates match what we think are acceptable timelines for Dutton and Jebb.'

'We have a sighting of a stout lady with an enormous handbag talking with a young boy in a cap and blazer on Nottingham Victoria station on the afternoon of the day Gordon Dutton vanished.' Trinder put a finger on the report in question.

Vignoles read the report. 'The boy's cap colour could match those of Bishop Osmond,' he remarked. 'What else?'

'This one looks like it could be Jebb. A boy in a school cap was seen standing outside Central at about 7pm with what the witness called a jolly, smiling, plump, grandmotherly type of lady.

The witness said the boy was crying, but being comforted by what appeared to be his granny, so the witness walked on.'

Vignoles read the remaining reports himself. He leaned back in his tilting chair, which gave a creak. 'So, perhaps what we have is an older woman who lures the boys away with cake or comfort.' A faint memory of something pricked his mind, but he couldn't trawl it up.

'That's what we think,' Trinder replied.

'This is a needle-in-a-haystack job if ever I saw one,' Vignoles said pessimistically.

'Not necessarily,' replied Blencowe, grinning through his beard. He fished out another exhibit from a pocket: a plain postcard with some typed notes. 'Michael Tibbott furnished us with his address when Jane first encountered him. He also happened to mention in passing that he lives with his mother, at an address not a stone's throw from here. Jane checked this on the electoral roll and saw a Mary. E. Tibbott listed in the same house. We're considering the possibility that she lures the boys home and Tibbott...' He tailed off, not wishing to finish the sentence. He handed the card silently to Vignoles.

'You think his mother...?' Vignoles felt queasy.

'I don't know. We are struggling to even contemplate it. It does sound extremely unlikely, even rather bizarre. But we've got to consider the possibility and investigate, guv.'

'Do we know what Mrs Tibbott looks like? Would she happen to be a stoutish lady?'

'We don't know. Benson and I took a walk past the place earlier,' Trinder added. 'It's in a small industrial area close to Talbot Lane and few, if any, other people reside there. It was once a bakery with a private dwelling attached, and probably retains the bread ovens, because we could see a chimney sticking up from a brick-built addition on the rear of the house.'

There was a moment of silence as this spoken bombshell exploded. Everyone present was thinking the same thing: that Gordon Dutton's body had been burned.

'If Tibbott is indeed a killer, then Jebb might be in his house right now,' said Vignoles, suddenly animated. 'There's no time to lose. John — you and I are going there immediately.' As he shrugged on his overcoat, Vignoles gave Blencowe some hastily-spoken instructions. 'Call the Badger and tell him all you've told me. We'll need his approval to put a day and night watch on their house.

Find out if the Nottingham, Grantham and Leicester civvy police have anything in their witness reports of schoolboys being seen with friendly, matronly, grandmother-types.'

Whilst Vignoles spoke, Trinder donned his hat and coat and was ready.

'Right, John, we'll make this a casual call, pretend we're following up on the tip-off about Twist. We'll act friendly and exceedingly grateful, and so he'll invite us inside of his own accord. We don't have a warrant and we'll need a sight more than just those cards to get one, but if there is even a tiny chance that these people are the culprits, we need to get down there now. A boy's life could depend on it.'

CHAPTER THIRTY-FOUR

Frog Island

Fuller Street was a double-ended cul-de-sac of ugly, low, brick-and-concrete business premises tucked away from the busy thoroughfares of Boar Street and North Gate Street. At one end lay a row of weed-infested railway sidings, insecurely protected by a rotten wooden fence and a gate that had long since given up swinging on its hinges. Vignoles and Trinder could hear the roar of water cascading over Hitchcock's Weir at a point where the Grand Union Canal joined the River Soar. This was out of sight, just beyond the rusting rails. For a street so close to the city centre, and in such close proximity to the Great Central viaduct that strode purposefully across the neighbouring roads, it was a curiously secret place. Without a map it would be hard to find.

Nobody was likely to enter Fuller Street unless he had a specific reason to do so. Perhaps to take his car to Herring's Motor Garage, a place so cramped it could barely house a brace of Morris Travellers beneath its corrugated asbestos roof. Or perhaps to enquire at the shabby, blue-painted delivery door of Norton Hosiery Ltd which, judging by its decrepit appearance, was suffering from a severe lack of business. There was, however, a great deal of fading buddleia growing around the building. Here and there a space had been cleared in anticipation of redevelopment and, in a few places, a modern construction had arisen; all fawn-coloured brick and metal-framed windows, without a hint of ornament or style. Perhaps in ten years time the area might have fully revived and found its feet, but it still had some way to go. Vignoles accidentally kicked an empty Heinz tomato soup can into a pool of oily water in the gutter.

'I can't imagine anyone does much trade down here,' Trinder remarked.

'Is that Tibbott's house?' Vignoles pointed at a narrow brick building with a concrete path running beside it that led, via a sharp dog-leg, to the edge of the canal. Some thin stands of willow edging the canal offered the only softness in this harsh environment. 'Surely nobody lives in that?'

'Around the corner is an older part, built to be a dwelling house and perhaps a shop. Selling loaves and buns first thing in the morning to workers.'

'I can see why they went out of business, John — there's nobody about.' The street was almost silent save for the sound of water rushing over the weir, a low hum of what might be a generator hidden in one of the buildings, and the sound of falling rain. 'Is this Frog Island?'

'Part of it.'

'Should be left to the frogs.'

'It's what the town planners call "ripe for redevelopment", guv. The perfect place to hold someone against their will, I reckon.'

Vignoles could feel his jaw tense. He looked at the dirty windows along the side of the bakery, each metal frame covered by security grilles. 'Hmm… bars to stop people getting in.'

'Or out. It's old, but secure.'

'Ideally, we need to convince a magistrate to give us a warrant. In the meantime, we'll just have to do the best we can. I imagine Tibbott's at work, so we'll be dealing with his mother. I'll get us inside somehow — the rain might help us with that — then stall her, and you can make an excuse and get snooping.'

Trinder was pulling on his leather gloves and flexing his fingers as if readying for the boxing ring. Vignoles hammered on the door with a heavy iron knocker in the shape of a snarling lion. It sounded hollow, as if the house were empty. He peered through the letterbox into the dimly-lit hallway, with the floor of a typical Victorian-patterned tile. It was devoid of furniture, but a frameless mirror hung on a chain on one wall. He closed the flap and was about to knock again when he heard the sound of feet shuffling. The door opened a crack.

'Not today, thank you. I don't buy from hawkers.' Her big, round face was flushed as though she were hot. Her eyes were guarded, a broad hand grasping the door firmly.

Vignoles smiled and lifted his hat. 'I am terribly sorry to disturb you, madam. Am I correct in thinking that I have the pleasure of addressing Mrs Tibbott?'

'Yes, that's right.' She softened in response to his charming tone. The door opened a little wider.

'My name is Charles Vignoles and this is my colleague, John.' He beamed an ingratiating smile. We were wondering if Mr Michael Tibbott was at home.'

'No, sorry dearie, he's out working all day, as usual. Delivering around and about in his van, he is.'

Vignoles formed a crestfallen expression. 'Of course. Oh well, never mind. We just knocked on the off-chance. He's been such a huge help to us, Mrs Tibbott, so eager to assist in our enquiries.'

'What enquiries?' She opened the door fully and folded her arms across her voluminous chest, which was encased in a floral-patterned housecoat. A waft of yeast and dough accompanied the motion and Vignoles noticed a sprinkle of flour on her sleeve.

Vignoles produced his warrant card. 'Police enquiries, Mrs Tibbott.' He noticed that she did not flinch at his revelation, yet she seemed to plant her feet more firmly on the step. 'And I know that Michael would jump at the chance to assist us further.' Suddenly her face transformed into a smile. 'Oh yes, he's a most helpful boy. Always willing. A good, honest sort is my Michael.'

'Indeed,' replied Vignoles, injecting a surprising amount of smarminess into one word. 'If only there were more good citizens like him in this world.' He sighed loudly. 'Perhaps you would be so very kind as to let him know we called.'

'I will. He'll be sorry to have missed you. I have to dash now, dearie: I've got to get my dough into the oven. Goodbye.' She began to push the door towards them. Vignoles suddenly put up his hand to catch her attention and distract her from closing it.

'If I might be allowed to trespass on your time for just one moment longer, Mrs Tibbott, I'm wondering...' he made a point of looking at Trinder as if seeking his opinion, '...if perhaps you might also be able to help us. Living so close to the incident in question...'

Her eyes flickered for a moment. 'Incident? Has something happened?'

'Oh, yes. A very serious crime. You will have read about it in the paper, I'm sure.' The rainfall intensified and the droplets bounced off their hats. It was fortuitous timing. 'Perhaps we might step inside, out of this downpour, just for a moment, if you don't mind?'

'Oh, how rude of me to keep you gents standing outside, getting all wet.' She shuffled out of the way and ushered them in. 'Come on through to the kitchen and have some nice, hot tea.'

'What an excellent idea!' Trinder chipped in as he crossed the threshold, matching Vignoles's amiable tone. His eyes, however, made a note of everything as his shoes squeaked on the cold tiles. Mrs Tibbott pulled a door firmly shut as she passed it, making Trinder wonder what she was so keen to hide from them.

The two policemen were relieved to take off their drenched hats and damp overcoats and sit in the warm around the kitchen table. Their hostess lit the gas under a huge kettle then laid out everything needed to make tea for three. Two bread tins were filled with dough that had risen to a great height. Vignoles made himself comfortable on a chair beside the table, and politely invited Mrs Tibbott to carry on with her baking and not let them get in her way. He gave off an aura of being relaxed and completely at ease, as a friendly associate of her son, not a prying detective.

'I'll just pop these in the oven and then a lovely big pot of tea will be on its way for you.'

Trinder saw his chance. 'Oh, thank you, Mrs Tibbott. We policemen do love our tea, but it can have its — ahem — consequences. I wonder if I might use your, um...' Trinder asked with feigned coyness.

'Of course, dearie. Just through there and down the corridor. It's an inside one,' she added, proudly. Trinder slipped out and closed the door behind him.

Vignoles was carefully inspecting the room whilst trying to look as though he only had eyes for Mrs Tibbott and the baking tins. 'This was once a bakery, wasn't it?' Vignoles began, as though chatting merely to pass the time. 'Did your husband run it?'

'Yes, that's right. But I lost my Duncan at Dunkirk.'

'I am so sorry, Mrs Tibbott. I had no idea.'

'There's plenty of others had it the same. And as time moves on it eases the loss. I've got to thinking it's almost funny, in a way. Not funny that he died, but how. I mean, he bought it from a Jerry shell, and yet there he was, in the catering corps. But a bomb doesn't care if you're carrying a gun or making soup, does it? My father-in-law started the bakery, then Duncan worked it, and then I took it over in 1940. But times got hard and, what with those awful national loaves and the shortages, business around here all took a turn for the worse. I only bake for me and my boy now.'

'Oh, it was a real family business, passed from father to son to widow.' Vignoles tried to sound genuinely interested in the commercial and family aspect of it, so that his next question would not appear to be what it was: a crucial one to the murder enquiry. 'Do you still have the bakery equipment, the oven, and so forth?'

'Most of it.'

'I noticed the chimney.'

She fell silent and frowned. There was a watchful stillness behind her eyes. Vignoles knew to change tack.

'You've doubtless heard that the remains of a boy were found below the railway viaduct.'

'I read something, somewhere,' she replied, vaguely. 'I'm not one for following these things. Can't be doing with all the doom and gloom in the papers. Have you caught whoever done him in?'

'Not yet. Living in the area so close to where it happened, I wonder if you might have seen anything, Mrs Tibbott, or if you were by chance at Leicester Central station last Saturday?'

She changed the subject. 'Where's your pal got to? He's been gone a long time.'

'I'm not surprised,' Vignoles said light-heartedly. 'He drinks an awful lot of tea when we're out on enquiries. Must have a stern word with him about it,' he joked, giving her a wink and smile. As if on cue, the kettle started to wail. Mrs Tibbott filled the teapot.

Vignoles had to find a way back to his questions without making it into an interrogation. He again laid on the charm. 'You know, Mrs Tibbott, you are exactly the helpful sort of person we need. If you were at or near Central station on Saturday you could really assist us with this case.'

'I might have walked past. It's on the way from the shops, you see. Why are you asking?'

'Might you have seen a young boy looking upset and being comforted by a lady?'

She was about to pour tea into the cups but, seeing Trinder's empty chair, paused. 'Shall I send a search party out for your man?'

'He'll be back any second, don't you worry. He loves a cuppa!' Vignoles smiled companionably. 'Funnily enough, the description we've been given of the lady was of someone of a similar age to yourself. Although quite obviously not you, of course. Perhaps you know her.' At that moment Trinder sidled back into the room.

'You're here — at last!' Her voice had an edge to it. 'Your tea's ready.' She poured out three teas and slid Trinder's across the table towards him.

'That looks like a lovely strong brew, many thanks!' he said brightly. He picked up the cup and saucer but did not sit down, choosing instead to drink it whilst leaning against the Welsh dresser. He looked relaxed, and idly inspected the piles of books and bits of decorative china displayed on it.

'So, did you see the lady with the boy, Mrs Tibbott?' Vignoles asked once again, drinking his tea.

'I've really nothing to tell you,' she replied, flatly. She seemed discomfited by Trinder not taking his seat but continuing to inspect her belongings. 'I wasn't there and didn't see anyone.'

'Oh, look! Train books. I just love trains!' Trinder suddenly piped up. His face was a picture of boyish enthusiasm as he lifted a picture-book with a big, red, express locomotive storming forwards, great billows of smoke trailing. 'And timetables, too!'

'Don't touch those!' Mrs Tibbott snapped. She stood up quickly. 'My son doesn't like anyone looking at his books.' She swiftly reined in her anger, replacing it with a fake apologetic tone. 'Sorry, but he even hates it when I meddle with them, and I'm his own mother.'

'These are great!' Trinder, acting the part of a thick-skinned bobby, continued as though she had said nothing. He flicked idly through various books.

'Do forgive my sergeant; he does get a bit carried away whenever he sees anything about railways. But he will be careful. He'll put everything back in its place, exactly as he found it.' Vignoles had risen and, whilst speaking, manoeuvred himself to stand between her and Trinder, partly blocking her view of him. 'Well, we have taken up more than enough of your very valuable time already, Mrs Tibbott. We really must be getting on our way now; you know how it is: places to go, people to see, villains to catch!' He gave a merry little laugh at his quip, purely in order to insert a pause. He was deliberately prolonging his leaving speech in order to buy Trinder more prying time.

Mrs Tibbott looked anxious as she tried to keep a beady eye on Trinder, tilting her head and leaning to one side in an attempt to see behind Vignoles, but his outstretched hand demanded that she take it, acknowledge his thanks and bid him farewell.

'And thank you so very much for rescuing us from the rain, Mrs Tibbott, so kind; and also, I must add, for the nice, strong brew of tea; that was just what we needed after being caught in that horrid downpour. And also, of course, we must thank you for your delightful hospitality, and for sharing with me the charming story of your family business.' He had run out of things to say to delay leaving. He toyed briefly with the idea of asking to use the lavatory himself but, after Trinder's suspiciously prolonged absence, it would make the true reason for their visit blatantly obvious. He thought of one final thing to add. 'If you remember anything that might help us, do please let us know.' He replaced his hat with an almost formal dip of the head.

'What was it you wanted to ask Michael? You never said.'

'All books back in place. No harm done! Right, we'll be off now!' Trinder deliberately cut off Mrs Tibbott's question. He walked briskly into the hall and made straight for the mysterious door she'd been so keen to keep shut against them. Unfortunately, she had followed him closely.

'No! Not in there!'

'Oops, sorry, I forgot the way out. Silly me.' Trinder's face was a picture of innocence as he removed his hand from the doorknob. *Dammit! If only the guv had kept her distracted for a few more seconds.*

Moments later the two men were striding down the concrete alley and back onto Fuller Street. The rain was teeming. With hands on their hats they sprinted as well as they were able in their heavy winter overcoats until they were back on Boar Lane. Once under the relative shelter of the dripping railway bridge they stopped to catch their breath. Trinder was panting as much from excitement as from the exertion.

'I've got something, guv! Those books on the dresser which she got so twitchy about. One was a soft-backed album with little coloured cigarette cards pasted in. I think a tea company made it. It was called *The Train-spotters' Album*.'

'The one with the boy and girl in blue and red on the cover? What of it?'

'It had a page missing!'

'So?'

'One of the few details in the Barrow Hill Mystery, that could have significance, but proved a dead-end for the investigators, was that a page torn from just such an album was found close to the crime scene. It led to some vague speculation that the victim was a train-spotter, although it could simply have been blown there in the wind or been dropped by someone unconnected to the crime. But it was logged and retained, and sits in a file on Blencowe's desk. Guess which page is missing from Tibbott's copy. Page five. The same page!'

Vignoles felt his heart miss a beat. A bus swished past in a stink of diesel and a crash of gears, obliging him to raise his voice. 'Excellent work, John. Now we need to match the shape of the tear along the page with Tibbott's book.'

'Also, I had a snoop around the old bakery. It looked as clean as a whistle, which seems odd for an abandoned business.'

'Very.'

'And that's not all, sir. She was baking her loaves today using the domestic range in the kitchen. So why was the bakery's bread oven warm? In this weather it should be as cold as iron.'

CHAPTER THIRTY-FIVE

38C Leicester North

Vignoles and Trinder stepped gingerly across the uneven, ashy ground and between the odd bits of discarded detritus that engine sheds breed. The locomotive shed lay some distance away, with a collection of black-and-green-painted locomotives smoking in a desultory manner in front of the gaping doors. The elevated tracks leading into the huge coaling shed were close to hand, and there was a long hill of neatly stacked coal to their left. They were tramping along one of the lengthy, uneven sidings used to unload this veritable mountain of shiny black gold, but as Mr White, the shed foreman, was explaining as they walked, this far siding was rarely used for unloading coal into the reserve stack now that coal supplies were more regular and reliable, and instead they used it to store locomotives in need of serious attention, or those condemned to be dragged away and broken up for scrap.

'I'm not too sure how much longer this one will have,' said White, 'she's getting a bit long in the tooth. Came down from Bulwell Common. I think she got down here by mistake, to be honest. Our lads don't like these sort much. So she got shunted down here out of the way and we've not got around to sending the old girl back.' He puffed on a cigarette, thankful that the earlier rain shower had passed. White's easy chatter was welcome. It was quite a hike from his office and neither detective wanted to fill the time with idle speculation about what they were going to see. Both men had a lot to consider and were each mulling things over privately.

Foreman White's call had come in as soon as they had returned to the office, buoyant about their success at the Tibbotts' house. There was no time even to take off their hats. They made straight for 38c, as Leicester North shed was more commonly known under British Railways ownership.

'She looks like an Ivatt C12. Am I right? Must be fifty years old.' Vignoles thought he recognised the type of locomotive they were being directed towards.

'And a bit more on top, inspector. She's almost a museum piece now. I'll confess to having a bit of a soft spot for the old girl. Handsome-looking tank engine and, if maintained properly, can do a decent job. She needs a bit of fettling, but the lads were none too eager to take her out or give her any attention.'

Vignoles managed a little half-smile of appreciation. 'So she's not failed, then?'

'Nah. Just a touch wheezy around the glands and there's a bit of knock from the big end, but nothing to stop her doing a turn. Been down here a week. Nobody's paid her any heed. Not until this morning, that is, when I lost two engines as failed in quick succession, so we looked around to see what we could pull together. I got one of our cleaners, Stan Mitchell, to prepare her fire and give her a check over before I sent a crew along. He's waiting by the engine, as we reckoned you'd want to quiz him.'

'Mitchell raised the alarm?' Trinder asked.

'That's right, sergeant. About 0938, give or take a minute.' His scrupulous exactitude made Trinder look up from watching where he placed his feet. 'We were running very late as we'd tried our best to patch up the two failures. Then I got the shout from Mitchell, but first I had to check it wasn't a joke, because I didn't want to waste your time on a mere prank. So I interrogated all my staff, but everyone denied all knowledge.'

Vignoles raised a hand and brought them all to a stand some distance from the engine. Two uniformed constables were standing near a long length of rope strung between two lamp posts and looped over the post of the perimeter fence and over the buffer of a crippled wagon parked close to the end of the siding, thus forming a cordon. A group of railwaymen smoked and talked quietly beside a row of coal wagons on a parallel siding. 'I want to take in the whole scene before we approach,' said Vignoles. 'So, the engine is out of view unless one walks around here, or looks down from the back of the coal shed.'

'Which has very few windows,' Trinder noted, 'and they look like they've never been cleaned since the day they were put in.'

'So, unless your men are unloading coal wagons, this is a hidden corner,' Vignoles remarked.

'Only used for old engines, clapped-out wagons and — very occasionally — the breakdown crane.'

'Who has been on the engine since the discovery?' Trinder asked, taking notes.

'Only Mitchell and his chum Earnshaw.'

'Eddie?' Trinder exclaimed, 'is there anything he doesn't get his nose into?' He rolled his eyes and gave a slight shake of the head.

Vignoles had already spotted the young man in question, standing, hands in pockets, beside a very grubby younger lad, presumably Mitchell. He beckoned them to approach, nodded to acknowledge Earnshaw, and addressed his workmate. 'Engine Cleaner Mitchell? I understand it was you who made the discovery.'

'Yes sir.' He looked about seventeen and had a comical smudge of black on the end of his nose which, taken together with his dark brown eyes and overly prominent ears, made him resemble a surprised teddy bear. 'I was told to clean out and build a fire, so I carried some kindling and rags over here in a barrow. You can see the barrow just there, sir. I placed some of the kindling on the footplate, then entered the cab, and that was when I found the note. He's got it.' He pointed to a constable, who saluted Vignoles and handed him a plain white postcard. 'I left the other, not dissimilar exhibit in situ, where it was found, until you arrived, sir.' He spoke in the stilted manner policemen felt they needed to adopt.

Vignoles read aloud from the card. 'Have a good look at your engine. What you might find? Where was this?'

'I found it pushed part-way behind the pipe dropping down from one of the gauge glasses,' Mitchell continued. 'Just sitting there, bold as anything. I took it down and looked to see if there was something on the back. It looked new. All clean and fresh.'

'What did you do then?' Vignoles asked.

'Well, I reckoned it was a prank by one of the other lads. We do lark about a bit sometimes...' He responded to his foreman's admonishing glare with a sheepish expression, but continued. 'Thought it were a dead cat or seagull stuffed down the chimney or summat.'

'What did you do next?' Vignoles asked.

'So I looks in the firebox, using a bit of burning rag to get some light, but it was just ash and old fire. So I walks around the engine — I needs to check the smoke-box, anyway — to see what char was in there and clean it out. Well, that's when I saw it.'

Vignoles and Trinder looked at the locomotive. The door at the front of the boiler was standing ajar, but they could see nothing amiss or unusual.

Eddie continued the story. 'We've pushed the door almost closed, because of the rain, you see; but I told Stan that this is now an official crime scene, so we had to leave it untouched and not let anyone else mess about with it, either.'

Vignoles was going to observe that they would decide if it was a crime scene or not, but held his tongue.

'That was a sensible decision, Eddie,' said Trinder.

'So after I saw the thing in the smoke-box, I happened to see Eddie nearby and whistled to him, to call him over.'

Eddie took over again, feeling the need to explain his proximity to the locomotive. 'I'd worked into the shed on my engine, to take water, as we'd already done an early run, and I had a bit of time until my next turn. I'd heard that number 67397 was out the back and I fancied taking a peek. I've only see a couple of these sort before, when I've been to Annesley shed, and so I was dead keen.'

'Are you in the habit of mooching about instead of looking after your engine?' White wondered what image Eddie was presenting to the detectives. He glowered at the young fireman.

'We know all about Eddie's habits,' said Vignoles, giving White a reassuring look. 'He even has some experience with police matters.' He kept his voice deadpan, not wishing to give the young man more credit than was strictly necessary.

'Stan called me over and showed me what he'd found inside the smoke-box. Then he showed me the card he'd found in the cab. It all looked fishy so I stood guard whilst Stan fetched the foreman.'

'I wasn't too happy,' said Foreman White. 'I'd got Eddie's engine booked to move off and he'd gone missing! Well, never mind all that now.' He blew air out between his teeth in a long, drawn-out whistle that served as illustration of a frustrating morning that looked as though it was about to turn worse. He lit another cigarette.

'We'll take a look now,' said Vignoles. 'Mitchell and Earnshaw, come with us. Everyone else stay here. We want as few pairs of boots trampling about as possible.' As they approached the sombre, black-painted engine, glossed by streaks of recent rainfall, both detectives inspected the wet ground of compacted coal dust and ash for possible footprints. They wore gloves against the cold and Vignoles told Mitchell and Earnshaw to put theirs on.

'Were you wearing gloves when you looked inside?'

Mitchell nodded. 'And in the cab, sir.'

'Good. Our forensic officer might be able to get fingerprints among all this ash, oil and grease.' They heaved themselves up onto the front footplate and Trinder opened the heavy metal door wide. Peering inside the cylindrical smoke-box, they saw another plain postcard. It appeared unnaturally bright and white, lying on a few dried and brown leaves and twigs, placed in turn upon a neat bed of grey ash. It was a carefully contrived cameo that clearly held significance for the person who had assembled it. They stood silent for a few moments, the atmosphere leaden and heavy, their nostrils filled by the acrid stench of burning. They could easily read the clear, bold letters written in black ink, apparently in the same hand as the other card.

'It starts with a poem,' said Vignoles, 'and I feel sure I recall these lines from somewhere or other.' He read aloud. 'No burial these pretty babes/Of any man receives/Till Robin Redbreast piously/Did cover them with leaves.'

The words evoked in Vignoles a vivid recollection of standing on the stage at school on speech day. It must have been 1919 and, as a nervous thirteen-year-old, he had recited it from memory and won a prize of a tortoiseshell propelling pencil. He still had it somewhere. 'It's from the traditional children's tale *Babes in the Wood*. Then under that we have 'R.I.P. G.D. and J.J.'

'I've been mulling on that, sir,' Eddie piped up in a serious tone, 'and I reckon it might mean Gordon Dutton and Jimmy Jebb, you know, those boys I read about in the paper.'

Trinder did not reply, but glanced meaningfully at Vignoles. *Did this mean there was no hope of finding Jebb alive?* The day seemed to turn colder in an instant. Trinder arranged for the scene to remain secured and for interviews and statements to be collected. They then walked back to the office, discussing the new development.

'That card, guv, it's almost like the killer wants us to find him.'

'Or her,' Vignoles added, almost under his breath.

'You think *she* could have done that?' Trinder looked aghast.

'I'm not sure what I think, John. Perhaps I'm just reminding myself that we still have no hard evidence that tells us Tibbott is the killer. Hence the reason he is still walking free. But Fireman Earnshaw's connection to Dutton and Jebb is hard to deny, and the implication is that the ashes of Jebb are lying in that smoke-box.' Vignoles looked tired. If that really were so, then they had failed the young lad. 'The killer remains a step ahead of us.'

Trinder was nodding in agreement. 'But why leave such a clue other than to lead us straight to whoever did this? The handwriting can be matched to a sample of a suspect and prove they wrote it. I think they're playing a horrid game of cat and mouse.'

'Then we cats had better make ourselves prize mousers!' quipped Vignoles, in a voice that lacked mirth. 'Let's see if the forensics officer finds anything useful to make an identification, although what was there looked even less promising than the Dutton remains. Get Blencowe, Benson and Lansdowne out on enquiries. They need to find a witness who saw a stranger in the yard in the last seven days; that is, since the loco was berthed there. If we are really lucky they will hear about someone matching the description of Michael Tibbott — or his mother.'

Chapter Thirty-six

Leicester Central

'This could prove useful,' Benson said to Trinder, who was standing beside the vast desk she shared with her fellow officers. 'I finally managed to interview the council workmen who prepared the site for the archaeologists.'

'Aha,' he murmured, half-listening as he leafed through some papers he was holding.

'They identified Michael Tibbott on site on two separate occasions.' She knew the name would get Trinder's full attention. 'The first time they saw him he looked embarrassed and walked away without saying anything. They thought he had nipped around the back for a you-know-what and was surprised to discover them at work.'

'What date was this?'

'September 24th. They had only just come on site and were carrying duck boards around to the back.'

'Hmm... that's three days after Dutton vanished. We could surmise that is after the time he was killed.'

'Tibbott might have been checking how he'd left the site. We know Dutton's remains were in place before they commenced digging, so this helps to give us a timescale.'

'We often hear that those who commit particularly dreadful crimes like to return to the scene. But he must have got the shock of his life to see it being turned over.' Trinder, deep in thought, absentmindedly tapped his pencil against his chin. 'However, rather than flee and never be seen there again, he chose to return later. When was it he returned?' He used the pencil as a baton to make the point.

'The next morning. Not long after 9am. What is more, he stood around for some time asking the men about what they were up to. He came across as a curious bystander, which they are used to, and so they thought nothing of it, even when he paced around the area asking where the dig was going to take place. The men had a drawing supplied by Professor Wildblood and showed Tibbott their plan of work, which drew more questions about the size of the dig and how long it would last.'

'So, you think he was worried about the ashes.' Now the pencil was pointing at Benson.

'I think so, sarge. Most intriguing of all, just as he was finally leaving he asked if they were planning to remove the rubbish and litter. They told him that was not their job to pick up mess left by others, and off he went.'

'So we've got him visiting the beginning of an archaeological dig and asking questions, just like other nosy members of the public. There's nothing to prove he knew Dutton's remains were there.' Trinder changed tack. 'Any luck on the 38c enquiry?'

'Oh, yes! Tibbott delivered a set of spark plugs to the assistant shed foreman, Arthur Parkes. He has an Austin A40 that was playing up. We even have another witness, as well as Mr Parkes, who saw him there.'

'Hm... all very well, but Tibbott had a legitimate reason to be there.'

'And we've not found anyone who saw him go anywhere near that engine, though, sarge.' Benson looked almost apologetic. 'Perhaps his delivery gave him the chance to scout out the lay of the land, and then he went back after dark to place the ashes and cards.'

'Possibly. But an empty box used for car components would easily contain the ashes. It would be small and light, so he could move quickly, so I think our theory that nobody takes any notice of a familiar and safe figure holds true. Remember the experiment I did with Mavis? The people at the shed were accustomed to seeing him about. If he did walk down to the far end with a small box, perhaps it wouldn't stick in their memory.'

Benson was nodding agreement. 'What about Mrs Tibbott?'

Trinder pulled a pained expression. 'It's hard to fathom. Did anyone see her at the engine shed?'

'No. And a woman would stand out as unusual and attract attention. I say, sarge, if Tibbott is a killer, do you really think his mother can be involved?'

'She could be the lure perhaps. Not doing the dirty stuff.' Trinder did not look or sound especially convinced.

'Either way, it's quite sick-making.' Benson stared at the floor, as if this might help explain the inexplicable. She lowered her voice. 'Do you think Michael Tibbott is the killer, sarge?'

'We have only scraps to go on, but things are pointing that way.'

'You think he killed Dutton at his house and cremated him in the bakery?'

'Maybe.'

'What about Jebb?'

'After reading that postcard, the guv is starting to lose faith that we'll find him alive. I'm trying to remain optimistic. We've got every bobby keeping a lookout for him and appeals in the papers, but no sightings as yet. But we have to keep the faith until forensics prove otherwise.'

Trinder turned to walk away, but Benson stopped him, her expression grave. 'Do you think he'll strike again?' He looked down into Benson's eyes, shiny and bright behind her glasses, imploring him to offer some reassurance. Lansdowne and Howerth, who were seated nearby, quietly and studiously processing piles of interview reports, had both looked up and were observing him expectantly, for they, too, wanted to hear his reply.

'Yes, I do think he – or they – might do it again.' The sound of the big office clock marked time. 'But for now I think they'll just watch and wait, because they know we are sniffing around them, and will assume we are keeping them under surveillance. They will be watching us scrabbling around, and will enjoy our discomfort and annoyance at having found no concrete evidence against them. So, perhaps we have a bit of time.'

'Ooh but I'd like to arrest Tibbott right now! Then we'd have carte blanche to take that old bakery apart. I can't stand the thought of those...those monsters staying free a moment longer.' Benson's face coloured with anger.

'We all feel the same, Jane; but we need to gather as much information as we can first. We've got to make sure that when we do swoop, a good lawyer doesn't get them off the hook a few hours later because all we had were a few flimsy suspicions and theories that could collapse as easily as a house of cards.'

'Sorry, sarge. I do know all that, of course; it's just that sometimes this job can be so blummin' frustrating!'

'We will get there in the end, Jane, but by patience and solid hard work, not by jumping the gun. Keep a level head and just keep chipping away. Get more detail, more sightings, more witness statements, like you have from those workmen. Make more connections; perform more cross-referencing. It's all adding up, slowly but surely. We will get him, you know. The guv always gets his man!'

CHAPTER THIRTY-SEVEN

London Road

Jane Benson and Max Hawkes sat in a cosy corner of the Marquis of Wellington on London Road. The pub was a safe distance from their digs and from the station. This was a deliberate choice on Jane's part: she didn't want their landlady, a fellow lodger, one of her colleagues, or any of the station staff to see them out together.

Hawkes had dialled their landlady's number from a callbox in Sheffield to inform her of his intended time of arrival home, but then said he needed to speak to Miss Benson. This aroused the landlady's suspicion that something was 'going on' between them, and so she insisted on taking a message to pass on instead. Hawkes repeated his request, Mrs Mason again refused, and the impasse was only resolved when Jane trotted downstairs and made it clear that she'd overheard and understood that she was wanted on the phone, leaving her landlady with no choice but to hand over the receiver. Mrs Mason then moved barely a yard and, under the guise of pretending that her barometer needed some urgent tapping and inspection, blatantly eavesdropped. Hawkes said he had no pennies left and was about to be disconnected, and hastily suggested a time and place to meet; Jane, desperate to flee the listening ears of Mrs Mason, agreed just before the line went dead.

'You do understand,' Mrs Mason said coldly, 'that I disapprove of relations between guests of the opposite sex.' She made the word sound like some manner of Old Testament curse of affliction.

'We are only meeting for a friendly drink, not that it is any business of yours.'

'It is when it is conducted inside my house, or over my telephone line, in my hallway!'

Hawkes laughed as Jane recounted the story. 'Oh dear. She really is the absolute limit. Sorry to have ruined your reputation.'

Jane sipped her drink. 'We might be in for a bit of a reception later, though. I can't see her letting us sneak upstairs together unchallenged.' She felt an odd sensation. She'd said it: she'd said that they would inevitably return home later as a couple. That was odd, and it was not what she'd planned.

'Better steel ourselves with some more of this fine ale, then,' he winked.

'Any excuse.' She felt the need for some Dutch courage. 'Thanks for coming in and making that statement to my inspector. I hope it wasn't too much of an ordeal for you.' She had managed to make herself scarce whilst he was in the office.

'Nothing to it. I just repeated what I told you. Was it useful?' He looked hopeful as he sipped his beer.

'It was a small detail that needed following up. One of many.'

Hawkes looked crestfallen. He'd hoped his contribution had held more significance and she would be appropriately grateful. 'I see. So that Dutton chap was not the prime suspect, after all?'

'No one ever said he was. I'm not going to share case details, but one thing you must be clear about is that the boy's father is not the killer.'

'Well, that's a relief, at least. I'm glad I didn't share a carriage with such a murderer.'

'So, what happened at the audition?' She wanted to change the subject.

'Passed. Sailed through. It was nothing challenging. I start mid-December. They've got a lot of extra midweek bookings as Christmas approaches. I'll come back Fridays for my job at the Green Cockatoo, of course, and stay here till I'm due back in Sheffield. I'll find temporary lodgings up there. If all goes well I might be working at the Cockatoo until spring.' He watched her reaction closely.

'It would be a shame if you left Leicester.'

'You think so?' he asked, gratified at her comment.

'Yes, you need to stay here a little longer, at least until Lucy and I can make a second visit to the club.'

Hawkes felt disappointed with her reason. 'Don't leave it too long. The job here could end just like that,' he said, clicking his fingers. 'That's the way it goes in my line. But if it does, you could always visit me in Sheffield.'

'That might be difficult, what with my shifts,' Jane replied quickly.

'Take a couple of days off and stay overnight.'

Jane was taken aback at his suggestion. She fell silent. The implication seemed to occupy the space between them. She drank some more beer and could feel her head spin a little.

'You get settled in up there, and we can see how things go.' *That was nicely vague reply*, she thought. 'And we all get so busy around Christmas, don't we? Family, friends; you know how it is.

And besides, I will need to see our murder case closed first.' She formed a pained expression. 'Leave out of town is cancelled for the duration.'

'Really?' Hawkes gave a low whistle.

'It's one of the most chilling cases I've ever encountered.'

'Are you close to solving it?'

'I think we may be, but it's complicated. One of the most difficult parts of police work is knowing in your heart who is responsible, but not having the evidence to arrest that person. You still need to work hard, gathering the tiniest of details before you can do anything. If you don't do this frustratingly slow groundwork, then all your efforts are wasted.'

'How do you mean?'

'The case may not get to court, or, worse still, it gets to court and then collapses on a technicality. A guilty person could walk free and, thanks to the law of double jeopardy, we don't get another go.'

Hawkes was nodding his head and looking thoughtful. 'Is that when you can't be tried twice for the same crime?'

'That's right. There are good reasons for this law, but it brings added pressure for us. We must not mess everything up by being hasty. The problem is, we are looking at an evil, merciless child killers. If we drag our heels too long then...'

'... they may strike again?' offered Hawkes.

Jane nodded and took a swig from her glass.

'You said "killers". There is more than one?'

'We suspect two may be working in concert.'

'Jesus.' He drained his glass. 'That horrible thought calls for another drink.' Jane smiled weakly and did not try to stop him revisiting the bar. Left alone she realised that she had again slipped into discussing the case — not that it really mattered; after all, it was only Max, but rules are rules. She drained her glass and vowed to change the subject.

An hour-and-a-half later they were ambling along New Walk. The rain had long ceased, replaced by a more welcome frostiness that made their breath appear like steam. The piles of sodden autumn leaves lining the footpath were starting to crackle as they dried and stiffened in the cold night air. The air smelled of damp earth and cosy coal fires. The ornate gas lamps threw a gentle light on the trees and park benches, and on the gravel that crunched satisfyingly under their feet.

At length they came to the park gates, emerging onto an avenue of spacious Georgian houses. 'It finally feels Christmassy. Look, someone's put up some decorations.' Jane pointed to a wide bay window of an elegant house, the curtains drawn to reveal a grand drawing room with an oval dining table, six straight-backed chairs, mirrors on the walls and many lighted candles. Paper-chains and boughs of holly and ivy were draped across a heavy mantelpiece, whilst the table boasted a great centrepiece featuring a log with holly and other greenery.

'That's quite a place,' Hawkes remarked. 'Looks like they will be having a houseful.'

'Ooh, I'd love that so much. A houseful of friends and family over for Christmas. It's my dream. One year our inspector and his wife invited Lucy and me to their house for Christmas.' Hawkes slid his hand around her waist and gave it a little squeeze. She didn't resist. 'We even stayed over. It was just so delightful. Somehow they had rustled up food supplies that we could hardly believe. There was so much, and yet rationing was still in full swing.'

'Sounds lovely. For me, I'm afraid that Christmas means working till after midnight on 24th, crawling home half-cut, sleeping it off for most of the day, a quick bite of turkey, then back to work in the evening.'

'So you're working the whole time?'

'Yep. Someone has to provide the music for all the dinner-dances and parties. Still, it pays pretty well.'

'I'd never really thought about the bands going without any Christmas fun.' She fell silent, picturing the pretty, glamorous young women who sang with the bands, like those three she'd seen at the club. The drink flowing freely, kisses under the mistletoe, that might lead to... who knows what kind of fun? Hmph — she knew what! Perhaps he chose a different girl every year. Maybe he was lining her up to be his 'Miss Christmas 1952!' A voice in her head warned her to be on her guard. Perhaps she should remove his wandering hand. However, another — far louder — voice told the other one to shut up and let her enjoy the moment. Life was brief. Too short for nagging, sanctimonious voices of conscience.

In unison, and without a word being spoken, they each stopped walking and faced one another, standing beneath a lamp that threw its hissing light down upon them through the branches of a tree. The tall spire of St Stephen's reached into the not-quite-black of the city night sky. Jane felt his hand rather high on her waist, the other was around her shoulder and against the collar of her coat. As she had turned to face him, his hand had brushed lightly against her breast. She really ought to push it down to her hip. He began stroking her side, up and down, ever so gently, and even through the layers of coat and dress it felt extremely pleasing. She looked up at him, his face softly illuminated. He was just a little bit too handsome to be trusted; a little bit too charming to be taken seriously as a potential boyfriend. What was his past, romantically speaking? What plans did he have for the future? She realised that she didn't really know very much about him at all.

What she did know was that he was holding her close and she felt no urge to resist. His hand slid inside her coat and her heart almost missed a beat when he began to caress her breast with firm but thrilling moves that could not be seen by any passer-by. She let out a slight, involuntary gasp of pleasure. She really should stop him... this was outrageous behaviour. The scandal, if anyone were to see... There was a gentle pressure on the nape of her neck and she moved closer, her lips already opening, ready and willing to be kissed.

Chapter Thirty-eight

Leicester

'I think a girl next.'

'A girl?' Mrs Tibbott paused in scrubbing the kitchen table with sugar soap. 'That would be a nice change. I'd like that.'

'I thought so.' His eyes were filled with something dark and sinister. He was smiling, but there was an unfathomable cruelty deep inside. 'But, of course, a girl brings her own problems.'

'In what way?'

'There's not so many girls as boys hanging around the railway. They don't wander about on their own, either.' He giggled in an oddly childish manner. 'And I want to keep the railway theme going. It's more interesting to stick to the same idea. Don't you agree, Mummy? Then we'll really be something special. Unique, that's what we are.'

'Of course, we are, dearie,' she said, but frowned, and the circular motion of her arm moving the cloth around the table surface slowed momentarily. 'What about the schools?'

'Very risky.' He sucked air between his teeth. 'Hard to separate one from her mates. They're like sheep: all herding together. Do you remember when we watched that sheepdog trialling up in Cumbria?'

'Ah. Now that was a nice trip.' She paused in her cleaning. 'Pity it rained so, but that's Cumbria for you.'

'They explained how to separate one sheep — the one with a ribbon around its neck — from the others.'

'Shedding, they called it.'

'That's right. At the school gate it would be much the same. Quite a skill to shed one giggly girl away from the crowd, and without being noticed. Not easy. Not even for us.'

'She might have a nice pretty ribbon around her neck, though.' Mrs Tibbott now took her turn to giggle as she bent back to scrubbing away with the cloth, her vast bosom swaying. 'I bet you'd like that.'

'I might!' He formed his cold, emotionless smile again. A pike under water might share something in common. 'Tempting though it is, we must stick to the places we know. And shedding is our mission. Engine-shedding. Haha.'

'You are a one for your little jokes, Mikey.'

'We need to find ourselves a suitable railway girl. A girl will warm to you from the start. You're not the sort to frighten them, and you can befriend her. Win her confidence. I think we take her in broad daylight. I've got a bit of an idea.'

'I bet you have.' She stood up, dropped the cloth in the pail by her feet and stretched her back.

'We'll be remembered as the *Railway Killers*.' He pulled himself up and puffed out his chest. 'Imagine that in lights in front of the pictures.' He motioned with his hand as if pointing out the words on a cinema façade. 'When they make a film about us! Great big posters with our faces on them. Can you see it? A train steaming out of the dark, a young kid screaming, and great big bold letters with the actors' names. I wonder who they'd get to play me.'

'They'll be doing nothing of the sort. Sometimes you are quite the limit.' She gave him a cross look.

'That last lad was almost too easy. That's why I thought a girl. Really test ourselves.'

'What about a nice meat loaf for supper?' It was as if she was not listening.

'Lovely.' He licked his lips. 'I want to give those stupid detectives a right royal run around.' He laughed with a coarse, ugly sound.

'I don't know, Mikey. Maybe we should stop a while. Draw breath a bit. You seem to be in such a rush all of a sudden. I'm worried the detectives are becoming a bit of a nuisance. I don't like what's in the papers today. And why did they call in to see us?' She pointed a finger at him as she asked the question. 'They were friendly enough, but what did they really want?'

He looked mildly discomfited. 'You said it was to confirm something I'd told them. There you go, that's proof that I've got them in my pocket.'

'Have they been back in touch?'

He shook his head. She gave him another hard stare, then looked away towards the store cupboard in the wall. 'Treacle tart and custard for afters?'

'I'd like that. Now don't you worry, I've got everything under control. The dad's copped it for the first one and I stitched that cripple Twist up nice and proper for the second.' He looked smug. 'I've got them running about like blue-arsed flies, to be honest! Haha.

'Michael! What language!' She glared at him, eyes flashing. 'Wash your mouth out with soap!'

'Sorry mother.' He sounded contrite, but ruined the effect by smirking and had to turn his face away. The sound of his sniggers seemed to act like a switch being thrown. She stooped and thrust her hand into the zinc pail, grasped the steaming-hot cloth, dripping with dirty, soapy water and with this oddly menacing weapon advanced towards him. 'Wipe that stupid smile off your face!'

'I said I was sorry!' He spun around to face her, back against the sink.

'Don't answer me back.' She weighed the sopping cloth in her strong, chubby hand. With surprising alacrity she took a step forward and suddenly thrust it into his face in a swift, practised move. He made no attempt to resist the inevitable, but raised his arms pathetically, as if in surrender. 'Open! Open your mouth! Bad boy!'

He twisted his head to try and evade the cloth, but she forced it hard against his lips, letting dirty liquid rush down his chin. Although his arms were strong enough to push her away, he made no attempt to do so. This punishment was horrible, but still preferable to having her hard fists pummel his kidneys.

'The sooner you give in, the sooner it is over.' She pushed harder, her considerable weight winning out, his mouth slowly opening, his neck bent painfully backwards. The cloth was pushed inside and he started to retch, spluttering and flapping his arms in distress like a beached seal, face turning crimson and chest jerking in convulsive movements. Her voice was flat and quiet but laden with cruelty and menace, her hand ramming the cloth deeper with each word, like a series of punctuation marks. 'You. Vile. Nasty. Boy.' She watched his Adam's apple bounce up and down as he was forced to swallow the dirty water. His eyes were rolling, the whites showing with fear as he retched deep and deeper. She suddenly pulled away and he span about, clawing at the cloth and spewing foamy water and vomit into the sink, coughing and gasping air into his lungs in between deep convulsions, all of which made him choke and be sick again.

'Let that be a lesson to you!'

He nodded frantically and gulped air. 'Yes... sorry.' He hung his head then retched again.

Suddenly, all traces of anger and violence evaporated. 'Clean that up, will you, dearie? Make it all nice and clean for Mummy.'

Her voice had returned to its soft tone, and it was as if nothing had happened. 'I'll stick the kettle on and make us a lovely, fresh pot of tea. I bet you would like that, wouldn't you?'

He nodded his head in reply whilst rinsing out his mouth by cupping his hands under the running cold tap. 'Yes, please, Mummy.'

'We'll have a sit down, then, and you can tell me exactly how we are going to catch ourselves a pretty little schoolgirl.'

CHAPTER THIRTY-NINE

Nottingham Victoria

Dorothy Feakin fussed with her daughter's coat, adjusting a collar that needed no adjustment and flicking away an invisible piece of fluff, constantly inspecting and checking that Susan looked presentable. Her spectacle frames curved upwards in a cat-like, fashionable style, the little brilliants set in the frames flashing as she bobbed her head backwards and forwards and from side to side in little jerky movements, the better to inspect her daughter's attire. There was something of the mother hen about her, and Susan, though long used to her mother's ways, was tiring of the attention, aware that they were standing in full view of the other passengers waiting on Nottingham Victoria station.

'Mother, please!'

'I just want you to look your best. We can't have you arriving at Aunty Mo and Uncle Jim's looking a disgrace.'

'Leave the poor girl alone for five minutes. You'll wear her coat away if you worry at it any more.' Mr Feakin was sympathetic to his daughter's plight. He gave her a surreptitious roll of his eyes that made her giggle. 'Have we time enough for a cup of tea?'

'I think it's due any moment, Dad.' Susan glanced at her watch. She was very proud of this timepiece and took every opportunity to check it, enjoying the way it looked so perfect on her thin wrist. So delicate and gold against the soft, dark-blue leather strap. Of course she knew it was not real gold, but that didn't matter. It looked like gold and was quite simply the nicest and most perfect thing she owned. Except, perhaps, the charm bracelet that Aunty Mo had given her for her communion present. But the watch was definitely more useful. She loved the tiny blue dial with the golden hands, each tipped by a tiny shining stone that she liked to think were diamonds. 'I bet it will come out of the tunnel soon!'

'Ok, let's have a bet. I say in one minute; how about you?' Her father was a cheerful, enthusiastic, easy-going man, always ready for a joke, a witty saying or a snap wager on the most unlikely of things, like whose twig would appear from under a bridge when they played Poohsticks. He also enjoyed a flutter on the horses, football and games of dominoes down the Headless Woman of a Friday night with his chums.

'Oh really, Lawrence. How childish are you?' His wife pursed her lips. This was frivolous nonsense, and set a bad example.

'What do I win?'

'A mint!'

'I will guess eighty seconds. Starting from... now!' Susan was only too happy to flick her eyes between the fragile second hand sweeping around the dial and the gaping black mouth of the tunnel.

'Have you got your ticket? Is your purse safe?' More imaginary fluff was flicked away. 'The guard is going to take care of you till Woodford Halse. Don't forget.'

'Yes, mother...'

'Dot, Susan is top of her class in Physics, Maths, Biology and French. I think she can manage to get out at the right station.'

'The guard will look after your suitcase, and he will hand you over to the stationmaster at Woodford, who will put you on the train to Cheltenham and tell the guard to look after you. I've packed you a cheese sandwich and an apple, so don't forget to take them out of your case when you change trains, because you'll be peckish by then.'

'Yes, mother...'

'How are we doing for time, Susie?' asked her father, watching the tunnel with a twinkle in his eye, willing the train to arrive.

'Forty seconds...'

'Come on, come on!'

'Is that it? No; it's just a goods train, so I still stand a chance.' Susan gave him a quick smile.

'Stop it, you two.' Mrs Feakin looked impatient. 'Listen, Susan: Uncle Jim will meet you at Cheltenham in his new Vanguard. If there is any delay or any problem and if for any reason Uncle Jim is not there waiting, I want you to—'

'Here it is!'

'Oh yes, look: it's coming in on our track. What time?'

'Sixty-eight seconds. Well done, Dad. You win.'

Lawrence dug in a pocket of his Oxford bags and pulled out a hand clutching something. 'Here you go, love, I'll give you my winnings.' He emptied the coins into one of the side pockets of her coat with a little tinkling sound. 'Get yourself a bottle of pop and some chocolate.' He then added, as an afterthought, a clutch of Fox's Glacier Mints.

'Ooh, thank you, Daddy. Look, it's got a name.' She read the brass name-plate as the green-and-black painted engine hissed slowly past. 'It's called *Derby County*.'

'Pretty decent team.'

'Did you hear what I said, Susan? Phone home if there is any problem, there is a callbox right outside the station. Dial O to get the operator and ask for a trunk call. She will tell you how much money you need to put in the slot. I've put three shillings in your purse, just for this, so don't spend it on anything else.'

'Do stop worrying, Mummy.'

Lawrence Feakin was walking briskly towards the rear of the train of carmine-and-cream coaches that was squealing to a halt, one door already swinging open as an impatient traveller stepped out. The guard lifted a huge perambulator, partially wrapped in brown paper, from the goods compartment adjacent to his cubicle in the brake composite coach. He briefly inspected the delivery note tied to the handle, then looked up to see the Feakin family looking at him expectantly.

'Hullo! Are you the little miss who's coming with us till Woodford, changing for Cheltenham?' Mrs Feakin approved of the chirpy railwayman and was relieved to hear that he was fully conversant with the travel plan. She had explained everything to the booking office clerk a few days earlier, giving him detailed instructions and insisting that Susan be in the continuous care of railway staff throughout the journey — most particularly when she changed trains. She had insisted that the clerk repeat everything back to her, twice, as her husband became increasingly embarrassed at her delaying the couple waiting behind them — a middle-aged lady and what appeared to be her son.

'A Mr Grenville is supposed to be collecting this here pram. Expecting it today. Leastways, Mrs Grenville is expecting... someday soon, haha! Tell you what, miss, we'll put your case safely in here and then you go and take yourself a nice seat near me. Make yourself comfortable whilst I get this train on the move and then I will pop along after and see where you are and that everything's all right.' Susan felt relieved. The way her mother had been talking, it sounded like she was expected to sit on her suitcase in the guard's draughty old goods compartment for the whole journey.

'You *will* keep an eye on her, won't you? Make sure she gets out at Woodford, and don't forget —'

'Mother, *please*!' Susan thanked the guard and, after her father had carefully stowed her case beside a set of large tea chests and a brand new Raleigh bicycle, she walked a few steps along the platform until she came to an empty compartment. She climbed in, dropped down the window and, leaning out, gave her mother a peck on her cheek, breathing in the familiar scent of her perfume.

'Aren't you lucky to get a compartment all to yourself? Oh, my little girl is so grown up now!' said her father, giving her shoulder a little squeeze.

As the expensive new pram was being wheeled away by a rather young-looking father-to-be, the guard stood with one foot in his doorway and the other on the platform. A chain led from his waistcoat pocket to his lips, ending with a whistle that he blew loudly twice as he flapped a green flag mounted on a stick in the general direction of the engine.

'Bye-bye!'

'See you soon!'

'Take care!'

The train pulled away and *Derby County* soon got into its stride; the huffs and puffs becoming softer and more regular. Susan noticed the sound of hushed voices and footsteps in the corridor. She felt disappointed: people were shuffling through, looking for somewhere to sit. The train was quite full in the middle section, as usual. Her dad always said that, if you want to bag a compartment to yourself, it was best to wait at the far end of a platform, and get aboard either just behind the engine, or in the last coach. It had worked today — till now.

The compartment door slid open and a rotund woman thrust her equally rotund face in the gap. 'Hello! You don't mind if we join you.' It was not a question, so she did not wait for an answer but made the gap wider to allow her broad hips to pass. A younger man followed close behind — Susan guessed he was her son — carrying a string shopping bag containing some carefully wrapped paper parcels and another bag that seemed equally full. He gave Susan a little nod of the head and proceeded to help his mother remove her coat and fold it neatly before laying it almost reverentially on the string rack above their heads. He did the same with his own coat and hat, but the woman kept her pale blue hat — that looked like a hydrangea blossom — firmly on her head. Eventually, after a minute or so of more fussing, accompanied by much sighing and other such expressions of settling in for a long journey, the newcomers sat down. Susan pulled out a paperback and wedged herself comfortably in her corner seat. She gazed out of the window as the train traversed the viaducts and threaded across the clattering, elevated rail junction of Weekday Cross. *What a funny name that is*, she thought.

'You reading *Jane Eyre*?'

Susan felt obliged to look across at the beaming, plump, pink face. The question did not need answering, as the title of the book was on show, but she was brought up to be polite to her elders. She suspected that this was an opening gambit to draw her into conversation, so she smiled and nodded, then instantly looked away, picked up her book, opened it, and adopted a studious expression, hoping that this would signal her reluctance to chat.

'Are you enjoying it?'

'I've only just started it, but I like it so far.'

'Ah, that's nice. You like it so far! Isn't that nice, Mikey?'

'It is.' The man was looking at his fingernails, but he gave Susan a quick glance. He did not seem remotely interested in her reading habits.

'Mikey's my son. We're going away for the weekend.'

Susan gave a wan smile.

'Are you off to anywhere nice?'

'Cheltenham.'

'Did you hear that, Mikey? She's going to Cheltenham. How about that? Can you believe it? Cheltenham!'

Susan resisted the temptation to groan and shut her eyes. Was this woman really going to repeat everything she said? She'd better say as little as possible.

'What good luck to share the journey with a nice girl like you. You see, we're going there, too!' The woman gave a huge grin, causing dimples to form in her cheeks.

Susan swallowed. *What rotten luck.*

'Has your mummy gone to the buffet car?'

'There isn't one on this train, mother, as I keep trying to tell you.' Susan noticed that the son was not very polite.

'My parents aren't on the train; I am travelling alone.' Susan found she rather enjoyed saying that out loud; it made her feel very grown up.

'Mikey loves the trains, don't you, dearie?' She looked indulgently at her son, but he appeared to be fuming behind a motoring magazine that he had pulled from his coat pocket. Susan thought he looked too old to be spoken to like a child. She could understand why he was trying to hide his face.

'Yes mother. It's the best way to travel.' He slowly lowered the magazine and addressed Susan. 'Did you happen to get the name of the engine, miss?'

'Yes. It's *Derby County*. My father says they are a jolly good football team. I thought at first that it was named after the county, but he says it isn't.'

'If it was, then it would be *Derbyshire*. But he's right that this class of engine was named after football teams. You see, there's *Huddersfield Town*, *Liverpool* and *Nottingham Forest*, then there's...'

Susan lifted her book in a manner that she hoped did not look too rude, and turned a few pages whilst politely half-listening as he proceeded to list football teams. It sounded like the radio on a Saturday afternoon, only there were no scores. Her father liked to do the pools and religiously followed the mellifluous voice of the announcer, pencil in hand, as he checked off the results. Although she preferred netball or hockey, she would often join her father and mark off the score draws for him. It was a comforting and homely thing to do together at the mid-point of the weekend, even if she was not too concerned about the results.

She was startled out of her reverie by the touch of a soft, podgy hand on her knee. 'I said, would you like something to eat, dear? I always come prepared for a journey, with plenty of lovely grub. I've got sausage rolls, scotch eggs, pickled onions, a pork pie...'

'I highly recommend the pie!' her son interjected. Having finished reciting football teams, he carefully unwrapped a huge and quite delicious-looking pork pie.

'I've also got cheese and crackers, ham and mustard sandwiches and a cherry pie. It's better hot, of course, but beggars can't be choosers.'

'And we have a flask of tea to wash it down,' her son added.

'That is awfully kind of you. But I...'

'Don't be shy! We'd feel awful tucking in with you just sitting there, starving. Here, have a slice of pork pie.' The thought of, indeed the smell of food, had made Susan feel hungry and her cheese sandwich was in her suitcase in the luggage van, so she accepted the offer with a grateful smile.

And so Susan Feakin found herself drawn in. The pie was mouth-watering and infinitely preferable to her mother's undoubtedly bland sandwich. The tea had exactly the amount of milk and sugar that she liked, all stewed together nicely in a Thermos to make a rich brew. It reminded her of the tea they took on long country rambles or to picnics in Bradgate Park, just outside Leicester. She had looked forward to quietly reading her book, and had initially resented the interruption, but munching quietly on a huge slab of the best pork pie she had ever tasted, whilst a jolly lady chattered away cheerily about this and that, was no hardship. And, as an added bonus, since they were travelling to Cheltenham, she no longer needed to worry about the journey at all: she would just stick with them. She didn't need the guard any more. In truth, she never had needed him; as Head Girl and vice-captain of the netball team, she was quite capable of changing trains unchaperoned. Her mother was such a worry-guts, but she would feel relieved if she knew that Susan was tagging along with this kind mother and son. She watched as the motherly lady busied herself laying out another slice of pie, two little sausage rolls and a large Scotch egg in front of her. This was more than she could eat, but she felt grateful for the lady's generosity.

The guard suddenly appeared in the corridor and slid the door open. 'Everything all right, miss?' He caught sight of the giant, crusty pork pie sitting in splendour upon a sheet of white paper dotted with tell-tale grease spots. 'Cor, that's the way to travel in style!'

'You're very welcome to a slice.' The son waved a hand towards the guard, inviting him to partake.

'Very kind, sir, very kind indeed; but I'd better say no. Can't be seen eating pie on duty!' he guffawed.

Tibbott carefully wrapped a thick slice of the pie in a torn-off piece of the white paper. 'Go on. Take it for later.' The guard needed no persuading; he accepted the package and swiftly secreted it in his capacious uniform jacket pocket.

'Thank you most kindly, sir. Well, I can see the young lady is safe and being well looked after. She certainly fell on her feet when she met you! It's a way to go yet before Woodford Halse, miss, so you can relax and enjoy your picnic.'

'We're also changing at Woodford for Cheltenham, so we can keep an eye on her the whole way,' said the lady, beaming a broad smile. The guard looked pleasantly surprised: that was one less thing for him to worry about.

'I shall leave you to it, then. I'll pop your case out at Woodford, miss.' After sliding the door closed he ambled back to his little private compartment, eager to consume his slice of pie in total peace.

CHAPTER FORTY

Woodford Halse

Violet Trinder did not consider herself the nosy type. She was observant and interested in her surroundings, but preferred to note the changing seasons rather than the everyday goings-on of the village. It was the arrival and departure of the swallows and swifts that caught her eye. The trees turning, then dropping their leaves; the different flowers in the hedgerows that lined the lanes radiating from her little town were more to her interest. She had come to notice the regular passing of the many different trains — especially the *Master Cutler* express, with its gorgeously exotic umber-and-cream Pullman cars —using them to measure out the hours of the day. She was even becoming a dab hand at distinguishing one class of locomotive from another simply by the sound they made.

Of course, she could not help but take some notice of the daily comings and goings of Woodford residents as they passed her window or entered her shop, causing the bell above the door to tinkle. It was good for business to remember to ask Mrs Wyatt how the plans for her daughter's wedding were progressing; there was potential for a lucrative order. Passing comment on how well Miss Jones from the station refreshment room suited her latest dress, then artfully showing her some newly-arrived fabrics that would look equally fetching, paid dividends.

However, when compared with those she stood alongside in the bread and meat queues, Violet was almost ignorant of the intimate workings of the town. The capacity of others for observing, noting and dissecting every last word and action of their fellow citizens left her amazed. Not only that, but everyone repeated these inconsequential and unnecessary observations to anyone who stood still long enough to listen. There seemed to be an endless thirst for scandal and intrigue in a place where there was actually very little. So old Mr Jenkins had been to the library twice that week and his leg was looking worse? He might need an operation. What do you think about that? She thought nothing about it, other than *just leave the poor man alone.* She really did not care if Terry Neil's motorbike was parked outside Coulson's shop most evenings because he was taking every opportunity to see their daughter. Maybe Miss Coulson was indeed angling to ride pillion with him into Banbury on a Friday night? Back very late they were, last Saturday. An observation made with much tut-tutting and clicking of tongues. After midnight — or so they'd heard... And so it went on.

With regard to the last item of gossip, Violet happened to know it was closer to one o' clock, and that they'd spent an inordinate amount of time standing very close together in the rain outside the back door. But she was not going to share that accidentally observed detail with anyone.

It was therefore unsurprising that Violet had taken most of the day to decide that there was something odd about the van. She had noticed it parked there first thing that morning, of course. It was quite hard to miss, being a box van painted in a rich, dark blue with bold cream lettering on the sides. As she stood at the shop window, mug of tea in hand, taking in the view before getting down to work, she could see that the vehicle was clean and tidy. Quite surprising, bearing in mind all the rain and the filthy roads of recent weeks. It had come down from Leicester, judging by the motor-supplier's details painted on the side. Delivering spare parts for cars. That made sense. It was pulled up on the opposite side of the road from her shop, not far from the entrance gates to the railway station but, more significantly, close to the little motor garage right next door to her shop. He must be delivering to them. Unlike some of her fellow citizens, she did not need to know what was being dropped off, nor indeed what the driver looked like. She made no attempt to find out, and promptly pushed it out of her mind.

However, a hour later she wheeled little Robbie out of the shop in his pram and put the 'Sorry closed, back in ten minutes' sign on the door. He was in a lively mood, burbling and pointing and making all manner of communicative noises as he sat up, a red toy tractor close beside him. He seemed to be pointing at the vehicle across the road and so Violet stopped and together they repeated the word 'van' a number of times, Robbie's version being closer to 'wan'.

Violet returned to her shop after buying the provisions for their evening meal, a job that had taken somewhat longer than the rather optimistic ten minutes expected, largely due to the succession of people who had insisted on cooing and making odd noises to Robbie, who replied by whacking the tractor and saying 'wan', which confused everyone. As she was unlocking the door Violet momentarily wondered at how long the delivery was taking, and the apparent absence of a driver. Even her curiosity was starting to be piqued. She looked towards the garage, but there was nobody in view. It was a while since a car had pulled up beside the rusty petrol pumps, whilst the same two old cars were still gathering raindrops at the side of the forecourt in the hope that someone might buy them. There was a light on inside the main workshop and she could just see the back end of Colonel Sharp's Daimler. It was a very small building, and so, unless the van driver was in the tiny back-office, then he was not there. She shrugged her shoulders and hurried inside as another squall of rain started to fall.

In the early afternoon Mrs Wyatt called in. Colours and fabrics were discussed and patterns spread across Violet's broad wooden cutting table. It was agreed that the customer would take away three patterns to show to her daughter, along with little samples of eminently suitable fabrics that Violet had ordered in on the off chance.

'...any more and she'll never make her mind up. Best give her a limited choice or else she'll be dithering over this for a month of Sundays. What a coincidence that you stock almost exactly the colours and patterns we've been discussing.'

'Well, they are so very in vogue at the moment. It would be good to make a decision fairly soon, as a bridal gown and bridesmaids dresses will take time to make. I would hate to rush them, and would want at least one, but preferably two fittings.'

'I completely agree. Ten weeks to go and already there seems far too much to do.' Mrs Wyatt looked despondently at the rain pelting the plate glass window and dripping from the canvas awning. 'Goodness, I'd better hang on here a moment and see if this will pass over. Hm... I wonder who's expecting a delivery. That van's been there most of the day.'

'It must be to do with the garage. But I've seen nobody around and I'm pretty sure they've taken nothing out the back.'

'You have to wonder sometimes. There's no urgency in folk these days.'

'Oh, I know.'

'Hm... that young girl looks strange. I wonder if she's ill?'

'What girl?'

'The one climbing into the mysterious van.'

CHAPTER FORTY-ONE

Leicester

'It took some wrangling, but the magistrate has issued a search warrant for Tibbott's place.' Chief Superintendent Badger was seated beside Vignoles's desk. Despite the grim matter in hand, he was enjoying delivering this piece of dramatic news. With conscious deliberation he extracted the valuable document from his black leather briefcase and handed it over to Vignoles. 'My colleagues on the other forces were in complete agreement with our point of view. I think the beak had little choice but to agree.' He gave a little grunt of satisfaction.

'Well done, sir. Are you sure we should show our hand at this stage? I'm worried in case they've covered their tracks and we find nothing. That could rather leave us empty handed and on the back foot.' Vignoles was cautious.

'There's only one way to find out. You've convinced everyone that they took the children back there and then probably murdered them in the same place. So get the men in and rip the place to pieces. Strip it clean. Sift every last piece of ash in those bread ovens. Nobody can clean a place to perfection. If they took the children there, we'll find proof. The Leicester Constabulary are pulling together a search team as we speak. There will be ten of their best, plus their forensics chaps in support.' Badger made a point of inspecting his expensive wristwatch, an act that involved nudging an expanse of brilliant white, starched cuff held together with a silver cufflink to one side to expose the dial. 'They'll be ready in an hour, but I want you in there first. Give them directions and ensure all finds are passed across to yourself. Keep me informed the moment you find anything.' He gave Vignoles a steely look. 'There's a lot riding on this.' Vignoles felt he hardly needed reminding of that fact, but held his tongue. 'You'll be needed back here I dare say, so get one of your men to stay down there the whole time. We're gearing up to be in there a day, maybe two if so needed.'

'Very good, sir.'

'What about the Tibbotts, sir?' Trinder was standing to the other side of the desk. 'Do we arrest them now?'

'Yes and no. We shall aim to divide and rule, sergeant.' Badger savoured the sentence and paused for effect. 'We arrest Mrs Tibbott now and start questioning her. On her own she might be easier to break down. Thanks to the cooperation of his employer, we know the son will be out on deliveries all day. We have his schedule, so we know where and when to spring the trap.' Trinder nodded approvingly. 'From this point onwards, I don't want them to see each other. We keep them apart.' Badger looked inordinately pleased with his plan.

'Do we know if she's at home now?' Vignoles asked, reaching for his hat.

Badger fidgeted with his gloves on the desk, not wanting to meet Vignoles's gaze. The self-satisfied look of moments ago seemed to drain out of him. 'I'm given to understand that she is in Leicester at the present time.' His voice was oddly flat.

'That sounds rather vague. Does that mean she's not at home? I thought the Leicester boys were watching her.' Trinder appeared surprised.

'That was their part of the plan.' Badger blew air out of his mouth in an impatient expression. 'Early this morning, after her son went to work, she left Frog Island and walked towards the city centre, carrying a bulging shopping bag. Then they lost her.' His brow darkened. 'Bloody amateurs.'

'Presumably she'll return home soon with her shopping,' Trinder observed, collecting his hat and coat.

'I admire your positive outlook, sergeant. But why was her shopping bag already full?' Badger was conceited, but he was a good detective at heart.

'She said that she still baked bread for personal consumption, but perhaps she also sells some loaves, at a market or to a shop or cafeteria,' Vignoles offered.

'I hope you're right.' Badger looked mildly relieved.

'If we leave a line of police cars and a Black Maria outside their house, she'll spot them and make a getaway,' Trinder observed.

'She won't get far; not with the number of officers posted down there.' Badger was trying to regain his confident manner. 'They've got three motorcyclists on the road, as well. They'll be ready to arrest Tibbott when we give the word.'

Vignoles turned to Trinder. 'Sergeant, get descriptions of Mrs T to every stationmaster in our region, just in case she tries to slip away.' He looked out onto the station concourse from his office window as he buttoned his coat, then left.

'Woodford Halse. This is our stop.' After screwing the lid on the Thermos flask, the man rose and retrieved various items from the overhead luggage rack. All three stood in the narrow space between the bench seats, donning coats and hats as the train slowed, the brakes biting at times and the momentum threatening to send them flying in a heap. The enforced proximity meant that Susan Feakin could smell the woman's strong, sweet scent and the cigarette smoke clinging to the man's clothes. He had opened the compartment door whilst Susan tried hard to concentrate on getting her arm into her coat sleeve whilst still clutching onto *Jane Eyre* and her hat, all without losing her balance. She felt giddy and a bit dizzy.

And why was she suddenly so drowsy? Oh dear, her eyes felt terribly heavy. When she stood up it really hit her. All she wanted was to curl up in that comfy corner seat with the warm air enveloping her... and sleep. Sleep... She rubbed her eyes, which felt like they had giant grains of sand in them. The hustle and bustle of collecting everything somehow brought her to the platform, where she stood, feeling oddly detached from reality. The guard was saying something. He was smiling, but her eyes were blurry and finding it hard to focus. She said something polite in return, but it was little more than an automatic response, and then he was gone. She looked around in a mildly confused manner. 'My case... I need my case.'

'I've got it here, miss. Don't you worry.' The man was leaning towards her and his voice seemed too loud. She frowned and forced herself to concentrate. He was holding up the case, but he wasn't the guard; he was the kind man... and there was his mother. Goodness, she was so tired. It was almost impossible to think clearly. She watched the train steaming at the platform's edge. She let the banging and clattering of the station go on around her without paying it any heed. There was a whistle, then she watched a drift of steam rise in the cold air from between the coaches and heard the snort of *Derby County* as she pulled herself into motion and eased her carriages away from the island platform.

The station fell quiet. A whistling porter strolled past them with a brown parcel dangling from a finger of each hand looped through the brown twine tied around them. A stub of hand-rolled cigarette hung from his lips. There was a sudden breath of hot air accompanied by the sound of a coffee machine roaring as the door into the station refreshment rooms opened and closed with the tinkling of a bell. A young woman had stepped out carrying a mop and bucket and then entered another door further along the station. There was a metallic sound as the bucket handle struck its side as it was placed, none too gently, on the floor.

Susan felt rooted to the spot. Her feet were like lead and her legs lacked the strength to move.

'Come along, dearie. Just down these steps.'

Susan lifted a hand to her forehead, which felt slightly damp. Was she coming down with a fever? 'No, we need to wait here. My connecting train comes in... here...' She concentrated hard on placing the words in a sensible order. The man was pouring tea from a Thermos flask and insisted she drank some, even though she was no longer thirsty and felt like she was swimming in the stuff.

'No, dearie, we have a better plan,' said the woman, brightly. 'We can get you to Cheltenham quicker than the slow old train.'

'You can?' She rubbed her temples. 'But how?' They were encouraging her to walk slowly towards the glass-windowed arcade that covered the broad, wooden steps leading from the platform down to the road below.

'Mikey has his van parked just here — just outside the station gates. He's got to drive across to Cheltenham to make a delivery, you see. We'll be there in a jiffy.'

Susan gave her forehead another gentle massage. Her head was pounding. Despite her best efforts, her mind kept wandering off as if in a dream. She felt the woman's bulk press close and a soft but powerful arm slip through hers. 'Don't you worry, we'll go straight to the station at Cheltenham, so you can meet your uncle there. We'll stop on the way and phone to let them know you'll be early. I found your uncle's number in your coat pocket, dearie, so we'll take care of everything, don't you worry...' She babbled on in a reassuring manner and Susan felt herself being guided onwards. Even if she wanted to resist, she was powerless. The force exerted was gentle, but unstoppable. She had no choice but to descend the steps. It was all she could do to stop herself tripping and falling. All she really wanted to do was sit down... lie down. Close her eyes and give in to blissful sleep...

* * * *

The two burly policemen carried between them a solid beam of wood with a steel-reinforced head. It looked weighty. Using the handles fixed on each side, they made a couple of exploratory test swings between them, their legs adjusting to the kick-back, before they gave a short count and rammed it hard against the door. It made a deafening boom and the door shuddered on its hinges, followed by a splintering sound. After a count of three, they repeated the assault. This time the door eased back further and clean shards of wood showed around the frame. Vignoles could feel his ears ringing. A third attempt sent the door flying open, the men almost falling into the hall, moving their feet rapidly just to remain standing. They stepped aside to allow a stream of other officers to flow into the house, each calling and shouting — surely an unnecessary effort, thought Vignoles, since nobody was home. However, this yelling seemed to be the current practice, so he let them charge inside and bawl. As the dust settled and the tramp of booted feet diminished, he and Trinder followed.

They went straight to the kitchen. Trinder anxiously picked up a pile of railway books from the dresser, placed them on the table and leafed through. 'Got it!' He held up the small, soft-backed booklet filled with small cards pasted onto demarcated places on each page. The cards had paintings of different classes of British steam locomotive. He flipped it open to the right place then extracted a large envelope from a voluminous inner pocket of his overcoat. He carefully removed the page that had been filed away as evidence in the Barrow Hill case and laid it alongside the neatly torn edge where a page had been removed from the booklet. Vignoles had been watching him intently and they both peered closer.

'An exact match.' Vignoles gave a grim smile of satisfaction.

'One more detail — and another nail in his coffin.'

'Perhaps. But his defence will remind the jury that he was there on legitimate business and, as a rail enthusiast, he had every reason to own such a book and take interest in the engine shed. It will be claimed as pure coincidence that he lost a page where he did.' Vignoles shrugged his shoulders. 'I'm just playing devil's advocate.'

Trinder looked around, considering where next to search, the sound of random bumps and bangs from other rooms revealing that his colleagues were getting down to business.

'What have we here?' Vignoles was going through each railway book systematically, flipping each individual page to see if anything was concealed between them. 'A 1950 shed book. Gives the numbers of every locomotive and where they are shedded. For serious spotters only, rather dry reading for anyone else.'

Trinder nodded. 'The kind of book the likes of Dutton and Jebb would own.'

'Except this one has *Peter Whitwell* inscribed in a boyish hand. He's added *Chesterfield*, but there is no address.'

Trinder pondered this for a moment. 'Barrow Hill is not far from there.'

'We need to check with the local constabularies to find out if a Peter Whitwell has gone missing in the last two years. That could give us a way in. Killers often keep mementos as trophies.' Vignoles had checked all the larger books as he was speaking and found nothing else to capture his interest. He pulled open a drawer and picked up a small volume lying inside. Although externally it looked exactly like his own, he felt instinctively that it was the same copy Tibbott had been holding when they had met on Leicester Central. He opened the hard cover to reveal the fly page, and read the inscription out loud. '*This book belongs to G. Dutton. If found, please return to owner.*' Vignoles felt his skin crawl; he made a rueful expression. 'He forgot to put an address.'

'But that's not why Tibbott didn't return it.'

'No, John, it was not.' He scanned a few pages where various numbers were carefully underlined in red or blue. On closer inspection he noticed that the colour of the ink was not the only difference. There was a subtle variation in the way the lines were made. It was obvious that two people had annotated the book. One had been very careful, the other more slapdash in drawing his lines. No train enthusiast shared a spotting book. 'He even had the nerve to carry this around and use it, John.' Vignoles shook his head in disgust and fought a sudden urge to vomit. 'We're getting closer. We've found something of Dutton's in Tibbott's house, and we can place Tibbott at the dumping site. We have a possible name and a link to Barrow Hill shed. And we know Tibbott was near there on at least one occasion. We have him at Leicester shed and also close to where Jebb was abducted, and at the right time.'

'And the mother was seen with Jebb outside Central. I'm sure we will find more if we dig deep enough,' Trinder added. 'We've got enough to nail him.'

'Put Blencowe in here until they've finished ripping the place to pieces. We need to get to work on the Tibbotts. There is no reason to delay any longer. If they haven't located the mother yet, find out why it's taking so dashed long. Leicester is not that big. And we need Michael Tibbott in handcuffs. We need him off the streets — and the railways — before he can do any more harm.

CHAPTER FORTY-TWO

On the road

'A nice clear run we're having.'

'Clear of heavy lorries, but did you see that car that just went past? That was police: plain clothes dicks in an unmarked car.'

'How can you tell?' She leaned a little nearer the windscreen and peered through the relentless drizzle at the empty road that unwound in their headlights. 'I can hardly see a thing.'

Tibbott tapped the side of his nose. 'I can smell them, even from in here.'

'If you say so. But they were going the other way, nothing to do with us.' The windscreen wipers squealed each time they swept from right to left; the rubber had corroded on one, and so it left an arc of water across her line of vision.

He bit his lower lip and swung the big steering wheel, shifting the heavy gears. 'There was a motorbike cop a few miles back. Just sitting there in his black rain-cape and white helmet at the side of the road. Did you see?'

'No.' She settled herself back into the corner between the cab door and the back of the bench seat. 'What do you think it means?'

The van swung around a series of reverse curves, the black hedgerows on either side blocking any view, although the night and the falling rain ensured that their vision was reduced to the twin beams of the weak headlights. 'I'm trying to think it out. Why would he just sit there in this weather? It was like he was waiting for something. Maybe for a van to pass.'

'Perhaps the detectives were driving out to meet up. Pass on some information.'

'What information? What do they know?'

He shrugged his shoulders and checked his mirror, a naughty twinkle in his eye. 'Dunno.'

'Hm... but if they were looking for us, they'd have stopped us. Not driven past. That don't make any sense, son.'

'I'm just wondering what's going on, that's all. We might need to rethink things. I'm not sure we can wait too long before — you know what.'

Mrs Tibbott had twisted around on her seat and was peering through a small window that gave onto the large space in the back of the vehicle. She shone a pocket torch through the glass onto something bulky hidden beneath a dark blanket. 'She's stirring. I think it will wear off soon. The dose was not strong, as she only took one cup.'

'That's OK. We don't want her completely out.' He gave a wolfish smile across the cab. 'And even if she does wake up, she can't get out, so don't worry. We're not far from Leicester, but I'm thinking we won't go there. Not now. I've got a feeling in my bones they might be expecting us to do that.' Tibbott leaned forward, the better to see through the rain and try to read a finger-post pointing down a narrow lane. 'I could really murder one of those sausage rolls, if there are any left. I always get ravenous just before we do it.' In the dark cab, the slight glow of light from the dashboard made his toothy grin appear devilish.

'There's two left... here you are.' She handed one across. 'Are we going to pull over?' There was a poisonous glint in her eyes.

'I reckon so. A quiet little spot down a country lane, where no one can see the van. In this dirty night, we'll be quite alone.'

She fell silent for a while and watched the relentless swish of the wipers. 'Do you think they've rumbled us?'

'Not sure. Maybe they've found something.' There was something shifty and nervous about his expression as he glanced at her quickly across the cab.

'Found what? If you did like I said, they'll never get a clue.' She waited for his response, but he said nothing. 'Perhaps we should stop. Let her out and call it a day. Let this one pass.'

'What? And have her spill the beans!' Tibbott spluttered and spat bits of greasy, flaky pastry down his front.

'All right. Then we have to be quick about it. You've got me properly spooked about those police motorcyclists. Do you want some cheese?' Her change in tone was dramatic. 'I've got a lovely bit of Cheddar here.'

'It's a shame to rush things.' His words were mashed up with half-eaten sausage roll. 'Especially with us having a girl...' The indicator ticked and he turned the van off the main road. 'Go on then. A nice bit of cheese will set me up nicely.'

CHAPTER FORTY-THREE

Woodford Halse

Violet said goodbye to Mrs Wyatt. Hers was not only a valuable order, it would also be enjoyable to make, so, all in all, it had been a good afternoon. She went back to her worktable. Before her client had visited, Violet had been doing some hand sewing work that really needed finishing, and so she sat back in her chair, with the desk lamp shining over her shoulder to illuminate the tiny stitches. But her mind kept wandering back to that parked van.

What was it about that inconsequential moment that had struck such a chord? It was nothing of note. Just a family with a sleepy daughter getting into a delivery van. It could be of no interest to anyone. Not even to the gossiping inhabitants of her village. She had no idea why Mrs Wyatt had thought it worthy of comment. But Mrs Wyatt had noticed, and even called her over. Was that not indication enough that there was something... Violet paused between stitches to think how best to describe it... something a little *odd* about them. No; the three seemed quite normal. So why was she wasting her time thinking about them?

The child seemed dazed and had been helped into the cab. The others sat each side of her on the bench seat, but she did not speak to them; she just stared into space. Violet had got a clear view of the girl's pale face because a light blue Alice band held her hair back. Either the girl was sickening for something or they had just met her after a very long, tiring journey. A suitcase that had been placed in the back of the van seemed to support that theory.

Violet sewed a while longer, but her mind kept returning to that little cameo. For some reason it brought to her mind something her husband had said about a dreadful murder case he was working on. He'd not spoken about it recently, which made her think that it was turning nasty and he'd chosen to not bring its unpleasant aura into their home.

But one little detail had stuck in her mind. The prime suspect was a man, and they suspected his mother of working in collusion. She was a decoy or an accomplice in some manner or other. It was both surprising and hard to countenance. John had mentioned that they lived in Leicester, and that the son drove a... *Yes! — that was it! A delivery van. Oh golly gosh!* Violet winced as she pricked her finger. John said the man delivered car parts to the motor trade. She sucked on her perforated digit, but deep down she was processing the little pieces of information and they surfaced, pricking at her conscience rather as the needle had her skin. The man and woman seemed to fit what few descriptive details John had mentioned to her, but the problem was, they did not look remotely like killers. It was not credible that such an ordinary-looking mother and son could be capable of such vile acts.

Hearing Robbie whimper she went to fetch him. Whilst feeding and changing the boy, her mind continued to mull on what she had seen. Should she report it? Bother her husband at work when he was so busy? He might waste valuable police time investigating her silly notion, and attention would be diverted away from catching the real killers. On top of that, it would be ever so embarrassing when it was proved to be nothing but her over-inventive imagination. John would have to explain — shamefacedly — to his colleagues that his foolish wife had thought she'd witnessed child killers kidnapping a new victim, right outside her shop — indeed, right outside a police sergeant's home — when in reality they were just an ordinary, decent, law-abiding, innocent family. She could feel her face burning at the mere thought of how embarrassed she would be.

She put Robbie in his playpen and returned to her sewing. Another good reason for saying nothing was that, according to police rules, John should not have revealed any details of the investigation, even to his wife. She wondered exactly where the fine line fell between mentioning a case's existence and breaking the rules. It might prove awkward if she reported this couple as matching a description that John had given her, because then questions would inevitably be asked about John's probity.

Violet was not concentrating properly on the demands of her fine needlecraft, so she got up and put the kettle on. Whilst waiting for it to boil she picked Robbie up and supported him on her hip. Swaying him slowly back and forth, she gazed out onto the wet street, noticing that the street lights were now alight and reflected in the deepening puddles. The White Hart hotel across the road had some fairy lights illuminated in the window in an attempt to drum up some pre-Christmas trade. The colours were pretty and she pointed them out to Robbie, who responded with glee.

But the scene failed to quieten her nagging suspicions. What was the relationship between those three? He was about the right age to be the girl's father, and the older lady could be his mother. Three generations out for a drive. Or maybe the lady, who could be mother or grandmother, and the girl, who could be the daughter or the granddaughter, were being given a lift by a van driver. *A van driver...* That is definitely what John had said... Violet allowed her chain of thought to reach its dreadful conclusion. She felt her throat constrict and go dry. She held her son a little tighter and kissed his chubby, warm cheek before again replacing him in the playpen. As the kettle reached boiling point and began to whistle, she turned off the gas and listened as the high note slowly faded and died. Instead of filling the teapot, she paused for a minute, chewing on her lower lip and drumming her fingernails on the enamel hob of her stove. No, the risk was too high. She could not live with the guilt if she failed to act and something happened to that child. And so, an hour or so later than she should have, Violet lifted the receiver and put a call through to the railway detective department.

Chapter Forty-four

Leicester

'Sir?' Lucy Lansdowne knocked lightly on the door. Both Vignoles and Trinder looked up. 'There's someone to see you. The gentleman claims to have information about the missing boys.'

'If you could take a statement and his details, I'll join you shortly,' Trinder responded. They were busy drawing up a plan of action to arrest Michael Tibbott and their work could not be delayed.

She hesitated. 'I'm afraid he's insistent that he speak with the DI in person. Immediately.'

There was a loud commotion and the sound of raised voices coming from behind Lansdowne. Mrs Green's strident tones were admonishing someone, followed by a louder shout, a curse and the heavy, irregular stomp of feet.

Vignoles looked at Trinder. He raised an eyebrow and they both turned to watch as Lansdowne barred the doorway.

'I'm sorry sir, but you cannot come in here! Please wait outside.'

'I told him, inspector! I told him not to come a step closer or there would be ructions.' Mrs Green's voice was piping up somewhere out of sight.

'So, here you are! I told her I wanted to see you. There's no time to waste.'

'Mr Twist, to what do we owe this unexpected visit?' Time was pressing and there was no point in arguing about his unceremonious and unwelcome entry. It would be better to just find out what he knew and send him on his way. 'If you promise to calm down, you may take a seat and tell me why you are here.'

'But make it snappy. The DI is a busy man.' Trinder was less accommodating. He offered the old soldier his chair and chose to stand, towering over the ugly little man. Lansdowne stood in the doorway. Vignoles could see Mrs Green gesturing with impatience in the background, and then with a shrug of her shoulders that implied 'be it on your head', she flounced off.

'I reckoned you needed a bit of help. Got a fag, mate?' He looked up at Trinder with his strange wonky smile, lazy eye looking somewhere in the top corner of the room.

'Don't start that again.' Trinder glared back at Twist.

'All right, all right, keep your hair on. But you might be thanking this old cripple in a minute. Might change your tune to something a bit nicer.'

'I appreciate the time and effort you have taken to come here, Mr Twist.' Vignoles spoke calmly. 'It cannot have been easy.' He darted Trinder a mildly admonishing look. 'And I don't imagine you did so in order to waste our time.' He clasped his hands together and looked at Twist with an expectant expression, daring the man to deny his assertion.

'Precisely! You see, the penny's starting to drop — at last.' The strange figure nodded in an exaggerated manner. 'Mebbe you're not so stupid, after all.'

'You will not speak to the detective inspector in that manner,' snapped Trinder, outraged.

Vignoles raised a hand. 'Sometimes we make mistakes or overlook things. No one is infallible. So, what did you come here to tell us?'

Twist was nodding his head appreciatively. There was a hint in his mannerisms to suggest he was enjoying calling the shots and holding the attention of the detectives. A telephone started to ring in the main office.

'I admire a man able to admit his failings. That's wise, that is.' Trinder cleared his throat and gave Twist a look that urged him to get to the point. 'Yes, yes. You see, it's like this.' Twist settled back in the chair and made a play of better adjusting his metal caged leg, wincing as he did so. 'Ooh, the damp. It plays havoc.'

'Indeed.' Vignoles gave a brief smile and raised his eyebrows, indulging Twist in his little performance. But Twist was now straying close to the edge of his patience, not helped by the telephone that was still ringing incessantly.

'You hauled me in like a criminal. I would say like a *common* criminal, except it was nothing of the sort, was it. *Common* my blown up foot! You were accusing me of killing that boy. Now, that's not nice. Not nice at all.' He wagged a finger in the air.

'There were good reasons for questioning you, and we were following a tip-off.' Vignoles was calm. The man had grounds for his grievance and deserved an explanation. Vignoles noticed that Lansdowne had left. He hoped it was to silence that darned phone.

'In your haste to accuse me you forgot to ask me what I knew.' Twist shook his head slowly, eyeing Vignoles and then Trinder in turn. 'You never once considered what I'd seen.'

'We asked how you dealt with Jebb and his friends. We needed to understand how the burnt remains of his train-spotting book were found in your incinerator.'

'And I told you straight. But then you sent me packing.' Twist stopped and an uneasy silence followed, made all the more intense by the telephone bell having ceased. 'See? You're doing the same thing again. You're not asking the right questions, detective. Why didn't you ask me about who you're interested in? I might know more than you think.'

'What do you mean?' Trinder's voice was quiet. All trace of annoyance had gone.

'If that poor lad was outside my place and someone snatched him, it stands to reason I might have seen who took him.'

'You see all the comings and goings along the lane, and you are usually at home.' Vignoles's voice was flat and emotionless. He knew they had made an awful blunder, but he could not allow himself to consider whether the delay had resulted in Jebb's life being lost.

'Who put you on to me?'

'A member of the public gave us your name,' Trinder replied, 'but, as you know, we cannot reveal our sources.'

'Tell you what, sergeant, shall I describe him? Because I know exactly who he is. Yeah, that surprised you, didn't it? I don't know his name, but I'd recognise his face anywhere.' Twist smirked. 'I always seem to be the one doing all the work around here.'

Trinder opened his notebook. 'Fire away.' As he wrote down the surprisingly accurate description that Twist provided, he could feel the hair on the nape of his neck rise. The man described was Tibbott.

'When and where did you see this man, Mr Twist?'

'Got you hooked now,' he sniggered. 'Three times, I saw him. Two were before that Saturday the lad went missing. The one you accused me of messing with, in case you need reminding. He was walking about near my house. "Prowling" would be a good word for it. He smiled at me and whistled a silly tune and he looked all innocent and friendly when he saw I'd clocked him. But I knew there was something fishy about him. Knew he were up to mischief.'

'Can you provide exact dates and times?' Trinder asked, pen poised.

'No. I weren't writing nothing down. Why should I? But I reckon it was the two Saturdays in a row before the one in question.' Trinder screwed his face into a scowl as he tried to mentally untangle the sentence and place relevant dates beside his notes. 'Late afternoon time he was there. It were going dark,' Twist continued. 'The second time was when he had no choice but to talk to me. He told me he'd been down to look at the engines.'

'Scouting out the lay of the land,' Trinder observed, whilst looking at Vignoles.

Vignoles nodded. 'It's a very plausible excuse for being there. What about the night you met Jebb on his own? Was the man there then?'

'No. I didn't see him at that time. Not that late, leastways.'

'Do you mean to say you saw him earlier in the day?' Vignoles asked.

'Yes!' Twist looked exasperated. 'That's why I've stumped all the bleeding way here to tell you. Like I said, I saw him three times in total. And the last time was when I went to the shop for my paper. Now, you know where that is, because you checked me out good and proper. Asked enough questions in there, didn't you? They've not been the same since. Sent me to Coventry, they have. All unfriendly and sniffy they are with me now, thanks to you lot!'

'I know the feeling: we make few friends in our line of work,' Vignoles commiserated. 'Mr Twist, what was the man doing when you saw him, when you went for the paper?'

'I saw him in his van. Pulled up at the side of the road, right opposite the shop. He was letting her get out.'

'*Her*?' Vignoles sat bolt upright.

'The big lady. She got out and waddled off. She had a surprising turn of pace, as it happens. I'd not seen her before. But I saw her later.'

'Where was that?' Vignoles asked.

'Not long after the boy ran off. I sent him packing and went back in my shed. But, blow me, didn't I hear footsteps and heavy breathing outside. I thought the cheeky little monkey was back. He's got a nerve, I thought. So I opened the door quietly and had a look out. Working out my strategy, I was. But what I saw instead was the big lady going past. She looked to be minding her own business and not stopping near my house. I thought it a bit strange, though. I mean, there's only the loco shed down the end and no women work there. I can't see a lady like that being a train-spotter.'

'In which direction was she going?' Vignoles asked.

'Away from the shed, following the lad.'

Vignoles and Trinder looked at each other. 'Did you see her go in the other direction? Going down towards the shed?'

'No. But I suppose she was probably down there before I got myself back home. I walk much slower than she does. There again, you're the detectives. You can work all that out.'

'Was she lying in wait, do you think?' Trinder's question was directed at Vignoles.

'Mr Twist, you have been exceedingly helpful.' Vignoles stood up as he spoke. He noticed that Lansdowne had returned to her spot in the doorway. 'WPC Lansdowne will take you along to the interview room, provide you with a nice, hot cup of tea and some biscuits, then take your statement down in writing. We need what you have told us formally recorded, as I am sure you can appreciate.' He glanced at Lansdowne, who nodded that she would do as instructed. 'When you have finished, Lansdowne will get you a cab home, at my expense.'

'Thanking you most kindly, detective. Tea and biscuits would go down very well. As would a smoke.'

Vignoles turned to Trinder. 'Do you have any cigarettes, John?'

'Um... yes, of course.' Trinder dug into his jacket and fished out a pack of Players. 'Take the lot. It's half full.'

'A scholar and a gentleman you are, sir.' The fishy grin was no less unsettling than it was heartfelt.

'Sir?' Lansdowne spoke quietly to Trinder as Twist was easing himself up out of the chair. 'Could I have a moment? There was a telephone call for you. It sounded pretty urgent.'

Chapter Forty-five

Towards Leicester

Driver Tommy Besson and Fireman Teddy Doig were experienced footplatemen. A solid fifty-four years service between them — and counting. A foul night with poor visibility posed no problems for them: they never let inclement weather conditions delay their train.

They were Great Central men through and through and could boast of starting and stopping their engines as smartly as anyone in any link in the land. It was a matter of intense pride between all crews brought up on the traditions of their line that they wasted the least amount of time in the necessary acts of calling at stations. Many of the King's Cross crews reckoned themselves the best, working as they did on their busy suburban lines dotted with multiple stations. There were impressive stories about the men working out of Liverpool Street on equally crowded commuter lines, and all were deserving of respect, but Besson and Doig were having none of their claims to be the tops. They had even taken to timing their starts and stops and working out their averages and tabulating the results, challenging their rivals to provide a more impressive set of statistics.

Not that tonight was the right time for note-taking or an especially impressive performance. They were still quick, but they were not reckless. That was the whole point: any fool could set his train hurtling off into the night without a care for safety, but did they know where the next semaphore was if the lamp flame had blown out? Or when the next fog signal would crack like a pistol under the wheels?

However, even Besson and Doig could not know what lay waiting for them further down the line that evening.

Their engine was a 'good un', as Besson would tell anyone who'd listen. *Sir Clement Royds* was getting a little long in the tooth, but they'd been looking after the old thing since before the end of the last war, and knew its every quirk and foible. They were always working on the engine when on shed or with a lengthy lay-over; tightening something here, adjusting this and oiling that. On top of which, the engine was now sporting a brand new coat of lovely green paint and looking quite splendid. They were both immensely proud at just how fine 'he' was looking. They had agreed to drop the convention of calling this particular engine 'she', as it sat most uncomfortably with the male name it carried. However, this single, mildly unconventional quirk aside, they were both very much traditional enginemen. Always insisting on a clean white shirt each morning (worn with a tie in the case of Besson, and with a red-and-white spotted neckerchief for Doig) and their overalls and jackets had almost all the colour washed out, such was the diligence of their hard-pressed wives. And none of this knotted handkerchief nonsense, either: only peaked caps were acceptable. As far as Besson was concerned, a hankie on the head made a man look like he was on holiday in Filey. Smart, proud and professional, and with a locomotive that lived up to its billing as one of the Director class, they made a crack team.

Chuffing merrily in front of its rake of gaily painted coaches, their loco was a lovely sight for the few who saw it pass on its way north. Bowling along the smooth permanent way of the London Extension, the two pals were quietly smoking and concentrating on doing their respective jobs.

'Weather's bad!' Doig eventually shouted across the cab.

'Aye, it is.'

They had nothing more to say. Besides, conversation was not easy above the roar of the engine. Besson narrowed his eyes to better discern the next signal aspect. Doig was right: the rain was heavier on the rubberised canvas sheet strung between the cab roof and the tender. Visibility was shortening; he'd best be particularly alert. Just in case.

* * * *

DS Trinder, having returned his wife's telephone call and taken down all the details, passed them on to his boss. 'Vi says she saw what may have been the Tibbotts right outside her shop at about 3pm, sir. But she says the van was parked there all day, from about nine o' clock. She didn't see anyone load or unload anything and it never moved until she saw a man, a woman and a teenage girl get into the cab and drive off.' Trinder and Vignoles exchanged knowing glances.

'Benson! Do you have Tibbott's delivery schedule?'

'Right here, sir.' She handed Vignoles a list which the owner of Draper's Deliveries had provided. 'According to this, he was due to deliver in Woodford last thing today. To a garage on Station Road.'

'That's next door to our place,' Trinder said gravely. The thought that a murderer had been so close to his loved ones made him shudder.

'So, he's ignored the list and gone to Woodford first thing,' Vignoles observed. 'Why would he do that?'

'I'd say he drove down this morning, parked the van and took a train back north, guv,' Trinder replied. 'Mrs Tibbott meanwhile slips away. She somehow loses her police tail, which suggests she knew we were on to her. She cuts back to a station — this station, perhaps.'

'Maybe. You think she travelled elsewhere to rendezvous with her son?'

'It looks that way, guv. Gosh, it almost feels like they're daring us to catch them,' Trinder exclaimed.

'That explains why we are still waiting for her to be pulled in by uniform. The constabulary are going to get it in the ear for letting her give them the slip.'

'But who's the girl, guv?'

'We don't know. Benson has checked, and no alerts have been received to look out for a missing female. I'm praying that this was an innocent family outing — perhaps the girl is a relation. Benson, make some enquiries about that.'

'Right you are, sir,' Benson replied. 'Also, I'll call all the places Tibbott was due to make a delivery today. That way we can see if he visited any this afternoon after they left Woodford. If they did, it might give a clue as to where they are now.'

'Good thinking.' Vignoles handed her the work-sheet. 'My guess is, he's trying to create an alibi. He can prove he was in Woodford on business and is hoping that nobody as observant as Violet had noticed that he was absent for most of the day and that his van was lying idle.'

'I wish she had not delayed so long in placing the call.'

'Doubtless she has her reasons. But who is the girl?' Vignoles balled a fist and punched his other palm in frustration. 'If she's not a relation she could be in mortal danger. We need to know where they picked her up. And we've got to find out where they're taking her. Her life may depend on it.'

'I think I can answer that, sir.' Blencowe had hurried across to join them, having just hung up his desk telephone. 'That was Nottingham City Police HQ. A lady named Feakin has reported that her teenage daughter Susan has failed to arrive as expected at

Cheltenham. The girl changed at Woodford, but failed to catch her second train. The station staff saw a girl of her description leave the station at around 3pm with a man and a lady.'

'That's her!' Trinder almost shouted. 'That's just before Vi saw them get into the van.'

'Where was she travelling from?'

'Nottingham Vic,' Blencowe replied.

'The sheer nerve of it: their carriage must have passed our office window!' Trinder looked outraged.

'What a bloody shambles.' Vignoles looked pale. 'We're the ones left with egg on our face. But never mind us, it's only the poor girl who matters now. Blencowe — mobilise everyone! We need every officer the combined forces can muster. Circulate descriptions of the van, the Tibbotts and the missing girl.'

'Yes sir!' Blencowe barked back.

'Put all stations on alert, in case they ditch the van later and return to the railways. For now, they're on the road, so I need a car.'

'We could requisition the chief's,' suggested Trinder. He was a good driver, and this might be his one and only chance to get behind the wheel of a rather tasty Jaguar.

Vignoles grabbed his hat and spoke over his shoulder as he hurried out of the office. 'I'll go and tell the Badger the news. He's in the refreshment room, taking tea. I won't be long.'

* * * *

PC799 Claypole swung his motorbike off the road, the headlight illuminating the large letters painted on the back of the stationary van. *Kar Kare is Our Koncern*. It was unforgettable, and had attracted his attention. He cut the motor and kicked down the side-stand, but left the headlamp burning. There were no street lights for miles and the night was wet and pitch black. Before Claypole dismounted he drew out his heavy torch and clicked it on; then, wedging it between arm and body, he pulled off a gauntlet and extracted his notebook. He was sure he was right, but it was always best to double check. *Draper's Deliveries.* Yes, the name was correct and looked to be the right make of van. He'd found them.

It was an odd place to stop, though. He put the notebook away and instinctively looked at his wristwatch. It was good form to make a note of the time. He didn't hurry and was deliberate in his actions. Nobody had yet stepped out of the van, the lights had not been illuminated, nor had the engine fired up. The scene seemed to exude an aura of slightly ominous stillness. He had best be careful and weigh everything up before wading in.

Gauntlet replaced, he slowly approached the van, his tread cautious and his eyes alert beneath his helmet. The rain was driving down hard and pattering into the sodden surface of the lay-by, whipping the pools of muddy water into a frenzy of ripples. The steep, grassy slope of the railway embankment was a looming black presence to his left; an even more intense blackness that seemed to make itself felt rather than actually be visible against the opaque night. He swung the torch to and fro, looking under the vehicle and into places his bike's headlight could not reach. Drawing closer he noticed that the latch securing the rear van doors was not fastened and it hung loose. He glanced around, but nobody was there. His noisy approach on the motorbike would surely have drawn attention. He swung one of the twin rear doors wide open and shone his torch inside, illuminating piles of boxes marked with labels pasted on them. Some new vehicle tyres were securely tied to one side. A shiny exhaust unit with a brown luggage label tied to it lay on the floor. There was a strong smell of rubber, new metal, oil and corrugated cardboard. His torch beam caught the end of a dirty mattress. A scrunched-up woollen blanket lay on top. He heaved himself inside and approached the mattress, careful where he placed his wet, muddy boots. He would not go too close, and would be careful not to disturb anything, in case it was evidence. Someone had been sleeping in there; he saw a damp patch on the mattress and wrinkled his nose at the slight odour of urine.

A small suitcase was placed neatly to one side. He squatted on his haunches, carefully lifting his cape free of the floor, and peered at the label: *S. Feakin,* mouthing the words softly to himself. He stood up, climbed out and pushed the door shut, then took a moment to once again scan the area. But the road was still empty. His bike's headlight beam, sliced by countless drops of rain, illuminated a red pillarbox on a wooden post. What looked like an elm tree was towering behind it at the far end of the lay-by and a ragged hawthorn hedge edged the bottom of the embankment.

Who in God's name would come all the way out here to post a letter? He shook his head at this irrelevant thought then walked along the side of the van, past the closed passenger door and around to the front of the van. He shone his torch onto the maker's name on the radiator to confirm it was the make and model that they were looking for. It was best to be thorough before he called this in to head office. His sergeant would give him a right balling out if he'd failed to check all the basic facts.

He angled the beam higher to inspect the Road Fund Licence disc and suddenly jumped with fright. The shock went through his whole body like a convulsion and he instinctively launched himself out of the path of the van, fully expecting the engine to suddenly fire up and for the mad, staring, angry-looking man behind the wheel to slam his foot down hard on the accelerator.

The man's mouth was snarling and his eyes bulged with manic rage. His face was pressed so hard against the windscreen that the tip of his nose was bent by it and had turned paler than the rest of his skin. PC Claypole felt nervous. He tensed up and beneath his cape switched his torch to his left hand, freeing his dominant hand to reach for the truncheon at his right hip. Once he had grasped it he felt much more confident. 'Step out of the vehicle, please, sir.' There was no response; in fact, the driver did not even stir. Claypole repeated the request, but louder and sterner. He waited. Nothing happened. He used his torch to make exploratory passes across the grimacing face. There was a lifeless quality to the eyes: they glistened but did not blink. His facial expression would later be described in Claypole's written report as one of 'shocked disbelief'. But, whatever it was, Michael Tibbott was long past caring.

* * * *

As the train swayed, the passenger held on to the edge of the bar counter, but the steward, long used to the motion, merely adjusted his stance. 'A gin and tonic for your lady wife,' he said, placing it on a coaster. 'And for you, sir?'

'A bottle of pale.'

'Very good, sir. Rotten old night, ain't it?'

'It is indeed.'

The steward placed a glass on the counter and filled it carefully with pale ale. 'But we're snug as a bug in here. The rain won't slow us down, and we'll arrive dead on time, as usual.'

'Hubby and me are off to Manchester to visit my sister and search the shops for Christmas presents. At least, we girls will; I expect Bernie and Gareth will spend most of their time in the RAFA club.' She rolled her eyes.

'Darned right, we will! Can't be doing with crowded shops. Quite maddening. He's got a fine clubhouse. Be a shame to waste it.'

'Ooh, I love a turn around the shops, when I get a chance between shifts,' the steward remarked, wiping a cloth over the counter, despite it already being spotlessly clean. The husband thought the man had an effeminate manner about him and was in all likelihood a pansy. But the ale was a top brand, and he took a quick sip to prevent spillage as the carriage twitched. 'To your good health, steward!'

'Yours too, sir, and madam.' He smiled and nodded in the wife's direction.

'Put a whisky chaser on my tab, too, if you will. May as well get my visit off to a flying start, eh?'

'I need a top up as well,' the wife giggled, her glass already half empty. The narrow bar was warm and the train was running well, so why not get tipsy and just fall into a taxi at the other end?

* * * *

'Cause of death?' Vignoles was holding a black umbrella above his head, the fabric rattling with the heavy rain. His pipe was rammed into a corner of his mouth.

'I need a closer look to be sure, but I favour a shortish knife. Sharp and pointed. Perhaps with twin points.' The doctor paused, removed his spectacles and polished them with a cloth as he considered his next observation. 'We found crumbs of cheese on the floor and seat, so a cheese knife could prove to be the weapon of choice.'

An eyebrow was raised. 'Stabbed from behind?'

'Yes, and with considerable force. A short knife would need to make maximum penetration. I expect to find marks on his back that indicate that the hilt reached the skin. But therein lieth the intrigue, inspector: he would need to be leaning forwards over the wheel in order for that to be possible in such a confined space. The shock and pain thrust him perhaps further forward against the windscreen, leaving him as he is now, but he was already exposing his back and leaving it open to attack prior to death.'

Vignoles and Trinder gazed at the scrunched-up figure of the late Michael Tibbott, the bulk of the corpse still resting on the steering wheel. 'He was either peering to check something external, in front of the van, or fiddling with something on the dashboard.'

'Well, whatever he was doing he was relaxed, or at least not in a defensive posture. He was completely unsuspecting. The wound penetrated his heart, I am sure, but it was not instantly fatal; he may have taken a minute or so to die.' The doctor held up a hand. 'I am sticking my neck out for you with this theorising, as I know you chaps need as much as you can get right now. The point is, I can't help but feel he was oddly compliant. Almost too relaxed.'

'Compliant? What do you mean?' Trinder asked.

'Lethargic. I need to get him into the lab to give you the full gen, but if you push me for a guess right now, I'd say he was drugged. His pupils are very dilated. I'd like to test what's in this flask.' The doctor held up the smaller of two Thermos flasks found in the van. 'This was on the bench seat alongside him. I can't smell anything, but I'll explore further.'

Vignoles felt puzzled: of those he feared they would find dead, Michael Tibbott was not even on the list. It was, clearly, a deliberate killing: a case of murder. Had Susan Feakin realised the danger she was in and made a pre-emptive strike? If so, then she must be a feisty young lady because that would take not only immense courage but also an unambiguous realisation that she was trapped in a life-or-death situation; a teenage girl would surely not strike such a hard and fatal blow by accident. But where was Mrs Tibbott whilst her son was being stabbed? And where were she and Susan now? Three people climbed into the van at Woodford, and now there was only one.

The doctor's comment about drugs was intriguing. Violet Trinder had described Susan as seemingly half-asleep. That pointed to her having been given some kind of narcotic to keep her quiet and compliant. But there again, surely Susan could not have stabbed Tibbott so forcibly if she was doped up. Unless the drug had worn off sufficiently...

'Where the heck are they?' asked Trinder, scratching his head. 'The girl was probably in the back on that mattress for some of the journey, at least. But what happened next?'

'The effects of the drug eased off. They stopped and moved her into the front and fed her bread, cheese and tea, by the look of it.' Vignoles was throwing out a possible sequence of events, but without any conviction.

'Then Susan saw her chance, grabbed the cheese knife and stuck it into Tibbott's back,' Trinder suggested.

'I don't think there was sufficient room for her to do so, what with three in the cab.' Vignoles was trying to visualise it. 'Mrs Tibbott presumably sat between the passenger door and Susan. She would hardly just sit there and let it happen. Maybe the mother was not in the van at the time.'

'Or, if the mother had for some reason been powerless to prevent the girl's attack, having established that her son was dead, she set out in pursuit of the girl, who, presumably, was making her escape. Of course, it could have been his mother who killed him,' Trinder pontificated further. 'If the girl was in the back of the van, then there was enough room in the cab for the mother to stab him.' Trinder fell silent for a few seconds, thinking hard. 'They pull over into this lay-by for whatever reason, and whilst they sit here eating she... she starts to realise the true horror of her son's depravity. It nauseates her and she decides enough is enough. It has to stop. Perhaps she slips him some drugged tea — previously used to pacify the girl — waits till it kicks in, then stabs him.'

Vignoles weighed up the various hypotheses, his head cocked to one side, puffs of aromatic smoke rising from his pipe. 'I don't know, John. What kind of people are we dealing with? Nothing about them makes any sense. It's undiluted madness, lacking any logic.'

'Or, having stabbed her son, she takes the girl and leaves.' Trinder was not giving up. 'So, they hitch a lift. To all the world they are simply a mother and daughter in distress: standing in the pouring rain and clearly in need of help. They'd surely be picked up by the first driver that spotted them. Perhaps they told the driver a story about their car having broken down.'

'That is possible. We'll issue an alert for local forces to watch out for two females of their ages, perhaps in a vehicle, possibly hitchhiking. Mrs Tibbott might realise she has to avoid the railways, in case we've got the staff looking for her.' Vignoles peered into the sheets of rain, his spectacles already heavily spotted with water. 'Is that a light I can see through those trees? Probably a farm. Did they take shelter over there, perhaps?'

Trinder needed no prompting. He called the motorcyclist across and moments later man and machine were en route to the farmhouse.

'Sir!' One of the constables approached, draped in a voluminous waterproof cape that made him look like a giant, shiny bat. 'I found this. It's sodden, but quite clean.'

'A blue Alice band,' Trinder said grimly. 'Vi said Susan was wearing one; a blue one.'

'Where did you find it?' Vignoles asked the PC.

'Over there, sir. By the bushes.'

Trinder followed the constable's pointed finger and crouched low, his coat trailing in the dirty puddles, shining his torch on the ground. 'Footprints. Quite small ones.' The beam flicked up to the hawthorn hedge and a gap that revealed a sturdy wooden fence. This ended a little short, however, and there was enough space for a person to squeeze through to the grassy slope of the railway embankment. 'It's a steep climb. Surely not?'

The constable stepped through the gap, careful not to trample what might be evidential prints. One of his colleagues had joined them and his torch helped survey the wet grass. 'I think there could be marks. It looks like someone might have scrambled up there.'

'A heavy, middle-aged lady and a half-drugged girl, going up there?' Vignoles considered the likelihood. He looked upwards into the teeming rain at the great bulwark of embankment. It made no sense to ascend this unappealing incline. The railway was out of sight and the steep slopes of black wet grass felt oddly ominous and oppressive.

'Get up there and have a look around,' Trinder instructed the constables decisively. He wanted action.

* * * *

Sleeping heads lolled, rocked by the motion of the train. An elderly cleric, spectacles perched on the end of his nose, held a book open on his knees, head bowed as though he were concentrating hard on the translation of the Anglo-Saxon poem. But his eyes were closed and his hands were slack on the pages. Next door a young couple, newly married, snuggled close, delighting in their own empty compartment. His hand cupped her breast discreetly beneath her opened coat. She moved deliciously in his hand as the train swayed. Her eyes were closed, but she was not asleep. Along the corridor, the guard perused the sporting pages in the *Daily Express,* picking up a few tips from the form guide and making a pencil mark beside the horses that caught his eye. He glanced at his watch. Bang on time. Besson and Doig: 'the Old Reliables', he called them. He smiled to himself and toyed between placing a shilling on My Best Girl or Spill the Beans, both running at Wetherby.

* * * *

Susan Feakin tried to keep her eyes open but the rain stung them, and even turning her head to the side gave little respite, as the rain just streamed into her eyes in rivulets. Her hair was loose and matted, now free of the hairband that she had lost when it snagged on a thorny bush, and a spread of her fine blonde hair was catching one eye, tormenting it and making it weep. Her mouth was gagged by a piece of cloth and it was all she could do to hold back the convulsions that made her want to retch. Her chest heaved again and again, but she knew she must not vomit. She'd surely choke. She was lying on her back, a piercingly cold steel rail crossing the base of her skull whilst the multiple bolts securing the rail fasteners dug hard into her neck. Her spine was twisted as she lay along the wooden sleeper, her ankles tied with rope to the other rail. It was excruciatingly painful and her lungs felt constricted. But she knew that it was all soon to end. Cut off in an inescapable instant. There was no chance of survival. The fear was unbearable. Her heart was pounding as if it would burst any moment and her intestines were burning as if covered in quicklime. She tried vainly to cry out but it was impossible. She bucked and fought against the knots but they refused to ease. Rain and salt tears covered her face. If she could just faint and let it happen when she was blissfully unaware of the pain and fear it might not be so bad. But to know... to hear the train coming, feeling the ground vibrate and the rails shake as it approached, would be sheer torture.

* * * *

The two constables in their capes made slow but steady progress. Their feet slipped on the lank, slimy grass and in the mud that lay beneath. Their torchlight raked the ground and marked their progress. Vignoles walked away. Once on top of the embankment, the constables would signal if they found anything. He walked to the side of the road and stared into the night. There was a bridge some distance away where the road ducked under the embankment. He considered this. If you wished to climb up to the railway — and heaven only knows why you would — then that was surely the place to choose. The brick-and-stone abutment would provide a recess, a gutter, with a hard, low wall to one side offering support and guidance. It was a far better proposition. He was not quite sure why Trinder had suspected that Mrs Tibbott and the girl were up there, but somehow he sensed the sergeant's instincts were right. But they were climbing in the wrong place.

'Down here! We should try along here. There's a bridge.' He indicated with his arm to Trinder, who shouted back that he understood, and then tried to call to the two constables, who were close to the top. Getting no response he waved his torch at them, hoping they'd see that he and Vignoles were moving further along the line. He then followed Vignoles, making sure his torch beam showed clearly. The one remaining constable was to guard the van and flag down the reinforcements that must surely be not too far away. It was not a long walk to the bridge. The van's headlights might well have illuminated it before it had pulled over, alerting the occupants to its proximity.

'It would be far easier here. Look, it's been used. Probably platelayers use it occasionally. Or maybe even the two women.'

'Here goes, then.' Trinder wasted no time.

A faint whistle carried on the night air. It was distant; barely audible. 'Take care, John: there's a train coming.'

'Righty-o.' He was already making good progress, proving that this was indeed a far more viable route. Vignoles started after him. They were close to the top of the embankment when they heard the constables' urgent police whistles. Repeated blasts that demanded attention. Vignoles and Trinder paused and looked back. Torches were bobbing in the thick night, the motion suggesting the men were running, their whistles still sounding.

'They're coming our way.'

'Get up top! The girl must be up there!' Vignoles was worried. A fast-approaching train in this crow black night was potentially fatal. They were all in jeopardy, even if they kept off the track.

'Stop her!' One of the constables was running along the slightly sunken drainage cess at the side of the rails. 'The Tibbott woman's on the other side! I can see her!'

Trinder swept his torch across the double track. There was the unmistakeable form of Mrs Tibbott. Without a coat or hat, despite the teeming rain and the cold, she was standing close to the up line, immobile as if lost in thought. 'Get off the line!' shouted Trinder as loudly as he could. He quickly glanced each way, but could see little. There were but a few tiny dots of house-lights low down, but otherwise, on their elevated position, all was dark. There was no sign of the train, so Trinder sprinted across the tracks, the constables thundering close behind. Vignoles was frantically searching the area with his torch, but his battery was fading and the yellowing beam was not throwing far through the rain. 'The girl! Where's the girl!'

A short train whistle. It was much closer now.

Vignoles ran along the line, away from the direction the constables had gone. She must be here, somewhere. There was a commotion coming from across the tracks, but he took no notice. Mrs Tibbott was not his concern right now. 'Where is she?' He was speaking aloud in an attempt to release the tension building inside.

'Over there!' Trinder's voice was distant, but his stronger torch beam carried. It picked out a strange, twisted bundle of clothes across the down line.

'Christ almighty.' Vignoles ran as fast as his heavy coat and shoes would allow. He heard more shouts and calls and what was probably the tramp of the others joining him. How much time was left? Please let it be a London train, because that would pass on the other track. As he drew closer he could see it was a teenage girl, her lithe body twisting and flexing in futile desperation, her neck across the rails like the classic silent movie scene. 'It's the police!' he called, to give her hope as soon as he could. 'We're coming! Stay calm!'

Trinder was faster, cutting across the parallel running lines at a speed that probably surprised himself. He dropped to his knees and began struggling to untie the knot near her face. He glanced up at Vignoles with fear in his eyes but carried on trying. 'The rain has made them so wet... it's hard to... I can't...' He carefully removed the cloth from Susan's mouth. She immediately began sobbing and crying out.

'Help! Please, untie me! Quickly!'

Vignoles tried to undo the rope securing her ankles, but it was impossible. He felt the sleepers quiver as the rails made a faint singing sound.

'A knife! We need a knife — urgently!' Trinder was yelling at the top of his voice.

* * * *

'Green. Set for a clean run in!' Besson nodded. He'd seen the signal light but always appreciated getting confirmation from his fireman. He nudged the regulator a touch. No need to shut off just yet. They could poach a few more seconds. He knew the line like the back of his hand. Their steed was in fine fettle and was making the satisfying steady churn of valves and pistons working smoothly and efficiently. The rails clicked and clacked and the injector burbled as Doig put some more water in the boiler. Besson kept his eyes fixed ahead, watching the rain sloshing off the sleek boiler and streak past the cab side.

He shifted forwards on his hard wooden seat. What was that? He could not quite interpret the odd little lights dancing around. Doig, ever alert, noticed the subtle movement and instantly knew his driver was tensing, instinctively placing his hand on the regulator ready to shut off steam. He was expecting the unexpected. Doig could see nothing from his side of the cab, however. They were on a gentle curve and his sight-line was across what he could only guess was an elevated vista of open country, but it was so inky black that he might as well stick his head in a sack.

Besson was on his feet now, whistle cord in hand. The scream of steam through the brass whistle was long and urgent. He repeated it. Besson was not a man to play games with this warning instrument. The regulator was slammed shut and he was winding the engine down through the gears. Doig stood by the handbrake tower, ready to screw it down if asked. Besson shook his head and waved a hand to warn against its emergency application. It was too late. If they were going to strike something on the line then such additional braking would make no difference now. A hardened pro knew when to try to effect an emergency stop and slam the engine into reverse gear with catastrophic results to the motion and wheels; but such a man also knew when it was futile, and only likely to make a bad situation worse. Sound the warning, apply the brakes and let the train slow at a safe rate; brace yourself, and hope God was watching. The engine note changed and the train was starting to lose speed, but not enough to tip the odds.

'There's men on the line.' Besson was grimly dispassionate. If his last long scream on the whistle failed to make them move, then whoever was on the track would be cut to pieces. It would at least be swift. But the aftermath would be stomach-turning and distressing. At the back of the train, the guard put down his paper and frowned. They should not be slowing down in this section, let alone braking so hard. He could smell brake dust in the air. In the buffet car the steward felt the unmistakeable tug of gravity as the brakes were applied, and adjusted his stance to counter the train's movement. A customer pulled a dubious face at him and moved his glass close to his chest. 'Probably just a temporary speed restriction, sir, nothing to worry about,' he said nonchalantly, idly polishing a glass. Just seconds later they were exchanging worried looks because the carriage had begun shuddering as the brakes bit even deeper and the engine's whistle started to repeatedly scream warning notes.

The vicar opened his eyes and blinked. He was disoriented. 'Ah, we must be there already,' he muttered to himself as he felt his back pushed deeper against the cushions. He peered at his watch. 'Rather early, by my reckoning, and why all the clamour?'

In their empty compartment, shut off from prying eyes, the newly-weds clasped each other in an urgent embrace, mistaking the sudden rocking of the carriage for the fervid rhythm of their own passion.

On the footplate there was a grim acceptance of the inevitable. It was going to be hard to feel the thump. To hear that tell-tale sound. It would be short and surprisingly soft. And yet it would haunt them both to the end of their lives. It would be a perpetual torment, relived over and over until they were almost maddened by the memory. And there was nothing more either of them could do but wait.

* * * *

The constable hacked at the rope like a man possessed, using his pocket knife with panic-induced frenzy. Now and again he drew blood, but this was no time to worry about the little nicks he was making in the girl's pale skin. He worked until suddenly the last strand fell apart and her hands were free.

'Quick — give it here!' Vignoles shouted.

The roar of the engine was increasing by the second, its whistle wailing like a banshee. The constable and Trinder waved torches towards the advancing executioner in a futile gesture, imploring the snorting iron horse to stop and yet knowing it was far too heavy to do so before it reached them.

Vignoles fumbled and the knife fell from his cold, trembling hands. He retrieved it and again slid the blade into the rope. He felt the running rail vibrate. He shouted to his colleagues: 'Get clear, all of you! NOW!' As he hacked and sawed, Susan beat her bloodied wrists on his back in blind panic. Trinder clasped his arms around her, pinning her arms to her side, and held her in a tight bear hug to give Vignoles his one last chance to save her. 'Hold still, love, hold still.'

At last the rope gave way and Vignoles fell backwards in an almost comical tumble. With no time for anything but instant, extreme, instinctive actions, Trinder clutched Susan even tighter as he rolled himself across the rail and into the cess, pulling her on top of him then rolling over her so his body covered hers from head to toe. Her face was pushed roughly into the hard ballast as he shielded her. 'Close your eyes tight, Susan! Keep still. I've got you!' In the jumble of coats and limbs his hand somehow found hers. He grasped it and squeezed it tightly. 'Stay still, love. Just hold onto me.' He twisted his head about this way and that to check that no part of himself or Susan was near the running rail. His heart lurched in horror as he spotted his guv'nor lying on his back, completely motionless, in the four-foot — right in the path of the gigantic, roaring, wailing, unstoppable steam locomotive, now merely yards away. It was too late to save him.

As the front of the engine passed over his head, Vignoles saw its bulging cylinders, their lethal copper drain-cock tubes pointing like daggers towards his head. How low they were! He screwed his eyes tightly shut and felt hot steam and a wave of air crash over his body. The noise was so loud it hurt his ears. So, this was how he would die: under a Great Central train. They say that, when you are about to meet your maker, your whole life passes before you. In Vignoles's case, it wasn't his whole life, but a mere vignette of a day when, as a rookie PC, his first job was to visit schools to warn pupils of the dangers of playing on railway lines. One wide-eyed little boy had put up his hand and asked, 'Mister, would someone be chopped into little bits if a big engine ran him over?' He'd looked gravely at the child and admitted that, yes, this would indeed be the inevitable outcome. How ironic that, decades later, this was exactly the fate that should befall him.

It felt like an eternity as the loco, the tender and a seemingly interminable string of coaches passed over him. At last he opened his eyes and looked around. Susan was sobbing in Trinder's arms. Two constables stood nearby, shouting and gesticulating wildly.

Vignoles struggled to stand; his legs felt like jelly. He stared down at his hands and then his feet, relieved to find no part of him was missing, or even injured. A young PC spoke to him; his face was wan, almost green. 'She... she stepped right out in front of it, sir, Mrs Tibbott, I mean, sir. Calm as anything.' He turned away and suddenly threw up. Vignoles noticed the train had stopped. It was some distance down the line and a row of heads, illuminated by the carriage lights, was poking out of the windows, pale faces peering backwards, trying to work out what was happening. The dark-capped guard was walking in the four-foot towards Vignoles, shining his lamp along the ballast.

Trinder had taken off his coat and placed it around Susan's shoulders, his left arm lay on top, still holding her close. He spoke softly and in reassuring tones. 'It's over. It's all over, love; you're safe now. Quite safe.' Susan did not respond. She was in a terrible state of shock; shivering uncontrollably and muttering nonsense to herself. 'I have to change at Woodford. Is that my train? Where's my case? I don't understand.'

'Neither do I.' Vignoles mouthed the words so quietly that nobody heard him.

CHAPTER FORTY-SIX

Talbot Lane, Leicester

WPCs Benson and Lansdowne had returned to the dig site to oversee the closing down of the abortive hunt for the missing Plantagenet king. They attended in case something previously undiscovered relating to the Dutton murder investigation should turn up. Neither the policewomen nor the archaeologists were expecting any unpleasant surprises; indeed, the day had a distinctly end-of-school-term feel to it, in stark contrast to the tense and unsettling atmosphere of earlier visits.

The canvas awning had been taken down, as had the scout tent Professor Wildblood had used as his makeshift office. Both were now lying folded and trussed in a pile, together with the collapsed trestle tables and camp chairs, storm lanterns and other paraphernalia. There was much bustling about as workmen lifted the mud-caked duck boards and carried them to a lorry on Talbot Lane. The men were whistling and joking, apparently oblivious to the fact that this had been both a crime scene and the last resting place of a Roman. The grave, now empty of bones (these having been carefully moved to the university) was being filled in by the two female archaeologists, who were both busy with their shovels, replacing the earth in a fraction of the time it had taken them to remove it. The professor was fiddling about with a camera mounted on a tripod and was making it clear that he would quite like to be left alone, perhaps to reflect on his unsuccessful mission. Winter sunlight filtering through the trees and gaps between the buildings was giving the place a much needed lift, and last night's frost had hardened the ground and minimised the muddiness, to the relief of all.

The WPCs wore smart black uniforms with wide belts that cinched their waists. The soles of their otherwise pristine, sturdy, flat-heeled lace-ups were edged with fresh mud. They were seated on a makeshift bench formed from a wooden plank with a piece of hessian sacking thrown over it, balanced on two empty barrels that had once held sump oil. The ground rumbled as a heavy coal train passed overhead. Each nursed a mug of hot tea as they quietly discussed the violent conclusion to the Tibbott case. Neither was yet able to fully comprehend how the story had played out. Words seemed inadequate and both felt numb, shocked to the core, and unable to find any rhyme or reason for the depraved acts against innocent children that had been committed by the Tibbotts, nor for the murder and suicide that ended their lives.

'Seeing the parents in such distress is what really hits me, Jane. I can't offer any explanation or rationale to them. How terrible must they feel? Confused, repulsed and distraught by turns, I imagine.'

'I know, Lucy. They look so helpless, so lost.'

They fell silent for a while, watching the other pair of women fill the ancient grave. At last Lucy spoke.

'Do you think the voices of the living can be heard by the dead?'

Jane frowned. 'Isn't it usually the other way around? In séances ghosts speak to the living.'

'If you believe in such supernatural events, then the dead would have to be able to hear the medium calling them in order to answer, wouldn't they?'

'I hope they can — hear the living, I mean. I could take some small comfort in knowing that the Tibbotts' victims could hear how much they were loved — still are loved.'

Jane considered this for a few moments. 'Do you think anyone ever tried to speak through a medium to poor little Peter Whitwell, the Barrow Hill victim? He ran away from a Dr Barnardo's home. Unloved and unwanted.'

'It's heartbreaking enough that he was even in such a place, let alone dead with no one to mourn him. His parents, if they are still alive, might not even know. Or care.'

'Rest in peace, Peter. We were too late to save you, but at least now you will be laid to rest properly.' Jane sipped her tea, thinking of the tiny urn in which his few ashes were placed. Thoughts of Peter inevitably led them to discuss Jimmy Jebb and Gordon Dutton. They spoke in sad, hushed tones, and at one point Lucy pulled out a lace-edged handkerchief and wiped away a tear. Three victims dead and another left bruised, battered and scared out of her wits. Jane remarked that it would take Susan Feakin a very long time to trust anyone again. Lucy expressed relief at the almost miraculous survival of both their sarge and their DI on the railway line. She shuddered as she impressed upon Jane just how lucky Vignoles had been to escape with his life.

'The whole train went right over him. *The whole train*! Can you believe it? And not a scratch on him!' She concluded that God must have been watching over both men. They both fell silent for some minutes, each thinking her own thoughts about life, death, God and miracles.

Lucy began to feel a desperate need to throw off the heavy, miserable atmosphere that had settled upon them; she wanted to think and talk about something cheerful and light-hearted. She suddenly recalled an earlier conversation with Jane and decided to pick up where they had left off.

'So, come on, spill the beans about you-know-who.'

'Oh, that. It was *so* comical, Lucy. It reminded me of a farce I once saw at the theatre, in which the secret lover rushed out through the French windows in a blind panic — just as the husband entered stage left.'

'So what exactly happened? I want to know every detail.'

'Well, Mrs Hawkes turned up out of the blue.'

'So, all the time he was flirting with you, he was married? Oh, Jane, I am sorry; although, to be honest, I am not all that surprised. An itinerant jazz musician, moving from town to town...'

'She's his wife in name only.'

'But they are still married, Jane, so you need to watch your step. So, come on, how did you find out?'

'Well, I arrived home from work to find a strange lady on our doorstep, having a bit of a shouting match with Mrs Mason. And Mrs M quite surprised me.'

'In what way?'

'She had no sympathy with the lady — who, I soon realised, was Mrs Hawkes. She was shouting: *Who do you think you are, banging on my door and causing a scene like a fishwife!* She was really on her high horse. I expected her to shop Max in a flash and turn all sniffy and sanctimonious towards me, but, when it came down to it, she was curiously protective towards her lodgers. Quite an eye-opener. And for some odd reason, I also took an instant dislike to the lady...'

'...hmm, I wonder why that was?' interrupted Lucy, nudging Jane lightly in the ribs.

'So I told her he'd gone away and we had no idea where. And so, between us, we "headed her off at the pass", as they say in the westerns.'

'Then what?' Lucy's eyes were wide.

'I slipped past her and ran upstairs to warn Max, and, well, I have to say, I've never seen anything so funny. There he was, quite frantic, in the act of lobbing his holdall, shirt-sleeves and socks half tumbling out of it, straight out of his bedroom window and then, without looking round at me, he scrambled out himself. As he dropped down out of my sight I dashed to the window and saw him dangling from the drainpipe on one arm, just like a chimpanzee at the zoo! The look on his face when he saw it was only me — ooh, it was a picture! He'd heard someone hurrying up the stairs and thought it was *her* — his furious wife!' Jane was giggling so hard that it was a struggle to continue the story. 'He stayed dangling like that whilst he asked me if she'd gone, and I warned him that she was still on the doorstep, arguing with Mrs Mason. He said that, now she'd found his address, he'd have to move out, and told me to pass on his apologies to Mrs M for his hurried and unexpected departure.' She laughed again. 'It was just so funny conducting a conversation with someone hanging twenty feet up in the air, clutching a trumpet in one hand.' She howled with laughter, tears filling her eyes. 'Then he gradually inched his way down the pipe to the ground, and, with a final, cheeky wave of his free hand and a kiss blown to me, he was off, running helter-skelter down the alley that leads to the road at the back of ours. It was hilarious, Lucy, you should have been there!'

Lucy had been giggling along with Jane and wished she had been there. She would quite like to see Hawkes running away like a lily-livered coward.

'It must have been quite a jolt for Max to realise that his past had come calling', she said. 'A bit of a kick in the stomach, maybe also a punch in the heart.'

'Then I went downstairs, looking the absolute picture of innocence, to try and help Mrs M. Mrs Hawkes was demanding Max's forwarding address!'

'But you didn't let on where he was?'

Jane looked coy. 'Well, I know he is about to start a residency in Sheffield. So I told her he'd got a new job — in Leeds!'

'You little minx! You lied to protect him!'

'*Lied* is rather too strong a word, it was more a momentary lapse of memory. Both are large Yorkshire cities, so it's the kind of mistake anyone could make.'

'Do you know where he is playing, or where he is staying?' Lucy had become suddenly quite serious.

'I don't know the exact details.'

'It's lucky you work in the detective department, then! I'm quite sure that, given time, you will be able to trace him.'

'No need for such subterfuge.' Jane smiled widely. 'He gave me the telephone number of his digs up there, just in case I felt like visiting him at short notice for the weekend. Hmm... I find I've lately developed quite a fondness for smokey, noisy jazz clubs, especially if they have a red-hot trumpeter in the band.'

'But you should not be chasing after him, Jane. My mother says a girl should play hard-to-get. Men don't like girls who make things easy for them.'

'Oh Lucy, you seem to forget sometimes that it's almost 1953! We have a young queen on the throne, and that is going to change everything for women. For instance, did you hear that there are moves to try to get us designated as *detective* constables instead of WPCs? I wonder if that means women will be in with a chance to become sergeants one day...' She pondered this exciting thought for a few seconds, then continued. 'You mark my words, one day women will be equal to men. We'll be able to go where we like, when we like, and do whatever we want with whomever we want.'

'Surely you don't mean that you are going to *you know what* with *you know who* — are you?'

'Of course not,' Jane reassured her friend, 'I shall be staying at a respectable hotel, in a single room with a single bed.' Glancing sideways at Lucy, a cheeky grin spreading across her face, she added: 'Well, at least for the first few times...'

'Jane Benson — you little devil!'

'Oh, why not be reckless and foolish now and again? You only live once, as they say, and after these last few terrible weeks I think it's time I started to make the most of the one life that I've been given. Just promise me you won't say a word to anyone.'

'Oh, my giddy aunt! Just remember the old saying, Jane: *if you can't be good, be careful!*'

Jane chuckled at Lucy's words, then fell silent and looked far away into the distance, barely registering the archaeologists with their shovels moving around the grave mound, tamping down the soil. Her lips formed a slight smile. She was remembering a long and passionate kiss on the New Walk in the lamplight...

CHAPTER FORTY-SEVEN

Leicester

The day dawned frosty and cloudless. It was one of those winter days to embrace and enjoy, even though the air had a sharp edge that demanded gloves and a thick scarf. The crunch of Vignoles's heavy shoes on the gravel path was well defined on the iron-cold ground. The low winter morning sun cast lengthy shadows but lacked the heat needed to clear the hoar frost that etched the outline of each browned leaf and every prickly stem of the many brambles. The tracks of the railway that lay beyond the dense barrier were perfectly delineated, almost as if the sleepers and rails had been dry-brushed with the faintest touches of white paint. Everything looked clean and fresh, and the air bit deliciously into Vignoles's lungs as he inhaled deeply for the first time in weeks. He was finally free from the hideous, sickly smog that had so blighted the city.

Even the old house and its ramshackle environs were much improved by the attentions of Jack Frost's paintbrush. True, the smoke curling from chimney pot and incinerator was still yellow as pus, and the yard remained strewn with all manner of discarded rubbish; the windows continued to be masked by years of sooty grime and temporary repairs but, somehow, on this fresh December morning, it looked better. Old, tired and unloved, yet Vignoles could see that, beneath its shabby veneer, there was still a home to be made inside. It was filled with junk and dirt, it was hopelessly cluttered and disorganised, but at least a fire was warming it. It was rather like the man who was at this moment pottering around in his shed. Unappreciated and deeply unattractive; scarred and damaged and dressed in clothes that stank and desperately needed replacing — or, at the very least, a long, hot, soapy wash. But, beneath all that, there was a real person. Misunderstood and perhaps not easy to like, but still deserving of a respect he rarely, if ever, received. A man too many people found easy to judge and to shun. Little wonder he was sour and combative.

Vignoles stood at the rusty gate and called 'hello' through the partially opened door of Twist's black-tarred shed.

'What d'you want?' The voice came from somewhere inside.

'Just a chat, if I may.'

'All polite now, are you?' Twist's ugly face appeared at the door. His hands, encased in fingerless gloves of an indeterminate colour, held an oily rag. 'Not barging into my house like a herd of elephants now, then?'

'Not today,' Vignoles replied, with an apologetic smile.

Twist grunted an acknowledgement of sorts, then stepped out of the shed and leaned against the low wooden fence. 'What brings you down here? I've done my bit. I helped you out.'

'Indeed you did, and we're very grateful.'

'So, you caught them, then.'

'In a manner of speaking. It all ended rather badly. You will have read it in the paper, I suppose?'

'Nah. Not got around to it.'

Vignoles raised an eyebrow. 'Well it was a horrid, sordid tale from start to finish. I am just sorry that the good name of Lance Corporal Twist had to be mixed up in all that.'

'*Mr* Twist will do.' He darted a sharp look at Vignoles.

'You sell yourself short.' He pulled out a carton of cigarettes — an expensive brand bought especially for Twist. 'Smoke?'

Twist's staring eye locked onto the packet. 'Don't mind if I do.' Vignoles peeled off the wrapper and tapped the box to make two cigarettes protrude. Twist accepted one and Vignoles put the other between his lips. He struck a match and offered it to Twist first. The pair puffed their cigarettes alight and each watched companionably as a blue-painted express engine steamed noisily past, its name-plate hidden by the thick clumps of bushes, but the limpid sunlight striking the boiler and making it shine like a jewel as it passed, the deep maroon and rich, creamy yellow of the following coaches cheery and vivid. It was a very pretty sight.

'When we searched your premises, we found something of interest. It made us stop and think.'

'I've got plenty of curious stuff, that's for sure. You lot might even have done me a favour, turning the place over like you did.'

'How so?'

'It got me thinking how cluttered up this place is. There's too much bloody stuff to find a place for. I might incinerate the lot.'

Vignoles looked at Twist, momentarily shocked by the chilling parallel to the Tibbotts' evil actions. 'Not everything. Some things are worth hanging on to. But a good spring clean can do you a world of good. My wife reckons nothing beats a good clear-out.'

'Fumigate, more like. More of that blinkin' delousing spray

might be needed, haha!' Twist seemed to find the thought amusing. He scratched his armpit. 'Tell your missus she can come over and get to work whenever she wants.'

'But buried under all that rubbish, beneath the mouldy old papers and bottles and boxes, I found something that needs to see the light of day and be celebrated. It might need a bit of spit and polish, but it would glint beautifully in this lovely sunlight.'

Twist fidgeted, looking more embarrassed than annoyed.

'I made a few enquiries based on what we found. I wanted to know more about Lance Corporal Twist and his experiences on the Western Front. You hide your light under a bushel, sir.' He paused. 'Or more accurately, under mountains of rotting clothes. I want you to know that I appreciate the service you've given our country, and everyone in our office feels the same.'

Twist made a dismissive noise. 'None of your flippin' business. What good is it, anyway? It don't pay for my bread and milk.'

'No, but your army pension does.' Vignoles looked at Twist. 'I do apologise profusely for accidentally invading your privacy, but you were decorated with the George Cross, which is awarded only to the very bravest men.'

'Stupidest, more like.'

'I also read what your commanding officer wrote. You did everything humanly possible, despite terrible personal injury, to try and save the lives of two of your pals.'

'I just had to get on with it as best I could. That's what you do: you help others, with no thought for yourself. I'm no hero. Anyway, they still died.'

'You three were the only men in your unit to survive a mortar attack, and, despite the situation seeming hopeless, you struggled for hours in appalling conditions, whilst suffering agonising pain from your own injuries, to get them both back behind your lines and into a field hospital. That they subsequently died was not your fault. You refused to give up on them. No one could have done more.'

'They were the only true friends I ever had, and they're all gone. What's the point now, though, with me like this? It's not as if anyone cares if I live or die.'

'But people would if they were given the chance to get to know you, to understand that you are a war hero, a man deserving of respect. But unfortunately everyone is met immediately with angry words and harsh stares, before they can even say hello.'

They smoked in silence for a while, a fragile companionship strung between them. It was as thin and delicate as the spider's web between the gatepost and the wall that was now glowing as if on fire in a raking shaft of sunlight, and yet which might break at any moment. Vignoles spoke.

'As for the boys who tease you, well, anyone causing trouble from now on can expect a severe reprimand. They might even be hauled into the juvenile court. You just make sure a constable is made aware of any foolishness. But this comes with one proviso: that you do not scare or attack anyone from now on. You will desist from launching any more of your assaults with your stick.'

Twist shrugged his lopsided shoulders, but there was a tacit acceptance in the gesture. On the other side of the scraggy hedge and fence, another loco came to rest with a sigh and hiss of steam. Vignoles moved his head to try and read the number and name-plate. 'If we got this hedge trimmed back, this could make a darned fine viewing spot.'

'Bloody hell, don't encourage more of the little blighters down here!' Twist almost choked on his cigarette.

'Why not?' Vignoles looked at Twist, a smile forming. 'You can lean over this wall and pass the time of day, instead of trying to beat and antagonise them. They're simply excited kids who just want to look at trains. But you need to understand that they are nervous of the unknown. And your war wounds can appear frightening. If they knew you were a brave soldier who cared deeply about his comrades, I think they'd see you quite differently. Say a cheery hello and ask them if they've seen *Ypres*, the very engine over there, unless my eyes deceive me.' Vignoles peered between a narrow gap in the hedge.

'I know all about Wipers. That's what they called that place. The railway named some of the engines after the worst battles. There's *Wipers*, *Marne*, *Somme*. And then of course *Valour*, a tribute to all the men from the railway that got killed.'

'Aha! So, you *do* know the names of the locos.' Vignoles was surprised.

Twist shrugged. 'I see them as they go past.'

'The youngsters would really appreciate you telling them what you know. It might even encourage them to be less hasty to judge. You could help them understand why that lovely engine bears the name it does. You might be pleasantly surprised at what good company the young spotters can be.' Vignoles stubbed out his cigarette. 'Here, you keep the packet, I much prefer my pipe.' He passed the cigarettes over the wall with a broad smile. 'I'll have a word with the railwaymen who look after the line, see if they can tidy this area up a bit.'

Twist grunted but did not argue. He was looking at the engine simmering beyond the hedge.

'I might come down here myself one day and spot some engines.' With that he tipped his hat, turned away and walked briskly along the cinder path, eager to get some warmth back into his limbs.

Chapter Forty-eight

Woodford Halse

Vignoles and Trinder were seated in the snug of the White Hart hotel, each with a pint of Everard's Tiger on the table between them. A log fire was burning in the grate with little, cheerful flames, bringing welcome warmth and the scent of wood-smoke into the room. Even the few short steps across the road from Trinder's home had been enough to suck heat from their bodies. Now, with overcoats and hats removed, they settled back with relish into the battered but comfy club chairs. A Christmas tree stood in a corner, draped in paper chains, strands of gold-and-red tinsel and a mismatched collection of glass baubles that reflected the garland of tiny blue, pink and yellow electric lights. Behind the gentle murmur of conversation, a jukebox was quietly playing a selection of songs from the hit parade.

It was a Sunday lunchtime, and the pair had been banished to the White Hart by their wives, who wanted them out of the way whilst they prepared to roast half a leg of lamb with all the trimmings, entertained little Robbie, and discussed preparations for the coming Christmas break.

'Your good health, guv!' Trinder raised his glass.

'And yours, John. I would like to be able to drink to a case satisfactorily resolved, but I'm not sure we deserve such self-congratulation. We were more like onlookers, watching a horrific drama unfold. We identified the cast of characters and even the intended victims, but were powerless to halt the action. To be honest, I feel more frustration than satisfaction.' Vignoles looked sadly into the flickering flames.

Trinder wiped some froth from his moustache. 'Not entirely powerless: we saved Susan Feakin from certain death.'

Vignoles looked up. 'And for that we can give heartfelt thanks. I hope that, given time, she'll find a way to come to terms with her terrifying ordeal.'

'I can't believe it turned out that Mrs Tibbott killed her own son. Why do you think she did it?'

'I find it hard to fathom anything about those two twisted, disturbed creatures. Nothing makes sense. And that's what I mean when I say it feels like we stood by and watched them act out a grotesque horror story. They were teasing us, deliberately luring us in, dropping clues that any criminal serious about evading capture would never have left. It was schemed and planned and I can only conclude that they fully intended it to have a climactic and sinister end. Once the chase was on, there was surely no escape for either.' Trinder waited patiently as Vignoles drank some beer and pondered his next words. 'It was as though they were willing it all to end. Almost forcing us to hunt them down and corner them.'

'Was it mother or son calling the shots? My inclination is to suggest the mother. She took control in the end and set everything up for what — at the risk of sounding trivial — was effectively her grand finale. It was all so... well, staged.'

'I am inclined to agree.'

'Once he was dead there was no escape for her, even if we had not arrived at the scene in time to save Susan, she could never have wriggled out of that. Is the coroner satisfied that Mrs T took her own life?' Trinder suddenly looked worried.

'Yes. *Death by misadventure* will be his ruling, so we are given to expect. We cannot say for certain that she deliberately chose to stand in front of the train with the intention of committing suicide, but she ignored clear commands to step aside and repeated warning whistles from both ourselves and the locomotive.' Vignoles paused a beat. 'No direct blame will be attached to the constables for her death, although we must brace ourselves for a stern rebuke in not removing her from danger. She was murderously deranged and armed with a small, but nonetheless deadly, cheese knife.'

'But it was dark, raining and the situation escalated rapidly. We all had to act on sheer instinct. Without that constable's penknife Susan would have died. It's all very well for these police investigator chaps sitting around in suits drinking tea at their leisure in a nice, warm, safe office, nit-picking our every move then telling us what we should or shouldn't have done. It's so easy to be wise after the event, guv, to judge with the benefit of hindsight. They should try being there at the time!'

'I understand your frustration, John. But we are professionals and trained to assess high-octane situations. Perhaps we should have taken Mrs Tibbott into custody as soon as we suspected she was involved. Few, if any, will mourn the passing of the Tibbotts, but two more human lives were lost, and the Badger's investigators might conclude that we could have predicted and therefore prevented that.'

'Hmph!' Trinder supped his beer. 'That's hardly fair, guv — we aren't issued with crystal balls to tell the blinking future. And do they realise that you risked your life to save that girl? You deserve a medal for gallantry!'

'You did every bit as much. It was a darned close shave for both of us. Have you told Violet exactly what happened?' His voice sounded gentle and the eyes behind the glasses looked kindly.

'I spared her the scarier details. I mentioned your part in saving Susan, of course, but I gave her the impression that the train was a good distance away.' Trinder sounded apologetic.

Vignoles smiled with relief. 'Then our stories match. I also gave a censored version of events to Anna. There is no point in alarming our wives. They know the job can be dangerous, but we must protect them from the gory details. If they knew some of the scrapes we get into they'd worry themselves half to death every time we went on shift.' He looked hard at Trinder. 'You are a father now, John, so you have to be even more careful. Dicing with death was very foolhardy.' He held up a hand to stay Trinder's reply. 'Yes, I know, we were *both* reckless.'

'We saved a young life, guv. And for that I am unrepentant.'

Vignoles gave a wry smile and lifted his beer in an ironic salute before drinking.

'We also played God out there. We both made the choice to focus on saving Susan, when one of us could have opted to push Mrs Tibbott out of danger.' Trinder felt a tiny pang of guilt and fell silent. He wasn't sure if Vignoles was admonishing him personally or merely voicing what he expected Chief Superintendent Badger to say at the enquiry. Vignoles lit his pipe and continued. 'Please do not think me overly critical, John, but we must review our actions and be prepared to account for each and every one of them when we are hauled up in front of the Badger. There were aspects of our actions that night that could be improved upon. But ultimately I, too, have no regrets. Heaven knows we failed Jimmy Jebb. The poor mite ended up in a locomotive smoke-box, so the very least we could do was prevent the death of another child.'

Vignoles took a deep draught of beer before he continued. 'You remember old Mr Twist.'

'I'd like to forget him, if it's all the same to you.'

'Remember what we found when we searched his house?'

'You mean his medal?' Trinder recalled being shown an envelope clearly marked as being sent from the War Office. It was a display box containing a gleaming medal. It had been buried beneath a mountain of old bills and newspapers.

'Yes. The George Cross. A very important honour, awarded only to the most deserving of men. I was intrigued, and did some digging about how he won it. Vignoles fell silent for a moment, as if gathering himself. He then told Trinder the story of Twist's courage on the battlefield, relating how he had dragged his two wounded comrades to safety, despite having suffered dreadful injuries himself.

'My goodness! He really is a genuine hero. Who would have imagined it?' Thoughts of Twist prompted Trinder to light a cigarette. He smoked in silence and felt glad he had given — albeit under orders — his last pack of cigarettes to the old war hero.

'I paid him a visit yesterday,' Vignoles continued. 'He was still his usual charming self, of course.' Trinder smiled at the mild sarcasm. 'I asked him about his medal.'

'Did he talk?' asked Trinder, having heard that Great War veterans usually remained silent about their experiences.

'As you might expect, he spent most of the time moaning about us leaving his house in a state. But something he said struck a chord. When I mentioned the George Cross he said he was no hero, just someone faced with an emergency, and he'd had to just get on with it as best he could. He said, "that's what you do: you help others, with no thought for yourself." It reminded me of us on that railway line.'

'Then let's raise a glass to the man!' said Trinder, his actions matching his words.

'I've asked the civvy police to send a constable past his house now and again, and generally keep an eye on him when they can. I don't suppose a leopard can change his spots after so many years of raging against the world, but perhaps knowing a bobby might appear at any moment might restrain his worst excesses, and stop kids from taunting him.'

'Blencowe told me that Mr Dutton has put his house up for sale, guv. He's staying up in Glasgow permanently and the wife's going to live with her sister.'

'I suppose divorce is inevitable, and, in this case, I think to be welcomed. Their lad was the only glue holding them together.'

Vignoles wanted to banish thoughts of marital strife and child murder from his mind. This was a Sunday, after all, supposedly a day away from thoughts of work. He changed the subject. 'Mm, this Tiger's certainly on form today. A fresh barrel, I bet.'

Trinder smiled. 'Shame to not make the most of it, then!' They quickly drained what was left in their glasses and, without prompting, Trinder visited the bar and soon returned with refills. They said nothing for a while, but simply drank, smoked and listened to the latest recording of *White Christmas,* this time sung by Eddie Fisher backed by Hugo Winterhalter's orchestra. Its soft, mellow tones, combined with the beer and the cheery fire, lulled both detectives and turned their thoughts towards happy topics.

It was Trinder who spoke first. 'Have you noticed that Jane seems in a very jolly mood recently?'

'Yes, I think I have. She has quite a spring in her step. She was even singing to herself the other day.'

'She was looking really down in the dumps for a while. I wonder why the sudden change.'

Vignoles chuckled. 'You can never switch off your detective brain, can you, John?'

'Just taking an interest in the wellbeing of my officers, guv'nor.' Trinder smiled.

'Far be it for me to fuel your inquisitiveness, John, but when Anna asked Jane if she would be joining us for Christmas, she offered a regretful refusal. She is, apparently, already engaged for the holidays and, moreover, uncharacteristically coy about what her plans are.' He paused again. 'Coincidentally, Jane has recently become a convert to jazz music in its many forms. All of a sudden she is quite passionate about it, apparently, according to Lucy. As someone possessing considerable knowledge, who may be considered an authority on the subject, you might like to offer her a few pointers and play her some essential "cuts" from your extensive collection of recorded discs. I'm sure she would appreciate that.'

'Well, she certainly kept that quiet. Good show!' Trinder was delighted. At last he'd found someone amongst his colleagues to share his love of music. He'd never had much in common with Jane, but all that would change now. He was already imagining having some great chats, and introducing her to all styles of jazz, teaching her to appreciate the various merits of the many different musicians and singers currently making recordings — especially the American artistes. Perhaps she could come round at the weekend and listen to some discs with him and Violet. She was a bright girl, and would make a willing pupil. 'Hm... I wonder what prompted her to take up this new hobby, guv.'

'I've really no idea, John,' replied Vignoles with a twinkle in his eye. 'But I imagine she will especially enjoy music with a good trumpet lead. Now, let's go and find out how that lovely joint of lamb is coming along.'

~ THE END ~

~ The Inspector Vignoles Series ~

Blood and Custard is the seventh novel in the series, which comprises:

Each title is available from UK booksellers, including those online. The GCR bookshop stocks all titles and sales help to support the Great Central Railway.

Books direct from the author

Individual, signed copies are available at £8.99 plus £2.75 postage (total £11.74). If you missed the other six novels there is a 'catch up bundle' available for just £50, post-free, each one signed by the author. Please send a cheque to Stephen Done, 28a Holland Road, New Brighton, Wirral CH45 7RB stating clearly which books you require. To pay by Paypal or bank transfer, please email hastings.press@gmail.com or telephone 01424 442142.

Reviews of previous titles

'The best of the railway detective novels on the market. The series continues to go from strength to strength with every new release. First rate.' *Steam Railway*

'A fast-paced and closely-plotted crime thriller.' *Oxford Times*

'I love it! A real page-turner.' *Daily Mirror*

'Stephen has originated the new literary genre of Post-war Austerity Gothic.' *Liverpool Daily Post*

'Move over Aidensfield, the new Heartbeat could be here!' *Daventry Post*

'Torn Curtain is detailed and fast moving, with an incident on every page. And it is all beautifully told against the background of austerity and tension between East and West at the time.' *Mainline magazine*

'An absolutely riveting story. It has all the elements of a cracking yarn — tension and suspense that wills the good guys to hurry up and catch the villains.' *British Railway Modelling*

'Not just splendidly-paced crime thrillers, not just delicious treats for all steam train enthusiasts, but really vibrant social portraits. I intend putting them in my *Best Read of the Year* slot.' *Ewan Wilson, Waterstone's*

'All Stephen's books are well grounded in their time, with plenty of railway and social detail to colour the scene, but never so heavily laid on to get in the way of a good yarn.' *A. Jones*

Coming next!

THE MOUNTSORRELL MYSTERY & OTHER STORIES

The eighth book in the Inspector Vignoles Mysteries is the first collection of short stories featuring DI Vignoles, DS Trinder and the other much-loved members of the British Railways Detective Department at Leicester Central. This varied collection begins in 1953 with the title mystery, then moves forwards and backwards in time, but always along the route of the former Great Central Railway.

Stephen Done's website
www.inspectorvignoles.ukwriters.net

Facebook page
The Inspector Vignoles Mysteries

Publisher's website
www.hastingspress.co.uk